Blood Fire

of **Banja Rouge**

There Will Be Pain

Blood Fire of
Banja Rouge

Kelvin L. Singleton

Copyright © 2018 Kelvin L. Singleton

All rights reserved. No part of this book may be reproduced in any form or by any electronic or mechanical means including information storage and retrieval systems without permission in writing from the author. The only exception is by a reviewer, who may quote short excerpts in a review.

This book is a work of fiction. Names, characters, places and incidents either are products of the author's imagination or are used fictitiously. Any resemblance to actual events or locales, or persons, living or dead, is entirely coincidental.

ISBN 13 Paperback: 978-0-9979041-2-3
ISBN 10 Paperback: 0-9979041-2-7

Printed in the United States of America

Cover and Interior Design: Ghislain Viau

To the resilient women who have been like mothers in my times of need. May God bless and keep Aunt Casandra Roper, Aunt Hazel Washington and Aunt Carrie Gordon all the days of their lives.

Prologue

Every country on earth experiences dark times of blood and strife. This ugly truth also applies to the land of Haiti, a French stronghold in the Caribbean where people of African descent no longer consider the island a haven once transformed into a hub for slave trade and harsh slave labor.

August1791, the successful slave uprising of the Haitian Revolution in Saint-Domingue is the long-awaited threshold of freedom and peace. The revolt of black African slaves finally ends with the French defeated at the battle of Vertières in November1803. Ultimately, the eradication of slavery leads to the creation of the Republic of Haiti. Even so, this is not where disparity ends, giving rise to the great disconnect between darker skinned inhabitants and the lighter skinned mulatto descendants of French colonists. Whether a person is considered to be one of the haves or have-nots, enslavement comes in multiple forms as well as many colored masters.

Undoubtedly, modernization and political aspirations of a more recent age is still carved from the long-lasting effects of racial malice when shaping the policies concerning the fraught and bereft. These particular days in Haitian history, the murky days of

Duvalier, tell very different stories from the romanticized tails of legendary pirates, and the heroes of the stolen masses.

Less than two centuries following the Haitian Revolution, François Duvalier's avarice, paranoia and insatiable lust for power catalyzes the submergence of the beleaguered people beneath a light-dimming shadow when he seizes total control.

In the mid-1900s, Haitians are forced to withstand ghastly crimes against humanity at the hands of the most affluent family Duvalier, owners of the lion's share of the sugarcane industry in this, otherwise, impoverished country. François Duvalier lives like a king in the capital palace with a wife thought barren for many years. Simone Duvalier often feared for her life and marriage, until she gave birth to their first son, Jean-Claude. Jean-Luc, the second born son, becomes all but a bygone footnote; a nearly forgotten ember in the bloodstained inferno of Haiti's gloomy history.

Because the overseer of the virtual slave labor in the sugarcane fields is a brutal taskmaster named Luckner Cambronne, President Duvalier promotes him to lead his security forces. Once commissioned to raise an army by any means necessary, Luckner employs vicious, unscrupulous tactics to fulfill his duties. Culling the young and strongest field workers, he presses them into the military service of that rag-tag army. Yet, glummer days are to come.

Subsequently, sugarcane production suffers because of labor shortages brought on by raising the army. Therefore, with President Duvalier's blessings, Luckner Cambronne leads a campaign of terror on the Haitian people unlike anything in the country's history.

President Duvalier, referred to in hushed shadows as Papa Doc, engages the services of the Vodou. These staunch believers of several voodoo cults intimidate and subdue the people by threatening horrifying curses upon entire families. Fearing for their very lives, most will yield to the will of a dictator, whose iron fist affords little mercy to outspoken troublemakers. Even so, some among the populous advocate armed rebellion to challenge the brutal tyrant's regime.

Meanwhile, other elders seek peaceful resolutions. Conscripted liaisons are asked to negotiate what most believe to be a better way by actually employing workers with reasonable monetary compensation. In addition, they suggest that citizens should be allowed to enlist in the Haitian armed service of their own accord. These completely reasonable approaches may have solved the problems of the people and its dictatorship, but the decorum of diplomacy fails miserably. Its failure leads to bloodshed.

Ceremonially drenched in the blood of woefully mistaken ambassadors of detente, the Haitian Vodou create the much-maligned Tonton Macoute to terrorize the people. Grown men, children, and entire families, are soon murdered and kidnapped in the depths of dark night. This reign of dread is legendary, almost mythical, as masked boogeymen snatch people from the streets in gunnysacks. Most of the Tonton Macoute's victims are never seen nor heard from again. With impunity, these depraved marauders are allowed to murder, rob, kidnap and rape anyone they please. Even President Duvalier secretly fears them, creating an arm of military intelligence just to spy on the Tonton Macoute should they ever become a threat to him.

* * *

The day finally comes when the patriarch of the Rouge family is approached, but he brazenly refuses to join Duvalier's campaign of terror. This upstart condemns the kidnappings and killings with no fear of reprisal.

The only reprieve offered, in light of Kwaban Rouge's emphatic repudiation, is also unacceptable; he will never leave his home to live in exile. The insulted dictator targets Kwaban Rouge for death when this commoner declines to surrender his children to Duvalier's servitude as a secret exchange for his life. The threat is very real. Nevertheless, the rebellious Kwaban Rouge is a powerful voodoo priest. He is most prized, and highly revered by the people of his small provincial village.

The loyal villagers' willingness to crush and furiously repel each attempt to capture or murder Kwaban Rouge are unforgiveable snubs to the absolute rule of François "Papa Doc" Duvalier. Over the years, many villagers give their lives to protect the defiant one, who only wishes to live in peace. For quite some time, he gets his wish. The raids cease because the rebellious nature of this particular village seems more troublesome than it is worth. Much sooner than later, word of Kwaban Rouge's example sparks a rash of noncompliant revolts across the land.

In 1969, on the night of Kwaban's 50th birthday celebration, voodoo priests in Duvalier's service gather in a secret room at the sugarcane plantation. As the orange sun fades upon the Caribbean horizon, they cast spells of invisibility upon Luckner Cambronne and the Tonton Macoute, imparting blessings by bathing them in the fresh blood of human sacrifices.

They take this blood, stoked with powerful enzymes of utter fear, from most unwilling subjects. The sacrificed are not simply beaten into unconscious submission, however. Their murderers allow them to scream and struggle in the throes of torturous pain while hanging upside down. Under the threat of red-hot iron, the fangs of poisonous spiders, or the bite of venomous vipers, their hands are hacked off just above the wrist.

The exsanguinated victims quickly fade as their blood collects in bowls made of pure gold, taken from the treasury room by President Duvalier himself. He alone keeps the key to the national treasury around his neck, a king's ransom Duvalier hoards for himself while many of his countrymen live in utter poverty.

Armed with machetes and guns, Luckner Cambronne launches his most vicious assault on Kwaban's village, taking them by complete surprise at the height of the birthday festivities. Even so, the men of the village fend off the direct attempt on Kwaban Rouge's life, rushing him to safety. Most unfortunately, Kwaban's wife, Aiala, their daughter, and two eldest sons are cruelly and publically murdered by the Tonton Macoute as a warning to all those who resist the will of President François Duvalier. After beheading Kwaban's family, their bodies are further mutilated and displayed in pieces upon the rocky hillside.

During the violent mayhem and butchery, the young and the strong are kidnapped for indoctrination into the armed service or enslavement in the cane fields, where they are beaten often and worked until their hands blister and bleed. Regrettably, for Kwaban, his youngest son, nine-year-old Banja Rouge is among the missing and feared dead at the hands of the Tonton Macoute. They do not find Banja's body after days of searching.

With fire in his eyes and rage in his heart, Kwaban converses with the spirits, desperately searching for answers among the souls of the dead as to his son's whereabouts.

One violently stormy night, a frightened young man, starving and severely injured, makes his way back to the village only to die in his weeping mother's arms. Before he passes through the thinning veil, beyond what they refer to as the *Reach*, he tells Kwaban Rouge of his missing son among the slave labor of Duvalier's cane plantation.

The dying young man proudly describes his cousin, Banjalanah, as strong and defiant of his taskmaster's whip and brutal beatings as they force him to work day and night with little to eat. However, he warns that it is only a matter of time before they discover Banja's identity, which will mean certain death.

Kwaban, distressing over the plight of his only living child, again, consults the spirits. This time, the father seeks his son's essence among the living, and the cruel spirits grant a vision of Banja chained and depleted.

Kwaban Rouge gathers the faithful to elicit help in rescuing Banja before death claims him. Shamefully, some refuse out of fear, but the stoutest and bravest see it as their duty to a man who serves this community ceaselessly.

Fassa, the machete wielding blacksmith, with bulging arms and a fearless heart, roars his allegiance. Before helping Kwaban Rouge to forge a plan to rescue the child as soon as possible, he shames those who show cowardice when a young man's life is at stake. However, there is one among them, whose loyalty is to his own captured son and teenage daughter.

The craven traitor steals away this very night, seeking out Luckner Cambronne to trade this information for the release of his children.

After traveling many miles to betray the identity of Banja Rouge, as promised, Luckner Cambronne takes this turncoat to his son and ravaged daughter. Their emaciated, fly-ridden bodies lay tossed among the corpses in a mass grave because they tried to escape. The highly disillusioned father is tortured and enslaved, taking his son's place in the fields of death where blood often feeds the crops. It is fortunate for the others that he had not stayed around long enough to know and betray the strategy for the rescue of Kwaban's son.

With guards doubled along the most direct routes, hidden pathways weaving through forests and craggy cliffs facilitate the exodus of a father in search of his only surviving child.

Assuredly, Luckner Cambronne informs President Duvalier of his discovery. François Duvalier leaves the capital palace with his eldest son, twelve-year-old Jean-Claude, traveling to the plantation to pit the boy against Banja Rouge. Surprisingly, Banja summons the strength to hold his own in this carnal contest against a much larger boy. While baring his teeth like a wild animal with blazing, penetrating eyes, Banja Rouge nearly defeats Duvalier's eldest son.

Bloodied and shamed by the stench of fear, Jean-Claude is tossed a stout club that drastically turns the tide against the brave younger boy. As François Duvalier proudly watches his eldest son bludgeon

Banja Rouge with a wooden club that gives him a decisive advantage, Kwaban Rouge and his men run throughout the night to the plantation to search for his son with hope in his eyes.

When they find Banja brutalized and chained, beaten within an inch of his life, Kwaban rages against the heavens and weeps bitterly with his broken, fading son in his arms. Distraught and enraged, he lays claim to a curved, ceremonial blade and proceeds to behead many of the nodding guards of the plantation. Those who do not slumber on their watch are terrified by sudden, shrill cries in the night. Kwaban Rouge and the others kill them all with a swift and deserved severity.

Soaked with their blood, Kwaban would have stormed through the armed checkpoints on his way to the presidential compound, but Fassa wisely stops him from committing what is surely suicide. Besides, there is no time and the distance is too great. With the dawning still eastward the Haitian horizon, they free everyone they can find, leaving the beheaded body of the traitor where he lay.

After stealing several vehicles to maneuver perilous routes away from this bloody place. The vehicles are never to be found. Some are even pushed over cliffs when they could drive along the back routes no further.

Fassa and those who stay behind to destroy the vehicles and disguise their escape route, scurry to catch up with Kwaban Rouge and those helping to carry the dying boy to a secret place of ritualistic significance.

Far away and hidden within a clandestine cave, its floor formed by blood red clay, Kwaban prepares for an agonizing blood ritual known as *Collage au feu* or the Fire-bonding. Few of the Rouge bloodline have found cause or the courage to perform this excruciating ritual. Fewer survived it with life, mind, body and soul, intact.

Many hours later, a quake seizes the earth as two massive tornados ravage the presidential palace. Jean-Luc, the youngest son of François and Simone Duvalier, awakens to a world in complete turmoil before disappearing within this furious cataclysm.

Whether near or far, they find no sign of him, forced to accept that the five-year-old boy fell victim to the destructive forces of nature.

In the recesses of his wicked heart, after being informed of the state of the cane field guards and escaped prisoners, François Duvalier knows that the legends of old have risen to claim his son. Terrified that he has angered the gods, he keeps these thoughts to himself.

President François Duvalier never tells Simone what he witnessed when he burst through the door and tried to rescue Jean-Luc, who screamed for his mother.

The infamous Papa Doc never mentions those eyes within that furious deluge. He never mentions the voice of great horned serpents, with glowing, glowering eyes that threatened and hissed at him. He never mentions seeing the opaque form of the revered priest he has offended repeatedly because his immense pride would not allow a lasting peace between them.

* * *

Deep within the cave, battered and bruised, Banja Rouge experiences a montage of swirling, disconnected images during intermittent bouts of painful consciousness. There are phantom dark lights whisking and darting about. With the sound of Rada drums pounding throughout, someone familiar dances for what seems like hours, twirling about like an angry ballerina before a ring of fire. The curved blade glimmers red from the reflection of the fire, the clay floor, and the taint of blood. There is the inevitable darkness, and voices calling from its depths to choose life or death. Finally, there is freedom from all pain, freedom from all fear. Silence.

Suffering feverishly, wounded and curiously burned during the ritual to save his son, Kwaban Rouge watches as Fassa seals the body of a boy child and an ornamental box in a wooden coffin. Kwaban Rouge weeps as villagers lower the coffin into an unmarked grave. Once covered with fertile earth, he struggles toward the graveside. With his left hand, he digs a deep hole in the center of the newly turned soil. Tightly clenched in his bleeding right hand, thirteen uprooted briars bristle with needle like thorns, which he tearfully plants in the hole at the center of the grave. He packs the soil about them before spreading them out in a near perfect circle. By clenching the bleeding fist in the center of the thorny arrangement, Kwaban waters them with his blood as he softly weeps.

Tired and weakened by his infected injuries, he places his arms about the shoulders of Fassa and a child, who help him home. The men hold vigil as the women of the village tend his wounds, attempting to abate the delirium of fever that takes hold of Kwaban Rouge, despite age-old remedies.

When President Duvalier dies in his own filth and sweat, exactly one year later, Jean-Claude is named his successor, but the country is actually ruled by Simone Duvalier. Around 1970, she forces the hated Tonton Macoute to disband, ordering Luckner Cambronne into exile for carrying out her dead husband's commands with such unquestioning voracity. Under the constant threat of revolt by the people, she adopts a softer touch, hoping to quell the troubled waters of Haiti. Simone Duvalier prays that her son will learn from her example. Unfortunately, however, traits of his father will often dominate his relationship with the Haitian natives.

For many years, Jean-Claude dreams of that night at the plantation. While writhing in restless sleep, he dreams of a young boy holding the hand of a scarred man. That boy wears the face of his younger brother, but his eyes are the same as the angry man as he raises a gleaming, blood-soaked blade overhead.

Chapter 1

Halloween Ghost Story

The golf course of the prominent Ryland Hills neighborhood is reacting to the unusually cool late October weather in the Piedmonts of Rock Hill, South Carolina. The grass is dry, already greying like dying hair across the ground. Due to the hottest summer on record, it falls short of the plush green carpet of the well-groomed grass local golfers are used to. No one gives it a second thought because today is Halloween.

The usual hordes of trick-or-treaters seem absent because the threat of foul weather looms. However, many of the neighborhood's children have gathered with their parents at the pristine home of Dr. Joseph Silver, Piedmont Hospital's Psychiatric Director.

Dark clouds are congregating over Charlotte, North Carolina to Rock Hill, South Carolina, threatening to rob Halloween of its mischief and costumed fun. The wind is picking up and the temperature chills as lightning dances in the distance. For the past few years, the weather patterns have been a bit erratic and unpredictable in comparison to established norms.

Groups of grownups, some of them costumed, gather for small talk throughout Silver's home. The youngsters are chaperoned by two adults and a sixteen-year-old girl with a huge crush on Dr. Silver's son. Children of various ages are in the pool house where paper goblins and glowing skeletons hang draped with imitation cobwebs. The watchful chaperones dole out cups of punch, a wide assortment of candy, and frosted cupcakes. These are the ingredients essential to the making of a major sugar rush as 'The Monster Mash' plays over the speakers. While one of the chaperones gathers the children still playing outside, the grownups in the house are imbibing and eating from the caterer's excellent menu selections.

It is difficult to ignore the bouncing white ball of a tail. Dressed as a Playboy Bunny, ears, makeup, airbrushed nose and whiskers affixed, Allison Silver closes the refrigerator door with a tray of her special rum balls in hand. She playfully kisses her husband on the lips before planting one on his boss's cheek.

Before walking away to rejoin the guests, Allison offers Nathan Clarkson some of her stoked rum balls and scolds, "Gentlemen, this is supposed to be a time of celebration. More accurately, maybe it is just another pagan excuse to celebrate. Anyway, under the threat of unimaginable penalties, shoptalk in my kitchen is forbidden during such an excellent party. However, since I am in a fantastic mood, I am prepared to overlook this infraction. In return, dear husband, I expect some very special attention when this costumed hotbed of decadent gossip is over. Oh my God, the fish are practically jumping into the boat today. It's like listening to the very-local local news." She giggles. "Well, do we have a deal?"

Dr. Silver looks at Allison and then Medical Director Clarkson with a smile before they all burst into laughter. Slightly blushing, he says, "We have a deal."

With a wicked little smile, she says, "Well, since you've chosen to throw yourself on the mercy of the court, you may resume your shoptalk. However, be warned, sir, ignoring our guests for very much longer only serves to draw further penalty from the high-court of Bunny Land. Alice is going to send you down the bunny hole." She giggles, wiggling her bunny tail as she hops away.

Clarkson smiles and winks at him. "Well, it sounds like someone is in big trouble—the lucky kind of trouble —for a change. She's a great gal, isn't she?"

Silver takes a sip of cognac and jokes, "Sometimes, punishment can be lots of fun. Especially when she's in a hot, rum ball type of mood."

They both chuckle and resume the private conversation. While stroking his hairline with his index finger, Clarkson peeks at the target and whispers, "Speaking of fresh fish jumping into the boat—one of them is watching us. I think she's about to take the bait."

Dr. Silver tilts his head and pretends to scratch an itchy eyebrow with his left pinky finger, whispering with the glass of cognac blocking his moving lips.

"Uh huh. She's been taking nervous glances from time-to-time. I think we've tortured our colleague long enough because the good doctor is approaching as we speak," Dr. Silver whispers in reference to an anxious Dr. Luna Patel.

Clarkson asks, "Is she?"

"Uh huh." Dr. Silver hums under his breath.

Dr. Luna Patel, nervously, steps up into the kitchen. She raises the hem of her black gown to make sure that her heels do not cause an embarrassing slip. Her smile is forced, but sheepish.

"Hello, Executive Director Clarkson. How are you, Joseph."

Clarkson turns as if surprised. "Luna, Happy Halloween. We were just discussing your unfortunate predicament."

He hugs the woman and gives her a light peck on the cheek; something he never does. Because the greeting lacks his usually cheerful smile, it feels more like the kiss of doom. When Dr. Silver gives her a hurried little hug and backs away as if she has a rash, it really feels like the kiss of death.

Silence encompasses all as she holds her breath. Meanwhile these two men contain their giggles.

As Clarkson assumes a serious demeanor by crossing his arms, Dr. Silver looks to the floor with a morbid sigh and shakes his head as if he has bad news.

Finally, she can stand it no longer and asks, "Joseph, please tell me. Will someone say something about the review board's decision?"

Silver now crosses his arms before saying, "Well . . . Nathan, do you want to . . . ah . . . no?" Clarkson shakes his head to the contrary and contemplates the fine craftsmanship of the cabinets, adding to her angst.

Dr. Luna Patel is obviously on the hook, being reeled in by the two pranksters. She quickly approaches her boss and touches his arm. "Please, tell me," she says on the verge of tears.

Dr. Silver looks at Clarkson, dubiously, before they burst into laughter.

Luna punches Silver and says, "You bastards." She bends at the waist, clutching her chest in relief.

Clarkson points at her and says, "Boy, you are too easy for this type of work."

Silver adds, "Had you going there for a moment, didn't we?"

Luna says, breathlessly, "Have you two been sneaking those suspicious glances at me all this time to make me feel as if the sky is about to come crashing down just for laughs? How cruel of you. I was really beginning to sweat." She places her hands on the granite countertop of the island and shakes her head with a relieving exhale. "If I wasn't wearing deodorant, I'd be stinking up the place by now."

"Trick-or-treat!" Clarkson says, raising his drink to the glamorous Indian doctor. "Now you have been properly indoctrinated into one of America's most pagan holiday traditions."

"I thought I was done for, and vulnerable to my first medical malpractice lawsuit," she says.

Clarkson asks, "Or is it April fools?"

"No, you're fine. You are just fine. The Kettleman boy's murder/ suicide was exacerbated, undoubtedly, by his parent's abuse when they removed him from our care against your advice. Possibly, with lots of therapy, your patient might have survived to recover from the damage they inflicted on him over the years, but only if he had more time to open up about what was really troubling him. The Medical Examiner told me that there were definite signs of physical and recent sexual abuse during the initial exam of the body. The autopsy eventually revealed several old fractures. His suspected torture and killing of small animals was a classic warning sign. It was evidence of what he wanted to do to his parents, but he kept all of that rage bottled up until they finally popped the cork. Had he shown some definitive resistance to going home, you would have had the right to invoke legal interventions with our full support. However, it is now pretty clear that the young man wanted to go home with them so he could exact vengeance. There is little doubt that he used that silent, disconnected time in your care to plot his retribution."

"I really wanted to help that patient, but he seemed too deeply traumatized to open up. With just a little more time, I believed he would have responded enough to have him removed from the abusive home. Perhaps it is as you say, I'm just being naive. Obviously, the Kettleman boy navigated the step-by-step path to homicide in his mind. He wanted to inflict maximum pain. Murdering both parents in that a fashion before committing suicide at the tender age seventeen . . . such a shame," she says with more than just professional regrets. "Did he actually drug and sodomize both parents with wine bottles, forcing them completely inside only to shatter with a baseball bat when they woke up?"

Dr. Silver considers her words with a cringing grimace and nods to affirm her inquiry. "The ME's grapevine passed down the fact that the parents were very accomplished methamphetamine addicts. The mother kept up appearances by using lots of makeup to hide her rundown facial features. The husband . . . well, he just looked like a grizzled old man beyond his years. I admit that I now feel a certain twinge of guilt over this case."

A sudden lightning flash fills the world with electric brilliance, but an immediate thunderclap transforms them all into turtles as their necks try to recede, flinchingly, into their torsos. The quiet, civilized conversations of the Silver's guests now hush as booming thunder rolls on like the angry footsteps of God.

Darkness, sudden and complete, sweeps the lights away like dust before an anxious broom. When an unknown child shrieks, those with children quickly move toward the rear doors, heading for the dark pool house just as the rising wind brings frigid rain.

Dr. Silver seeks to avert any panic by saying, "Please be calm everyone, it's just a power outage. I believe I heard a transformer blow in the distance. Not to worry, the backup generator will kick in shortly. Please don't rush. I'm sure the children are just fine."

As he goes to the drawer for candles and flashlights, the generator revives the lights inside the house. However, the pool house requires a manual connection to its power supply since it is not usually essential in a crisis situation. He joins the worried parents through the driven rain as the violent squall rages overhead.

With flashlights and candles distributed throughout the pool house, the frightened children are all accounted for.

One child, six-year-old Cindy Hollander, has fallen and scraped her knee. She is the child that cried out while taking a spill at the foot of the fireplace. The mother consoles the frightened child, but fear of stormy weather is always a contention.

From somewhere, another child, an infant, is crying. Everyone looks anxiously for the source of the sound but sees no one. In a moment's pause, ominous footsteps slowly descend the stairs of the loft. Soon, as they all seem to hold their breaths, an unfamiliar woman appears holding a frightened baby. As she quiets the infant, Dr. Silver picks up Cindy and sets her upon the table to inspect her bruised knee by candlelight.

He goes to a pantry and takes out a first aid kit to disinfect and bandage the minor injury, which seems to hold the attention of everyone in the room. As he picks up the child to hand her to her mother, lightning flashes and thunder rolls, causing Cindy to clamp onto Dr. Silver's neck and shut her eyes with a helpless whimper. He quietly shushes the child, consoling her, as he looks the mother in the eyes and smiles.

"She's still very anxious during thunderstorms, I'm afraid," says Cindy's mom. "I'll take her now, Joseph."

He waves her off and says, "It's okay, there's no need to rush her." He gently strokes the back of Cindy's hair, feeling her restriction slowly loosening as the storm front quickly moves away.

Wearing a trench coat, Allison Silver arrives with blankets and extra beach towels for those who got wet. When someone takes the burden, she asks, "Is everyone okay?" She looks at her husband and then the girl's mother. She says, "I am so sorry, April. You are drenched. Please take a blanket to warm yourself."

A howling wind surrounds the pool house as the blankets and beach towels are shared among the soaked guests.

Dr. Silver smiles at his loveable wife. He asks, "Please. Can I get everyone to take a seat? Guys, there are stacks of chairs behind you. Just open the double doors and you will see them. There are also beach towels behind the closet door to the left."

As Dr. Silver lights the fireplace, three men pass out the cushioned, folding chairs and beach towels.

With the fire lit, he says, "Well now, we aren't going to let a little bad weather ruin our Halloween party, are we? It's just grumpy old Mother Nature doing her job, but she's a little upset because she wants to go trick-or-treating like everyone else. I suppose this is her way of doing both, and the joke is on us." The parents chuckle and the children smile, even Cindy. He touches her nose and asks, "Cindy, are you ready to go to your mommy now? I think she can use a hug, too. You don't have to be afraid anymore because we are all together now."

The child, dressed as Dorothy from *The Wizard of Oz*, smiles and nods her head so he puts her down. April Hollander welcomes the girls into her arms and whispers. "Are you okay now, sweetheart?"

"Yes, mommy, I'm fine."

"Then what do you say to Dr. Silver for tending your booboo?"

The child runs back to Silver, hugs him and says, "Thank you for helping me. I was really afraid, and my leg feels much better now."

The guests cheer and clap as Joseph kisses the child on the forehead and says, "You are quite welcome, Dorothy." She smiles because he recognizes her costume.

His wife kisses his cheek and checks on the woman and the infant, who is quietly drinking her formula in her mother's arms. As his thoughts wonder toward the lightning and the events of the recent past, including the infant's cries when the storm front passed over, Dr. Silver shudders.

"Well, now let's see. Children, do you know what we used to do for fun when we were kids on many Halloween nights?"

One rambunctious young man, with a missing front tooth, answers, "You and my uncle threw toilet paper all over grumpy old peoples' houses when they didn't have treats to pass out!"

This statement brings a guilty blush to Dr. Silver's bearded cheeks and roaring laughter from nearly everyone else. He raises his hand to confess, "Guilty as charged, Billy. That is too rich, very good. However, besides wasting our parents' precious toilet paper, our granddad would take us into the deep woods where we started a roaring campfire. We roasted marshmallows, ate lots of chocolate, and Grandpa's favorite graham crackers. In fact, I'm pretty sure that's how s'mores came into being."

His guests chuckle at the probable embellishment.

"The very best part of our Halloween camping trip was when Grandpa told us Halloween stories. Some were really scary, but not all of them. We were a bit older than most of you back then, so I won't tell you any of those. However, I do have a very special story in mind that I am simply aching to tell someone, if your parents will permit me the honor. Would you like that, kids?"

"Yeah!" is the resounding retort of the audience, parents included.

Dr. Silver looks to the woman with the infant now sleeping comfortably in her arms. She looks down at the child with a smile before nodding. Dr. Silver kneels at her feet and gently presses his palm to her cheek. A tear wells in her eyes as he kisses the sleeping infant and gently caresses her head. Allison Silver sits next to her with a sad, yet hopeful smile.

Dr. Silver stands and says, "Then it's unanimous, so everyone gather around. Let's see. Since we don't have any marshmallows or graham crackers, Martha, would you please share cupcakes and refreshments with our esteemed guests?"

When the guests are settled and comfy with their kids sitting in their laps or nearby, Dr. Joseph Silver says, "As I said, this is a very special story. You all know what doctors are, right? We are all men and women of science. Some are involved with the sciences of the body. Others are involved with the science of the mind, as am I. Often times, the two distinctions are not so easily defined. Sometimes, because of our jobs as scientists, we tend to lose sight of the things in this world that science cannot explain, prove, or disprove. I'm talking about matters of faith and God, things like that."

Cindy Hollander says, "I like God. He's sending me a little brother soon."

Amongst the cheers, little Billy says, "Me too. Yesterday, I found five dollars on the sidewalk. My dad said that God gave it to me for being a good boy, and he let me keep it all by myself." He looks to his dad, who whispers in his ear. "Oh yeah, it was tax . . . tax . . . it was tax-free." The parents laugh aloud as Billy's father ruffles his hair with pride.

With the firelight at his back, warm hearts all around, and lighted pumpkins everywhere, Dr. Silver kisses his wife and begins the PG rated version of this Halloween story.

Chapter 2

Enemy Closer

The weather is blustery, with frigid gusts as midnight approaches on December 18, 2012. A dark figure blows into those cold palms, leaning against a tree at the edge of the parking area. Instinct makes her reach for the weapon as a slow moving vehicle crunches along the gravel drive.

DEA unit leader, Supervisory Special Agent Paige, accompanied by Special Agent David Phunts, eases to a stop and turns the headlights off at a boat landing on Lake Wylie. They sit quietly, waiting in the moonless dark as night birds call. Eyes are upon them, watching from a short distance with a night scope. She uses the shrubbery to maneuver into a better position, standing behind another tree to get a good look at the passenger. His presence is a distastefully interesting surprise, but, tonight, living on the edge has its upside.

Moments later, Phunts looks at his watch.

SSA Paige grunts and says, "She's already here. Agent Rodriguez has been watching us for at least five minutes now."

"Rodriguez? I thought you transferred her out of our unit for knocking Agent Pembroke out with a flying knee to the jaw," Phunts asks. "Where the hell is she?"

SSA Paige grunts and says, "She missed, and Pembroke's trip to the hospital was just a ruse."

"Why the subterfuge?" asks Phunts.

With his hand on his weapon, Paige ignores the question and glances up at the rearview mirror. He raises his black eyebrows and smiles when he says, "She's very close now."

Phunts squints through the windshield, slowly panning to the right. When he turns toward the passenger window, peering into the darkness beyond, Phunts nearly soils his pants. He flinches when he realizes that the undercover agent is staring right at him.

"Christ!" Phunts shrieks. "Shit!"

She smiles, knowing that she got him good. However, for various reasons, she truly despises this man.

Paige unlocks the doors and says, "Told you. You know, for a veteran officer of the DEA, you are not very observant, Phunts. One of these days, someone is going to sneak right up your ass and put a gun to your head."

Deep cover Agent Paula Rodriguez hears him as she climbs into the back seat of the black SUV and shuts the door. There is the unmistakable odor of diesel fuel on her clothing.

She blows into her hands and says, "Probably sooner than you think. Can I get some heat, boss? It gets a little chilly out here, especially if you've already crapped your pants."

Phunts retaliates by saying, "Funny, Rodriguez. One of these days, your ghost impersonation is gonna get you shot by friendly fire."

"That'll be the day, Phunts. I never actually considered you a friend."

"Why are we meeting here a week before Christmas, Agent Rodriguez?" asks Paige. "What have you learned?"

Agent Rodriguez says, "First things first, gentlemen. Before I say one more word, I respectfully ask that you turn your cell phones completely off and place them in this signal coffin." She takes the seven-inch box from the large front pocket of her black hoodie, which she opens and places between them.

The unit leader glances back at her, but complies. While doing so, he asks, "Becoming a little paranoid, agent, or are you just being diligent?"

"I believe it was you who taught me that it's better to be little of both, sir."

"Indeed, I did."

Agent Phunts sighs, begrudgingly, and says, "Man, are you shitting me?" He looks at his boss and asks, "Are we actually taking orders from her now?"

Agent Paige says, "Just do it, Phunts. I'm certain there is good reason, so submit to the request without griping." When Phunts complies without further complaint, Paige latches the box.

Rodriguez puts her phone on mute and prompts a specially designed application before leaning forward to pass a small wand over her boss's body. Satisfied, she does the same to Phunts, only more thoroughly. The needle jumps. She looks at the screen and prompts the application to search. She discreetly sweeps the rear

24

compartment and looks at the screen again. She double checks its readout and sighs. "I've learned a lot, boss," she says while opening a map. "The Mendez Cartel has decided that they have starved out the Southeast long enough. They're gearing up for a major push into all key cities in South Carolina, North Carolina via Charlotte, and Georgia via Augusta to Atlanta. This is big, sir. All of the local dealers from Charleston to Mecklenburg County, from Bankhead to Columbia are hungry for product. They are giving the fed centers like Virginia, Washington, and Maryland, a wide berth, pushing for eastern Tennessee and back dooring into Alabama, Louisiana, and North Florida. Marijuana is in high demand and they have tons of it. I'm not talking about Mexican swag. They are going to push hydro at reasonable prices—if such an animal truly exists. I suggest you get the paper chasers to look into lobbyists pushing expand legalization in southern and southeastern states. When Washington and Colorado legalized last month, Mendez put his legal bots to work right away because it's a strong pipeline for laundering dirty money while competing with completely legitimate operations. I have a short list to start your search. That is just the tip of the snowcapped mountain. Plans are in place for movers to start transporting heavy white, and weapons, whether they like the idea of hauling guns or not. The bigger the risk, the bigger their payoffs will be. These heavy mules know two things. If they change their minds, or try to quit and run, their entire families will die. In addition, all hustlers in afore mentioned areas are thirsty, starving for blow. Dealers will have less travel time without worrying about being screwed with that overpriced, recompressed crap. The so-called drought was just a way to raise and keep the prices outrageously high. The new prices will seem drastically low by comparison. It will be like a sale on Christmas snow from a northern blizzard. When you add lower prices, less competition, less risk, and better product to the table of contents, it's pretty much a book. End of story."

"Is that all, or do you have anything concrete . . . names, places, dates? Instead of conjecture, how about a little solid investigative work?" asks Agent Phunts with more than just a hint of disgust. "Jeez. What a colossal fucking waste of our time, Rodriguez. What you've got here amounts to all huff and no puff."

"SSA Paige, boss, as both my trainer and handler, you once said 'ours is a dangerously stressful job that can get to anyone at any time.' That's why you had your hand in a position to draw down as I cautiously approached this vehicle, is it not?"

Paige nods and says, "Undoubtedly, agent. I stand firmly by those words."

"Besides teaching me to trust no one, you taught me that we should all express ourselves when issues need to be voiced, so we can continue to perform our duties fully focused on completing our missions. Do you remember that, Special Supervisory Agent Paige?"

His sharp instincts and intuition tell him that she is about to expose something unexpected. Paige looks into the mirror and says, "I stand by those words as a way of life—a way of staying alive —so go ahead. Get your guns off, Paula."

As she literally reaches for her gun, she says, "Thank you, boss." The sound of a weapon being unholstered and a lethal bullet shuffling into the chamber in the back seat causes Agent Phunts' ass cheeks to tighten up. Ordinarily, a bullet is already poised in the chamber, but the sound of the shuffling slide is strictly for dramatic effect.

As Agent Rodriguez leans forward between the front seats of the SUV, she uses her right hand to place the barrel of her weapon to the back of Phunts' head. He freezes as the cold steel touches his scalp.

She twists her neck to make the bones crackle. With a sneering revulsion in her voice, her dark brown eyes grow darker and deadly serious.

Her boss slowly looks to his right when she says to Phunts, "I'd like to see a gutless, bitch-made, brownnosing *puta* like you wearing a face like mine and an ass to die for, maneuvering these danger zones full of *vato loco* without getting fucked in the ass or sucking cock on the first day in the trenches. I hate these drug smugglers as much as I hate dirty cops. Racist, chauvinistic, misogynistic white bread pigs like you always add to my stress level. You are constantly disrespecting, demeaning, and undermining my work ethics. Right now you are sitting next to a fucking African American man, who is your superior in every way imaginable, which eats you up inside. Look at him, Phunts. He hasn't even lifted a fucking finger to save your near-death ass. Without a shadow of doubt, you are at the mercy of a Latino woman who can run circles around you on her worst day, bitch. If I was pregnant and going into labor, I could still stomp a gaping mud hole in your sorry ass so I strongly suggest that you package the hostility before I decide to demonstrate the indiscrete definition of the word. I would like to finish this debriefing so I can get out of these funky clothes, drink a tall glass of vino, and fall asleep in a steaming bubble bath before possibly getting laid tonight. If one more disrespectful word parts your lips, I will unflinchingly let this Glock 40 solve my many problems with your continued existence! Do you know with whom you are now fucking, Phunts? Do you know who you're fucking with, mothafucka?"

Agent Phunts raises his hands and says, "Okay, Paula. You are right. I've always been a bit harder on you because I saw your great potential. I'm sorry. Obviously, I. . . ."

"Shut up. I'm not finished because you've been up my ass since I joined this unit three years ago!" she barks. "Do you really think you can placate me with insincere patronizing remarks right now, Phunts? Look to your left. Look!"

Phunts complies, wordlessly. She activates a scrambler to nullify any transmissions before saying another word.

She divulges, "Our unit commander is a fine ass brother, isn't he? Do you realize that I'm secretly in love with him, or that he's the only thing that keeps me focused while people are being murdered and beheaded all around me by these evil fuckers? If you piss me off again, I'll have to kill you both and set this car on fire to get rid of the forensic evidence. Now then, knowing how I really feel about our team leader, please don't speak again because it's the only way we can all play our roles in the twisted little drama that's really about to unfold here. Do we have a deal?" Phunts merely nods.

Paige raises an eyebrow, fighting to contain both his concern and a contritely wry smile. Agent Rodriguez presses the gun harder into the crown of Phunts' head and grabs Paige's tie to draw him close enough to plant a passionate kiss on his lips. She looks him in the eyes and whispers, "If you never knew how I felt, you know now, *papi*." Agent Rodriguez slips her hotel keycard into the inside pocket of his blazer.

She places a tape recorder on the console between the two men up front. Without warning, she snatches Agent Phunts' weapon from the holster, handing it to SSA Paige before deactivating the scrambler on the seat with the touch of her finger.

"Just what the hell do you think you are doing?" Phunts protests, angrily. "You have had your way, your say, and your fun, but the games are over, Agent Rodriguez. This bitchy little tirade now constitutes blatant insubordination and an assault on a fellow Drug Enforcement officer."

With Special Supervisory Agent Paige's handkerchief, she reaches into Phunts' blazer pocket and removes the pen recorder that he activated just before he saw her peering into his window. She shows it to her boss, whose shocked enlightenment is unmistakably evident by the anger in his eyes.

Before deactivating the stealthy recording device, she speaks directly into it. "This is deep cover DEA Agent Martina Ruiz of Zero Unit—AKA—Agent Paula Rodriguez—AKA—Natalie Hernandez. My official designation is Alpha Demonica 001. Attending my debrief is Special Supervisory Agent Daniel Paige and highly compromised Agent David Robert Phunts, who I am now placing under arrest for accessory to murder and treason by way of betraying members of the base unit. This message is only a footnote to Agent Phunts' willful and unsolicited recording of highly classified material solely meant to undermine an intelligence gathering operation concerning the criminal activity of the hybrid Mendez Columbian/Alba Mexican Drug Cartel. Because I've successfully linked the Mendez Cartel to a powerful faction of the Mexican organization led by Manuel Mendez's cousin, Senior Roberto Alba, this unauthorized recording corroborates evidence that proves Agent Phunts has been selling his information to the subjects of said criminal organization. Agent David Phunts is and has been on the take. End transmission."

She jams the pointed device into Phunts' headrest and shows the cellphone's screen to Paige as she scans it with the wand. The shortwave transmitter is indicated, telling her where its receiver could be found. Only now, it begins to beep. The agent reaches for the go bag in the back, using the handkerchief to unzip it and remove the recorder. She shows Paige Agent Phunts' recorder disguised as a pack of cigarettes before turning it and the pen transmitter off. She bags it and the pen, before giving it to her superior.

While keeping the gun on Phunts, she presses play on the tape recorder that she placed between them earlier. "Sir, this is a voice activated recording made at my request by the Defense Department's Whisper Operations Center. It's coming." She takes out her handcuffs and drops them in Phunts' lap.

With urgent authority, Agent Paige says, "Talk to me, agent."

"If what I've already revealed doesn't convince you or our superiors, this highly classified recording from the DOD's WOC will prove that Agent Phunts is dirty. He's been feeding one of Mendez' lieutenants information on our ops for quite some time. However, since you never told anyone who I really am, he could not adequately track me through your layered firewalls. Under your guise of reassignment, no one knew where or what I was doing undercover for the last eighteen months. Thinking I was someone else's problem and long gone, he could not rat me out. Otherwise, I'd be sliced into little pieces and fed to the dogs by now. Thank you for the extra safeguards, sir. Your cautious protocols kept me alive. I believe that you took it upon yourself to remain as my personal contact because you had suspicions of a leak in the unit. You just didn't know it was your buddy here. So thanks, again, sir."

Paige says, "No need, Agent Ruiz, because you are right. Had I known, Phunts would not have accompanied me to this meet. However, because he is so close to the fire, we will season him to taste." He directs his attention to the silent man in the front seat to say, "If pictures are worth a thousand words, then your facial expression and utter silence says much more. Doesn't it, Phunts?"

Agent Phunts begins to sniffle and water spills from his eyes as soon as the recording begins to play. Phunts recognizes the conversation and drops his head in shame. That is all Agent Paige needs to put the cuffs on him. He reaches down and removes Phunts' ankle holster while Paula holds the weapon on him.

Once certain that Phunts is completely disarmed, she places a restrictive tie wrap around the head support and his throat before drawing it tight enough to assure that he will not try anything in transit. She is tempted to cinch it tight enough to cut his breath off completely, but that would be going too far.

"I have a loudmouth tweeker, who likes to watch, on the hook. As last reported, I've been working him for more than a year now. He has juice, but gets high and flaps his gums a little. That is how I knew there really was a mole. His namedropping finally set me on the right path. By affording me the latitude and security clearance to requisition wiretaps within the DOD without navigating the normal channels, my intelligence gathering has paid dividends, sir. The first four shipments are supposed to be worth more than a hundred mill each. I'm gathering intelligence on the routes and our best place to intercept as quietly as possible. You will know the timeframe when I do, but the evidence leads me to think that Phunts is not the only one on the take."

Agent Paige reacts, "Two moles in our pod? Are you certain? Do you have a positive identity?"

"Negative on the ID, but I'm certain that Phunts is not the only rat in the nest. I don't believe they are in contact, for all the obvious reason, but he or she exists, sir. My closet tweeker, Mac, is an independent trucker with two brand new Peterbilts that have identical tricky trailers. I've fully demonstrated my ability as a diesel mechanic, who is more than willing to kick some ass when necessary, so I've maneuvered into a ride along position because little things just keep going wrong with the engines when I want them to. This scheme also involves several piggyback tow trucks for eighteen-wheelers and luxury RV's with phony mechanical issues. Some of them come with hollowed out engine casings. No guts or moving parts, just empty compartments for hauling contraband. Professionals have stripped down and gutted these vehicles to haul maximum loads. The subsequent shipment schedules are going to be more staggered after they establish control with the initial loads. Few drivers know enough about each other to rat, but not mine. Because he recruited at least ten other independent truckers, he is the nexus. But there are two problematic concerns."

"What's that?" asks Paige.

"This miscreant is closely related to the mayor of Tega Cay and the chief of police in Rock Hill. They have been covering Mac's sorry ass for years without even knowing how deep and deviant he really is. Those words came from his very own lips. When the time comes to take him down, I must caution against involving the locals. All I need is the time and place of the switch out. It is happening soon and within a one hundred mile radius. Please be ready to move when I make contact again. I've planted discrete GPS burst devices on top of both trailers and cabs, which only activate to transmit coordinates when I prompt them to do so. I'll know it's time when Mac makes an overnight run without me. If we can keep it clean and tight, without it leaking to the press or the bad guys, we may get all these bastards."

Paige shuts off the recording when he realizes that Phunts compromised a recent operation that resulted in the death of an agent and the wounding of two others in an ambush. The hit squad was waiting for them. He asks, "Is that everything?"

"No, sir."

"You just kissed me full on the lips, Martina. I think we can drop the sirs for now."

"You're the boss," she says with a smile and salute. "Nearly every drug affiliated murder from Charlotte, North Carolina to Atlanta is being committed by the cartel enforcers. They're going out of their way to implicate rival OGs to clear a path for themselves as distributers. They have a few handpicked, well-connected brothers, White boys, and *vato*, feeding them intelligence on who they will want eliminated from their own hoods and whom to blame it on. Anyone known to be a snitch gets whacked as a preemptive. At least forty unsolved, seemingly unrelated killings are actually connected to this conspiracy. These people are serious. The Mendez Cartel's contraband is already within U.S. borders, and they have warehouses bought and paid for by dummy corporations everywhere. The cost of looking the other way has already been negotiated at trucking weigh stations and with dirty DOT patrol officials along all the routes to be taken. This is what I know. When the mules finally get the call, the trucks will pass muster at the weigh stations on route to the switch out zones. Once the truck is allowed to pass, the designated off-duty DOT patrol officers will collect the final payoffs and distribute the money. Depending on how many of them are in on it, Mendez will pay up to half a mill per scaling station. These men are well-organized and dug in from top to bottom. It may take days or months, before they are confident enough to move the shipments to distribution points, so be ready at the drop of a hat. These disks contain evidence of everything I've just reported to you and more. There is one more thing. Mendez has at least one man or woman posted at nearly every rat-infested hotel in tri-county areas surrounding drop points, especially lodges in a position to visually monitor police precincts or intercept narcotics' communication bandwidths." "Why?" her superior asks.

"They are lookouts for us because, naively, DEA stings have been known to include local and state police as perimeter backups. These lookouts are comprised of couples, muscle, and the techno geek with surveillance equipment. If law enforcement looks like they are massing for a bust, or if coded chatter heightens, they will know, even if it has nothing to do with our shipments. I hope that I'll be able to give you the heads-up in time to be ready without layovers at public hotels. I won't be allowed to ride along when the contraband is moved to an unguarded switch out point, but anything is subject to change. The contraband I am expecting to escort is located somewhere between Rock Hill or Fort Mill, South Carolina and Charlotte, North Carolina. Once I zoom in on which property and route they plan to use first, I'll holla back loud and clear."

"Is all of this documented and substantiated?" Paige asks. "I mean airtight."

"I learned from the best, didn't I?" she asks. "Manuel Mendez and his Mexican associates are blood relatives. That is how a mixed Columbian and Mexican Cartel has been formed and operated without unnecessary blood in the streets for the last few years. The drug wars of the west coast and the Southwestern Border States have nothing to do with Mendez's people, other than the fact that they are secretly instigating the beef between these factions as a distraction to law enforcement. The map and GPS coordinates indicate all of the seemingly legitimate warehouses that we have hauled merchandise to and from, slowly working our way east. The red zones indicate the ones with heightened, state-of-the-art security where the vehicle and our persons have been heavily swept for transmitters and tracking devices. There were times that I was allowed full access, but not in what I believe are the hot zones. However, I have noticed the logos of three distinct import/export shipping companies: La

Carta International. Northern Transit Incorporated, and Moraga Shipping."

"This is excellent work, Agent Ruiz." He winks at her, smiling.

Agent Ruiz stares into his eyes. As if she has just relieved herself of a heavy burden, she sighs and says, "Thanks. This has been a long haul. I can't wait to put a cap on this because I need a serious rewind, sir. I'm just a little worn down by taking chances, being quick on my feet, and living with the fear of being betrayed by one of my own." She pats the keycard in his pocket. "Please feel free to use everything I gave you tonight. Oh yeah, the senior DOT patrol officers with gambling problems, large debts, mortgages, and very sick family members are the most susceptible targets of the cartel. Dig into their financial records and personal lives, certain things will jump out at you. Former Agent Phunts here has betrayed our unit and caused the death of at least one fellow agent for filthy blood money. If left up to me, I would squeeze his bitch ass like a lemon and leave him in the sun to dry rot. But I know how this works, and sometimes the slime still rises to the top by making deals." She backs out of the car and disappears before Phunts knows she is gone. The smell of diesel fuel lingers.

With Paige staring at him, Phunts snarls through his teeth, "That jalapeno eating bitch has had it. This time, she's going up on charges for assaulting another DEA agent. She is clearly off her fucking rocker from being under too long. Those tapes . . . the recordings are a part of my own undercover operation because I don't trust her. Come on,
Paige. How long have you known me, man? You know me."

Paige looks down at the gun and backhands Phunts with it, knocking out his left canine. "You didn't even know she would be here tonight. I kicked her out of the unit remember? I should have known that a prick named Phunts couldn't be trusted. You are the reason Agent Costa lost his life, why his children will grow up without a father. You are the reason Agent Mora will never walk again. You are the reason Agent Stickler will never be the same in the field because she had her hands wrist-deep in blood and guts for an hour to keep Agent Mora alive. I am going to see that you get what is coming to you for these betrayals. How long have you been reporting our tactical operations, Phunts?"

"But I. . . ."

Paige's serious eyes tell him to forget pleading his case. Phunts knows that there will be professional exile, prison, or death at the end of this road. With overwhelming evidence against him, Phunts will lawyer-up before cooperating because he needs to negotiate a safe future for is family, calculating a slim chance at getting into WITSEC. Before they move fifty yards, Paige stops and reaches behind Phunts' seat to cinch the tie wrap even tighter. He also removes the knife that Phunts always carries in his left pocket; an oversight he can ill-afford. He takes his own cuffs and secures Phunts to the door handle. Satisfied that his prisoner can barely breathe, he drives on.

Paige's coded message arranges a classified transport at a private airport.

Four hours later, Agent Paige lightly knocks before using the key. He slips into the dim lighting and pauses when he feels a naked someone in the shadows behind the door. He raises his hands, looking down at the wet footsteps on the carpeting. Slowly, he turns toward the object of his desire, the object that desires him.

Chapter 3

The Gains of Loss

The high school sports programs of the upstate are hotly contested from Rock Hill to Fort Mill and Tega Cay, South Carolina. Within these three small towns, the elite of football and basketball talent always seem to amass spring-loaded runs for the state championships year in and out.

The Northwestern High School Trojans have taken the AAAA class State Football Championship for the second time in three years, hanging their purple and gold banners proudly about the city of Rock Hill. However, the 2012 Northwestern basketball teams are left in the dust of the Fort Mill Hornets and the Tega Cay Archers in this battle for a shot at the state hoops banner. For the first time in state history, two small towns, separated by only two miles, are taking top seeds with both boy and girl teams.

Fort Mills' poorly constructed city charter, combined with the struggling economy, have set the stage for Tega Cay's acquisitive mayor to re-annex the blue-collar township. The red tape and court appeals are done with now, so this will be the last year that these schools compete because they are being combined at a new facility in August of 2013. Standing between each other and the final battles for the South Carolina State Championship, tensions are running high. The ultimate bragging rights will belong to the winners, whose mascot will stand atop the new high school. The chance of these teams splitting the wins is a strong possibility, however. This is a dilemma for those who wish to influence the outcome.

* * *

The dinged and dimpled, white 1996 Ford F-150 rumbles up the driveway, knocking a little protest as the ignition shuts off. She is running a bit rich. As the noxious exhaust fumes rush by the driver side window with the mid-March breeze, Banja Rouge proudly watches as his son and daughter take turns shooting balls on the court off to the side of the house. At age seventeen, these fraternal twins have somehow managed to inch out the old man's 6"3' frame.

Kysing Rouge, his daughter, is shooting with the white, green, and black ball her dad bought at the final WNBA game in Charlotte, North Carolina. The father/daughter outing took place on Kysing's eleventh birthday in early November of 2006. That short trip across the Carolinas' border remains a memorable occasion.

She is wearing white warm-ups, shooting flawlessly from the free-throw line. Her brother, Kilarin Rouge, dribbles the ball aggressively between his legs before maneuvering to take the three point shot. Wearing the red and black warm-ups he got nearly three years ago, when the Miami Heat beat the Charlotte Bobcats by one point, he rises for the jump shot as if elevating over a defender. Kilarin "Killer" Rouge confidently releases with a high arch at the apex, just as his sister's ball begins to rotate through the air in slow motion. With a nanosecond between them, there are double swishes from the white net when both shots slip through without touching the rim.

Kysing turns to smile at her brother, who is standing directly behind her with his shooting hand still in the air and a comical grimace etched upon his lips. Kysing laughs at him.

The thought suddenly occurs to them that they never heard their balls bouncing from the concrete court. When they look forward, their dad is standing beneath the basket, palming both balls with his huge hands.

Banja smiles at them and says, "Good shots." He dribbles the ball in his right hand and asks, "Anyone up for a game of cutthroat?" The father shrugs off the dusty shirt he had tossed over his muscular right shoulder as his kids approach him for a hug.

Without warning, both Fort Mill High juniors will snatch the balls from their father. Kilarin dribbles outside of the key, spinning to take the ten-foot jumper. Kysing dribbles backward to execute a crisp crossover before going around her father for the easy layup. The challenge is on.

Thirty minutes later, with the score tied 20 all, Banja backs in. They are all huffing and puffing, but the kids have him bracketed as he carefully dribbles to avoid their long arms swiping at the ball. He is trapped between the two trash-talking kids when they force him to pick up the dribble at the top of the key.

Taking a page of trash-talk from her brother, Kysing asks, "What ya gonna do now, old man?"

"That's right. What you gonna do now, pops?" Kilarin taunts. "We got ya. One of us is gonna win, but it won't be you, old...."

The father feints a blind hook shot to get them to react. He slings the ball at the backboard. Banja pivots, hopping between their crisscrossed legs as the basketball slams into the backboard. When the ball rebounds toward them, he grabs it in midair, coming down before taking flight for the two-handed jam with a defiant roar. Game over!

"Ugh!" the winded kids grunt in unison, knowing they've just been had.

Moments later, drenched in sweat, all three are lying in a triangle with their feet touching as they do thirty sit-ups on the cool pavement. Once done, they sit upright with their feet still touching. Their father reaches for both their hands and pulls one at a time to stretch their backs to complete a proper cool down.

With body heat steaming from his short hairs and lathered scalp, Banja Rouge lets go and says to them, "Good game, children. Try to remember that there is always something to be gained by your losses."

"Oh . . . really? What could that be, dad?" Kilarin asks of his father's seemingly conflicted statement.

"I can't wait to hear this one, dad," Kysing replies with a smile, knowing that the paradox is about to unravel. These young, highly competitive athletes have never known losing to provide anything remotely resembling an upside.

Banja Rouge looks them both in the eyes. With careful deliberation, he pinches the tips of his index finger and thumb of the right hand, as if he's about to conduct a symphonic orchestra. With the three remaining fingers freely pointing upward, he paces the back and forth movement of his hand with every word from his lips.

With a slight Haitian accent still eking through, he says, "Leave everything you've got on the court, and never underestimate a smaller opponent's desire to win. Although your ball handling skills and height advantage over many players are good assets, they can become your greatest liabilities when you forget these things. When your opponent makes a successful move on you, do not close your eyes and wish to forget it. Instead of wishing it away, open your mind's eye to it. Absorb and relive every fluent aspect of their movements in slow motion. Calm your beating hearts, and like ripples upon still water, allow yourselves to see it repeatedly until you realize a strategy to counteract the moves that your opponents will surely try to duplicate. Surprisingly, children, competitive players are often unprepared to defend their very own moves. Learn to counteract as well as use those same moves to your advantage. We may not win each challenge on the court or in life, but you are only truly losers if you forget to take something positive from every defeat or setback." The proud father smiles because their eyes reflect the absorption of his words of wisdom.

Yara Rouge has been watching from the kitchen. She raises the window over the sink and shouts, "You're all going to catch pneumonia sitting out there. Dinner is almost ready so get washed up!"

As the sun descends, Banja retrieves his shirt to walk arm in arm between his loveable children. Soon, the famished Kilarin breaks for the door to wash up first.

Kysing holds onto her father and says, "Thanks for the advice, dad. It all actually makes sense now. I'll try to remember that tomorrow, when we take on the Artichoke Archers."

He laughs before kissing her on the temple. "Artichoke, as in perfecting the art of choking? I get it. That's hilarious."

Yara sweeps her long hair behind her ear and moves toward the backdoor to greet her husband just as Kilarin bursts in.

"Mm. Smells great, mom," he says, hurrying to the bathroom to wash his hands. "Proteins and carbs, I love spaghetti night!"

"And you'll have none of it if you don't take a shower first, young man. You know I don't play that, boy." She smiles and mumbles under her breath, "He really thinks that his pitiful flattery is gonna change things around here. Good try though."

She opens the door as Banja reaches for the doorknob to let their daughter in. Kysing enters, pausing just inside the door. She closes her eyes to inhale the aroma of one of her favorite meals.

"Oh my goodness. Mom, I love you, but I think I love your spaghetti more." Her parents will chuckle, but they laugh heartily when she adds, "Can I have spaghetti as my first boyfriend? There aren't any rules against dating food, right?"

As she runs for the bathroom, Yara looks Banja in the eyes and smirks. She is smiling when she asks, "Had a good talk out there?"

He nods his head and smiles back. "We always have good talks. Especially, after I've kicked their butts on the court."

"I know because I was watching from the window," Yara says while placing her hands on her hips, disapprovingly. "Mr. Rouge, what have I told you about hypnotizing your own children with your Jedi mind tricks? I saw those subtle, rhythmic hand motions you use to captivate those kids as you speak in that calm, soothing voice."

Banja laughs aloud as Yara attempts to hug her hardworking husband.

"Careful, baby, I'm a bit grimy," Banja warns.

She kisses his lips before wrapping her arms about his broad shoulders. "Since when has that ever deterred me? I love the smell of wood chips, sawdust, and sweat on my husband after a hard day at the lumber mill. Mm. It makes you smell so manly."

"Pine Sap Cologne. A very novel idea, but it will probably be very sticky. I love you, baby."

"I love you, too. Still, I'd buy it for my man. I bet other women would, too," Yara teases. "How was your day?"

He sighs, despite a slight smile when he says, "Good. Actually, they let a few people go today."

"Oh no," she says. "Are things getting worse?"

He reassures her with a happy grin. "Not to worry. Things have been sluggish for a while, but it has been picking up, lately. Anyway, this was not exactly a workforce reduction. It was more like a jerk-force reduction. However, my job is more secure now that they fired the only other person who can fix and load those debarkers with minimal help."

"Are you talking about that mean, racist guy that always tries to get under your skin?" she asks as they approach the stairs. "You've never referred to any of your co-workers as jerks, other than him and his cohort."

"That mean old drunk got himself and his supreme buddy fired after lunch for mumbling racial insults in Callahan's Diner while the boss's daughter took lunch with a new African American buyer, who works for several big housing contractors in Rock Hill, Columbia, and Gaffney, South Carolina. When they heard him, she nearly lost a substantial contract because Grumpy was wearing a Gannett Lumber uniform at the time. As the story goes, Sandy Gannett gave the new buyer a standing discount on the first ten bulk orders. I hear he cleaned up, too. Jumped on it like a rapist in heat."

She laughs, but feels a measure of guilt because the fired workers' misfortunes will also reflect on their families. "Lord, please forgive me," Yara says.

He takes Yara's left hand while wrapping his left hand about her waistline to spin her about.

"On the upside, the boss called me in and gave me a raise. He actually apologized for not firing Jack Mansur much sooner. Tim Gannett didn't have to do it, but he explained that we were all forced to work with that asshole because he thought the company still needed the antiquated sourpuss. He said that my putting up with it all of this time was worth the raise alone. Also, because I kept the other minority workers from kicking Jack's ass on company property, I had earned a real promotion."

She claps her hands, gleefully. "Really? But I thought. . . ."

"Don't get too happy yet, baby," Banja warns. "Because no good deed goes unpunished, he will be depending on me to work quite a bit of overtime until others qualify for the vacant jobs. That means I will be training senior and newer employees to replace Jack "Sour Britches" Mansur as well. However, you can relax because we're going to be okay as long as Gannett Lumber stays in business. In fact, he is planning to expand the operation. The extra money will come in handy. We can reduce our debts and pay down on the mortgage. Between the companies represented by today's new buyer, there are twelve new subdivisions under development. That means lots of work in the near future simply because Sandy Gannett railed down on Jack like the wrath of God right there and then. Oh, Yara, it was a thing of beauty. Mr. Belfort appreciated and respected how Sandy immediately handled the situation with Mansur and pledged exclusive contracts with Gannett Lumber, and personal recommendations to his associates in the business. He spent upwards of 3.2 million dollars in lumber orders for respective contractors."

"If a new client comes to spend that kind of money only to be insulted, I'd say Jack Mansur earned it. Now, paying down the mortgage will be nice, but I think we should get you a better truck. I think old Libby has hauled more than her share. Besides, honey, you deserve this. I mean, I don't know how much money you're going to get as a raise, but it doesn't matter. Let's do something just for you for a change. Okay, baby?"

"A newer truck would be nice. Are you sure about this?"

"No. No. Not newer. I mean brand new. You da man now, honey. You've gotta represent."

"Brand new? Maybe, let's look for next to brand new also."

"You know you don't need my permission, Mr. Rouge. Just my approval." They laugh. "And, besides, I've already been vetted as the new mortgage loan officer at the local Wells Fargo, just a few blocks away. I will no longer have to cross the state line just to fight Charlotte's aggressive drivers and bad traffic. Your father will finally join us so he can spend some time with the kids before graduating next year. Things will be wonderful."

"That's great, Yara. Things are really looking up."

When Banja gets this squirrely, conflicted look on his face, she asks, "What's the matter?"

"Father—finally joining us in America. Our children soon graduating. Wow. Where has the time gone?"

"Wait! What about the kids' basketball playoff games?" Yara asks, fearing that he will miss the important occasions. "I mean, do you have to start the overtime and training right away?"

"Not to worry. Two of Mr. Gannett's sons played ball for the Hornets before going to college. He understands how important it is to me. Besides, the mayor of Tega Cay is his cousin and Gannett hates his guts. I will not have to start working longer hours until Monday so all is well. I will be a bit late for Kysing's playoff game on Friday, but I'll be there before the game clock hits zero. I will be able to see most of Kilarin's game on Saturday."

"Good. I'm glad, and I know they will be thrilled to see you there."

"So will I, Yara. You know, Mr. Gannett admitted a little jealousy of me today, as we sat in his office and had a drink. It was just a beer, and he insisted I have a drink with him as the new go-to guy."

"The Mecklenburg side of the family probably owns half of the upstate, and the other side of it probably owns the rest. Why on earth would he be jealous of you, and still give you a raise? That just doesn't ordinarily compute these days."

Banja smiles at her and says, "He went through my employee profile while considering my raise and promotion to managing supervisor. Of course, I'll still have to get my hands dirty, but I'm the boss. And I intend to make myself invaluable to the company." "Go on," she says in anticipation.

"Mr. Gannett was surprised that I am actually forty-three-years-old. He thought I was somewhat younger, therefore he is a little envious because I seem to wear it so well." He flips his imaginary hair like a smoking hot chic and puckers her Botoxed lips.

"I see," Yara Rouge says while squeezing her husband's firm, muscular shoulders and biceps. She smiles and pats his bottom as she says, "Yes, sir. I am definitely the lucky one here. You are quite the specimen, Mr. Rouge. I sure would like to get some fries with that shake."

They laugh and kiss. The kids have showered, and now it is his turn. On the way upstairs, he tells them not to wait, knowing that the water will probably go cold halfway through his shower. This is simply a way of delaying the inevitable onset of heartburn. Banja is not sure if it is the spaghetti sauce or the garlic bread that disagrees with him. Maybe it is the combination of the two. In any event, he will eat whatever Yara puts on his plate before sneaking back into the kitchen for some of that soothing pink stuff.

When he comes back downstairs, his family is sitting at the table. They have not eaten as a sign of respect, waiting for him to come downstairs, despite the grumbling stomachs of the twins. Because Yara has shared the good news, they cheer for the breadwinner of the family. They join hands, waiting for him to close the circle. Curiously, there will be no heartburn for Banja Rouge tonight.

Chapter 4

Kysing's Rock

Banja Rouge crosses the state line with Sandy Gannett, who is flying out of Douglas International Airport to Los Angeles to check on her ailing favorite aunt, Kathryn. Her aunt lives on the east coast, becoming ill while visiting a daughter and grandchildren out west. Banja kindly sits with Sandy until her flight is announced. In the meantime, they discuss the public firing of yesterday. She congratulates Mr. Rouge on his promotion and fully endorses him as her father's choice to replace Mr. Mansur.

"There just isn't any more room or excuses in the world for the tolerance of such outright intolerance. Just because it isn't their burden to bear, too many people just act like they are deaf and dumb. The business world, in general, has allowed too many people like Jack Mansur to use their positions or their race to torment people in the workplace. Gannett Lumber and Building Supplies, I'm ashamed to say, has been just as guilty of turning a blind eye to it. But no longer. That's a promise, Mr. Rouge."

"Call me Banja, please. And thank you for the kind assurances, Sandy."

She looks at him and says, "Until the shame of it washes away, I feel I must address you formally as a sign of respect and utmost regret, Mr. Rouge. Of course, since I'm the boss' daughter, I insist that you continue to address me by my first name. Deal?"

Banja shakes her hand and says, "Deal, Sandy." Her flight is called for boarding.

Before leaving, Banja purchases a ticket for his father to travel from Haiti. Until recently, Kwaban has declined a second visit, but the yearning for his family has steadily grown like a knot in his gut. The fact that he is missing the growth and development of his maturing grandchildren is the argument that Yara and Banja have successfully used to convince him to come to America for good. When the ninety-year-old grandfather is ready to fly the friendly skies, he can pick up his ticket at the newly reactivated Toussaint Louverture International Airport in Tabarre, a commune of Port-au-Prince.

Upon his return to Fort Mill, the truck gurgles to a stop in the gymnasium's packed parking lot. Banja considers the flight receipt, smiling to himself as he puts it in the glove compartment. When he gets out and walks toward the Hornets' gymnasium, his stomach squirms as the sound of rowdy, rumbling fans shake the packed stands to the steel rafters. He calls his wife, whose phone vibrates to warn her of his arrival. Yara tells her son to watch for his father, but answers the phone screaming in Banja's ear as Kysing drives the ball to the basket against her defensive nemesis, Stacie Mecklenburg.

When Kilarin stands to wave at his father, he disappears amongst the fans' raised hands as Kysing ties the game again. As the cheers subside, there are some not so subtle boos from the crowd because it is obvious that at least two opponents fouled her.

After Banja sits next to his wife, Yara asks, "Baby, what took you so long? You almost missed the entire game."

Banja looks up at the scoreboard and says, "I'm sorry, honey. Traffic was bad going and even worse coming back because of accidents and rubberneckers. I hate going into Charlotte on Fridays."

"Well, as long as you made it. Did you get it taken care of?"

"Yes, the ticket will be waiting for father at the airport. Of course, it costs more than they quoted on the phone, but at least it is one way this time."

The tall center inbounds the ball and the speedy point guard dribbles down the court for the Tega Cay Archers. She is very shifty, drawing extra attention from the Hornets' defense. She loops the ball back to the top of the circle where Stacie Mecklenburg is free to take the three point shot. When the center approaches to contest the attempt, Stacie rises to take the shot too quickly.

As the ball arches toward the basket, it looks to be a close miss. The referee blows the whistle and calls a foul on the Hornet's defending center. Even though no foul occurred, and Stacie's momentum clearly carried her inside of the three-point line before taking the shot, she gets three free throws to the angry boos of the home crowd.

Coach Candace Peeler runs toward the same referee and voices her angry opinion of his bad call, for which she promptly receives a technical foul. The Lady Archers' power forward makes the technical foul shot. Despite the home crowd's attempted distraction, Stacie "the Mech" Mecklenburg drops all three free throws to give the Tega Cay Archers a four-point lead with only 1:12 left on the clock.

The heavily biased crowd moans as the Tega Cay fans cheer for their team. Coach Peeler calls timeout, needing to bolster her girls and discuss how they plan to come back.

Kysing Rouge makes eye contact with Stacie as she leaves her rebound position at the key to huddle. The eye contact seems slow of motion as Stacie wipes her face. Slowed by adrenalin-distorted time, sweat slings from Kysing's chin as she says, "Good shot." She turns and goes to the huddle.

Surprised by Kysing's acknowledgement, Stacie's eyes seek the hardwood. She knows there was no foul, but took the shots anyway because that is the way it is done. Decent coaches always teach good sportsmanship, but never to look a gift horse in the mouth because referees are subject to making mistakes against all teams, eventually. However, she feels a twinge of guilt as she heads for the huddle.

Coach Peeler reminds her girls, "This game is not over. We have recovered from bigger deficits with less time on the clock, ladies. It ain't over until the fat lady sings, and I'm deaf today. This is how we will approach the situation."

Coach Peeler draws out the triangle offensive attack on her board.

With seconds left, she admonishes, "Do not leave this in the hands of the referees. We know what we are up against tonight, so I want you all to stay focused and rise to the occasion. Drive the rock to the hoop. Score quickly, and ram it down their fucking throats. Get back on defensive, immediately. Do you hear me, Lady Hornets? Leave everything you've got on that court or you will feel it tomorrow, and the next, and the day after that. We don't need favors from the referees to win because we are the Hornets, and we're better than them. Ram that rock down their throats. Let's go on three!"

The coach puts her hand out with the palm down and the team joins her. However, Kysing brings her right hand up from under to mesh her fingers with Coach Peeler, who looks to her star player with pride and confident butterflies churning in her gut. Kysing places her other hand atop the pile.

With sweat dripping from her smooth chin, Kysing shouts, "Let's go. Let's go. Let's go. Get it!"

As she turns away, Banja rises in the stand and shouts, "Kiss-kiss!" She hears and looks at her father, who is holding out his hands as if they are the claws of a tiger. She smiles and exhales a deep breath with her eyes to the floor as she takes her position. She looks up at to the opponent's basket and pictures her next move.

The Hornets inbound against pressure, passing out of the uncalled hacking fouls of the Archer defenders. The forward takes the ball across the line, moving aggressively toward the basket. As she approaches the top of the key, Kysing moves in from the corner. Help comes too late from the weak side. The forward dumps the ball off. Kysing roars as she takes flight and jams the rock down their throats, even though the rotating center fouls her on the way up. Still, there is no whistle from the referees when Kysing Rouge comes down hard. The crowd groans because she is slow to get up. Her family, like the crowd, now holds their breath.

When she rises to shake it off, the fans go wild. The crowd shouts Kysing Rouge's well-known nickname.

"Stinger! Stinger! Stinger!" rises to the ceiling. Their chanting voices, vibrating the steel rafters above, urges Kysing and the rest of the team on. With her name reverberating high above, the entire team's energy level rises as if the crowd is giving them a piece of themselves so the Hornets may persevere. In unison, they have become the sixth man.

Dana Smead, the Tega Cay Archers' head coach, directs a damning glare at the head ref. As he runs the sideline, she keeps pace, warning, "Don't you do it to me, Arnie. Don't you fucking do this shit. Let my girls win or lose on their own merits. Do you hear me?"

Kysing blocks the power forward's attack. The ball is rebounded by Stacie "the Mech" Mecklenburg, who launches for an easy layup, but Kysing Rouge is the real machine here. She recovers in time to reject the shot off the glass right into the waiting arms of the Hornets' teammate. Samantha Green is about to drive the ball the other way, just as Referee Arnold Pol places the whistle to his lips to call goaltending on Kysing for what was a clean deflection off the backboard. The ball was clearly on the way up when Kysing Rouge slammed it into the backboard, so goaltending would have been another bad call on a long list of bad calls in this contest.

"Damn it, I will tell Susan about that floozy living behind Callahan's Diner if you blow that whistle. You can bet your castrated balls on it. I will do it, Arnie. I will do it, so help me!"

What comes out is a deflated, half-hearted late whistle that draws everyone's attention and instant recrimination from the frustrated crowd. He cannot just wave the whistle off and allow play to continue, so he points to a fictitious wet spot for the mop girl to dry up. Collectively, the crowd issues a united sigh of relief.

A timeout is called with twenty-seconds on the clock. Both coaches are drawing up plans to counter the opponent's efforts.

The rowdy crowd goes dead silent when the players prepare to inbound the ball. Their heartbeats are one, clasping their hands together to will this team on to the State Championships in Columbia, South Carolina.

The opponent contests Kysing's inbound pass. She fakes the overhead pass to the forward, while the point guard searches for daylight. There it is—an opening. Kysing bounce passes to the point guard, who drives to the basket. She dishes the ball to the power forward that comes from the corner to dribble under the basket into an apparent trap. She leaves her feet, surrounded by the raised hands of taller players. She is not trying for the layup, firing the high velocity rock out to Kysing Rouge, who drives toward the basket just outside the key. She feints a quick shot, but fades away as her double-teaming opponents leave their feet. With contact assured, the Stinger rises with confidence, eyes locked on to the target. Swoosh! The crowd goes berserk as the defenders come down on her to bring the reluctant, but unavoidable whistle.

The score is tied seventy-nine all. Yara Rouge buries her eyes in Banja's jacket, afraid to watch. With one second left on the clock, Kysing approaches the foul line for her free-throw shot. One basket and they will go to the South Carolina State finals. Both coaches want to take a timeout, but they have none left to call.

Kilarin prompts his mother to watch. "She's money from the line, mom!" Yara cannot bear to look.

Kysing Rouge wipes her sweaty palms on her soaked shorts, wiping her face in the crux of her forearm. When the ref blows the whistle and gives her the ball, the world is silent. As she bounces the ball with her right hand, she holds her left arm backward in the general vicinity of her family. Her fingers are the claws of a predatory animal.

Banja Rouge smiles to himself.

She assumes the posture. Drowning out all things in this universe, her eyes slowly rise to the target. One mock shot with her right hand and slightly bent knees, Kysing Rouge is ready to claim her destiny or immense disappointment. Kysing inches closer to the line and takes a blow as sweat drips from her. She bounces the ball twice and pauses to look up. The basketball leaves Kysing's hand, slowly rotating as more sweat drips from her chin. Swoosh, and the crowd roars!

Only one second remains for the opposing team. With no timeouts left, they attempt a quick inbound pass and shot that goes errant.

Kysing "the Stinger" Rouge has made the game winning shot, and there is absolute bedlam in the gymnasium as the fans pour onto the court like an avalanche. The Fort Mill Hornets are going to the South Carolina State Finals to compete with Byrnes High, another fiercely competitive upstate rival.

Chapter 5

Robbed, Not Defeated

Every now and then, he hears the angry echoes of other teammates banging chairs or slamming doors shut, but it makes no difference to his state of lonesome dejection. As Kilarin Rouge sits in the dim gymnasium, head bowing low, he quietly weeps. The echo of, "There's always next year, kid," holds no solace for him because his team was just cheated of the chance to take that bus ride to Columbia, South Carolina.

His dream of playing in the Carolina Gamecock's coliseum and winning the state title have been, effectively, dashed against the rocks of despair in the wake of a close, but crushing defeat at the hands of biased referees. Not a better team.

With his tightly braided locks falling from his shoulders, he holds a sweaty towel against his eyes while fighting the urge to cry out in the dimness where hushed whispers seem to echo all around.

Standing in the lighted hallway to the locker rooms, Banja Rouge and Coach Tom McCardell quietly discuss Kilarin's distraught state of mind. Both are angry, feeling for the disappointed junior, who has been a starter with the same Hornet teammates for three exciting years. This is Kilarin's team. This cohesive unit was built around Kilarin Rouge by an excellent coaching staff that developed more than a one-man squad.

The approach of footsteps means nothing to the young man.

They reach the youngster, standing before him, wordlessly, until Banja kneels and touches his son on the shoulder. The startled young man rises from the depressive malaise to look into his father's eyes. Kilarin's pain is deeply infectious. He hugs his sympathetic father, fighting back the abject tears of sullen disenchantment.

"We were worried when we couldn't find you, son," Banja says. "We searched everywhere we could think of. Your mother and sister were frantic until I just told them that you are here. If I had taken Kysing's advice from the start, I would have been here sooner. You are not in this alone, Kilarin."

"I'm sorry for taking off like that, dad," Kilarin whispers. "I couldn't face anyone after . . . after letting everyone down."

The coach places his hand on his star player's right shoulder and says, "Never once, son. You've never, ever, let us down."

As Banja sits with his arms around Kilarin's heaving shoulders to console him, Coach McCardell's cell phone chimes and vibrates in his shirt pocket. He turns to answer it. "Hello, this is Tom. Yep, we found him. He is okay, just hurtin' something awful right now. You are? Come right on in, George."

The coach walks away and grabs four folding chairs with thick rubber boots that will protect the polished surface. He takes them to center court and heads for the overhead light switches.

Banja says, "You didn't let anyone down, Kilarin, especially your family. That includes your team and fans alike. I am very proud of how you played. I'm proud of how you met this contest with maturity and determination. You gave your heart and soul in the face of overwhelming adversity, son, so never feel as if you've let any of us down because nothing could be further from the truth." He hugs Kilarin Rouge, who returns the gesture in a touching moment between father and son.

More footsteps are approaching, ending somewhere on the Hornets' home court. Coach McCardell interrupts by saying, "Rouge. Number eleven, front and center, young man."

Kilarin and Banja look to center court where a tall stranger stands beneath the dim overhead lighting next to his coach, who beckons them to join them. They stand to walk arm in arm toward his coach and a man they have never met, but there seems to be something familiar about the stranger.

"Yes, coach?"

Coach McCardell displays an open palm to introduce his lifelong friend. "Mr. Rouge, Kilarin, I would like to introduce you to someone you may want to speak to. Before we begin, I only ask that you both keep this meeting on the down low. Agreed?"

"Sure, coach."

Banja says, "Agreed. What's going on?"

The tall gentleman in the kakis and white dress shirt reaches out to shake their hands. The coach invites them to sit as he says, "My name is George Boxer, gentlemen. You may have heard of me, since my name seems to carry a sort of mythical air about it in these parts. I say mythical because I don't do television or radio interviews. Tonight, I could be your magic unicorn, son. As my good friend, Coach McCardell suggests, we have been friends since grade school. What he hasn't revealed is that I'm a scout for the North Carolina Tar Heels, among other school affiliates, and I've been watching you play for three seasons now."

Kilarin's heart skips a beat. He turns to his father and smiles because he has heard of this man. Mr. Boxer's reputation for scouting athletic talent is legendary in the south, but, until now, he has never seen him up close.

"Really?" Kilarin replies with a lump in his throat.

"I grew up in these here parts, and I am all about the rock, son. I've come to believe that you have what it takes to make a positive contribution to any one of the teams that I represent. Now your coach tells me that you have your heart set on playing for the Carolina Gamecocks. That's an admirable aspiration, but I think you can do better."

Kilarin is about to burst, "Yes sir, but...."

Banja holds onto his son's arm, feeling his surging enthusiasm as he strains to stay seated.

George Boxer splays his fingers with open palms, assuming a look of seriousness as he says, "Son, this is the part where your absolute silence regarding this meeting comes into play. I need both your words that this conversation will go no farther than the four of us and your immediate family, whom you must also swear to secrecy.

Do I have your solemn oath on that? Can you gentlemen all look me in the eyes and swear this to secrecy?"

They do, even the coach pledges to say nothing.

"What is it?" Banja asks.

"I am sort of an independent talent scout—a freelancer — with very strong ties to both schools afore mentioned and others. In this case, I guess you can call me a quadruple-dipper when trolling for basketball talent. However, even independents have rules of engagement when it comes to contact with students. If I actually adhered to the rules, I'm sure I'd be breaking quite a few by just being here."

"Are you really allowed to scout for opposing schools?" Kilarin asks. "Wow!"

"As I mentioned—in the eyes of some —I'm a man with clout because of my meticulous eye for talent. My affiliation with these particular universities carries weight, but I practically wrote the contracts that dictate the terms. Therefore, I seek the talent that fits the team, with a mind to anticipate their future needs based on the strengths, weaknesses, and productivity of their present players. I'm also forced to give strong consideration to graduating statuses, and injury reports. Hard data, logistics, and my enchanted crystal ball work quite nicely together. For example, if the Carolina Gamecocks are in need of a savvy point guard or power forward, that's what I scout and place. Presently, Anthony Mackey and Tyrel Poinsett are both healthy and academically sound in their sophomore years with Richards and Ballenger behind them. If the North Carolina Tar Heels are in need of a beast to play center, then that is the position I scout. Speaking of beasts, son, I must admit that I haven't seen your kind of unselfish passion for the game in a long time. I commend you on your maturity in controlling your temper in the midst of one bad call after another when it was amply clear that yours was the better team. It is obvious that you were all robbed tonight. However, in my eyes, you are undefeated, young man."

"Thank you, sir." Banja says. "I believe my son really needed to hear those words from someone other than his confederates."

"Oh. Please believe me when I say, I'm not the kind of man who will blow smoke up your ass and tell you the fog is rolling in. I was here a year ago for the game against South Point. Your stats were off the charts, son. With 44 points, five steals, eleven assists, seven offensive rebounds, eight defensively, and six for six 3-pointers, Kilarin, you were a young man possessed. I have not seen a game so lopsided against a ranked opponent in all my years as a talent scout. You led your team to a 111 to 57 point victory that has stuck in my mind ever since. If it wasn't for injuries to two key players, you team could have gone all the way."

"Thanks for saying that, but...."

"No buts are necessary, Killer. I mean every word of it, and I plan to voice my concerns with the School Board's Athletic Commission on what I consider to be blatant biases against your team tonight. It may do no good, but as a man who makes a living by giving youngsters their honest to goodness shots at a future in the collegiate and professional sporting world, I feel it my duty to lodge a complaint because it deprives us all of the best athletes in the game. Referees are human and capable of honest mistakes, but tonight's gross ineptitude borders on criminal at best. I have seen things like this break a player or an entire team's hopes and dreams, draining the desire to thrive at what comes naturally and with hard work. It takes the joy out of it for the players and fans alike, so someone has to step up and state the facts. See I have several people in my employ, two of which are always posted on both sides of the court to digitally record the games that feature the players of interest. If need be, I can cover five to ten different games at the same time. So when I make a formal complaint about these crooked, back alley-bought referees, you can bet your boots there will be plenty of documentation to go with it. To keep you all isolated from any recriminations, I will not make it all about you, Kilarin, but the grand scheme of things in general."

"Even if it changes nothing, I'd still appreciate that, Mr. Boxer. You are right. I was just seriously contemplating whether it is still worth it when someone can just snatch it away whenever he likes. Tonight's loss really hurts. The entire team is talking about quitting."

"Actually, young man, that may not be such a bad idea when you think about it. A mass walkout could go far to convince those people that they can no longer turn a blind eye to the malfeasances in officiating high school sporting events," Boxer says with a glance at the coach. "Of course, something like that will only have to be a bluff to achieve the desired effect. However, with the entire school and the team's fans begging them not to quit, this can become quite a public embarrassment for some people. At the very least, those who were probably bought off will be placed under very heavy scrutiny while officiating in the Pee Wee League."

"Do you really think so, Mr. Boxer?"

"You can call me George, Kilarin. Trust me when I say that it would be a loss to the game of basketball and its fans if players like yourself walked away completely. Let us get down to business, shall we? Mr. Rouge, firstly, I'd like to ask your permission to speak to your son about his future in the game of basketball."

"Of course," Banja says. "It is fine with me, as long as my son wishes it. How about it, Kilarin?"

"Yeah. Yes, of course."

The coach smiles at them.

"Now then, your coach tells me that you're actually only one credit from graduating, assuming you pass all your courses this semester. Is that correct?"

"I may only have a B-plus average in Calculus, but I'm aces otherwise, sir."

George Boxer sits erect and looks at Banja with a smile when he says, "Respectful, too. You just passed two tests just then, young man. You were honest about your grades and still called me sir. I like that. It is a sign of good rearing by good, attentive parents. Something that goes lacking these days."

"I appreciate the compliment about his upbringing, George," says Banja. They chuckle because Kilarin's father is proving his manhood in a way that still exudes respect.

"Coach McCardell, can Kilarin's academic transcript and PSAT and ACT scores be made readily available?"

Coach McCardell nods an affirmation. "Of course, George. I can fax them and his complete high school transcript to your office by Monday morning."

"Thank you, sir. That will certainly make things easier if we are to move forward. You see, when presenting a prospect to a team, I like to walk in confidently loaded for bear."

"Just how tall are you now, without sneakers on?" asks George Boxer.

"At my last weigh-in and measurement, I'm six feet, five and a half inches tall, sir."

"And still growing, I bet. Six-five to six-eight is perfect for a ball handler. Just remember, the taller you get, you must work that much harder at retaining your dribbling and agility." He takes a pad from his breast pocket and thumbs through it. "You have grown seven inches since the first time I came to watch you play right here on this very court. Back then, your coach was kind enough to call me to say that he may have someone special to watch. Your squad scored over eighty points in that game. In my line of work, it pays to be a walking, talking stat sheet because it can be a fickle profession." He scribbles down the boy's current height.

Coach agrees, and Kilarin is bouncing off the walls. "What do you mean by it being fickle?"

"That's a good question, Kilarin. What I mean is that there are many talented ballplayers out there, but not all of them can hold it in the road in sunny weather, son. Sometimes, however, that talent pool dwindles like water in times of drought. I look for several specific qualities in the players I am scouting. Things like a player's temperament, family stability, maturity, recorded disciplinary actions and police records, are all precursors for me. But allow me to clarify one thing. When I refer to family stability, it's never about income. That would make me just another really stupid Republican." Boxer grins as the rest of them burst into laughter.

"No, sir. Some of the best players come from next to nothing. They become the best because they are athletically talented, well coached, and disciplined enough to be coached. Most of all they are hungry. Are you old enough to remember Michael Jordan and the Chicago Bulls?"

Kilarin nods with a smile at the silly question.

"Of course you are, but as great as MJ was, he isn't the subject of my point. The Bulls also had a player named Dennis Rodman. He was a wildcard as a Piston, but he was weapon for Phil Jackson in Chicago. Rodman wasn't the biggest or the best offensive player, but he had special talents. He was a great rebounder, but more than that, he had a talent for flustering bigger, stronger players by talking trash in their ears. He threw many players off their game, and got quite a few tossed out of games for throwing a punch at him for the insane things he whispered to them. He derailed one of the most productive players back in the day. Carl Malone to be exact. With Rodman guarding him, Malone just couldn't seem to deliver a simple bag of mail. Maybe a bit before your time, but there is always film to watch." The elder gentlemen chuckle because it is true.

Kilarin looks at his father and coach before saying, "One of your criteria for scouting ballers is finding the players who can resist that sort of thing. Stay on track no matter what frustrates them most."

"You are very sharp. Saw the bigger picture. I tip my hat to you, young man. Now, let us get back to business. As a junior you have already broken all the school's longstanding records and most in the state. You have my vote for MVP, that's for sure. Well, as Coach McCardell and I both see it, you have two choices of how to proceed. You can gut it out, try to stay healthy, and come back next year. However, as I understand it, your schools will be merging. The question you must answer is whether you want to be the same player for them that you were for Tom. Now, here is the significant part. In the state of South Carolina, you are currently ranked the number one player. You're nationally ranked below the 200 watermark— without having played for the national championship. You have no idea how phenomenal that is, son. In my book, that makes you a five star player, Killer. That puts you among the elite prospects in my eyes, and a Sneaky Pete at that. I'm no bottom feeder, gentlemen. But the cream doesn't always have time to rise to the top. The best ones often languish in the shadows until daylight breaks and they shine when given the opportunity. You are my Sneaky Pete, Kilarin Rouge. Nobody will see you coming."

"Wow. Thank you, Mr. Boxer. I never kept up with rankings, but—wow."

"Just don't let it go to your head. Now, option number two involves hard work, sacrifice, and resilience. As I understand it, you chose to skip or advance in English because of your birthday.

So, as a junior, you are already taking twelfth grade English. You can elect to graduate early without bothering with your senior year and sign a letter of intent for early entrance. It is a lot to consider, and there is absolutely no pressure to change your course. Either way, you have my support. However, I suggest you collect the applications now and begin the process. With a strong recommendation, I can practically guarantee you a full ride and a spot on either bench of the Carolinas. On the other hand, you can do the same playing for Kentucky or Duke. You just have to figure out where you really want to be and start working toward that end, depending on your test scores. Mind you, young man, if you should choose option two at any of the four colleges, you can kiss this summer good-bye because you will be in school while your friends are hanging out at the beach. After graduating high school this summer, you will get to relax a little before starting your freshman year in college. And you had better attend every class and show a GPA that guarantees that playing isn't going to become an issue. If you study hard and get a leg up on things, I believe you will outshine anyone competing for your position. Now I mean this, son. I need both your mind and body to continue as a well-oiled machine that works together on all levels. The college atmosphere has powerful distractions, such as Cindy, Mindy, and Bambi."

The older men laugh. Staying focused and wide-eyed, he whispers, "Duke? Kentucky? Yes. Yes, of course I can do it. No slacking allowed. I'll pull that B-plus up to an A by the end of the semester."

"We will give it a great deal of thought, Mr. Boxer," Banja assures. "Of course, my wife does have a say in this."

"I'd expect nothing less, Mr. Rouge." The scout takes two business cards from his pocket and hands them to the boy's father. "I want you to think long on this. You have my blessing to discuss it with your immediate family and coach McCardell here, but no one else. All bets are off if my name or the details of this meeting ends up on someone's social media page. You should know that Tom is your greatest fan, Kilarin. This private introduction is nothing less than the selfless act of a saint because he is willing to let a personal masterpiece move on to bigger things regardless of his own aspirations to take a state championship. You rarely find people of his caliber and coaching acumen, who are willing to do this sort of thing for a student that they have groomed from a cub. He will always have a personal stake in your future, so you should consider such things when standing alone at one of the many crossroads you will face in your life. Sometimes it's not about what Jesus would do, but what he wouldn't do."

"I will, Mr. Boxer. I promise to consider everything we have discussed tonight. Even if I feel like I'm gonna bust wide open, I will keep my mouth shut."

The scout furrows his brows and sits forward in his seat. With his hands clasped between his knees, Boxer considers the floor, contemplating the delicacy of things. Quite abruptly, he asks, "Any drug use, son?" He suddenly looks the boy, not his father, directly in the eyes. "Marijuana, cocaine, Molly, ecstasy, meth, mescaline? Any uppers, downers, alcohol?"

Without blinking, Kilarin Rouge looks into those serious eyes to proudly state, "No, sir. I have never experimented with drugs, Mr. Boxer. Never will. I may be young, but I've already seen a lot of my former friends spinout because of it."

Banja places his arms about his son's shoulders. Without hostility, he proclaims, "My wife and I have discussed the trappings of drug use and peer pressure to use them at length with both our children, Mr. Boxer. I'm very proud to say that my son is a good boy with a mind of his own. He has goals and high aspirations."

They join Mr. Boxer as he stands. "Patience and temperance, you both pass with flying colors. Well, Kilarin "Killer" Rouge, I truly believe that you are ready for this, son. You can bet your bottom dollar that I never stamp my sign of approval on just any old make and model. That is not to say there have not been some disappointments over the years. Remember, the Gamecocks can use you, but their mediocre showing and outgoing seniors casts a shadow on their recruiting options. I have no doubt that you can go there and thrive, but the odds will be stacked against you in the end. The North Carolina Tar Heels, Duke University, and Kentucky will give you an immediate shot. I believe your best chances at playing for the National Championship lies with the teams that Coach Roy Williams, Mike Krzyzewski, or Coach Calipari have put together in North Carolina and Kentucky. A scrappy, cerebral, go-getter like you will fit the scheme of things like that missing piece on the chessboard for either of the three.

You see, some of their best players, no matter what their national ranking by Rival, Scout, 247 Sports or ESPN, I probably placed them and the guys on the bench who spell them when tired. Their probable replacements after graduating or early enrollment in the NBA. There are times when I'm three layers deep, young man. That's why I don't have time for interviews and glad handing. Gentlemen, I look forward to working with you in the future." He shakes their hands once more and leaves.

Kilarin hugs his coach and then his dad. He thanks his coach for believing in his ability to handle this great opportunity.

Coach McCardell is a bit misty-eyed when he says, "Whatever you decide, Killer, I want you to know that you have my full support. They robbed us tonight, so I'll be forced to take the assistant coach's position next season because of Larkin Mecklenburg's dirty, underhanded dealings. There is no doubt in my mind that he's behind tonight's fiasco because he wanted his son Robbie to win so badly that he must have bought off or blackmailed the entire referee squad for tonight's game. Having two biased refs against your sister's team last night didn't do it so he must have really upped the ante just for you." "It hurts, but it's okay, Coach McCardell."

McCardell looks at Kilarin and his father and says, "You're right, son. Sometimes, one man's loss can be that same man's gain. Always remember that. I feel badly for the team, but for you most of all because you sweated blood on that court. You were unstoppable, unselfish, and tenacious in your determination to rise above the officiating bullshit. This is my way of giving you a chance to realize your dreams without helping our nemesis to achieve theirs on your back. The best revenge against crabs in a bucket is to prove you are better than those who would hold you back by walking tall. I want you to stand straight and proud, my boy. That being said, gentlemen, I'll let you get home to your family. If you do decide to go all-in, don't be surprised to look up and see me on the same sideline someday. You see, I've got a few options, too. Good night." He winks with a wily smile.

They shake hands and head for the door. Surprisingly, George Boxer reappears in the dim lighting of the hallway. As they approach, he looks Banja Rouge in the eyes to say, "I was so excited about meeting your son, I almost forgot my other reason for being here. I gave you two of my business cards because this offer also stands for your daughter. I've been scouting her as well. Because Kysing "the Stinger" Rouge is about to compete for a State Championship, it may be a good idea to hold off mentioning this until she has played her heart out without any undue distractions. Then again, it can be quite motivating. I will leave that decision to you and your wife's discretion. You have some very talented children, Mr. Rouge. I commend you and your wife for supporting them through these challenging times where so many youngsters get lost. I am sure that there are great things to come in their futures. I came back to let you know that the two schools I'm looking at Kysing Rouge for are none other than UConn and Baylor. Same opportunity, a full ride. Both teams have need for a skilled ball driver with a deadeye at the foul line. If you take no offense to the term, what both institutions are seeking is an aggressive attack dog, with both height and excellent ball handling skills."

Banja smiles when he says, "No offense will ever be taken for compliments to my children. You have given us wonderful news tonight. Thank you very much, sir."

"I gotta tell ya, when I saw her sling that ball at the backboard and split those defenders to take flight for the two-handed jam, I swear I almost crapped my britches. Few female athletes possess the agility and physical ability to execute such plays. I believe that the Stinger is a perfect fit for either program. With my recommendation,

UConn and Baylor are both prepared to offer her a full athletic scholarship. In fact, Mr. Rouge, I have them chomping at the bit. You have a good night."

Boxer tips his cap, turning away to leave them astounded by even better news. "I'll have digital trailers of both your kids' on-court accomplishments delivered to their coaches for your family's approval before I use them to present the players to the teams they decide to join. If you take the early option, that is. Once again, good night, and keep the faith."

* * *

Meanwhile, the Tega Cay Archers, their parents, and fans, are partying around a bonfire at Lake Wylie. The tent setup with lots of food, soft drinks and booze for the grownups have all been previously arranged.

With all the whooping and cheering going on, Mayor Larkin Mecklenburg toasts the team for beating the stuffing out of the Hornets by a paltry two points.

He holds his glass high with his son close at his side to toast, "Here's to the Tega Cay Archers. Heck of a game, guys. Next stop, the semi-finals and State Championship!"

Most people cheer him on, but not everyone is quite as ecstatic. Robbie, seems a bit sullen, but whoops it up for his father's sake. Claiming to be just a little tired from the game, he sneaks off with a couple bottles of beer to hang with his teammates. Robbie harbors a secret resentment, believing that his father lacked faith in his ability to win on his own. Though the sour subject will go undiscussed, he knows that Mayor Larkin Mecklenburg's fingerprints are all over their defeat of the Fort Mill Hornets. The boy now feels that he has to perform well at the state level to prove his true skills as a baller.

His sister, Stacie, is farther away from the rowdy well-wishers. Her boyfriend kisses her and tries to lay her down in the back seat.

When she rebuffs his efforts, he sweeps his blond hair aside and asks, "What gives, babe? I'm just trying to cheer you up."

He kisses her again, and slips his hand into her shirt. The angry girl loses patience with his lack thereof. She slaps the Archer's starting quarterback across the jaw and says, "I told you I'm not ready for that, Willy. I swear to God, you make me sick."

She exits, straightening her blouse and sweater as the horny senior moans his frustrated disappointment.

"Wait, Stacie. Come on, babe. Why can't we just . . . you know? Ugh!"

She suddenly turns on William Chalmers with fire in her eyes when she says, "I'm not ready, Willy. What part of that don't you understand? I haven't trusted you since catching you with that tramp, Missy Tyler. Secondly, our parents are just over there. Have some fucking respect, you knuckle dragger. In fact, why don't you just fuck the fuck off? We are done for good, Willy. Don't bother calling. No emails or text messages, either. I bet Missy is readily available to suck your sweaty cock. You are so fired. Jerk!"

With her ponytail swinging from side to side, Stacie jogs away. She wipes tears from her eyes, but she is glad to be rid of him for good. This time, she realizes that she really means it. There should be no forgiveness for his constant betrayals with other girls.

Mayor Mecklenburg moves away to hold conference with Mayor Riley of the defunct Fort Mill Township. As they shake hands in the shadows, they both look over their shoulders.

Riley asks, "Well, did you get everything you wanted, Larkin?"

Larkin replies, "Not quite, but close enough. Santa Claus is still coming early this year for us both, and this year just started. Now that I know you are a man to be trusted, I will endorse you for the job as Deputy Mayor." As he lights a cigar, the match flares up in the breeze to singe his nostril hairs. "And don't worry, Mayor Riley, I will happily give you the money to move your ailing wife to a better facility where she won't have to share her dinner with the rats and roaches. Such a shame about Karen's dementia. Truly, it is. You have my sympathies. She was always such a vibrant, engaging woman."

He walks away, shaking his head as if saddened by Karen Riley's diminishing capacity.

"What about everything else?" Riley asks. "You made many promises, Larkin."

Mayor Mecklenburg turns to consider the sheepish man in the shadows and returns to his side. He rocks back and forth on the balls of his heels and says, "No need for worry. Your staff will have jobs in the expanding administration. Ah, as many as we can absorb, keeping in mind the fiscal feasibility of course. On another note, Coach Tom McCardell will have to sit second chair, but he will still be coaching under Don Driver. However, that is subject to change within the near future because I must admit I believe McCardell to be the better coach. If my son wasn't graduating this year, he might have been better equipped to teach Robbie a few things while keeping Kilarin Rouge in line next season. Boy, those two kids sure do hate each other. Your female basketball coach, Coach Peeler, will become the head coach of the girls' team since she defeated us to advance to the state championship game. Anyway, I think Coach Smead is on the way out the door because she seems to have lost her team spirit. There now, I think that covers everything. Satisfied?"

In his mousy sort of way, the humbled mayor of the defunct township fights the instinct to cower completely before Larkin Mecklenburg. "Yes. I suppose I am."

"Joe, things sure are going to change around here. In addition to a lot of rezoning, there will be even bigger changes. Oh, ah . . . I convinced the school board to combine the athletic awards ceremonies. After we become state champions, of course. I believe it will begin a getting to know process between former competitors to solidify the fact that they are going to be one team now. Watching each other rewarded for their athletic accolades will establish a little respect between the players and their parents. Everybody wins. What do you think, Joe?"

"I think that is a smart play, Larkin. An excellent way to build a bond of respect between the players," Riley lies, knowing that it will only serve to embroil and refresh the resentment of those who were obviously robbed. It is also another way to remind everyone who is boss.

"Good, I'm glad you approve. We will prepare for four days after the State Championships have been won on March 29. On April 2, I'll have the media make a whole big deal of it in the cafeteria or the gymnasium of the new school. For the ceremony, we can have all the students arrive together on the Archer's new Streamliner team buses. Maybe I'll arrange to have fireworks and handout the trophies and scholarships for the outgoing seniors myself. The works, nothing but the best," Larkin says with a proud gleam in his eyes. He walks away, smoking his cigar with a smug smile.

Chapter 6

Gone Awry

As Agent Ruiz lies upon her stomach, rubbing her bare feet playfully in the air, the sheet covering her naked buttocks threatens to slip to the floor. Agent Paige seems a little winded from making love to a woman nineteen years younger than he is. She kisses his cheek and unfolds the map she takes from the nightstand drawer with a yellow highlighter.

She says, "Things have changed, but in a good way. Mac is being more forthcoming. More inclusive. It could be due to nerves or a heightened trust in me. Two days ago, Mack left without a word. He towed an empty trailer, leaving it outside of my surveillance range. Something he never does because it is his personal property. Yesterday the trailer moved back into range. In two days, we will be picking up a legitimate load of goods across the North Carolina border just south of Charlotte. These are the coordinates of his tagged trailer. Once there, we will switch out trailers to bring the tricky trailer that has been packed with the contraband back into South Carolina. When Mac disappeared without a word two nights ago, I suspected that things were ramping up. Another driver must have picked up the load of contraband and dropped the trailer at this location until it is safe to bring into the state." She shows him the GPS coordinates of the trailer on her laptop.

Agent Paige asks, "Are you certain of this, Martina?"

"Post positive. I contacted your quiet friend at the DOD, General Merchants, who tasked a satellite to keep intermittent tabs on this location. He has been very helpful. After dropping the tagged trailer out of my range, Mac bobtailed his way back to home base."

"Great."

"I followed your instructions to the letter, which was brilliant by the way. I just happened to call him twenty-minutes after his return to invite him out for a fat burger and coffee. His blood was up and he needed to unwind, so we had a few drinks instead. That's when Mac confirmed my suspicions about the timetable when I pretended as if I was considering other employment offers. He confessed that some high society bitch recently called for a reference because she is considering me for a job as a housekeeper. Agent Hammond was very convincing as a rich housewife, by the way."

Paige grunts and says, "I bet the conflicting thought of you wearing one of those black and white maid's outfits versus losing his mechanic really boggled his mind."

"You're instincts are on point. Mac is a little superstitious about changing partners so close to the payoff so he felt he had to convince me that our ship is finally about to come in. No choice but to tell me everything I needed to know. After picking up a load in a nomadic trailer, we will be traveling north on I-77 to do a drop and switch, then back down I-77 South to his off road warehouse just southeast of the new high school down this gravel road. Because of the road construction right here, traffic is being diverted this way. Anyone who owns businesses or lives in the new school area has to first take this old bridge or Interstate-77 across the Catawba River and then go back across on the new bridge into Tega Cay. If we wait until he is in the warehouse, we can effectively apprehend him because a crew isn't scheduled to show up for at least a day before divvying up the load. They want to make sure that this place is as safe as Mac assures. Don't get me wrong, Manuel Mendez is not that trusting so he had his men stakeout the warehouse for a week to monitor any incoming or outgoing traffic since Mecklenburg guaranteed the privacy of ownership. After no one showed up for a week, except for an elderly woman that Mecklenburg paid to deliver their food and laundry, they reported the place as secure. If that old woman knew that she was really running errands for armed drug dealers and killers, instead of immigrant workers, she would have shit her drawers. Before sending anyone inside, I strongly suggest that you have Agent Masters infiltrate the camera system that they have installed without Mac's permission. I stumbled onto them by accident so I'm fairly certain that they have captured my image. This is state of the art tech, so get Agent Masters on it immediately."

Agent Paige looks over the highlighted satellite map and formulates the plan in his head, calculating the amount of operators needed to lock this bust down as quietly as possible. He rubs his rasping chin and nods his approval.

He says, "Hm. Judging by this photo, this is very sophisticated, military grade tech. I will have our drones do flyovers of the target and surrounding area from the upper deck using infrared detection. Then, after Agent Masters and his tech-heads defeat the security system, I believe we will place tactical teams inside and outside of the warehouse. Manuel Mendez is notorious for planting *"hombre muerto"* or "dead men" inside to ride with the cargo. Sometimes, they will eat, sleep, and defecate inside storage units until delivery is complete. We will setup snipers and spotters in the surrounding woods here, here, here, and here to cover all sides of the warehouse. These men, as you know, are all experienced military operators, so lying in wait for long periods is nothing new to them. If there are any surprises, remember to keep your head down."

"You bet."

"Your thorough intelligence gives us the upper hand so we can make a quick and decisive bust without the Mendez Cartel ever knowing that we are on to them. We will hit them across the board in a coordinated strike. Looking at your cell photos of the inside of the warehouse prompts me to place sharp shooters in the rafters at the front and back because we don't know if he will back in, drive in, or loop around. Someone has to be in position to take the shot if heavily armed men occupy the trailer. I sincerely hope not because they will be expected to report in. Taking them alive, or getting them to cooperate will be nearly impossible. Anyone with family living in Mexico or Columbia knows that they will be in peril, so talking is not an option for these guys. You were also right about the scattered warehouses. The ones you have already given us are all under surveillance from Texas border towns to Florence, South Carolina to Jacksonville, Florida. Financial and taxation records trace these properties back to offshore corporations leading directly to a foreign entity called Macchiato Imports/Exports. Because the recon surveillance teams are backing your assessments to prioritize the targets based on the amount of armed security at these sites, our eyes in the sky, both satellites and unmanned drones, are tasked to that end. Good work, Agent Ruiz. Damn good work."

She rolls to her back with her knees rubbing together in the air, allowing the sheet to slip away from her wanting breasts.

Smiling playfully, Martina Ruiz says, "I just had you inside of me for an hour. When we're alone, do you think we can get beyond addressing each other as agent this or special agent that?" She places a fingernail between her teeth and smiles at him. "By the way. You should know that it is a real turn on when you speak Spanish to a Latino woman, papi. Even when you're talking about dead men."

"I see." He puts the maps away, shutting the laptop and moves toward her.

She stops his advances to ask, "Oh. What about that dirt bag . . . Phunts? Is he playing ball?"

"He's got no choice. His family has gone on an extended vacation to his in-law's home in Massachusetts—under our watchful eye —of course. Phunts is wired for sound and doesn't take a crap without us watching him. Your cover is secure. Under our supervision, he makes regular reports to a man named Alexi Vega. Our spooks have infiltrated and cloned Vega's phones so everything he unknowingly discloses and everyone he talks to is being recorded and scrutinized. Some are being tracked through the Voice Recognition Software Database and phone records that lead right back to Mendez himself. We will get him, doing our best to keep this lethal contraband from ever hitting the streets. We are working all angles on this bust by following the phone calls, the personnel, contraband, and the money. Our intelligence network strongly suggests that Mendez is coordinating these maneuvers from within the U.S. border. It is only a matter of time before we pinpoint him."

"You mean it's true? Is Manuel Mendez here somewhere? I thought that fat bastard was just blowing hot air."

"He will not slip back across that border without us knowing. The U.S./Mexican crossing is now equipped with high-speed, hi-tech facial recognition stations, and handheld facial scanning units to map anyone leaving or coming into the United States. Border patrol personnel will remain doubled or even tripled until we have them. No members of this Columbian/Mexican cartel, with the balls to set foot on U.S. soil that we already have any digital surveillance on will ever leave this country again. They are using scramblers, and SAT phones to coordinate, but our techies are hacking in to triangulate his position. Many private aircrafts, hangers, and pilots are subject to surveillance teams equipped with facial recognition technology. We have dispersed nearly five hundred agents throughout the mid-Atlantic, the southeast. All the way to southwestern border towns. Across the board, they are all the handpicked best of the best from Special Forces, CIA Black Ops, FBI, and DEA. Every man and woman is a shooter. The moment we pinpoint Mendez's location, we will move on him hard and fast."

She says, "Wow, that many."

"Twenty-five tactical agents are standing by in a warehouse at a government airport in Quantico, Virginia and outside of San Antonio. No one is allowed to leave or use unsecured, unmonitored lines of communications with their families or anyone. They are primed and ready to go at any given moment. At flight speeds of over 900 hundred kilometers per hour, they can be almost anywhere in an instant." He kisses her and backs away.

She looks at him, curiously. "What's the matter? Is there something you're not telling me?" she asks.

"Technically, Martina, even though you are the primary field agent, it goes against all protocol to share this much tactical information with you. However, I trust you implicitly. I believe that agents, who risk their very lives in the field to find credible evidence, deserve to be in the loop so that they know the benefits of successful missions as well as the consequences and resources wasted on failures and mistakes. Director Gleeson and I are pouring all of our juice into this one glass because I believe the intel is viable and warrants this massive homeland operation. Four hundred million dollars in drugs and weapons is nothing to sneeze at. Rarely do operations with such mass and breadth come off without losing a pigeon or two, but we have cast a tight net to minimize loss and casualties with an overwhelming force poised to take them down with extreme prejudice where necessary. This, my dear, is where futures collide with destiny for us both. It's either win or go home with our heads bowed low and our tails permanently tucked between our legs. We are in these trenches to do good, and this time we have to be playing for the winning team.. This transmission now ends. No more talking."

"Thanks for your complete confidence. Transmission received."

His buoyancy reassures Agent Ruiz, even though her gut reminds her that almost anything can go wrong when least expected; something he taught her. For now, in this private, naked moment, both souls wish only to turn off the mechanisms of thought. Tomorrow and destiny comes as swiftly as the wings of sparrows. Therefore, what is left of tonight should be spent on the needs of the flesh, on the simple caress of it, lived in the heat of it where sweat and sounds of moaning pleasure become all the immediate world.

* * *

The weather is nice…warm. It greatly differs from that night in December on Lake Wylie when Agent Phunts got his hands caught in the cookie jar.

McKenzie "Mac" Mecklenburg drops the load inside the secured yard of an auto parts manufacturing plant where many trailers sit. After the paperwork is signed off, he gets back into the cab and maneuvers into position to couple with a modified refrigerated trailer in the shade nearest the fence. Agent Rodriguez raises the heavy hood and checks the hot, idling engine of the Peterbilt cab.

Once Mac links the hydraulic brake lines and the trailer is locked down, he checks the padlocks on the trailer doors for signs of tampering. He rubs his hands with an oily rag as he inspects the tires and undercarriage. Now, he bangs on the side three times. Seconds later, he adds one more bang.

Meanwhile, the woman he knows as Natalie Hernandez whispers, "We're at the switch. We will be there soon, so be ready. Be advised, the target just signaled someone on the inside."

Mecklenburg stares at her ass with a grin. "What's that?" he asks, startling her.

Hernandez's heart skips a beat because she did not hear him approach. She straightens up and rubs her forearm across her jaw to leave an oily streak on her face.

She turns and looks down at him to shout, "I said, this thing is ready to be changed. Finally figured out the problem with the slight overheating. Your primary oil sender sensor needs replacing. I'll hook her up to the reader when this is all over."

"How bad is it?" he asks with concern.

"Not to worry, boss, she'll make it alright. It's an easy fix, and this is a short trip." When they drop the hood, she adds, "Did you like the view from down here?"

He asks, "What do you mean, Nat?"

Playing her role, coyly, Natalie Hernandez approaches and looks up into his big, drooling eyes to say, "I caught you watching my ass when I was up there. Don't deny it."

Mac blushes a bit and says, "Hell, girl, that's what a thing of beauty is for."

Her smiling dark brown eyes flirt with a man she despises. She reaches out to caress his cheek and says, "When I get my cut for all of these hauls across the country, maybe I'll let you do more than watch, you sick pervert."

She snatches the oily, sweaty rag from his hand and wipes her streaked face.

After licking his lips, Mac smiles and says, "Oh, I'm going to thoroughly enjoy that momentous occasion. Saddle up, Ms. Hernandez. It's nearly six o'clock. Traffic may be a bitch."

"You got it boss. Let's move out."

They get back into the cab where he checks the gauges to monitor the engine temperature. The powerful Peterbilt engine causes the tires to dig into the gravel to break out the heavy trailer.

* * *

The FCCH, or Federal Criminal Communication Hub, tasked to this particular op, is buzzing. Voice Recognition locks on and confirms a 99% match to Manuel Mendez's voice when he calls his lieutenant at a Motel 6 in Rock Hill, South Carolina. As they pray for mere seconds to triangulate the signal's origin, Paige orders the men in Virginia to gear up. They have finally pinpointed Mendez's location in an exclusive hotel in downtown Charleston.

Paige's men, all Spanish speaking agents, are watching the warehouse, poised to take down the smugglers as soon as the leader reports that the contraband is secure.

Twenty-five DEA tactical team members stow their backpacks and secure their weapons in the jet. They are airborne in less than five minutes.

In South Carolina, SSA Paige receives additional information from a liaison to the Central Intelligence Agency. Moments later, FBI agents invade DEA Headquarters, where they take Paige's counterpart supervisor of a separate unit into custody for treason and undermining an ongoing operation that puts DEA personnel directly in harm's way.

Agent Paige leaves the mobile communications hub and jumps into the SUV with three technicians as he quickly makes his way to I-77 North. He is listening, monitoring the situation in transit. Agent Ruiz drops subtle hints by calling out landmarks and mile markers as they travel south on I-77 back into South Carolina.

She says, "Carowinds. I have always wondered about that place. Have you ever been there, Mac?"

Mecklenburg looks into his side mirrors and says, "Not in a very long time. They are open seasonally, but I'll tell you what. When this is finally over, I will gladly take you there for a night you will never forget. How does that sound?"

"I think I'll greatly enjoy that momentous occasion," she says while twisting a lock of black hair around her fingers.

The wire she wears is a one-way communicator. Therefore, Ruiz has no idea that the agent, who hacked into Agent Paige's files, has compromised her. When the cameras of Mecklenburg's warehouse captured her image, the cartel's security operator decided to have their mole in the department conduct a deeper background search. The one hidden camera that she had not noticed caught Agent Ruiz discretely snapping a photo with her phone. Because this detail initially escaped notice, he decided to take no chances even though she was heavily scrutinized before passing muster.

The second mole, who has never seen Agent Ruiz, had nothing to work with until now. Using his security clearance, he digs into her second tier of fabricated identification as Paula Rodriguez, a convicted felon for drug trafficking. Paula Rodriguez, who, apparently, changed her identity to Natalie Hernandez, further intrigued the trespasser so he runs her through the agency's facial recognition protocol. It took some time, but he discovered that she is indeed Martina Ruiz, a deep cover agent sequestered from Paige's unit by an unknown handler for her own protection.

* * *

The new, customized team buses are loaded with members of the boy and girl basketball squads at their respective schools. Over the summer months, the abandoned high schools are slated for conversion for younger students from pre-school through eighth grade because their numbers require both facilities. The much older elementary and middle schools are a bit rundown on both sides of the tracks.

The Tega Cay bus pulls out of the school's parking lot, heading for that bothersome, roundabout route to the brand new high school for the Athletic Awards Ceremony. The mood is a bit sullen after Tega Cay's boys made it through two playoff rounds just to lose the State Championship in a total shocker. Woefully underestimated, the underdogs ravaged the Tega Cay Archers with a tenacious defense and lightning quick offensive schemes.

Wearing suits and dresses now, each person recalls their own memories of the disappointing embarrassment at the hands of the Spartanburg Warriors during a devastating defeat.

Moments later, the Fort Mill Hornets begin the trek to the awards ceremony in style, with a less dour atmosphere. By beating tough playoff competition, the Lady Hornets, led by Kysing "the Stinger" Rouge, have taken the South Carolina State Championship title. On March 28, 2013, in the South Carolina Gamecocks' Coliseum, the Lady Hornets earned the respect of all pretenders to the throne by taking the title game by storm. Coach Candace Peeler's strategy to drive nearly every shot inside the paint, paid dividends, forcing the tired defenders to double-team the unstoppable barrage by Kysing Rouge and her teammates. The Stinger was responsible for fouling out two of the opponent's best players by the third and fourth quarters.

Her feints to the basket, while dishing the ball out to the perimeter shooters netted flawless threes like hail falling from the sky in their one-sided destruction of the well-coached Summerville Green Waves.

Kilarin, Yara, and Banja Rouge watched from mid-court with unprecedented pride. When Kysing earned the Championship MVP, a prestigious accolade of high school athletics, she accepted with grace as she dedicated this win to her teammates, coaches, and twin brother.

Standing tall with the winner's trophy, she breathlessly proclaimed, "This win is also for my family. Especially my brother, Kilarin Rouge and the entire Fort Mill boys' team who were robbed of an opportunity to play for the boys' 4-A State Basketball Championship. I love you, Kilarin "Killer" Rouge!" As tears streamed from the eyes of both siblings, she kissed the trophy and raised it overhead with a hearty, "Woohoo!"

Thoughts of the memorable win raises the spirits of all who ride on what will become the female athletics bus when the new school opens in the fall. In an undeniably pro-karmic statement, the girls' victory is a validation to everyone that what is stolen can be returned to its rightful place and shared by all those deserving.

Ten minutes ahead, a dump truck, filled with construction site refuse, flashes its headlights to pass the Streamliner Bus carrying the Archers' basketball squads. After getting word that his pregnant wife is now in labor, the driver rushes to end a long day at work in time to be there for the birth of their first child. He floors it to beat oncoming traffic, switching back in front of the school bus. As the cargo shifts, a rusted slab of concrete, with ragged rebar protruding from it slides off the pile to crash on the road directly in front of the bus.

The bus driver shrieks a cuss word and warns, "Hold on, guys. Shit!"

There are screams as she breaks hard, causing the bus to bow. Despite her efforts, there are harsh thuds under the bus and then the back tires blow!

The seasoned driver does not panic, holding it steady. After forcing the damaged bus to the shoulder on the rims, the driver knows that this ride is over. Upon inspection, three of the four back tires are scrap. The rugged piece of concrete is lodged between the mangled right tires and the back bumper. Several concerned witnesses stop to check on the passengers.

The bus driver first calls the police to report the accident. Then she gets on the radio and says, "Unit two. Unit two, this is Unit one.

Please come in, Charlie."

There is a crackle and her husband says, "This is Unit two. Go ahead, Mandy."

"Ah, Charlie, we have a blowout situation on route. Caught some rebar from a dumper that shredded the rear rubbers. I'm smelling antifreeze. I think it caught a radiator hose, too." She looks at the right-side mirror and adds, "Yep. I see the greenish fluid leaking. We are done here."

"Jeez. Everyone okay, Mandy? Come back."

She wipes her forehead and answers, "Yeah, Charlie. No one is hurt. I've alerted the police, but I'm going to evacuate the bus just in case."

"What's your ten/twenty? Come back."

"We are about eighty yards from this poor excuse for a new Catawba River bridge. Come back," Mandy answers.

"Then you're in luck. We are right behind you. Hang tight, Mandy. Be there shortly."

"Thanks, Charlie. Do you think you have room?"

Seated up front, Coach McCardell and Candace Peeler are already wrestling with the question of room on unit two after hearing the conversation between the husband and wife bus drivers.

Even with both squads and a few cheerleaders aboard, there may be enough room left. Charlie Abrams looks over his shoulder to ask the coaches, "Well, after the way they treated you guys, I wouldn't blame you if you say let 'em walk. It's up to you, so what's it gonna be?"

The coaches look to one another and consent. Coach McCardell stands up. Facing the players, he says, "In the spirit of charity and the goodwill of sportsmanship, we will be picking up the Tega Cay team because they are having mechanical problems. So I want you all to behave yourselves and tighten up back there to make room." Of course, there are disconcerted moans and groans from the rival kids, but they comply.

As the bus slows to a halt, Coach Peeler stands to address the student athletes as well.

"I don't want any crap out of any of you. This, ladies and gentlemen, is simply karma at work. Enjoy it with straight faces. These kids will be your classmates next school year so let's all display a little decorum and maturity. Please be civil, even though we can whip their snot-nosed butts on our worst day!" She makes a fist and pumps it as if she has just scored a hole-in-one.

The kids all laugh and cheer. Anyone who did not fully understand the auspices of words like karma or fate, now has a new appreciation for the concept of the unjust not prospering.

The parents are already at the school, waiting to greet their kids. Much of their small talk centers on the poor timing of this ceremony with the roadwork and high volume of quitting time traffic. A rumor soon begins to circulate that a minor accident is the holdup.

After the coaches shake hands, they usher the students onto the bus in a somber, single file procession. Silently soured, they move as if this bus ride is a conveyer belt into a gas chamber that will end them all.

Walking alongside the functioning bus, they can feel the rival team's eyes looking down upon them. Most will elect to take the first seat they come to. The twentieth student to board is Stacie Mecklenburg.

The bus seems a bit cramped now, and silence fills the dead spaces like expanding foam that forces the air out. It soon appears that a couple of students may have to stay behind. As any young man should, Kilarin Rouge stands in the aisle to allow the tall young woman to shift one seat back for this short jaunt across the bridge. She humbly thanks him as he holds on to the stainless steel bars overhead. Robbie Mecklenburg elects to do the same, but he does not expect to be facing the unyielding glare of his nemesis. The graduating senior nearly turns away, but refuses to cower in front of all those who watch with intense anticipation. Kilarin Rouge, a mere junior, seems to have the upper hand as he flexes his jaw and stares Robbie down.

Charlie elects to stay with the wounded bus, allowing his wife to drive unit two to the award ceremony. When they make the roadside decision to switch, Mandy says to Coach Peeler and Coach McCardell, "I'm telling you guys, this is a bad idea, but one can always hope."

As fate would have it, the Stinger and the Mech are now sharing a row. There is a moment of quiet tension until Stacie decides to break the ice by saying, "I like your dress."

Kysing Rouge replies, "Thanks. I absolutely love those shoes. Are those Prada?"

"Thanks. They are Christian Louboutin, actually. I know they cost enough to be extremely comfortable, but I am so not used to wearing heels. They all seem to hurt like hell. Now I know what the Iron Maiden must have felt like as far as fashionable, medieval torture devices go."

Kysing giggles, but still says, "Nice, though. I like."

"Really? This is the first time I've worn them and it looks like we are about the same size. Tell you what . . . I'll trade you for an autographed jersey."

Kysing Rouge stifles her giggle, not knowing that Stacie Mecklenburg is serious. Silence creeps back in as they both clear their throats at the same time. Then, in a moment that seems meant to be, they both face each other at the same time to present their open palms and shake. "I'm Stacie Mecklenburg. Hi."

"The Mech, I know," says Kysing as they shake hands. "I'm Kysing Rouge. It's nice to formally meet you, without being sore, tired, and covered with an oil slick for sweat."

The brothers are distracted, surprised by the less aggressive attitude of the girls, but they quickly resume the stare down in lieu of a cat fight. For this split-second, they both feel slightly betrayed by their sisters for consorting with the enemy. For this fleet and feverish instant, they experience an accusatory, gnawing sort of annoyance. Because they love their sisters, it does not endure.

"The tire blowing out almost seems like fate."

Kysing Rouge asks, "What do you mean?"

"Here we are. I'm actually sitting with the Stinger. The freaking Stinger in the flesh. Congrats on winning state and claiming the MVP title. You deserved it. I really mean that."

"Thanks for saying that. I appreciate it, but I didn't do it alone."

"Are you kidding?" Stacie whispers. "Don't say anything, but I was there."

"Really?"

"My parents thought I was boohooing at a stupid sleepover. You were like . . . like a female version of Michael Jordon, Tim Duncan, and LeBron James, combined into one."

"LeBron who?" They giggle. "Thanks again for the high praise. With a nickname like the Mech, you are no slouch yourself. You've shredded a few defensive stances designed to stop you and only you. Good stuff, Stacie. "

Stacie says, "You know, I discovered something when I Googled you. Do you realize that we actually share the same birthday?"

"No way!" Kysing squeals. "You're just messing with me right?"

"I'm as serious as the day we were born." Stacie opens her purse and says, "Look. Here is my driver's license."

After realizing that she is telling the truth, Kysing smiles and says, "Wow. That is uncanny. I guess this makes us cosmic sisters."

"Ya think?" Stacie takes her hand and whispers, "Can I tell you a massive secret?"

"Sure. What is it?"

Stacie's skin flushes when she glances over her right shoulder and whispers, "I think your brother is so hot. God I've had a major crush on him for the longest."

Both girls giggle as Kysing glances over her shoulder.

Sensing that he is the subject of discussion, Kilarin smiles. Because his attention is drawn to their hushed conversation, his eyes soften as curiosity blooms.

Robbie notices and harshly demands, "What are you looking at?"

The tension meter jumps fifty degrees as the bus stops just before hitting the on ramp to the bridge where merging traffic crawls along painfully slow.

Kilarin's eyes narrow for an instant. Then he smiles and says to Robbie Mecklenburg, "Right now, I'm looking at a loser with a really cute sister. Are you sure you're related?"

The chorus of 'oohs' and 'ahhs' do not help matters much. In fact, it practically guarantees an escalation between two competitive people that have always disliked one another. There has always been a little posturing between them, visible in the discreet pushing and shoving on the court, but no real reason for animosity.

Before the coaches can rise to intercede, Robbie takes a hostile step toward Kilarin. At this moment, there are only two people in the universe, and Kilarin's anger rises to meet the other halfway.

Kilarin unbuttons his blazer, same as Robbie. Most spiteful words hurt when Kilarin says, "Big Papa's money bought you the divisional and conference titles, but his check bounced sky-high when you went to Carolina for the big dance. You got your butt whipped by a smaller squad as if you stole something. When you really think of it, that is exactly what you did. You actually stole a whipping. What?"

The statement draws lots of embarrassing laughter, the type of mirth that only accompanies the bitter truth of a contentious matter. Moreover, some of Robbie's teammates, those who considered him a bit of a ball hog and the reason they lost, are giggling or laughing aloud with no care for his bruised and bloodied ego.

In truth, Robbie Mecklenburg's overcompensation in an attempt to both win the game and gain his father's undeniable respect, caused him to make questionable, indecisive calls on the court. Everyone knows this to be true. His begrudging teammates, especially.

Instinctually, Tega Cay's head coach should have sent Mayor Mecklenburg's son to the warm the bench. His fear of reprisal, however, played the greater influence in his handling of the matter; allowing Robbie to continue was a bad decision.

Robbie sunburns. Each step taken with that bowing proud chin, and those upturned eyes, propels him into battle with an unspoken rage.

"What, Robbie? Don't bring me any of your daddy's wolf tickets because they will get cashed in back here. You can mean-mug me all the way to the floor for a dirt nap. Come and get it cashed in, Robbie "Rich Kid" Mecklenburg. You're only mad because it's all true."

The bus driver grunts with a wry smile cracking her lips, despite an effort to control her own biases for the blue-collar teams. Mandy Abrams looks at Coach Peeler and says, "Told ya back there that it was a bad idea, didn't I?"

Peeler resists the urge to grin because it simply would not assuage a situation that could turn into a full-blown riot. She knows her position demands that she intercede, but she is like a child anticipating Santa's arrival with a big red bag of exclamation points. A second or two more of this glowering loathing and she shakes her head to snap out of it. She is the grown up after all.

Concealed in obscurity, a Black teammate in the back disguises his voice to yell, "A fight! A fight! A nigga and a white!"

"Who said that?" shouts Coach McCardell. "I want to know who said that word right now."

Both girls quickly rise between their brothers before they can engage. Two of the coaches wisely take the girls' places to form a solid, adult barrier.

When Coach McCardell's eyes display his disappointment, Kilarin backs down and buttons his blazer. He says, "I'm cool, coach. I'm good. I felt disrespected and voiced what we all know to be true. One fly can only eat so much crap. I'm sorry, sir. It won't happen again."

Kysing Rouge asks her brother, "Are you okay, Kilarin?" In reference to the unanimous decision to finish high school early, she says, "Please don't blow it now. Remember, we have bigger, better things in store. Just keep your cool. No more chest beating, promise?"

With a sense of remorse, he looks at his twin sister and glances at her new friend, whom he may have insulted with nasty, hurtful remarks about her father influencing the outcome of the game between the boys' teams.

Kilarin Rouge says, "I'm good, sis." He whispers in her ear, "Please tell her that I'm really sorry for what I just said. I was wrong for that, and I apologize."

Kysing smiles and hugs him for showing his true character. While doing so, she whispers, "I'm proud of you, Killer. You should know she really likes you. I'm talking massive crush."

When the girls return to their seats, Kysing relays the message, which Stacie accepts. She turns toward Kilarin and touches his hand to relay her own message with a hopeful smile. Stacie cannot presume to speak for her brother, but she knows that Kilarin is right about her father. Both Mecklenburg kids do, experiencing a sense of shame to varying degrees. In fact, Robbie's total embarrassment no longer raises his ire. Rather, he acquiesces by secretly accepting the truth of the matter. In a way, the acceptance of truth can be a relief. He no longer desires confrontation with Kilarin, whom he envies as a slightly better basketball player. Had they ever really gotten to know one another, both would realize the benefits of mutual respect.

Meanwhile, Stacie's touching gesture eases the angst in Kilarin's eyes. Despite his best effort, a single tear falls from his eye as he stares into her bluish-grey oceans. He grasps her hand for an instant to convey his appreciation of her forgiveness before wiping the unmanly tear away.

Reminded of the school's upcoming tryouts for its rendition of Romeo and Juliet, Kysing smiles at them both with her own tears welling. Like William Shakespeare's star-crossed lovers, they could almost never be.

Coach McCardell witnesses the display and maneuvers himself into a position to block Robbie Mecklenburg's view until the touching moment passes. Lacking commitment and insistence, he politely clears his throat.

Once they are certain a clash has been averted, Coach Peeler moves back to her seat at the front while McCardell trades seats with one of the students in the middle of the bus. His bad knees are a bother today, so taking Kilarin's place standing in the aisle affects his decision to chance the strong, young kid's injury.

* * *

SSA Paige takes the Pineville exit near Carowinds Theme Park, crossing the highway just to get back on I-77 in a southerly direction. He floors it while racing through the traffic, running the emergency shoulder when necessary.

When the phone vibrates in his shirt pocket, Mac nearly jumps out of his skin. As Mac tries to turn it on, it rings again and leaps out of his chubby hand only to slide under the driver's seat as they go up the on ramp.

"I'll get the phone for you, clumsy," Hernandez says.

The identity of the second mole's contact before his arrest is no longer in doubt, which causes distress among those who are involved in this part of the sting operation.

Paige utters, "No, don't Martina. It's probably Vega!" Ordering the tactical team to take Vega down, he hits Martina's contact number on the cell phone just as she hands Mecklenburg his phone.

"Yeah, this is Mac." He listens for a moment, feeling the temperature on the rise with each broken syllable. Just as her phone begins to vibrate, Mac says, "Okay. I understand. No, sir, it is not a problem. I'm headed for the post office right now. I'll be sure to put that check in the mail in a few minutes." His heart begins to pound as his eyes darken.

He pretends to drop the phone again.

Agent Martina Ruiz looks at a one-word text message, which reads 'Komodo.' She recognizes the red flag just as McKenzie Mecklenburg draws the nickel-plated .45 from under the seat. She drops her phone and reaches behind her, but it is too late. Mecklenburg throws his considerable weight behind two vicious backhanded blows to her face!

Martina's weapon falls between the seat and door when he hits her hard enough to break her nose and fracture the right cheekbone. Blood gushes from her nostrils and lacerated cheek.

He drives his fist into her jaw and deploys the emergency breaks with the truck idling in neutral. He leaves his seat and grabs the injured DEA agent to rip her flannel shirt open. When he sees the flat microphone beneath the white T-shirt, his wide eyes frantically search the mirrors. A black SUV suddenly fishtails into view, scorching rubber as it quickly approaches.

"Oh fuck. Shit. You motherfucking bitch!" he shouts, pointing the weapon at her face. Agent Martina Ruiz is semiconscious when he rips the wire away and throws it out of the window. He watches the SUV as it sits on the shoulder at a standstill. He panics when their doors begin to open, tossing her aside to retake his seat behind the wheel. Mac throws the truck into gear and guns it with the pedal to the floor.

Nearing the center of the bridge, the coaches are talking to the students about teamwork and unity. They are pointing out the many benefits that a combined athletics program will produce once everyone finally puts the past behind them. Then, they hear distant screams and a crash of grinding metal as the Peterbilt powers through and over the slow moving vehicles blocking the way. Like a bull elephant in the rage of musk, Mac ramrods the temporary center lane meant for emergencies or roadwork vehicles.

Paige tries to pursue, forcing his way through the mangled wreckage in Mecklenburg's rampaging wake.

Chapter 7

El Legado de Manuel Mendez

Three expensive Cuban cigars smolder in the ashtrays of suite 322 at the exclusive Hollings Hotel in downtown Charleston where Manuel Mendez, Tito Cortez, and Ricardo Alba have suddenly abandoned snifters of costly cognac. Their garment bags lay askew, left to an uncertain fate while making a quick exit, but the motorcade is hopelessly deadlocked in traffic as Manuel tries to get to one of the barrier islands.

Meanwhile, circling high above, a surveillance drone is signal synched to track Mendez and Alba's phones. Two jets, one at the private airfield near the Charleston International Airport in North Charleston and the other at the smaller Johns Island Airfield have requested flight plans for Cartagena, Columbia and Nogales, Sonora.

Because Mendez's motorcade does not seem to be trying to get to I-26 or Dorchester Road, which will take him to the waiting jet at the airfield in North Charleston, analysts believe he is trying to flee the country via the Johns Island airfield where the private jet is fueled and ready to hit the tarmac. Although this airfield is technically closer, the congestive inner city and exiting rural traffic becomes a menacing hindrance to their need for a hasty escape.

Mendez has eight heavily armed men with him, but leaving the city at 6:15 places them in the middle of the heaviest of quitting time traffic. Finally, both vehicles are able to get to Maybank Highway on James Island, the first of the barrier islands just southeast of the Charleston peninsula. The traffic seems to lighten up on the Stono Bridge to Johns Island, but it quickly constricts on the other side as the merging southbound lanes bottleneck the griping motorists.

Mendez directs his men to bypass the traffic jam by driving on the shoulder, drawing the attention of a black and white patrol car along the way. The police officer turns around, calling it in as he follows along the shoulder with his lights and siren blaring. Suddenly he is taking shots, reporting the attack just before he's hit with automatic gunfire. His car veers into the marsh at the base of the bridge.

The unit leader communicates with the drone control center, relaying the information to Paige who directs them to take the initiative. Air traffic control grounds all outgoing flights at the airports, claiming that there is an inbound flight with engine troubles. As the bruised motorcade turns east on River Road, accidents jam the intersection at Maybank Highway. The second SUV carrying armed bodyguards crashes into a taxi and upends into oncoming traffic.

Mendez soon arrives at the airfield, where his private jet waits for permission to leave. As the rocking DEA jet begins its descent, Mendez's crew comes to a screeching halt inside the private hanger.

Manuel Mendez and his men quickly exit the SUV, heading for the jet, fully intent on taking off with or without clearance or an approved flight plan.

When the DEA transport stops, the tactical unit pours from the doors armed and geared up for war. With weapons at the ready as they approach Mendez's party, which they catch in the open, automatic gunfire rings out. The military trained DEA assault team, garbed in Technora Body Armor, advances as a single unit. Mendez's bodyguards go down one-by-one as he shuts the door on the jet. The pilot approaches the runway, leaving the others behind to cover their escape.

The unit leader and others use the fallen bodies to take cover, ordering his sharp shooters to take out the tires as the jet picks up speed. Leading the moving target with their scopes, two of them fire at the wheels. When the heavily burdened tires blow, the jet skitters to the right and plows into a fence. The last bodyguard falls from a headshot and two in the chest as the jet's engines begin to power down. Mendez and two powerful members of the cartel jump out and try to run for the woods. The snipers take their legs out on the move, convincing Mendez that he will never make it to safety. On his knees, he draws a weapon from his pocket and attempts to commit suicide, but a sniper takes the quick shot to the shoulder. Mendez crashes to the ground, his weapon lost. Armed men, handpicked by SSA Paige to capture him alive, if possible, quickly surround the three men. Mission accomplished.

With their hands raised, the pilots are escorted from the plane. Both swear that Mendez forced them at gunpoint to disobey the tower's grounding of their flight.

As a sweaty Mendez lays where he fell, clasping bleeding wounds, one of his cohorts spits at him.

Ricardo Alba's eyes burn holes into Manuel Mendez as he spitefully says, "*Manuel, cerdo . Te dicen que venir aquí era demasiado arriesgado. Su arrogancia se convierte ahora en la ruina de todos nosotros. La familia va a ser implacable!"*

The dead bodyguards are being checked for weapons, cell phones, and identification. As are the survivors. Undoubtedly, their passports are the real deal, but their identities are perfect counterfeits.

The tactical team's leader stands over the infamous Manuel Mendez, casting a late day, silhouetted shadow upon the injured cartel leader with his weapon strapped at ease. His men strip Mendez's jacket so the medics can assess the shoulder and leg wounds that they will dress on site.

Agent Edward Garza removes his dark glasses to look down on the captured cartel leader and paraphrases Ricardo Alba's words of condemnation in English. He says, "*Señor Manuel Mendez,* he's right you know. It was very risky and most foolhardy of you to enter the continental U.S., even with a half dozen phony passports. Because you wished to flaunt your immense power, arrogance has truly become the ruin of you all." He squats for a closer look into Mendez's eyes. "*La familia* will not be very forgiving. I believe you are probably all done now, but for the dying. You, sir, are now *hombre muerto*. However, when a man as powerful as you is caught in a seemingly untenable predicament, he usually finds some way to land on his feet. I'm sure that you will trade your limonada de los limones. But for you, Mendez, it will be just a little bittersweet from now on." He lights a cigarette, taking a few puffs before placing it between Mendez's lips.

"What are you saying?" asks Mendez, quietly. "Are you offering me a deal? Listen, I can make you all very rich men."

Agent Edward Garza replaces his glasses and says in a near whisper, "I'm certain that you can, but then we will become very poor in character. Your compadres are watching this conversation with great interest, my friend. I wonder which of them will be the first to dime you out because that's exactly what they think is happening to them right now."

Mendez resists the urge to look over his shoulder at the others, who cannot hear the chat, but he knows what they are thinking within his knotting bowels. Still, even though he feels his wounded counterparts' eyes crawling along his back and damp scalp, Mendez says defiantly, "Never."

Mendez flinches when Ricardo Alba shouts, "Traitor!" Agent Garza smiles.

Tito Cortez snarls, "Stinking traitor." He spits with disgust. "Before you sell your own mother out to these pigs, I will eat her heart. I will eat her fucking heart, Manuel!"

Garza looks down at Mendez, knowing his thoughts. His training serves him well by a simple insinuation that will pit them all against one another in the name of self-preservation.

"Medic, I want immediate assessments of the wounded prisoners," Garza barks.

The medics agree that the other two have sustained little more than flesh wounds, which are secure and non-life-threatening.

The airport's fire safety crew inspects the wounded aircraft, but no one is allowed inside without gloves and an armed escort. More sirens are closing on the airport. The officer that first reported the renegade motorcade has died from his wounds. The locals want blood, but this federal operation takes precedence.

"What about Mendez?" Garza asks. "Is it safe to transport him back to base, or are we hamstringed by his need for immediate medical attention? The likes of which will severely hamper our ability to keep this capture under cuff."

Agent Marcs, the senior medic that field-dressed Mendez's shoulder and leg wound, looks down at him and says, "No major arterial damage. Two routine through and throughs. He will live all right, sir. We won't have to share this piece of dog meat with the locals. I have a special cocktail that guarantees that he won't care if he's still facing a hundred years after the firing squad."

With authority, Agent Garza orders, "Alright, I want these prisoners, including the pilots, secured in our transport. They will remain deaf and dumb until command rips the labels off. Medics, make certain the wounded are hydrated. Quickly secure all weapons, photograph and bag the dead, which we will hump back to base with us for postmortem evaluations and identification. Johns, I need you and two men of your choosing to stay behind and secure Mendez's jet in this private hanger until our forensics teams can wrap it up and arrange proper transport. No one else touches that aircraft until forensics goes through it with a fine-toothed comb. Get to it, men. Let's wind it up."

Johns says, "Yes, sir." He turns away, drawing his two volunteers from the ranks.

"You'll be home by morning, men," Garza promises.

As per Garza's orders, tape covers the mouths of their prisoners. A wall of quiet darkness soon surrounds the prisoners when their captors secure sound barriers over their ears and black bags over their heads. Garza's men lead them, blindly, into the waiting jet. The wounded are strapped in before being intravenously hydrated, and sedated.

Garza makes a phone call that stops the approaching Charleston Metropolitan black and whites and the Charleston County Police in their tracks soon after entering the airport's gates. Ten minutes later, as airport mechanics and a wrecker tend to the wounded getaway jet's rehousing, the rest of Agent Paige's handpicked tactical squad rises above the tarmac with the catch of the decade.

* * *

The small bridge looks like a warzone of mangled steel and injured people as McKenzie Mecklenburg forces the powerful rig forward. As he steers with the heavy revolver in his right hand, fighting for control while destroying vehicle after vehicle, he glances at the pursuing SUV not realizing that Paige's men have mobilized to intercept him on the other side. For them, traffic is a problem. Still, Mac is hopelessly boxed in, but desperate men are capable of desperate and reckless acts.

Paige and his agents now find themselves blocked by a volatile debris field of shattered glass, burning rubber, and mangled metal. They are forced to pursue on foot with weapons at the ready.

Crashing onward, Mecklenburg loses focus of the motionless, wounded agent on the floor. Though bleeding and injured, the woman that Mac knows as Natalie Hernandez quietly watches him through tufts of disheveled hair. While Paige and the other armed men on foot distract Mac, she attacks, kicking at the gun hand from where she lies on the cab's floor. The gun goes off twice, sending .45 caliber bullets through the windshield and the cab's roof. The violent recoils rip a tendon in Mac's right wrist, snapping back hard enough to drive the hammer into the wrist joint. He yelps as the gun flies out of sight in the sleeping compartment in the rear of the cab.

With the accelerator to the floor, bouncing from car to car, he tries to fend off the wounded DEA agent's assault. He catches Hernandez with an elbow to the face, driving her back into the passenger side door. She reaches for purchase, accidentally opening the door to nearly fall out. Grasping desperately at the open door's handle and the bottom of the passenger seat with her head hanging dangerously outside of the cab, Agent Martina Ruiz struggles to hold on.

Mecklenburg's control of the vehicle is more difficult with a fractured wrist, but he sees an opportunity to rid himself of her by veering toward a bottled water delivery carrier. She gets clear and tries to stand just before he obliterates the left side of the much smaller truck, which flies over the railing and crashes on the riverbank below.

Mecklenburg holds it to the floor, gaining momentum, but the real estate is running perilously slim. The bus driver watches the mayhem in her rearview mirror with her mouth agape.

Finally, Mandy warns, "Everybody grab onto something. Oh Christ. Sweet Jesus Almighty. Hold on!" At first, she guns it, trying to outrun the deadly hulk. However, the driver decides she is better off trying to make room for it. She inadvertently leaves the wheel turned to the right, which will turn out to be a deadly mistake.

Meanwhile, Agent Ruiz throws several blows at the much bigger man. Using her martial arts training, she launches knee after knee into his shoulder, chest, and even his jowl. Nonetheless, hitting this man with all she has yields the same results of hitting a stern punching bag. Therefore, she rakes her fingernails across his eyes and goes for his gun in the back. Just as the agent reaches for it, he snatches her backward by the hair. She struggles out of his weakened grasp, driving a vicious forward elbow into his right jaw. The blow stuns him. She dives into the rear compartment and finds his .45. She orders him to stop the truck with the gun to his head.

Knowing that it is over, Mecklenburg blinks at her serious eyes in the mirror, and grins wickedly as he guns it straight for the rear of the big bus.

"Don't do it, Mac. I'll shoot. I swear to God I will shoot your fat ass!"

"Fuck you, you fucking cunt ass bitch!"

Wham! The truck jars the bus hard enough from behind to force its right front tire to ride up the low concrete railing. Ruiz slams into the dashboard, cracking ribs.

The entire world slows. Screaming students are tossed to-and-fro as the monstrous truck forces it up and over the sidewall of the bridge into support cables that snap like dry twigs in a dead forest. One of the broken steel cables whiplashes back like a spear, puncturing the bus's passenger side windshield to skewer Coach Peeler's body!

Even before Coach Peeler is impaled by the cable, both Kilarin Rouge and Robbie Mecklenburg are airborne, propelled toward each other by the sudden collision from behind.

After the bus rams into the wall of the bridge, the cable shoots down the aisle before suddenly recoiling in the blink of an eye. Kilarin is closer to the rear of the bus, but he is holding on to both overhead handrails when the truck hits them from behind. Therefore, his tight grip and arms serve as rubber bands might when kinetic energy suddenly reverses inertia.

Robbie is holding on with only one hand.

As the world slows to the speed of an unfinished thought, Kilarin Rouge's body spins through the air merely inches from the frayed cable. He jettisons pass Robbie, twisting toward the front window until a bundle of steel strands snap free to impale his body!

Just as it reaches the back of the bus, the bloody steel band holding the braids together splits and lodges in the center of the backseat as the cable cracks back. The braids separate, splaying out in all directions. In fact, both kids pass one another in midair a single nanosecond before the cable yanks all three through the obliterated right side of the front windshield. The splayed end or the braided cable snatches Coach Peeler through the shattered window just as the front of the damaged bus upends and teeters toward the rocks of the ebbing river below.

Stacie Mecklenburg's left arm slips between the seats, snapping when the bus jams. Though her arm is broken, it keeps her from falling all the way down the vertical aisle and out of the window. She screams in agony.

Kysing Rouge flies into the air and violently slams into the ceiling, landing on her stomach with enough force to fracture her ribs. Her face presses against the floor of the bus while her long legs dangle over the back of a seat, suspended in air. She is unconscious. The slightest movement—any shift of her weight—will cause her to slide off the back of the seat, right toward the damaged driver's side of the windshield.

Agent Ruiz aims from where she landed and pulls the trigger—twice!

Mecklenburg's blood splatters the window, horrifying the agent as she sinks back to the floor. Her eyes glaze over, as her mind becomes a fluid reverb of the past few moments. She always knew it could come down to this, but the training rarely adequately prepares law enforcement agents for the emotional blow back of the first kill.

When Agent Paige tugs at the bruised door, she nearly draws down on him.

"Agent Ruiz," he shouts. "Martina Ruiz, it's over, agent. Now put the gun down. Come on . . . ease it back. You can take your foot off the throttle now, Martina. That's right, ease back."

He climbs into the cab and slowly places his hand on the quivering gun, carefully removing it from her unsteady hands. With the weapon no longer a threat, he parts her hair so that her eyes and bloody nostrils are visible. Her eyes slowly rise as tears begin to fall.

He hugs her and asks, "Are you okay? I need to know if you can function because there are many badly injured people out there. They need our help. First things first. We have to secure this beast. Remember, there are people in that trailer back there."

Agent Ruiz snaps out of it and gingerly climbs down from the bloody, banged up cab. With sirens filling the air from every direction, steam rises from the mangled husks that have been scattered like jacks across the bridge.

While pressing a handkerchief against a bleeding head wound, a woman in a white skirt and a modest white blouse stumbles through the wreckage, pointing in the air.

"Help," she whimpers, faltering toward them. One of her heels breaks, and she collapses into Agent Paige's arms. Still pointing in the air, she groans, "Please . . . help."

Special Agent Paige reassures her by saying, "Yes, ma'am. Help is on the way. Just try to stay calm. You have a nasty head wound, so you must keep pressure on it."

Mrs. Bartels, the high school English teacher, looks at them both with widening eyes. Pointing upward, she begs, "Please help . . . students."

They follow the direction of her left arm and fingers to find that the woman is not delirious, but directing their attention to the three people dangling from a support cable over the swirling Catawba River and those jagged rocks below.

As the first ambulance and police cars arrive, Agent Ruiz blocks the dying sun with her hand and gasps, "My God!"

Dangling overhead, Kilarin Rouge and Robbie Mecklenburg are swinging back and forth on a support cable that has broken loose when the rampaging eighteen-wheeler created this path of destruction. When it pendulums to the left, Coach Peeler's limp, lifeless body swings beyond the bus's hulking mass.

During the carnage, an intact support cable tangled with the mangled bus's undercarriage and rear tires, stopping it from transporting the rest of the passengers to their deaths far below.

Battered and bruised, a terrified Robbie Mecklenburg struggles to hold on. His broken left leg refuses to wrap around the cable. His arms fatigue as he slowly slips down the thick cable, fearing that he is doomed to fall to his death.

"Please. Please, God!" he begs just as his right foot comes to rest on a ragged section of the frayed cable. When he places too much of his weight on those hardened strands, he slips and it lays his ankle open to the bone.

Horrified observers on the bridge and the opposing banks of the Catawba River gasp, collectively.

The pain is furious, but Robbie is strong in the midst of surging adrenaline. He holds on to redistribute his weight so that the upwardly curved wires support him by slightly piercing the leather heel of his right shoe.

Just as the youngster breathes a sigh of relief, red rain drips onto his forehead from above to mingle with his sweat.

As still as the dead, Kilarin Rouge is about ten yards above. His lacerated chin now rests upon his chest. His eyes are shut. The bloody hands dangling at his sides twitch, infrequently.

Like an angry nest of young serpents, strands of the gnarled, twisted metal braids of the bridge's support cable have punctured the right shoulder blade to protrude from the unconscious boy's chest. With the greatest of ironies, they are what is slowly killing him one drop of blood at a time, while holding him aloft like a severely neglected scarecrow.

Kilarin's left shoe is damaged where a one inch braided spare has been driven though, grazing his Achilles tendon and lacerating his foot to fill the black Wingtip with blood. The immense pressure inside of the stern leather shoe stems the flow to a degree, and he will walk again—if the maw of death lying below does not claim this young warrior first.

With black and reddish, sun-hardened clay boulders spread along the shallows like the teeth of a hungry beast, the shadow of death hovers for the promise of but one more soul to add among the torn and broken bodies that now feed the Catawba River with blood.

Chapter 8

Death Cry

Mayor Larkin Mecklenburg's boring speech about the integration of high schools and the overall reunification of Tega Cay and Fort Mill is running on fumes. In many ways, the condescending monologue insults several members of the audience, those who never voted for Mayor Mecklenburg. Thankfully, the mind-numbing solo nears a close, with him admonishing the parents to do what they can to assist in the transition by talking to their children and neighbors about the overall benefits of bringing the schools together. As a small peace offering, with the assistance of the School Board Superintendent, they unveil the new mascot. The future athletic teams will be called the Tega Cay Hornets, honoring the Fort Mill girls winning the State Basketball Championship.

Mecklenburg does not tell them that this small concession is really due to a lost bet with outgoing Mayor Riley. However, there is one small alteration to the black and blue hornet; its stinger shapes like an arrowhead.

Mostly, the crowd cheers for the new mascot. This is a shrewd move for a small town mayor, so is his naming of Fort Mill's Mayor Joe Riley as his interim Deputy Mayor. He announces a date for the first town hall meeting to formalize the decision. Anyone who opposes the idea may call for a challenge by vote. How that turns out will depend on how many Fort Mill fans of Riley show in attendance. Without their supportive turnout, he could be gone with the snap of Larkin's finger.

What most of them do not know is that Mayor Larkin Mecklenburg owns most of the acreage of the two mile stretch between Tega Cay and Fort Mill. Plans for massive property development are already in play. The mayor stands to make a mint by the annexation of Fort Mill.

The mayor's cell phone begins to vibrate in his breast pocket as many others begin to ring throughout the auditorium full of anxious parents, who are expecting the buses to arrive at any moment.

Allison Montgomery, a parent of the Hornets' point guard, looks at the breaking news on her cell phone and shouts, "Oh my God. It's the children!"

Mayor Mecklenburg and his wife are gone like a shot, leaving the others in the dark without so much as a word. However, the sports news crew waiting in the parking lot for the busses to arrive just moments ago have disappeared.

Over half of the tow trucks from the Rock Hill side of the Catawba River arrive to clear away the wreckage of this major traffic catastrophe. The atmosphere is still a bit chaotic as police officers struggle to divert the heavy traffic to allow first responders to move closer to the mechanical carnage. There are bodies—living and dead—everywhere, as plumes of smoke from burning vehicles linger like ghosts seeking the light.

The incoming traffic on the other side is cleared as quickly as possible. As trained drivers, police officers are asking most of the shocked car owners to allow them to drive their vehicles off the damaged bridge because time is of the essence for many reasons. The most dire of which, they still haven't the slightest clue.

Horrifying screams perforate the air as injured people suddenly regain consciousness in their mangled automobiles. Seasoned firefighters and EMT teams are working furiously to contain the situation. Some people will require physical extraction from their vehicles. First responders must stabilize and then extract some victims before tow trucks can haul off the ravaged hulks to make room for the emergency vehicles needed for the hardest jobs to come.

Firefighters are spraying fire suppression foam on the burning cars to keep them from exploding, which threatens to destabilize the bus filled with injured students.

On either side of the bridge, concerned and horrified people are praying, gawking, and calling family members to make sure they are not among the victims.

A black SUV breaks through the blockade on the northern side of the bridge with the flash of a badge and lights, essentially, ignoring the traffic cop's order to halt. Just as Rock Hill police officers approach the Peterbilt with their weapons drawn, Supervisory Special Agent Paige places Agent Ruiz in the capable hands of the EMT.

She grunts as the young Asian-American wraps and cinches her sore ribs. Because of her battered and swollen face, he strongly suggests taking her to the hospital for examination, but her mission is incomplete.

Paige runs toward the police with his badge raised, shouting, "Officer, please step away from the vehicle. Do it now!"

The officer ignores his warnings, while some train their weapons on Paige and the approaching men in the black SUV that just bypassed the blockade. When the defiant cop snatches the door open, despite the stern warning, McKenzie "Mac" Mecklenburg practically falls into his arms with a gaping head wound.

"Shit!" the officer shouts as he backs away from the apparent murder victim. Much to the officer's woe, he behaves like a rookie and vomits on the fat body of evidence that just flopped with a slushy splatter on the pavement.

"Officers, I am DEA Supervisory Special Agent Paige. This vehicle, though responsible for this tragic event, is off limits to unauthorized, on-federal personnel. The driver was a highly valued suspect attempting to flee, forcing my injured undercover agent to fire upon him to save lives. Please lower your weapons and back away. My men and I must take over now. We will access the dangers of moving this vehicle as quickly as possible, but you must first allow us to do our jobs."

The stubborn, local police officers are resistant and uncooperative.

Agent Paige is breathing hard when he says, "If you do not comply, gentlemen, I swear I will bring you all up on charges for the willful obstruction of a federal investigation. I know you want answers, but look around you. These are your neighbors and family members. Right now, they are in dire need of your attention. What we must do right this very second exceeds both your training and security clearances. Time is running out on those kids up there and in that bus—so move the fuck aside—and just let us do our jobs!"

Paige's men come to a screeching halt. Two will exit the vehicle with fiber optic equipment in black cases and automatic assault weapons. The other two are serious looking men, who are strapped for an all-out war. The Technora Tactical Assault armor is a convincing additive as they train their weapons on the men who are aiming at their boss.

The more senior of the police officers lowers his weapon to suggest, "Okay, men, let's remain calm. Apparently, we are all on the same side of the law. However, right now, their law looks a lot bigger and meaner. Holster your weapons and let these fed boys do their job. That's an order damn it!"

The nervous police officers comply as Paige says, "Thank you."

The officer who wisely defuses the potentially fatal incident, asks, "What the hell was this fat bastard hauling, nukes?"

SSA Paige looks him squarely in the eyes to say, "I'm sorry, Sergeant, that remains classified information at this point. However, I will warn you that this is an urgent situation that we may have to defuse."

Sergeant Wilkes snaps to. "Defuse?"

Paige nods his head and repeats, "Defuse. In the interest of more urgency, I will allow you to know what you need to get the lead out of the asses of your underlings. There may be explosives wired to go in that trailer at any moment now. Got me, Sergeant Wilkes?" Sergeant Wilkes is gone in a flash.

Paige's men, two of whom are garbed in heavy blast suites, move to either side of the trailer, breaking out their equipment. Firstly, they attach stethoscope type cups to the trailer to listen for signs of movement inside. Simultaneously, they affix Cobalt bits into battery-operated drills, which they use to bore quietly through the side panels of the trailer just inches above the floor.

Halfway through, Agent Starks says quietly into his microphone, "Sir, you may want to a take a look at this."

Paige approaches and reaches for the granular white powder seeping from the hole. He rubs it between his fingers and tastes. He whispers, "High quality cocaine. When you ease through, slide a stint inside before inserting the fiber optic lens. Get it done quickly. This truck has to be moved soon, but we must know what we're up against."

From the other side, Agent James speaks into his headpiece with hushed caution. "I'm through, boss. I detect no sounds of movement inside, so I'm inserting the fiber optic lens."

As he slowly inserts the fiber optic cable into the hole, Agent Paige joins him. He watches the monitor as Agent James maneuvers the lens to look inside the dark trailer.

"Now switching to low-light. Rear quadrant looks clear. No visible explosive devices detected high or low."

The other agent agrees from the opposite side after sliding a hollow metal tube through the drug packed wall to insert the fiber optic camera.

"I'm now checking the forward quadrant. Looks like they sealed the contraband in stacks of concrete bags. Several pallets of contraband material are secured by industrial strength cargo mesh and strapped down in the center of the trailer floor. Much of the cargo is dislodged and cast about the immediate area. Several bags have torn apart, spilling what looks like individually wrapped bricks of cocaine."

Agent Paige says, "Wait. Back up. Try the lower right quadrant, Agent James. There!" When he zooms in, Paige whispers, "There you are, *hombre muerto*. This one looks to have a broken neck."

Starks says, "Got another one on this side, sir. Judging by the amount of blood on his face, it looks like the shifting cargo may have crushed his skull. I believe there are just the two of them, sir. I think we are good. Wait. Wait one!" "Report!" Paige demands.

"This one just moved, and he has an electronic device in his right hand. It could be a cell or SAT phone. On the other hand, it's probably a detonator, sir."

Agent Paige says, "Fuck. Starks, watch him closely. James, give us your best eyes for another quick sweep of the doors. You have ten seconds to find anything out of place." Paige reaches down and grabs a black bolt cutter, heading for the rear of the trailer.

Starks warns, "Hurry, sir. He is beginning to stir. I think he's regaining consciousness."

"Shit!" Paige says, considering the dangers of moving this rig before properly securing the kamikaze smugglers.

"My sniffer is going off." Starks maneuvers the fiber optics to take a closer look at the bottom of one of the pallets where a blinking light catches his eyes. "Jesus!"

"What is it?" Paige asks hastily.

"I see it, too," says Agent James. "Sir, the doors are clear of any tripwires or motion sensors, but the bottom of each pallet of contraband is packed with what looks like military grade explosives. James crosses himself and kisses his crucifix.

The other two men are posted at the rear of the trailer with their weapons trained on the doors. Clark suggests, "We have dispersal canisters of nerve toxin in the truck, sir."

Agent Paige tosses him the bolt cutter and says, "There's no time. I'm going in. Pop it."

With his bulging muscles straining to break the hardened steel, Clark clamps down with the bolt cutters. When he breaks through and quietly flips the handle, Paige draws his weapon from the holster.

Paige's men advance, snatching the doors open for him just as the wounded smuggler sits up with a bloody grimace.

As if he is just emerging from a soundproof cocoon, the shrieking sirens now invade the air. It assaults the disoriented smuggler's intermittently hypersensitive hearing, and his head throbs from the unwelcomed barrage of noise.

The toxic odor of cocaine mingles with the fetid smell of feces and urine blooming from overturned buckets, whose tops came off near the rear doors of the trailer.

The sudden light from the open doors and the pain of his shattered, pinned legs prompt the smuggler to shriek what is to be his final death cry. He raises the detonator because they are coming!

The world of fluid motion slows to the throb of a single heartbeat.

The smuggler's wide, crazed eyes stare into his last evening's sunlight.

A silhouetted intruder rises to join him at death's door in this place where distorted time displaces the speed of movement. His head suddenly snaps back! His body convulses only once as the detonator falls to the floor, taking another heartbeat to strike the ribbed metal surface. His crossed eyes lock, staring up at the ceiling of the trailer as smoke clears the barrel of Agent Paige's weapon. A single trail of blood oozes from the wound in the center of the smuggler's forehead. Behind him, a high-speed blood portrait now paints the cache of weapons where his head rests. The hand that held the deadly device merely seconds before jerks, clenching shut as if the smuggler is fixed in the final second of his life. Though dead, he remains stuck in that moment when the firing neurons send the biochemical message to detonate the explosives.

Taking no chances, Agent Paige moves in, squeezing off two more shots at his chest. He skirts a pallets and draws down on the man with the broken neck, pumping one into the back of his head for good measure. He pivots without hesitation, aiming into all shadowy niches until satisfied that there are no surprises.

"Clear," he shouts. Only now does he take a meaningful breath. As he reaches down to retrieve and deactivate the detonator, his men move in to remove the charges from the explosives. Starks carefully inspects the other smuggler for weapons and booby-traps.

With an honest sigh of relief, Agent Paige approaches the exit. "This mission is not over, men. Remove the actuators from the explosive ordinance to be sure. We've got to move this wounded beast quickly."

He jumps down from the trailer, holsters his weapon, and bends at the waist to place both hands upon his knees.

Agent Ruiz, also known as Paula Rodriguez, AKA Natalie Hernandez, surprises her boss when she says, "I've got this, sir." Her nostrils are plugged with blood-soaked gauzes, distorting her voice. Her fractured, swollen cheek hurts when she speaks.

He turns, "Are you sure?"

She smiles a slight grimace and says, "Who better than me?" Paraphrasing a quote from one of her favorite science fiction films, she smiles sadly and utters, "I have to do this myself. Besides, in this jungle, we only get to keep what we kill, right?"

"Okay, Martina. You earned the right to see this through to the end. Roll her out gently. Then we must get you some serious medical attention. That's an order, Agent Ruiz."

She winces as she reaches for the bar to haul herself up into the cab. Agent Paige watches with concern, but allows her to finish her job because ancient is the hunter who wears the blood of the first kill. To complete this process, if she is to truly recover from the experience of righteously killing another human being, she must come to realize that it washes away. However slowly, it all washes away.

While climbing into the bloody seat, Agent Ruiz looks down at the body of McKenzie Mecklenburg. The memory of killing him flashes before her eyes. After drawing the door shut, she glances at the blood on her hands from the door handle and the driver's seat. When Agent Ruiz looks at the blood on the window, feeling it soaking into her jeans and the back of her white T-shirt, a cold shiver rattles up her spine.

Struggling to offset the onset of panic, she uses the windshield wiper, but quickly realizes that the red stain is on the inside. Agent Ruiz reaches into the back for a rag to clear the blood smear, finding one of Mac's sweaty flannel shirts instead. She quickly wipes the coagulating blood from the windshield and tosses the shirt to the floor near the ragged passenger's door, where it will soon slip between the crack to be flattened by the huge tires. When the claustrophobic moment passes, she swivels her crackling neck with her dark, puffy eyes focused through the small window of smeared blood.

When the damaged rig starts with a stubborn rumble, Agent Ruiz revs the engine and slowly backs away from the side of the bridge with a grating squelch. Once she turns the steering wheel and moves forward, the right front tire rub against the smashed frame and wheel well. This raises the stench of burning rubber as she forces it toward the far end of the bridge. As she passes the upturned bus, there comes a crumbling noise from a damaged bridge stanchion.

On the other end, armed men will guard it beside the road until Agent Paige has it towed away. They are all anxious to access the contents of the trailer, but there are still lives at stake here.

Paige looks back at all the frozen emergency personnel, who witnessed the deadly drama unfold when he courageously entered the trailer. When he whistles and twirls his raised right index finger to signify an all clear, rescue workers are jolted back into action.

As soon as Paige and his men clear the decks, two heavy tow trucks quickly move into position on the bridge behind the bus. They turn and back up before lowering the stabilizing drag braces. Moving quickly, they haul heavy cables across the lanes to hook onto the bus's undercarriage. Now, they draw the cables taught to secure the bus, preventing it from falling when the emergency crews go about getting inside to remove the injured, scared passengers.

Meanwhile, most of the frightened parents are gathered on the northern bank of the Catawba River. Mayor Mecklenburg finds something oddly familiar about the ragged eighteen-wheeler that passes by under guard of armed DEA agents, but he is too distracted by the immensity of the damage caused by it to realize that his own troublesome brother was the driver. He has no idea that McKenzie is dead.

His wife shrieks as she recognizes their son on her smart phone. The news helicopter zooms in on Robbie Mecklenburg as he struggles to hold on to the frayed support cable.

"My God, that's our son," she cries. As she thrusts the screen before her husband's eyes in tears, she begs, "Save him. You've got to do something, Larkin. Where is our daughter?"

The mayor looks at the live footage, shocked to see his only son suspended over the river where the support cable is now tangled with a live, insulated electrical cable that supplies the bridge with power.

Wind turbulence from the helicopter's main rotor is causing a badly frayed section of the support cable to dig into the power line's insulation as it whips back and forth.

A bird watcher among the worried parents on the north bank says, "Oh, dear God."

Without taking his eyes away from the cable, he hands the high-resolution binoculars to Banja Rouge to the left of him.

Banja asks, "What? What is it?" as he zooms in on his hanging son. He shouts, "Oh God, no. Please. That's Kilarin!" Sirens filling the air with chaos as they approach from their side, nearly drown out his voice.

Yara Rouge takes it from his hands as he trembles. After finding Robbie Mecklenburg through the lens and following the cable upward, she shrinks to her knees and begins to scream.

Yards above Robbie, Kilarin Rouge's limp form dangles from the cable. He is still unconscious. His chin rests upon his chest as his tattered blazer flaps in the wind caused by the news helicopter's churning blades. Like Velcro, his clothing clings to the cable where small, loose strands protrude. The strong buttons of his blazer are strained.

Kilarin is bleeding from several injuries, and he is beginning to moan his way into consciousness. As his upper body starts to lean forward, the bloody protrusion of his chest begins to slip back within!

After weaving its way to the scene through the backlogged traffic until it can get into the southbound lane, fire engine twelve finally arrives. Fire Chief Edmunds is leading it in his red car. Before allowing the ladder truck to move any further, he stops to assess the situation. His dispatcher calls to connect him with the civil engineer on the other side before allowing the heavy truck onto the damaged bridge.

A disheveled Mayor Mecklenburg and his frantic wife descend upon Chief Edmunds, demanding that he take action to rescue their son. Threats and harsh words exchange before abrupt apologies ensue.

Kilarin's desperate parents are quickly approaching just as the mayor shouts, "I don't care what you have to do, just get my boy down from there. Please, Chief Edmunds. Get him down safely no matter what!"

The fire truck slowly moves onto the bridge, just as Rock Hill's Chief of Police, the mayor's other brother, drives onto the bridge and orders the helicopter to get out of the vicinity because they are endangering lives. They move away seconds before the frayed cable works its way completely through the damaged insulation of the power line to make a lethal connection that neither kid would survive. Until moments ago, no one, in all this mayhem, has thought to cut the power.

Down below, emergency medical technicians and firefighters are cautiously descending the steep riverbank, hoping to find some of the ejected victims alive. Sadly, the first two are bloody and broken on the boulders near the river's edge where about three feet of water runs between them and the shore.

As a firefighter removes his gloves to check for a pulse in the driver of the smoking bottled water delivery truck, there suddenly comes a high-pitched searing sound. The firefighter recognizes this sound from his training and on the job experiences. His heart quickens and his eyes bulge, but his feet refuse to move him out of harm's way as the explosion erupts. His body flies through the fiery blast, smoking as he lands under the bridge, approximately twenty yards away. There, his fire-resistant suit and boots remain buoyant, displaying his burned and mutilated body for mere moments before he slips beneath the dark reddish surface of the Catawba River.

When the violent explosion ensues, the bus shifts above, causing many to moan with fright and despair. The damaged concrete wall and support column portend to crumble. Both tow trucks attached to the bus threaten to slide toward the edge of the bridge before stabilizing again. The tow truck drivers rush to the front of their vehicles to drag the cables from the winches, cinching them to the railing on the other side in case the bus shifts again.

Just as the concerned spectators and emergency workers breathe that ever-thankful sigh of relief, another support cable snaps near the top. The heavy braided cable careens from the skyward support, missing Kilarin Rouge's bleeding crown by mere inches as Robbie Mecklenburg watches in terror. He shuts his eyes at the last moment and clamps down on the cable with straining desperation.

Luckily, its wisps by, but obliterates the live wire a few feet from where it is entangled. Because she is closer to the powerline, electricity fries the dead woman's blood and internal organs in an instant. Sparking, electric fireworks rocket in all direction as people scream. The power to the bridge shuts off just as Robbie detects the current running up the cable through his hands. For a nanosecond, his heart and muscles are seized by its invisible grip, but he survives the current that nearly crystallizes the dead woman's innards below.

He opens his eyes slowly and looks down, now realizing to his horror that this is the very cable that impaled Coach Peeler. The very end of the cable that pierced her back now splays in many directions, like a snatch hook, grappling her midsection as her lifeless legs and arms dangle toward the river below. Because of her short haircut, Robbie can tell that her face is very pale because her body is nearly drained of blood. She is scorched and smoking where the cable disappears within.

The frightened kid whimpers, looking upward to avoid the scene, but there seems another dead body above him. Just before he shuts out the sight, Kilarin moves. The severely wounded boy's time is running critically short upon this precarious perch.

Kilarin moans, his eyes flickering toward consciousness. To varying degrees, pain racks his body from many points. He tries to raise his aching head as his ears begin to focus on the chaotic world beyond his fluttering eyelids.

He grimaces in agony, hearing a voice from below, shouting, "Don't move, Kilarin. Don't move!"

As he raises his head, opening his eyes to find himself dangling, panic takes hold. His struggle brings surging pain from his many injuries.

"Don't move or we'll both fall!" Robbie Mecklenburg shouts, desperately.

Tears begin to fall from Kilarin Rouge's eyes as he surveys the horizon filled with the lights of emergency vehicles. He tries to move, wincing from the pain. The young man's eyes eventually move toward the bloody metallic spear protruding from his chest. He whimpers with a hopelessness known only to the doomed. His dark brown eyes flicker as he descends again into the oblivion of unconsciousness. Once again, his chin comes to rest upon his chest. The bloody spear recedes a bit more, disappearing by inches into his body. He slips forward, completely unaware that he is moving closer to death.

Chapter 9

First Come, Last Served

As the ladder slowly extends with a firefighter in the bucket, Robbie Mecklenburg shouts at the man coming to rescue him. He glances upward, shouting for them to save Kilarin first. As the bucket bumps into the cable, just below the protesting young man, he shouts, "He's unconscious but alive. Get him first—before he falls."

As the latter comes to rest, the rescue worker shouts, "No way, son. Your dad will skin us all alive if we don't take you first."

"But I'll be okay. His time is running out, you asshole!"

"Calm down, kid, you're probably going into shock. I gotcha, kid. You're almost safe." With his left fist firmly clamped about Robbie's belted waistline, he informs the engineer through an open mic that he needs to swing two yards to the left. As he maneuvers the boom closer and quickly reaches for Robbie Mecklenburg with the right hand, Kilarin Rouge is no longer impaled. The bloody steel strands slip from his back, slamming him back into screaming consciousness. Now, only the entangled material of his blazer holds him erect. Finally, and most fatally, the buttons of his blazer break free!

With Robbie safely in the bucket, the firefighter gives the thumbs up, looking upward at the tricky angle as onlooker's cheers suddenly turn to screams of horror.

Robbie shouts, "You've got to go get him down."

The banded metal spear that protrudes Kilarin's shoe bends from his true weight. The last sound he hears is the shredding fabric of the blazer as he leans forward. Slipping back into oblivion, he spills toward his death.

The firefighter scolds. "Calm down, kid. I'll get him next, but we'll have to reposition the ladder to. . ."

Those screams now seem to erupt from the banks of the Catawba River as though amplified by loudspeakers.

Lathered in sweat, Banja Rouge falls to his quivering knees with his outstretched palms locked in an upward position as if he has been holding his son aloft with those bulging muscles straining against gravity. Yara's scream mingles with the others. Her shriek aches with the wretched knowledge that her son is the doomed teenager falling to his probable death.

A split second after Kilarin Rouge slips from the ragged blazer, he crashes headlong into the edge of the retracting bucket. His skull gushes when he hits the bucket, spraying both Robbie and the surprised firefighter. Wordless . . . stunned . . . they stare at one another. Kilarin tumbles toward the boulders below!

Mayor Larkin Mecklenburg and his wife get into the back of a squad car. The officer taxies them toward the fire engine, paying no attention to the heartrending cries of Yara and Banja Rouge, who continue to shout, "Kilarin . . . our son. Our son. Why God? Why?" Awash one another's tears, the mother and father of a lost child huddle in total despair amidst helpless sympathizers. Soon, their thoughts must turn to their missing daughter. Where is

Kysing Rouge? Could she be lying among the dead and broken bodies in the river below?

Trying not to stare down at the morbid sight of the latest victim, rescuers now fire threaded toggle bolts into the frame of the upturned bus. Cables are hooked to the bolts as the Jaws of Life cut away the rear top of the cab to allow the anxious rescue workers access to the injured passengers still clinging to life inside.

Kysing Rouge regains consciousness. Though a bit dizzy, she maneuvers herself into position to hold Stacy Mecklenburg from falling. They console one another while the squelching, grating metal of the cutaway is hoisted from the rear of the bus. Soon, a rescue worker barks instructions to the frightened passengers, warning everyone to stay put.

A firefighter reaches for a young woman, who panics as she regains consciousness. Quite contrary to her desire for rescue, she fights out of his grasp and falls. She screams, bouncing from seats to ceiling until she plummets through the vacated side of the windshield. She takes two others with her.

As tears fall from his eyes, Captain Timothy Braga warns them not to move. "We're here to help you. Please remain calm and we will get you all to safety. Is that clear?"

Amid the moans and groans, some will give positive responses. One among them keeps shouting, "Kilarin? Killer, are you there? Are you okay? Please answer me!" To her dismay, he does not respond.

Timothy Braga shouts, "It won't be long. Just bear with me for a moment. We must secure that open windshield so we won't have a repeat of what just happened. Your classmate panicked, but the rest of you must remain calm if we are all going home today. Do you understand me?"

Braga backs slowly out of the opening and keys the mike on his shoulder to advise his Chief of the precarious situation.

"What's it look like, Captain Braga?" Chief Edmunds asks from the middle of the bridge.

"Bad, sir. I counted at least six broken or dislocated limbs. They won't be climbing out on their own. Overall, I'd say that their emotional states are fragile at best. Quite a few are unconscious so I suggest we net that open windshield to keep anyone else from falling through. That girl . . . she seemed fine one minute. The next, she reacted negatively to my help. I have no doubt there will be more panic as we start hauling them out one by one. Christ. I had her. I had her and she just . . . she just. . . ."

"Calm down, Tim. Those kids need us to keep our heads clear. We will bolt nylon webbing across the entire windshield to prevent unfortunate accidents. We will lower you guys inside with collar hoists for those who are stable enough, then we will load the wire litter baskets. We will hoist them out vertically so make sure our people secure them with the crotch belts. Understood?"

"What about a crane, sir? Can we just hoist the entire bus back onto the bridge?

Chief Edmunds looks down at a long crack that practically forms before his eyes, wincing. "I considered that before conferring with Chief Egan, Chief Barker, and the civil engineers on the other side. That's a negative on the crane, Tim. It will require at least two units to do it safely and this piece of shit for a new bridge is dangerously stressed already. It would seem that those overhead support cables are more decorative than functional structural reinforcements. I can hear them singing on both sides. We can't risk it."

Braga says, "Christ."

"I'm afraid it gets worse, Tim. At least one of the weight-bearing columns below is visibly broken, and I'm looking at a jagged stress fracture in the center lane that has grown longer than Satan's tail." As if it protests the comparison, the jagged crack stretches between Chief Edmunds' feet. He quickly backpedals and shouts, "Shit on

toast. Get those kids out of there, Tim. Get 'em out!"

He looks at the squad car slowly approaching with the Mecklenburgs and says to himself, "What the . . . for the love of Christ." A crackling sound pierces the air.

Captain Braga happens to be looking directly at Chief Edmunds in the center of the bridge when he quickly backs away from Satan's tail. He responds, "Roger that, Chief. Urgency is the phrase of the day."

While waving away the approaching squad car, Chief Edmunds instructs, "I want two men to repel down the side to secure that compromised windshield before chancing four men, stripped down to the skivvies, being lowered inside to retrieve the victims. We cannot risk adding too much more weight than what's already tolerated. We will rotate the ladders of Fort Mill number twelve, and the Rock Hill two-five over the access, taking turns hauling them out as quickly and safely as possible. Get it done and bring 'em home, Braga. Edmunds out."

When Captain Braga begins to bark orders, it appears that his composure is once again intact. Often times, however, the only armor these heroes have at their disposal is the ability to project confidence with expediency.

* * *

Halfway down, Stacie Mecklenburg whimpers, "My arm is broken. I don't think I can hold on. My head hurts. Feels like I'm going to pass out."

Although her eyes are fluttering on the edge of consciousness, Kysing Rouge tightens her grip on the girl while positioning her body to prop them both up against the tow of gravity. Time is running out. If she slips into darkness, both may be doomed.

As if shouting will dislodge the bus, Kysing Rouge wraps an arm around Stacie and whispers, "Don't . . . don't pass out. You have to stay with me. Do you hear me, Stacie?"

Stacie whispers, "Yes. I'll try. Thanks. Are you okay? You don't look so good yourself." She cringes in pain.

Kysing smiles with a wince. "I hit my head pretty hard, and I think I injured my ribs. Other than that, I'm just peachy." She coughs just before vomiting, unexpectedly.

When the momentary sickness passes, Kysing Rouge reaches across Stacie to check for a pulse in Kilarin's coach, feeling the gross displacement of his neck vertebrae. Coach McCardell's head is lodged between the bottom of the seat and the retracting foot support right above them. His neck is broken; body hanging like a slab of beef. It sickens her to do so, but Kysing Rouge undoes his belt, drawing it free one loop at a time.

"What are you doing?" Stacie asks with a whimper of pain.

"Don't look, Stacie."

Stacie looks to her right, and screams.

Kysing is panting by the time she frees the belt from the bulky man. She says, "He's dead, and I'm fading fast. We need to secure ourselves until they come for us. I believe I am hurt worse than I first thought. If I go, I'm afraid I may take you with me. We need to move quickly. Are you with me?"

"Don't look now, but I'm pretty sure that both our dance cards are free," Stacie says. "I'm with you all the way. What do you suggest?"

"This is going to hurt like hell, but we need to free your broken arm and use the coach's belt to secure ourselves before either of us fades to black. I'm afraid that you will pass out and your full weight will pull your arm free while unconscious and helpless. Do you understand?" Kysing looks down and says, "We've got to stand on the back of the seats below us. I will depress the lever on your aisle seat and force it back to free your arm. You must try to stay conscious through the pain so we can both sit on the back of the seats below us. I will use the belt to tie us in somehow. Coach McCardell is a big man. I think it's long enough."

A moment later, there is a horrendous scream from the Lady Archer. When her badly swollen arm is finally free, Kysing uses the sash from her dress as a sling for Stacie's arm. Once Coach McCardell's long belt secures them, both girls pass into unconsciousness with their foreheads touching. Kysing's final thought concerns her brother.

As Kysing Rouge's bleeding head lolls to one side, she wonders if this is a dream.

Banja Rouge suddenly breaks away from his wife, running down the embankment to dive into the river. He soon rises, forced to walk against the current in the shallows. The deepest areas of this section of the Catawba River are four to eight feet deep at best, which he swims like a tireless mariner. His eyes are affixed on the swaying body of his fallen son, now lodged between two clay-red boulders near the opposite shore.

When Banja Rouge finally reaches Kilarin's broken body, his breaking heart rages at the sky. He rages at the God of heaven as burning tears flow down his flexing jaw. Held only by the supplanted ocular nerve, Kilarin's punctured left eye is lying on the bones protruding through his lacerated cheek.

As he raises Kilarin's shattered frame from the water, Banja's hopeless eyes are, eventually, forced to turn away from those glistening locks and a blood-red eye that shows no light; no life.

His male child is a sack of broken, grating bones, held together by punctured skin and stretched sinew.

The distraught father looks again to the sky and now to the bus hanging over the side of the bridge. Smoke from the burned out water delivery truck below has found its way through the broken windshield. Wondering of his daughter's fate, Banja begins to shriek her name, hoping against all odds that Kysing will answer. Because she is silent, he is truly forlorn.

Banja Rouge averts his eyes, looking at the whole of his son's slumping body in his hands.

His spirit is so distant. The father discerns nothing of Kilarin within. He struggles out of the water, forcing his feet to free themselves of the sucking mud. Fearfully, he searches every face of the fallen for Kysing, but she is not among these dead.

He slowly climbs up the bank as others come to help. The depth of despair muffles and mutes heartfelt words of condolence as the shoeless father slowly climbs the embankment. The smoky air, though filled with the sounds of sirens and screaming people, seems a sort of stifled chaos. Banja refuses to relinquish his son's body. Finally, he drops to his knees in exhaustion. His dejected eyes seek heaven once again, and then he finally lays Kilarin's broken body upon the ground.

Meanwhile, over the water, the sound of six bolts firing into the frame draws the injured bus driver from the haze of unconsciousness.

Mandy Abrams recalls the sight of the rampaging hulk approaching in her mirror. The images are broken and askew, but she remembers warning the passengers to hold on before the truck rammed into them. Two mistakes are hers to live with, clearly ensconced in her memory as she touches her bleeding forehead. She had turned the wheel to the right, toward the side of the bridge. Ordinarily, this would be a good thing. However, when the rig plowed into her rear, she planted her foot on the gas pedal instead the brake. The flashing thoughts come with a guilty moan and a whimpering, "Oh no. No."

Judging by the body parts she can discern, there could be three or more unconscious students on top of her. As she stirs, there comes a crackling sound reminiscent of ice about to part. She struggles to roll over, realizing that she is lying on the windshield where a running crack forms before her bulging eyes. Far below, a truck smolders. Three more crackling runs form and she screams as the glass shatters beneath her!

The heavy, tensile mesh prevents her and the others from falling to their deaths. Now she can hear the firefighters warning everyone to stay where they are. With her heart pounding, her blood pressure spikes and she clutches her chest.

Two by two, the passengers not so badly injured, are hoisted up the aisle to safety by cables fitted with horse collars and industrial strength nylon harnesses. Ideally, it would seem that the worst of the wounded should be withdrawn first, but they take more time to stabilize and safely extract. With the onset of panic being a constant threat to everyone, those less physically traumatized must go first to prevent any more disasters.

Clearly, there are far more passengers than expected. Captain Braga and his counterpart decide it best to hurry. Those who are unconscious could have spinal, neck, and brain injuries that require special handling that will not cause more harm or death. They must be strapped about the waist and secured to any sturdy fixture available, unless they show signs of regaining consciousness or their vital signs suggest life-threatening distress.

Due to southbound outbreaks of the A-H3N2 influenza virus, Piedmont Medical Center, among others, are quickly overrun with the wounded. Beds are scarce and those that are left must be reserved for the patients in need of immediate surgery. Many are transported to the facilities of the Carolina Medical Networks of Fort Mill and Pineville, North Carolina. Their triage statuses, which are subject to change, make a difference now that Piedmont is nearly overrun. Many are transported north as quickly and carefully as humanly possible.

By the time rescue workers get to them, Stacie Mecklenburg and Kysing Rouge have regained consciousness. They are found holding on to one another, their long legs cramping from pushing against the roof of the cab after the coach's belt buckle finally broke free from the strain.

As the two girls and a firefighter are hoisted from the cutaway, they rise into a world of unbelievable devastation. The dead are lined up on one side of the bridge as law enforcement officers take photographs and check their personal effects for identification, something usually done by the coroner. Those whose personal affects cannot be located, have the license plates of the vehicles they were found in attached to their wrists.

After walking the rest of the way, Stacie's parents are waiting as the hoist lowers them into the arms of the EMTs. A very compassionate officer helps Yara Rouge down the bank to a boat that ferries her to the other side to greet her only living child, who is oblivious of her brother's fate. As they take her to a stretcher, her mother approaches with tears in her eyes. They hug, briefly as Kysing Rouge is urged to lie still. Even now, her hopeful eyes are scanning the debris field for her father and brother.

"Mom?" she asks. "Where's dad and Kilarin? Mom?" Yara's sadness passes like a wave through her heartfelt tears and quivering lips. She remains silent as her daughter pleads. "Mom, where are they?"

The emergency medical team holds at pause as the mother's eyes involuntarily give directions to her daughter's grim inquiry.

When Kysing sees her tousled father upon his knees at Kilarin's side, she shrieks, "No, mom. Oh no, Killer. No!" She breaks free, despite her painful ribs, and fights to get to her brother as her mother tries desperately to stop her advance. The broken heel of her shoe causes her left ankle to roll, painfully. Still, she limps and stumbles forth.

Screaming his name, she slides to her bleeding knees. Her father's eyes are red from tears when he reaches out to hug her over Kilarin's battered body. She wails for her dead sibling, but he cannot respond. Kysing Rouge breaks free of her parents' grip and gently strokes his bloody cheeks, where both bone and skin are broken. While whimpering his name, she gently caresses the wet, glistening locks of his hair, but he is silent as she begs him to wake. A slight tremor seizes her hands as she kneels in the dust and gravel, weeping before she crumples upon Kilarin's chest and passes into silent darkness.

As EMTs hustle to secure Kysing Rouge on a stretcher, Stacie "the Mech" Mecklenburg watches as the girl who saved her life goes down. Her heart goes out to the Rouge family for their tragic loss as her parents hover. Apparently, Kilarin Rouge is dead. Stacie forgets her own pain for the moment because she now knows that her brother has survived. Meanwhile, her newly found friend's brother has not.

As they roll Kysing Rouge toward the same ambulance, the Mayor and his wife attempt to ride along. Cameron Reese secures

Stacie's gurney, but turns to protest their entrance. "I'm sorry, sir. We need to transport as many injured people as possible so I'm afraid you will have to meet us at Carolina Medical."

As his partner and the off duty volunteer approach the ambulance before attempting to board Kysing Rouge for the double transport, Larkin Mecklenburg scoffs, "What? That's our daughter you have there, and you nor God himself will stop us from accompanying her to the hospital."

He is standing in the way of the patient, who is moaning toward consciousness.

Stacie begins to cry, "But, dad, she saved me. She saved my life!"

"Sir, I'm going to have to ask you to step aside," Cameron insists while his partner waits patiently, as they are trained to be with distraught parents.

Larkin tries to bully his way into the ambulance. "I'm Mayor Larkin Mecklenburg and this is my daughter. That girl was able to run a few moments ago, so she can't be that bad off. Let her take the next one."

"I know who you are, sir. But I'm afraid that. . . ."

"Don't you presume to tell me what's what, mister." Larkin stares him in the eyes and lowers his growling voice to threaten, "Fuck with me and I'll make your life a living hell. If you do not get out of the way and allow us to ride with our daughter, I will have you all fired. When I'm finished, you won't be able to hold a job as a janitor at the most disease-ridden Mexican restaurant in the state!"

With what seems like panic building in her voice, Stacie pleads, "But she's really hurt, mom. Dad, where's your compassion? I wouldn't be alive if not for her." Her arm screams in her temporary restraint.

Larkin says to Stacie, "Baby, you quiet down now. You are badly hurt and probably in shock. We need to get you to the hospital to see about your arm. Just let me handle this."

Banja and Yara Rouge can hear the exchange. The upset wife feels her husband's rage building like static electricity in the air. As Banja's hands curl into fists, the intimidated EMT looks at his partner with a measure of acquiescence in the shadow of the mayor's job threatening tirade.

When Banja Rouge reaches his boiling point, taking hostile steps forward, Larkin's status will not save him from the bodily harm that is coming. Only his daughter's delicate touch halts this violent reprisal, but not before the Mayor sees death in this distraught father's red eyes. His penetrating gaze exudes, unmistakably, the crude and violent intensity of Black man's thoughts.

The two girls look to one another, both with their own measures of sadness. They wave goodbye as another ambulance slides to a stop to transport Kysing Rouge and a boarded woman with a neck injury. Her parents promise to meet her at the hospital, but only Yara follows because there is the matter of Kilarin's disposition to consider.

At both Carolina Medical Centers in Fort Mill and in Pineville, just off I-77 North, a few miles before reaching Charlotte, North Carolina, the emergency rooms are already filling up. All of the examining rooms are occupied. The older woman in the ambulance with Kysing Rouge fails to regain consciousness during the trip. The EMT suspects that she may have a broken neck, though they observed all precautions to secure her cervical vertebrae before moving her from the heavily damaged car on the bridge. After being thrown into the rear of her damaged SUV, she went unnoticed.

The precursory examination of Kysing Rouge is good, but woefully deceptive. Her motor functions, though she sustained abrasions and a head contusion, are excellent. Her sore ribs are not a hindrance and her airways seem clear. She follows the pen as instructed and her pupils contract when the intense light crosses her field of vision. After what she has been through, dealing with the very recent death of her brother, the elevated blood pressure stands to reason.

At the hospital, she is mistakenly placed near the back of the line for a CT scan. Although the parameters of the Five Tier Triage methodologies are observed, the extremely heightened elevation of her blood pressure should have served as warning of hidden dangers in a girl so young and physically fit. The need for ex-rays on the sore ribs she protects, while her eyes seem so saddened by her far away thoughts, is misjudged as emotional withdrawal.

Through her tears, Kysing Rouge wants to console her mother, but the teenager is too badly damaged herself. They hold each other and mourn Kilarin's death, missing Banja's strong presence as they patiently wait for proper testing, prognosis, and treatment. Moments later, propped up on a forty-five degree angle, the young lady drifts off to sleep. Her mother notices. Leaving her seat to caress her daughter's hair, Yara is thankful she has found a moment's peace from the slight headache and awful thoughts that will haunt them all in the coming days. What she does not know is that this is much more than simple slumber from exhaustion.

Banja, though distressed by dealing with the police and the management of Kilarin's remains, rushes to the hospital as soon as it is possible. He calls Yara for an update, but finds that his daughter still waits to be examined or admitted by a doctor. This angers him greatly because he is certain that Mayor Mecklenburg's children are not suffering in a corridor somewhere. The very tone of his voice serves as warning that he will tolerate no excuses when he arrives. Only the heavy northbound traffic heading into Charlotte will hinder him from being at his daughter's side. For some reason, through their uncanny connection, perhaps, Banja Rouge's spirit senses that Kysing's injuries are far more extensive than they seem. This would be a perfectly reasonable reaction of any father, but his spiritual connection to his children has always held most unique qualities. After the conversation, in which he implores his wife to be more aggressive, Yara feels a renewed sense of urgency because her husband has always had great instincts when it comes to their children.

She approaches a nurse who does not seem to have time to chat, which infuriates her. As Yara approaches the nurse's station with fury building in her eyes, a young Black nurse heads her off because she knows what is coming. Although it seems that some people are taken in an order more aligned by color than necessity, depending on who is running things, emotional histrionics will only set things back for Kysing, whom she triaged and suggested a CT scan. Head wounds are the worst bleeders, and the most difficult to accurately diagnose.

The head nurse downgraded the urgency, dismissing the younger nurse's opinion with no tolerance for questions.

This sort of thing is a growing contention between the two, building a head of steam with patients caught in the middle. So far, the head nurse's lax attitude toward any patient that Mesa Ntombi seems overly concerned about has not developed into any major medical missteps from which she could not recover. Today, though unbeknown to them, Kysing Rouge lies in peril because of it. What the young African American nurse knows is that there is the distinct possibility that the girl's wounds are far worse than they seem because of the amount of blood that has soaked and dried in her locks. That dried trickle on her forehead only hints at what lies within. She will need stitches for sure, after her hair is cut away. CT Scans for head trauma are basic and prudent, if not paramount with episodic unconsciousness, vomiting, and elevated BP.

Chapter 10

Bleeders

There are still two people in front of Kysing Rouge when her father strides in to raise holy hell about the slack attention his daughter has received. He rails down upon them, accusing them of placing her at the back of the line because she is African American.

The staff tries to calm him, self-assured that the complaint is just an unfounded accusation of a vexed father; it simply goes against hospital policy. In this case, at least one nurse knows this is not always true when that certain person is on duty. Nurse Mesa Ntombi has made a special plea to Dr. Casey Remington to check on the patient in question. He is quite busy, of course, checking only her chart. He promises to get to her as soon as the scan is complete, but his decision is based largely on a chart that has been re-coded, or downgraded, by the head nurse.

Kysing whispers to her mother that she really needs to use the bathroom. Because it has been hours since the accident and she refuses a disgusting bedpan, Kysing Rouge is assisted to a wheelchair. In very subtle ways, her condition is deteriorating before Yara's eyes. The mother, with the nurse's assistance, takes Kysing to the restroom where she is asked if she can stand. Kysing limps into the stall to relieve herself, holding her ribs with one hand and the handrail with the other. Without warning, her left hand trembles out of control. She cannot seem to stem its shaking, and her headache quickly worsens.

The girl quietly calls out to her mother when she finishes using the toilet, but she has trouble standing on her own. When the nurse and Yara Rouge come in, Kysing is wiping a trickle of blood from her nose. As they help her to the wheelchair, her vision blurs and she clamps down on her helpers' wrists.

"Baby?" her mother says. "Kysing, what's the matter? Talk to me."

During a moment of fading lucidity, Kysing looks fearfully at Yara to say, "Mom . . . something . . . something's. . . ."

At this very moment, Banja Rouge stiffens. He becomes quiet and alert, as if listening to a most calamitous directive.

The nurse tries to get her into the wheelchair, but when the girl's eyes suddenly roll backward and her body becomes rigid, it is already too late. Kysing arches, once. With her face toward the ceiling, she shrieks, involuntarily.

She shrieks again and arches her back so violently that her fractured ribs break. The snapping sound is horrendous. She begins to convulse even before falling to the floor. There, upon her back, the seizure takes complete control of Kysing's motor functions. The remaining urine in her bladder stains her gown amidst the most violent convulsions.

In urgent haste, the nurse quickly rolls the girl to the wrong side! Kysing's broken ribs separate to puncture her right lung. Her teeth are clenched too tightly for her tongue to slip between them, but she is in danger of doing serious damage to herself as her limbs quiver and flail. Her feet are vacillating pistons, pumping hard upon the tile floor as her body places her on her back despite her mother's effort to control her movements. Yara holds her down as the nurse runs into the hall. She reaches into a pocket for a communicator, into which she shouts, "Second floor CT. Grand mal. Code Blue—grand mal—women's restroom. Code Blue!"

* * *

Understandably, Banja and Yara Rouge are taking turns sitting and pacing in the waiting room area. Kysing's parents shed many tears between them, but these few hours without knowing their daughter's fate is maddening. Yara spends much of the time praying, whether sitting or wearing a hole in the floor.

Finally, a Thoracic Surgeon named Ross Oakmont emerges. He removes his headdress and looks toward the anxious parents with great concern in his eyes. He has to deliver bad news, something he never seems to get used to doing. He approaches them as though wading through water.

As the parents rush toward him for answers, he insists that they sit before he begins.

"What is it? Please tell us," Yara implores with mounting trepidation.

After they sit, the surgeon takes Yara's hand and says, "My name is Doctor Oakmont, your daughter's Thoracic Surgeon. I have good news, but I'm afraid that there is very bad news to follow. We successfully relieved the pressure and repaired the punctured lung; therefore, your daughter is free to breathe without self-collapsing or what's medically referred to as traumatic pneumothorax. In this case, every breath added more air between the ribcage and the lung, which, essentially, causes the lung to collapse. Once she was out of danger there, I then used what is known as a Synthes Rib Matrix to secure the broken ribs your daughter probably sustained during the bus accident and greatly damaged while seizing. It is the very best medical technology has to offer in regards to quicker mending time. We are, however, medicating her with powerful anticonvulsants because she has much bigger problems, I'm afraid."

"What's the matter with my daughter, doctor?" Banja asks impatiently. "Please, just tell us the truth." His eyes seek nothing less than honesty from Kysing's surgeon.

"Well, as you both know, once we stabilized her, we performed tests to ascertain the cause of the seizure since she's never had predispositions for the condition. We initially performed an EEG, or electroencephalogram, which further indicated the need for a CT scan. The CT proves that your daughter sustained some degree of intracranial hemorrhaging or bleeding in the brain, during the accident."

Yara clutches her chest, thankful for her husband's arm about her shoulder.

"Jesus. How can something like that go undetected? I begged those people to help us, but they were always too damn busy!" she shouts.

While calmly looking directly into the eyes of one parent or the other, Dr. Oakmont maintains a passive, even-toned voice, as he continues. He was expecting a reaction even more hostile than displayed because he knows that the hospital's triage protocols have failed this patient, placing her life in jeopardy.

"I understand you being upset, Mrs. Rouge. I do, but the length of time it took to rescue her from the bus in combination with the amount of trauma patients to arrive beforehand, made it difficult to ascertain the extent of her injuries. You sat with her all this time, as I understand it, but saw no sudden signs of deterioration until it finally presented itself. We regret this happened, but. . . ."

Banja shouts, "But what? Say what must be said, Doctor Oakmont, and stop treating us like fucking children. Is this not our daughter's life we are now talking about? Please, give it to us straight and stop worrying about diplomacy and lawsuits with your carefully chosen words."

The father is right to insist on expedient honesty.

Although he hopes to keep Mr. Rouge calm, this is to be expected. As a result of Dr. Oakmont's vast amount of experience when it comes to informing parents of their children's worsening conditions, he's come to expect the mothers to show the most pivotal of emotions. The fathers, however, have been more prone to anger and rage.

Doctor Oakmont rubs his forehead, gathering his thoughts while giving them a moment to calm down. His silence will prepare them for the worse, where there still may be an upside.

He says, "The CT Scan indicates that your daughter has a hematoma, but only an MRI MRA will determine the extent of the damage. The Magnetic Resonance Angiography will map the blood vessels to more accurately show where the damage is and its extent. We are keeping a watchful eye on Kysing every second. Once I repaired the damage, she was rushed in for the Magnetic

Resonance Imaging, which will tell us what we are looking at. My part is done for now, but the best neurological specialists are analyzing your daughter's results as we speak. She is heavily sedated, and we are administering anticonvulsants because the bleeder is putting intracranial pressure on her brain. This condition is serious, which must be handled delicately by experts of the field. All of this will be explained to you in greater detail. Right now, the important thing to remember is that we are doing everything within our powers to save her life. I understand that she is an athlete. Is that true?"

Banja says "Yes. Yes she is. Kysing is a basketball player for the Fort Mill Hornets."

"Oh wow. You mean your daughter is the Stinger, the State Championship MVP. I thought the name seemed familiar."

"Yes, that's our daughter and we are very concerned, Doctor Oakmont. Can you tell us anything more?" Banja says with a desired measure of calm in his voice.

"Well, besides having one hell of a ballplayer up there, she is young, strong, and in relatively good health . . . all things considered. These are always positive aspects while caring for any trauma patient. Please, remain calm and hopeful. We have specialized people dealing with this head injury and she will receive the best of care. Someone will take you to the ICU once all the tests are complete. We will keep her as comfortable as possible. Please remember, the human brain is a tricky, delicately intricate organ. There stands a very real possibility that the neurosurgeons will elect to induce a coma to reduce the stresses of maintaining all bodily functions so that the brain swell can self-correct. That remains only one possible option, but I assure you it is quite safe and routine. When she regains consciousness, please remember that at a parent should be one of the first faces she sees. Be strong for her. Above all, try to control emotional responses like fear and worry because positivity often plays a far larger role in a patient's recovery than most people are aware. Now then, I'm afraid I must leave you in the capable hands of my nurse, who will take you up in just a moment. Unfortunately, I have many more broken bones to mend." They all stand. Before he leaves, Banja shakes his hand and apologizes for being so forceful in his demands.

* * *

With mounting consternation and doubt, the female neurosurgeon lingers before the door to compose herself. This will not be easy, but it is long overdue.

In the dim imaging lab, Doctor Edward Conner considers Kysing Rouge's brain scans, moving from frame to fame with careful deliberation. When he notices what he has been looking for in a particular cross-section, he removes his glasses and places a small round manacled magnifier over the hippocampus region. He soon groans with concern, paying no attention to the person who now joins him in the lab.

He moves toward the computer monitor to zoom in on the corresponding cross-section, and studies it intently. The doctor standing behind him shifts the revolving pictures for a look at other sections of the same brain. With her glasses between her teeth, she thoroughly considers one image after another. The pace of her footsteps is all too familiar.

Without looking back to see who is there, Dr. Edward Connor notates before taking a moment to say, "Hello, Kora. Were you ever going to acknowledge my presence, or are you depending on the shock value as I turn around to ask who the hell is messing with my panels when there are free ones on the other side?" He still does not look back.

The female doctor stands there with her arms crossed, looking at his back. Without reply, she just stares at him with a hurt look in her eyes that she does not want him to see when they are face-to-face.

Finally, as he continues to type his notations, she asks, "How do you do it, Edward? How could you know it was I without as much as a glance? Were you told that I was called from Nason's Medical to consult or possibly more?"

Doctor Edward Connor continues to type, pursing his lips before saying, "Besides the fact that you have always had an unusual penchant for wearing those extremely sensible designer shoes, we were married for five years. During that time, I came to know every step of those tight calves in those Prada's of yours. Though it is not unpleasant, you have worn the same perfume for years. Zensuality, right? It wafts into my nostrils whenever you are at least fifty feet from entering the room. I knew by your scent that it took you a moment to enter the imaging lab."

She glances at the floor with a slight smile. "How have you been, Edward?" she asks.

"Fine," is his simple reply. "Yourself?"

"I've been okay, I suppose. Working endlessly, it seems." Her British accent always betrays her when she is uneasy, becoming more profound when she is upset or about to enter a fracas. She asks, "Edward, would it be too much to ask that you simply look at me when we are speaking to one another?"

With quiet deliberation, after taking another entrance into the lab, Surgical Administrator Irish Feeson listens to the exchange from where she stands around the corner. She knows that they were once married, but calling Kora Connor to help with this case based on the image reader's analysis was a difficult decision. She does not wish to alienate Edward, but together, they are the best at what they do in the region. She eavesdrops further, not expecting the conversation to become more dicey than cordial.

To answer her question, Edward Connor says, "I'm not looking at you because there is a brave young patient out there in dire straits. Also in truth, Kora, for six years, I studied you from head to toe. Now, I rarely look at you because I tend to see too much. And, frankly, it tends to disturb me."

She approaches until they are standing face-to-face, forcing the confrontation on terms that she needs, with or without his consent. "What does that truly mean, Edward? What do you mean by that?"

Edward grows annoyed at Kora's deliberate intrusion on personal space because he feels that she no longer has the right to do so. He tries to sidestep, but she counters. He turns away when the annoyance blooms into anger. Therefore, he answers her question, no longer trying to reign in his long chained hostility.

"Do you really want to do this now, while my patient's life hangs in the balance? Fine. Let's do this, you pompous, self-involved bitch!" He sighs long and hard. "I loved you, Kora. We had the world at our fucking feet . . . together. I do not look at you unless I absolutely must because I still see you—with him—in our bed! Does that answer your asinine question? Are you happy to know that I haven't found a way to safely remove entrenched, fire-seared, memories from my own brain without losing the capacity to perform even simple surgical procedures?"

She averts her eyes because he has finally said it, getting it off his chest for the first time since the wheels fell off the bus.

Irish Feeson has finally gotten the answers to questions she was too respectful to ask before. Right now, she feels ashamed for intruding.

"I'm sorry for forcing the issue, Edward. I realize that I made terrible mistakes and most egregious trespasses in our past."

Doctor Edward Connor's ire really comes to bear. These words, these long unspoken words have kept at bay for years. Now, she seems to want them to come out with the bitter venom that he has contained and drowned in work.

"Sorry?" he repeats as he circles her with a scowl of contempt etched on his face. "Sorry? It was a race to file for divorce. Your realtor still hadn't found a buyer for your old place, but you tried to take my home from me. Even though you were the one who lied and cheated, you still tried to take the home where I grew up in your preemptive strike. Even now, you have the nerve to force me to relive this fucking grievous bullshit!"

"I am truly sorry for everything, Edward. Truly. I am."

He takes a hot, seething step toward the slightly shorter ex-wife, who suddenly averts her proud eyes. A genuinely shameful sadness replaces that prideful defiance as her vision threatens to blur.

"What I really cannot understand is why you kept my name. If you could display such utter contempt for me, why would you? Is it a taunt, a sick little reminder that you will always hold a part of me hostage?"

Neurosurgical Administrator Feeson moves into the room, rounding the dim corner where she still goes unnoticed.

With her tears freely flowing now, Dr. Kora Connor, confesses, "Again, I deeply apologize. I was wrong, and then I made it all worse by being spiteful because you could not find it in your heart to forgive me. You would not even consider it, not even a little. When I was finally able to come to terms with things, unflinchingly, it required that I realize I had absolutely no right to expect that of you. I was so wrong for all the things I had done, before and after violating the sanctity of our marital vows."

"I see. Somehow, during that completely nightmarish episode in our lives, it was all really my fault. Is that how you rationalized your actions? Somehow, I managed to hurt your enormous British pride by not forgiving my wife for simply sharing a biological imperative with another man, so you took it into the deep end. What a fucking sleazy, worthless son of a bitch I've been!"

At this point, Irish Feeson thinks it best that she step in. She has never heard Edward raise his voice or use that particular type of profanity. She knows the complete story now, losing some respect for Dr. Kora Connor as a woman and wife, but not as a surgeon. Edward Connor is now displaying a level of anger that suggests volatility and violent reprisal. The way he is holding on to his clenched right fist suggests just how badly he wants to harm this woman. Obviously, harsh words are inadequate to quell what must have been fermenting in his soul since their horrendous divorce.

Each hurtful syllable spewing from his lips is much deserved, apparently. His ex-wife knows it. In an extremely complicated way, she is forcing this confrontation because they both need it. Oddly enough, her guilt requires that she help unburden her ex-husband of the emotions she knows he has been keeping contained like a penned animal.

However, the true weight of it, the density of his venomous rage after three long years apart proves to be a little more than she is prepared to withstand. Kora crouches to bended knees under the barrage of vicious, though true, words that Edward cannot seem to stop on his own now that the floodgates are open. She holds herself as if the room is frigid, knowing without a doubt that her own willful actions have tainted the soul of the nicest, most caring, and peaceful man she has ever known.

As she is about to clear her throat to let them know that they are no longer alone, Feeson hesitates when Edward Connor leans against the desk and shuts down. He slowly rocks back and forth in regaining his composure. He must have finally purged some vile rot that has festered in his soul, even when he shunted such thoughts into lead-lined rooms in his mind and heart long ago.

Dr. Edward Connor looks down at Kora crouching toward the floor with her tearful eyes affixed on the past misdeeds that destroyed their marriage. She is truly remorseful, and though he does not wish to recognize it, Dr. Edward Connor approaches from behind. He stands above her, placing his hands upon his hips with his eyes raised to the ceiling as if to question his own capacity to feel pity for her. With a sigh, he reaches down and takes both Kora's arms from behind to help her to her unsteady feet. He can now feel that this is no mere pretense of shame, but some deeply rooted measure of the unspoken truth.

She wipes the tears away, but they continue to flow as she tries to shore up her emotions.

"Thank you, Edward. I'm okay. I'll be fine."

Feeson backs away, receding around the corner to remain out of sight. Nevertheless, she continues to listen.

With her back to him, Dr. Kora Connor confesses, "I never meant to hurt you, Edward. I alone destroyed a wonderful and loving marriage for nothing more than my own vanity. I botched things up because someone, other than my husband, paid me a little attention with a few seductive compliments. I was such a fool, and I am so very remorseful. I have never forgiven myself for allowing my attorney to do her song and dance, all the while pretending to be the uncaring bitch during the divorce. Nevertheless, I swear to you, I was really dying every moment inside. I have been alone—literally alone—ever since that awful,

awful period in both our lives, Edward. Please believe me when I say that I kept your name, not out of spite, but what I now know is an unrealistic hope that you would one day find it in your heart to forgive and take me back. I kept it because I never wanted to give up on us, as well as a punishing reminder of my mistakes if you couldn't find it in your heart. God forgive me. I am so very sorry. Given my history, I don't expect you to believe what I have wanted to say to you during an eternity of lonely nights and wordless, solitary meals, but I still love you very much. I am so ashamed, but I love you. I still love you, Edward. You were the best thing to ever happen to me, and I hurt you deeply."

Irish Feeson wipes a tear from her own eyes and clears her throat to let them know that she is coming around the corner this time. At this point, both surgeons turn toward the resonance images as if nothing has happened.

Once she turns the corner, the surgical administrator asks, "Well, kids, how does it look for our young patient?"

Kora continues looking at the images when she says, "I've only just arrived to look at the cross-sections. I'm afraid I'll need a few moments more to get properly acclimated to this case." As an afterthought, she turns and shakes the hand of the woman who asked her to consult.

Edward moves toward the desk to task his notes. "How are you Irish?"

The older woman approaches and smiles at him, placing a firm grasp on his left bicep.

"Though all isn't sunny in this world, every now and again, something good comes of our trials. Whenever I see your handsome face hard at work with those gears churnings inside that brilliant mind of yours, Edward, I am given a sense of hope."

"Kysing Rouge is in trouble. The worst of it is a deep bleeder around the hippocampus, which was the epicenter of the violent seizure. Here is the HVA. The Hippocampal Voluming Analysis and incremental rises in the intracranial pressure will corroborate my findings. Also...."

Kora interjects, "If that isn't bad enough, she has a secondary hematoma. Here, in the Parietal Lobe. I have seen this combination of injuries before in sporting trauma patients, but this girl was not wearing a football helmet. Did she have a hat on or has she thick hair?"

"Hmm. I was told that you are very quick on your feet," Irish Feeson says to Kora Conner with a smile. She glances at Edward, conferring without hesitation. "Braids. Her head is heavily braided, which may have played a part in masking the severity of her injuries. But her highly elevated BP should have given reason to look a bit deeper. Her worse symptoms didn't become apparent until it was much too late."

"Braids. That's probably why her skull didn't split open like an egg," says Edward. "Even so, someone downstairs really dropped the ball. There is no use in denying that now."

"Yes. Yes, you are probably right about that. I have already made interesting findings in that regard. Someone in the ER will burn behind this. No matter how it turns out, the administration will face repercussions. Any half-assed lawyer can see to that. However, we like to think that saving a patient and giving them some chance at a reasonably normal life makes them and their families a little more grateful than legally aggressive."

"Well, there is that, but it's not my concern," Edward says. "Either I must perform the standard craniotomy and hope for the best after evacuating the hippocampal hematoma, or we induce a deeper coma and go in at the same time. A wide decompressive craniotomy may save this patient from drowning her own brain. Either way, I suggest we move as quickly as possible. Do you concur, Dr. Conner?"

"Together—perform both procedures—at the same time? Edward, do you think she's Iron Man?" Kora crosses her arms and looks to the tip of her right shoe, raising the toe as she considers the possibility of success. "Still, it has been done before, with injuries even more severe. Hmm, I wonder."

"If you two are fully compliant, we will have the necessary forms drawn up," says Irish Feeson. "But if you think this technique doesn't stand a chance in hell, I want to know about it right now. Let the parents decide whether they want a basketball player or a daughter back." She looks over her glasses, one to the other. Her second chin is always more profound when she does this, so she eases her gaze.

The doctors look at one another. Kora nods her head and says, "I think Edward could be right. It is risky no matter what we do. That rupture near the hippocampus will surely kill her, even if the procedure does not. How is her vision, any problems there yet?"

"Before stabilization, the patient complained about intermittent visual cessation. It scared the hell out of her, complicating matters more."

"Yes, I should say so. I agree, with Edward on this one. We should proceed."

"Edward, right now, I need you to use your outside voice," Irish says. His eyes are far away and calculating.

"What choice do we have? She can die either way, but to move now gives her the best chance at living with some quality of life. She will probably never play basketball again, and the probability of developing aneurisms will loom a constant threat over her. My colleague agrees that it is worth the risk so we are going in. My God, why is death or slower death, always the constant, unflaggingly loyal companion?"

"The parents have already lost a son to this tragic event. I don't think they will have any choices in this matter. And I fear death, or even a dreadfully slower death, will always be our constant companion to abide in this profession," Irish concurs. She exhales, but it is hardly a sigh of relief. "Okay then." She is about to turn and walk away, but the sudden alteration of thinking causes her to turn a full 360 degrees.

"Is there something else, Irish?" asks Dr. Edward Connor.

"I want both of you to discuss this with the parents. Live or die, this becomes both your burdens to bear, as well as theirs. Judging from the conversation that I overheard before making my presence known, I want you to assure me that you are both focused and there remains no personal distractions left to interfere. Yes, I am ashamed of my behavior. Ordinarily, I would never infringe on such a private and extremely passionate conversation. That is not normally my way, but neither I nor this hospital's administration, the parents or patient, can afford the trappings of divorcees at odds with one another. Clear?"

Edward looks away, his eyes seeking those of his ex-wife. "Did you hear everything, all of it?"

"I walked in and cleared my throat," she embellishes. "But neither of you heard me. Nor did you realize that I was standing just over there a few moments ago," Irish Feeson's admission now lacks the sense of shame she initially felt while eavesdropping.

"Edward. Kora. Can you both assure me that your personal lives will play no part in this endeavor? I need a definitive answer here."

Kora Connor looks at the tip of her right shoe with her arms crossed. Her embarrassment at having her completely unfettered confessions of shame overhead by a stranger is apparent. She looks at Edward and nods her head before confronting Irish's utterly reasonable and responsible inquiry. The look in Irish's eyes is not one of judgment as Kora Connor expects, but one of sympathy. Even hope.

"We will be fine, Mrs. Feeson," she answers first. "It was my fault, completely. I'm sorry that I used this forum to confront Edward and brought our personal lives into the workplace without warning you first. It shan't happen again."

"I'm fine, Irish. We're both just fine."

Irish Feeson, whose mothering instincts are now taking over, smiles at him. She approaches Dr. Edward Connor and takes him by the arm. She walks him across the room to face his ex-wife—the woman who hurt him to his heart—the woman he may still love despite himself.

"You two are going to be depending on one another with a fine and heroic young lady's life caught in the loom. Like it or not, you're both joined at the hip, and Kysing Rouge is like your own offspring. Whether that young girl dies on the table, dies in post-op, or miraculously lives to go on and have children of her own someday, she will become the glue that binds you two together. Whichever way this worm will turn, I hope that you will use the opportunity to heal at the very least. Now get going before the hopeless romantic in me begins to weep like a whimpering baby. If you were to see that, I'd have to kill you both. Headlong into the fray, doctors. Let's get to it."

As she walks away, Irish realizes that she still has the legal documents in her hands. She returns to find Kora alone. "Dr. Connor, these are your standard forms. It would be unethical and liable to have you interacting with these parents or the patient without signing them first, as we both know. I like to dot my Ts and cross my Is straightaway."

"How quaint. Yes, of course." As she signs all of the forms, keeping her eyes to the task, she says in a near whisper, "I want to thank you for what you said earlier. I admit that it was terribly embarrassing, and I felt harshly judged. Your kind eyes and smile, however, told me quite a different story. I thank you."

"I made the very same mistake once, which is not an easy admission. After months apart and living in hotels, my husband called me right out of the blue. It was a stormy, blustery night . . . raining birds, cats, and dogs. I will never forget. When he said that he missed me, and wanted me to come home, my heart filled with joy unlike any other time in my entire life. I wept like a child when Charles forgave me and said that he still loved me. No words have ever held such meaning for me. It was foolish of me to reduce such a sacred bond between man and woman down to little more than a biotic act."

Dr. Kora Connor signs the final page, placing her hands across her lips while considering these words. "I'm very happy for you, Mrs. Feeson. We don't all get second chances after making such dreadful mistakes."

Irish Feeson's warm disposition suddenly turns to a long mourned sadness. "No. No we don't, Dr. Connor."

"I hope things worked out well for you both," the doctor says to the tough administrator.

Irish looks away with tears welling in her eyes. "He died on the way to collect me and my things. A drunk driver was mucking about during the storm. Charlie never even made it to the hospital, never stood a chance. I waited and waited, but he never showed up. I stood just out of the rain, waiting in front of the hotel, never to know that the sirens I heard mere blocks away were wailing for my husband's broken body."

Kora places a sympathetic hand upon her shoulder, saddened by her tragedy after finding forgiveness. "I'm so sorry for your loss. How very awful that must have been for you."

Irish begins to buck up, backing away from that sadness and guilt. "We've all made mistakes in life, Dr. Connor. Not every wife makes the same as yours and mine, and even fewer live to know the forgiveness of a saint like Charles Emery Feeson. I have never seen Edward in sustainable relationships. I've observed him deep in thought from afar, where a kind of saddened loneliness accompanies his eyes. I now realize that he was probably thinking of you. However, he never lets on when I ask how he is doing. Over the years, I have come to think of Edward Connor much the way a mother thinks of a son. He still loves you. I saw it in his eyes after he railed down on you with a wrath, obviously, unexpressed before. Yet, when your genuine sorrow and regret nearly drove you through this floor, I saw it in his eyes. The sadness. The regret for hurting you that way . . . even deservedly so. Your back was turned, but I saw it in his eyes. Edward longs for you, but I am certain he fears he will never forget what happened. Any rational person, man or woman, must consider the unsavory possibility. Since I have already stuck my nose in it thus far, I may as well get neck deep. When this surgery is over, Kora, when there is that quiet need to be held, go to him. Let the chips fall where they may and be prepared to accept the consequences while remaining hopeful. You will have no better chance, dear. Bear in mind, however, if he takes you back and you ever hurt him again, you will have to deal with me. Now go on and get this process started. Edward has assembled excellent surgical teams. They have all been together for quite some time, developing multiple skillsets. They will see you through any crisis situations with unabridged professionalism."

Dr. Kora Connor wipes a tear away, thanking Irish Feeson with a brief hug. She heads for Edward's office where Kysing Rouge's parents will soon meet with them.

* * *

Irish Feeson decides to join the meeting with Kysing's parents to be sure this delicate matter is handled with optimistically sympathetic professionalism, leaving no avenue of discussion to neglect. Both doctors are taking turns speaking to them about the pros and cons of what they are proposing, itemizing the potential benefits and dangers with equally honest detail.

It is not until they mention that her daughter's entire head will have to be clean-shaven that Yara Rouge begins to cry because she knows that Kysing would do the same. She is distressed and this part is never easy for anyone involved. Doctors or parental proxies. The need for immediate action is expressed, but the parents are given time to discuss a decision that they must make together.

With a sense of urgency hovering over the fate of Kysing Rouge, they decide to allow the doctors to proceed by signing the necessary forms. Yara Rouge insists on resuscitation should something go horribly wrong. Their daughter deserves every opportunity to recover no matter the cost.

Chapter 11

Reap the Whirlwind

While Pauline Mecklenburg hoovers over her sleeping daughter, she recalls Stacie imploring her father to allow room for Kysing Rouge, who saved her life. Before sleeping so soundly, her injured daughter spoke to her about what happened while trapped in the bus with Kysing Rouge.

Stacie mumbles in her sleep amidst a bad dream about falling toward the damaged windshield of the upturned bus when Kysing Rouge suddenly grabs her by the broken arm. While straining to keep Stacie alive, she passes out and they both go crashing toward the river below.

As her mother strokes her hair, Stacie screams herself awake with a cold, sweaty shudder. The pain of her broken arm causes her to moan as tears fall from her eyes. Her mother consoles her, trying to ease the mind of the very troubled young woman. Pauline pushes the button, calling for a nurse because Stacie's pain returned fully when she awoke with both hands stretched overhead in dreaming simulation.

Once her daughter is again resting, comfortably, she decides to visit her son.

In the room next door, Robbie Mecklenburg is also suffering from his broken leg and stitched lacerations as his father slumbers in the chair. Pauline enters quietly and whispers to her son that everything is going to be okay. In time, he will heal and live out his days with no worries. As his pain medication is administered, Mayor Mecklenburg wakes from his fitful sleep in a very uncomfortable chair.

Paula, as many call her, looks at her yawning husband and says, "Honey, I think I'll go get some coffee and visit the chapel now that both kids are sleeping comfortably now."

He straightens himself and groans, "How are they?"

As Robbie slips deeper into slumber, she looks at her son and says, "They're both going to be fine, thank God. Just broken limbs, concussion, and nasty cuts. After a couple more days of observation, they'll be allowed to go home."

He gets up and places an arm around her shoulders. "Yes, that's good. Let me wash my face and I will join you. It will be nice to see Father Callahan after all these years."

* * *

After eight hours of delicate, but masterful surgery, Kora takes Irish Feeson's advice by joining her weary ex-husband for a light meal. Neither wishes to leave the hospital should something arise, remaining readily available within the walls of this great labyrinth of healing. Although most of their time in proximity of one another has been spent in torturous silence, she joins him, without invitation, as he showers. Slowly, and with great timidity, Kora approaches to wrap her arms around Edward. He hesitates before lowering her arms to the sensitive area on the small of her back.

They remain this way for quite some time before he finally kisses her in a way that fully reveals his longing. While the steaming shower drenches their skin, they quietly, but passionately, make love as her tears comingle with the cascading water. After the long fight to save a patient's life, Dr. Edward Connor and Dr. Kora Connor fall asleep in one another's arms in the dormitory. Even in this small bed, though it has been ages, they still fit perfectly together as if chiseled by a master sculptor.

Kysing Rouge lies perfectly still on the ICU ward where her worried parents keep vigil. In an extreme state of unconsciousness, her slightly swollen eyes remain shut, but she is breathing on her own. Her damaged, exposed brain rests beneath a custom fitted shield. The rest of her skull is clean-shaven, but most of her head is sequestered beneath bandages. A catheter is inserted into her bladder, connecting to a bag that collects her urine. Her Calvaria, the top portion of her removed skull, is tagged and sits in a cold storage.

Yara and Banja Rouge are holding each other when Kysing's left index finger twitches and she moans. They hasten to her side, speaking in anxious whispers to help guide her back. When the monitor alerts the nurse's station of the heightened brainwave activity, one of them meets Yara Rouge as she runs into the hallway to tell them that her daughter is coming around. Someone immediately alerts the doctor on call.

While holding her hand, the loving father whispers, "Kysing? Can you hear me, baby? I'm here, honey. Daddy's here."

As Yara rejoins them, she murmurs, "Dad, is that you?"

"Yes, love. I am here with you now and so is mom. We never left your side, baby girl. You must remain calm and go back to sleep. We'll be here."

As the nurse watches, urging caution until the doctor on call arrives, Yara gently takes her hand. Stifling her tears, she whispers, "I'm right here, baby. We love you so much. We love you so very much."

"Mom?" Kysing asks as she tries to open her eyes. "Why can't I see your faces? Why can't I see anything at all?"

Yara looks to her husband. Banja whispers, "The doctors say that you sustained a brain injury during the accident. They operated, but there is still a great deal of swelling. When the swelling goes down, you will see again. Trust me."

Doctor Redding nods his approval of how the father handles giving her the news about her impaired vision. He is cautiously relieved that the patient regained consciousness displaying cohesive verbalizations. However, he knows in his gut that she has emerged from the deep, on her own, much too quickly for it to be beneficial.

He needs to place her back under, and quickly, before. . . .

"How is Kilarin? Is he okay?"

Her perturbed parents look to the doctor for some indication of the path they must choose. He shakes his head to the negative, placing a precautionary finger over his lips. In this case, memory loss is the best thing for the patient.

Before her parents are forced to lie about her brother's condition, Dr. Redding asks, "Can everyone please clear the room so I can examine the patient. Please, this is important and I promise it won't be long. You will all be back at her side, momentarily."

He moves in to check on her. In the absence of Yara's tongue, Banja Rouge says with a quivering, "Your brother is resting. Hush now. You need your rest, too. We will be close by."

As they move toward the door, Dr. Redding whispers to the nurse, "I need to administer a bolus of Propofol because she shouldn't have risen so quickly. Contact both neurosurgeons and the anesthesiologist that handled the operation for an immediate consult. Then pray, nurse Pritchard. Pray."

The drug, Propofol, would allow her to breathe on her own, while returning her to a deep state of unconsciousness.

To their relief, Kysing smiles, and whispers, "I was so worried. I love you all so much."

The patient's reluctant parents walk into the quiet hallway where Yara buries her face in her husband's chest to muffle her weeping sorrows, holding him tightly as if to gain strength.

She looks into Banja's eyes and whispers, "How, Banja. How can we tell her a truth she will never accept? It will shatter her heart. It will shatter her mind. What do we do?"

What Dr. Redding can only categorize as short-term memory loss may be a blessing or a foreboding indication of greater brain damage than can be determined as of yet. However, and to their great despair, Kysing's brainwave activity and heart rate spike dramatically before the nurse returns with the powerful medication.

Her eyes are suddenly wide open and fixed as Kilarin Rouge's lifeless body flashes through her synapses. His damaged eye lying on the bones protruding through his lacerated cheek flares within her mind like an exploding cactus plant.

A tear falls down her cheek as she whimpers, "Oh . . . Kilarin."

A tremor takes control of her hands as Doctor Redding orders another nurse to administer a bolus of Nitrazepam and fifteen milligrams of Dilaudid. As the convulsions become more violent, they try desperately to hold her down to prevent the seizing patient from doing herself more bodily harm.

Suddenly raised from the comfort of slumber in each other's arms, Doctors Edward and Kora Connor quickly heed the urgent call, rushing to the ICU unit where their most recent surgical patient is now in the throes of a violent epileptic event. Despite all efforts, damage is now being done, and her life is most certainly in peril as her electrochemical brain activity runs amok.

The urgency on the returning nurse's face causes great concern for the parents, who are drawn to Kysing's door. They can hear their daughter thrashing about in her bed while Doctor Redding issues orders. The memory of her brother's death places Kysing Rouge in dangerous distress.

Her upset parents are helpless, forced to witness from a doorway just what the human neurological system is capable of when in total disarray.

***

The scrub nurse prepares to assist in getting Dr. Edward Connor into a surgical garment and gloves. For the moment, he is furiously scrubbing his hands while staring at the new MRI cross-sections. He looks at Kora, who is doing the same.

As she studies them, she says, "Oh, dear God. Edward. . . ."

"Yeah. I see it. Please, Kora, talk to the parents for me. Prepare them for the worst because I don't think our patient will survive. Her chance of coming out of this alive and merely paralyzed is next to none. Jesus Christ, how did this girl come up so fast? She should have been under for days!"

"Okay, I'll handle the parents. Then I'll join you as quickly as I can."

"Thank you. Hold on, Kysing Rouge, I'm coming. Just hold on, please." He is prepped, and the team follows him to the operating room.

* * *

In the quiet lobby, the flat screen holds the attention of everyone seated within listening distance. From the overhead vantage point, the news helicopter's camera images are enough to cause many to cringe. Smoke rises in the air from burning vehicles, as a man dives from his automobile's window on fire. He beats at the flames, but suddenly drops to his knees when he is completely engulfed. Dazed and confused, badly wounded people are stumbling from their battered vehicles.

The voiceover of a reporter accompanies the shot of the big rig that caused all the damage. Her emotionally charged words describe the destruction, the bus full of school kids hanging perilously over the side of the bridge, and two ejected passengers clinging to the broken support cable that skewered the dead woman at the bottom of it. The image of Kilarin's unconscious body hanging above the others brings burning tears from Banja's eyes. Now she reveals a final bit of information, something that catches Banja Rouge's attention.

The reporter says, "Again, we must caution all viewers that some of these disturbing scenes are quite graphic and unsuitable for young children. The young man that firefighters rescued from the bridge's support cable has been identified as Robert Mecklenburg, son of Mayor Larkin and Pauline Mecklenburg of Tega Cay, South Carolina. Unfortunately, the young man above him falls to his death before rescuers can retrieve him. Sources say that the young man is none other than Kilarin Rouge, the seventeen-year-old star of the Fort Mill Hornet's basketball team." With a final shot of the big rig, as a police officer pulls the doors open only to have a body fall out, she reports, "This is a scene of the eighteen-wheeler and the dead culprit who drove the killer vehicle into, over, and through cars caught on the bridge in evening traffic. Ironically, reliable sources have identified the owner and driver of the eighteen-wheeler that caused this tragic travesty as none other than McKenzie Mecklenburg, the brother of Mayor Larkin Mecklenburg and Rock Hill Police Chief Archibald Mecklenburg. This is a shocking twist to a tale of violence, mayhem, and thirteen unfortunate fatalities."

Dr. Kora Connor joins the beleaguered parents, who are full of questions. She looks them both in the eyes and says as calmly as possible, "We don't have much time, so please listen to me carefully. This most recent violent episode seriously complicates your daughter's condition. I am afraid that we have little choice but to go back in and try to alleviate the new damage caused by that last seizure. When she came out of it, I believe that the traumatic recollection of her brother's death caused a massive spike in neurological activity. Her emotional and physiological responses were too much to handle. The subsequent damage caused by the seizure are small ruptures to the brainstem and highly pressurized spinal fluid is now leaking inside, making the intracranial swelling exponentially worse. There are procedures we can perform to counter this problem, but I fear the prognosis is even worse. There is evidence of pituitary damage, and she has aggravated the injuries we have already worked tirelessly to repair. We have little choice but to go back in. You must bear in mind that in her already weakened state, our ongoing efforts to save her may ultimately fail."

Kora's heart goes out to them, knowing what helpless futility feels like.

Banja bolsters his weeping wife. He asks, "What are her chances, doctor?" His eyes are pleading for some hope.

"Tentative at best. I feel your anguish, Mister and Mrs. Rouge. Believe me, I do. But it is my sad and harshly painful duty to prepare you for the worst. On the grand scale, your daughter's initial injuries were comparatively small. The problem is where the damage manifested, and what it could do to her there. In this profession, we refer to it as rough terrain or bad geography because it is so difficult to navigate."

As Yara Rouge swoons, Banja steadies her on buckling knees. After helping her to sit, he asks, "Is our child going to die?"

Kora retreats. "We will do whatever we can to prevent that from happening. Like you, we want her to live through this. If there were no possible chance of her survival, she would be gone already. Now, I absolutely must prepare to assist in her care. Time is most certainly of the essence. I pray for a positive outcome, as should we all. We will do everything within our power to see her through this setback, but we have lots of work to do. Please excuse me."

A kindly and sympathetic counselor approaches to say, "Mr. and Mrs. Rouge, hello. Hi. My name is Andrea Dilligard, one of the hospital's counselors. My job is to make sure that we meet any needs you may have. I know that this is a very difficult time for you both as parents, but has either of you eaten since arriving?"

"No, we haven't," he answers.

"You must keep up your own strengths. If you'd like, I can arrange for something. Whatever you like."

Yara says, "No. No thank you. I don't think I can eat at this time."

"Nothing for me, thank you," Banja agrees.

"Well if you should have a change of mind, we have an excellent menu at your disposal when you are." Mrs. Dilligard forces a smile before asking, "Is there anything you need, anything I can do for you at all?"

"No thank you. You are very kind to offer," Yara says through her tears. "Wait. Maybe there is one thing."

"Just name it, Mrs. Rouge. What can I do for you?" Andrea Dilligard asks, relieved that she may be of assistance in some capacity after all.

"Is there a church nearby?" she asks.

"Why yes. In fact, in times like these, I always think it best to pray. No matter what religious preferences may be, we have a chapel downstairs that is always available to anyone who seeks a tranquil and divine place to pray. The chaplain's name is Father Callahan, a very devout and caring man. He has been here since yesterday's tragic events occurred. Would you like me to show you the way?"

Banja looks at his wife and says, "Yes please. That will be most appreciated. Thank you very much."

"There is really no need, but you are very welcome, sir. I will also dwell in the house of the Lord for yours and your daughter's sake. Mrs. Rouge, I fully understand what the emotional and physical toll has on the human body in distressful times like these, and because you haven't eaten, your blood sugar may be a bit low. Please indulge me by allowing us to transport you to the chapel by wheelchair. I saw you stumble a little earlier and I wouldn't want anything to happen to you. Will you agree to that for me? Please."

This sheepish, petite little woman displays a well-rehearsed smile that could melt chocolate if these circumstances were better.

Banja knows that his wife will refuse, but he thinks it best that she take this journey by wheelchair, considering the enormous stress. Moments later, they are in an elevator heading for the first floor.

Halfway down the aisle, Yara Rouge leaps from the wheelchair and runs to the altar to fall upon her knees. She clasps her hands and shouts aloud, "Why, Lord? Why? Please don't take my child from me.

Jesus, God, please. She is all we have left. Jesus, please!"

Her painful shrieks disrupt the quiet serenity of the chapel. Banja hurries to his wife's side. Mrs. Dilligard has experienced such things many times, taking a seat in the middle row to the right.

To the far left, in the first row, Father Callahan is speaking to Mayor Mecklenburg. In light of the disturbance by a bereaved visitor, it is his duty to console her. To quiet Yara's heart and ease her plight, if possible, Father Callahan excuses himself.

As Father Callahan approaches and tries to soothe Yara's angst. Banja helps her to a pew where the priest can comfort her.

Larkin Mecklenburg unwisely scoffs, "Some people just have no dignity."

His wife harshly reacts, even to her own surprise.

Quite out of reflex, she plants one across his cheek and shouts, "Larkin, how dare you?" Now aware of her public outcry, she lowers her voice to scold, "How can you be so callus? Stacie told me without a hint of doubt that their daughter saved her life. If not for that young lady's bravery and quick thinking, our daughter would not be in here with just a broken arm and a concussion. She would be in the morgue. We should be thanking them for raising such a selfless young woman."

Banja Rouge's red eyes fixate on Larkin Mecklenburg as he strides across the chapel with his fists clenched to unleash his fury. Just now, the chapel door opens as Rock Hill's Police Chief, Larkin's surviving brother, enters. As he moves up the aisle, his keen instinct into human nature locks onto the aggressive gate and posture of Banja Rouge. Following the Black man's angry eyes, Chief Mecklenburg locates his cowering brother in the corner of the front pew. He moves, instinctively, with a greater sense of urgency.

Banja ignores Paula Mecklenburg's attempt to thank him or apologize. He snatches Mayor Mecklenburg from the seat and slams his fist into his face. The mayor's wife pleads for him to stop. Banja hauls him from the floor to do more damage, ramming him into the nearby wall.

Father Callahan and Yara Rouge are drawn to the sudden commotion, only now realizing that Banja has left them.

Banja draws the threatening, spineless mayor in for closer inspection to say, "You dare those words, you heartless bastard? You insult my wife even as she seeks counsel with God in this Holy place. I heard what you said about us having no dignity! No dignity?"

The mayor's brother weighs in on Banja from behind, allowing the mayor to take a cheap shot that only enrages the bereft father. Banja is breaking free of the arm bar Chief Mecklenburg tries to cinch in, but it is hopeless until Father Callahan grabs him too. Even so, Banja still drags them, one step at a time, right up to Mayor Mecklenburg's red face to decree, "You greedy, selfish Mecklenburgs have been throwing your weight around long enough. My daughter may be up there dying because of your actions at the scene of the accident. My son is dead because you demanded that your son receive preferential treatment when it was clear that Kilarin was terribly in need of help. He was only ten seconds away from rescue. Ten seconds. And your own evil brother. . . ."

The police chief calls for backup. "That's it, pal. You're going to jail for assaulting a public official!"

Yara Rouge shouts, "Please don't!" She approaches to defend her husband, but receives a strong warning to stay back.

During all of this, Banja's eyes never leave those of Larkin Mecklenburg. With his lips curled back in a most wicked sneer, Banja swears, "One life taken for one life safe. Another life hanging by a thread, while one life is rescued. Nevertheless, I promise you this—I promise. If my child slips beyond the *Reach*— even if I must forfeit my very soul to the bowels of hell—you will reap the whirlwind!"

A police officer visiting an injured neighbor near the end of his lunch break answers the call and runs into the chapel. He pushes Yara Rouge to the floor and helps subdue Banja Rouge, whom he cuffs with a knee across his bulging neck.

Banja is dragged from the floor. Huffing and puffing from the struggle, Archie Mecklenburg orders, "Lock him up for assault. Get him out of here!"

Father Callahan intercedes at this point. "Everyone, please. This is a place of worship and prayer. Let's all just calm down."

As Paula Mecklenburg's eyes are met with those of the woman, who's been thrown to the floor, she says, "Stop it, Archie. Please, just stop this. My insensitive husband made several disrespectful statements about their tragic plight. Larkin alone is solely responsible for igniting this situation. Quite frankly, if it was me, I'd want his head, too."

She wipes burning tears away, walking toward Yara Rouge to help her to her feet. With her hands upon the woman's shoulders, Pauline looks back at her husband with shame and judgment in her eyes. "My unfeeling mate is out of control with power these days, and I do so apologize for his bad manners and utterly regressive behavior that is extremely unbecoming of a man of the people. Now, you let him go, Archie." After helping Yara up, she hugs her briefly and says, "I'm so sorry for this."

Larkin is silent, his eyes shying away from those of an angry, seething beast of a man. Officer Leach forces Banja to sit, sternly warning him not to move, almost begging him to stay put. He says,

"Chief Mecklenburg, sir, can I have a word?"

"What is it, Officer Leach?"

They move away from the others to talk. "Ah, chief, that is Killer Kilarin Rouge's father over there. Sir, the buzz is that your brother's actions are to blame in the death of their son. I was just upstairs visiting my neighbors and their kid, who was also on the bus that Mac rammed. According to Kerry Treadle, their daughter, literally, saved your niece's life though badly injured herself. They are calling her a hero, and the mayor burned the kid by taking her place in the ambulance transporting Stacie Mecklenburg. They say she has brain damage and is not expected to live."

"Oh dear God. Okay, now I get it. I suppose I see your point, Officer Leach," Archie says with a deep, foreboding sigh. "Jesus H. Christ in heaven. Why in the hell would Larkin instigate a confrontation with them at this time of bereavement? Stupid. Just pigheaded."

"Chief Mecklenburg, don't you think they have suffered enough for one day? The guy is just upset. I know I would be, and so would you if someone used his or her influence to place your dying kids at the back of the line on two separate occasions. This thing is already going to be a public relations nightmare for the mayor, but it doesn't mean that you have to be dragged into it. Sir, I really gotta tell ya, I don't want to be the one to haul this man in and lock him behind bars with a dying kid upstairs."

Chief Mecklenburg considers these words, scanning everyone involved. He knows his sister-in-law to be a meek and quiet woman. She seems to have the patience of a saint while married to his brother, a power-hungry, money-grubbing, son-of-a-bitch at times. He has never seen Paula go up against Larkin like that in anyone's favor. He considers the hurt in Yara Rouge's eyes and the anger in Banja Rouge's scowl, which never leaves Larkin. He has known his arrogant, heartless brother all of his life and realizes there could be some truth to the nasty little rumors circulating.

The kind of rage Banja displayed is not something that develops over someone eating your candy bar. The deciding factor in his agreeing to let Mr. Rouge go is the fear he sees in Larkin's eyes. It isn't always so apparent or easily detected, but one of the times Larkin Mecklenburg ever shows fear is when he's guilty of something. However, being the shrewd politician that he is, this behavior seems like something more. He never allows himself to show fearful intimidation in public. Nevertheless, from time-to-time, it betrays his dirty hands. This certainly seems to be one of those occasions.

Chief Mecklenburg sighs again and nods his head, bringing relief to Officer Leach. "Okay, cut him loose, but make sure that he stays in his lane. I will tolerate no more threats or physical violence. They can stay here and pray or go back upstairs as long as there is no more bullshit. Got it?"

"Understood, sir," says Officer Leach as he takes the handcuff keys from his pocket.

"Leach, give them my condolences please. We may as well start repairing the bridges where we can. I appreciate the heads up, son. Come to my office tomorrow after your shift is over. Your plea for understanding in this case makes you a candidate for a unique position our mayor believes will bridge the gap between law enforcement and the African American community. I think we need more officers like you for this detail."

Officer Leach flushes with pride and says, "Thank you, sir. I will report to you tomorrow. Thanks for this."

Rock Hill's Chief of Police watches the results, satisfied when a calmer Banja Rouge nods his head and finally takes his eyes off Mayor Mecklenburg, who trembles and cringes as if the man has an invisible grip on him from across the room. When his brother and wife approach with concern, a cold breath comes from Larkin's mouth as if he has just taken a puff from one of his accursed cigars.

Banja and Yara Rouge are just leaving the chapel when the Mecklenburgs look back and notice his piercing eyes glaring at Larkin one last time. When he is finally out of sight, Larkin nearly collapses, trembling from head to toe.

Pauline Mecklenburg asks, "Larkin, what's going on with you? Talk to me, honey."

"Cold," he chatters. "So . . . cold."

Father Callahan places a hand on him and immediately retracts. "My God, you're freezing. Come and have a seat."

"Maybe we should have a doctor come down and look at him," suggests Chief Mecklenburg. "What did he do to you, Larkin? Someone, call a doctor, please."

Paula watches as her husband shivers, afraid to touch him. Forcing herself to break free of the fear, she finally wraps her arms around a man who seems as if he has just climbed out of a deep freezer.

"Jesus. You're like ice. Please, somebody do something. Do something!"

A young resident and nurse hurry into the chapel. By the time she finishes the examination, Larkin's body temperature normalizes. To their bewilderment, he is better now. The resident and nurse leave to tend other patients.

Paula asks out of concern, "Larkin, can you tell us what just happened to you?"

He clears his throat several times before he can speak. A final shiver rocks his body as he says, "That man. He did something to me with just a glance, with only that evil, angry stare of his. It was as if the devil himself had seized my innards within his ice-cold grasp. I'd swear to it."

"What?" responds Pauline. "But he was handcuffed and seated yards away from you."

"Woman, listen to me. I'm not crazy. I know what I felt."

Archie Mecklenburg asks, "Is that why you were cringing against the wall even after we had him secured?"

Larkin shakes his head and gathers himself. "I can't explain it, but it felt as if his gaze had become a physical touch. I could feel his rage crawling all over my skin like hungry termites. I swear it."

The skeptical police chief looks down on him and scolds, "Maybe what you are feeling is guilt, Larkin. You've just insulted the parents of the very child that saved Stacie's life, and not for the second time as I've come to understand it. You should be feeling something, if you're still human."

Paula glances at Archie, wondering what this tongue-lashing is really based upon. She has always known him to be a man of compassion and patience where his brother is involved, but something has obviously changed.

"Now then. Paula, Father Callahan, I have some rather bad news and harsh words that should only be spoken between brothers. Can you two please excuse us?"

"What is it, Archie? What's going on?" Paula asks, refusing to budge.

"This, in part, is a police matter and confidential. I'm afraid that I must insist for now. Just for now."

Larkin considers these dreadful words and asks for privacy. Father Callahan offers Paula a hand, which she reluctantly takes and walks away.

Once they are alone, Larkin asks, "Now, what's this all about, Arch?"

His brother sits and faces Larkin with serious eyes. He asks, "Are you seriously pretending not to have a clue? Are you pretending not to know anything about the accident? Are you just playing one of your roles, Larkin? Because you best be warned that this is no time for lies or that psychological wordplay bullshit of yours."

Angrily, Mayor Mecklenburg shouts, "Will you just get on with it, man? What are you talking about?"

"I'm taking about Mac, Larkin."

"What? What the hell are you saying? I just spoke to him this morning—yesterday morning. It was yesterday morning. For Christ sake, what has he done now?"

Archie looks him in the eyes, suspiciously, gauging his reactions and answers for truth. He sighs because he still has trouble seeing through Larkin's more deliberate and calculated deceptions. The Mayor's tells are most apparent when surprised by unveiled truth. Archibald's rigid posture relaxes a bit, but not completely.

"Has no one told you? What, is this hospital one giant cocoon— see no light and hear no evil? Have you not been paying attention to the news?"

"Archie, the only thing that concerns me right now is our children. People have been calling left and right so Paula and I just agreed to turn our phones off. As for watching the news, it's just too damn depressing."

"Mac is dead. He's dead, Larkin. He is solely responsible for the Catawba bridge disaster."

"What? Mac . . . dead? He killed all those people? Dear Christ.""

"Are you telling me you've been living in a vacuum while his name is splashed all over the local news? Are you telling me that you didn't know?"

"Not a word of it. Really. Paula and I had so many well-wishing sympathizers and busybodies calling that we both agreed to turn our cellphones off. I just couldn't stand watching the news, seeing. . . ." He takes a deep breath. "I was too concerned about my children for that. Besides, I considered everything that happened yesterday evening as a police matter. What happened, did he have some kind of stroke?"

Archibald Mecklenburg shakes his head, dubiously. "God knows I'd prefer that to be the case here, but it's not that simple. Undoubtedly, Mac's rig caused all those injuries and deaths on that bridge. He nearly murdered your own kids because he was running from the feds. It was his actions that caused the worst traffic disaster in the history of both our towns, and I'm afraid that it will become a public relations nightmare for us both. Mayor Engle and I are doing what we can to downplay this info, but it's coming, Larkin. It's coming like that cooling air you feel just before a massive thunderhead sweeps through."

Larkin places his forehead in the palm of a hand and murmurs, "Oh dear God in heaven. The rig. That's why I thought it looked familiar, but there was just too much going on."

"It is customary for feds to inform and elicit the cooperation of local law enforcement when an operation like this is going down. You are the Mayor on one side of that bridge and I'm the Chief of Police on the other side. Mac's entire operation is smack dab in the middle of us both, so they kept the operation quiet because either one of us could tip him off and compromise them. After the fact, the feds were kind enough to let my people know why we had to be left out of the loop."

"But what the hell could he be doing to warrant that level of suspicion?"

Looking him sternly in the eyes, Chief Mecklenburg says, "Not suspicion, Larkin, but solid proof. Our misguided brother was transporting an inordinate amount of drug contraband and illegal automatic firearms for a dangerous, high priority drug cartel. From what my contact says, we are talking upwards of a hundred mill in drugs alone. He tried to kill the DEA agent, who was in the process of busting him, and she had to shoot him to stop his rampage on that bridge. His actions were deliberate.

Deliberate. If I've already found out that it is you who backed him in developing the warehouse property on Old Bohickit Road, and buying those trailers that were specially outfitted for hauling contraband, you can bet your sweet ass that others have or soon will. Those trailers were customized by professionals. They clearly registered as heavier duty material and extra weight, however, they contained hollow walls that concealed removable weights. These were not amateurs. I need to know what you know."

"What are you saying?" the mayor asks with a bit of annoyance. "Are you accusing me of financing his criminal operation? I gave him a hand, but I had nothing to do with the rest of it. I can't believe you would even suggest such things. When Mac and I last spoke, he was on an upbeat. He told me that he would soon repay me approximately half of the loans. But you know how he is." Larkin glances toward his wife, trying not to look.

Having gotten his answers, Archie looks at Larkin and says beneath his breath, "I can't always tell when you're lying to me, Larkin, except when you're worried about your wife being in earshot. I believe that you just sold me a passel of lies. I don't know how deep your end goes, but I suggest that you get busy cleaning up your mess and covering your ass before the shitstorm hits the blades and the crap comes home to roost. If I were you, brother, I'd invest in raincoats and adult diapers. If it comes down to it, you will be implicated or worse. Now I pray that I'm wrong about this, but after all of your misdeeds in life, it stands to reason that karma may require a reckoning. Our daddy was a moonshiner and a fast-talking con man. He was a straight-faced liar and thief. If anybody took on his ways, it was certainly you and Mac. God bless their souls. I pray that you find God's mercy to be an anchor as you are probably about to reap that very same whirlwind Mr. Rouge spoke of, earlier."

Larkin says nothing. His brother leaves after giving Paula a hug and shaking Father Callahan's hand. He heads upstairs to pay brief visits to his injured niece and nephew, who are both resting too quietly to disturb.

"Oh, Mac. Mac, what have you done?" Mayor Larkin Mecklenburg whispers as he rubs his forehead. Although he weeps for the dead, he will sweep the fear and sorrow away before his wife and Father Callahan return to his side.

Chapter 12

The Seeker of the Dim

Mechanically ventilated, Kysing Rouge no longer breathes on her own. To her parents' horror, she is surrounded by monitoring equipment, and the infusion pump that regularly administers a cocktail of different meds, including Thiopental. She is motionless, except for the rise and fall of her chest with that sucking, swishing sound that comes with each mechanically driven breath.

Banja Rouge stands near the window looking down at the world of motion below. He watches as the many cars rush by on the interstate with no awareness or care for their troubles. He looks back at his daughter, trying to reach her with his thoughts, but this is hopeless. She is too deeply withdrawn, too close to the periphery of the *Reach*.

Kysing's father has finally gotten Yara to eat something, but he is fasting to cleanse himself. He looks at his sleeping wife, knowing that the loss of both their children will probably splinter her fragile mind. He wakes her with gentle whispers as he kneels at her side.

"Yara, baby, can you hear me?" he asks while gently stroking her cheek. "I need to talk to you."

The exhausted mother climbs from the depths of slumber one milky level at a time. Her first response upon opening her eyes is that of fear.

She rises in the recliner, looking toward their daughter's bed, dreading the worse.

"Banja, what's happened? Is she okay?"

"Hush now. Sh. Nothing has changed," he reassures.

"What did the doctor say?" she asks. "I'm sorry, I fell asleep."

Banja kisses her softly and says, "You needed to eat and rest. You should go home for a while."

"No. No. I can't leave her yet. Did the doctors even come by?"

Banja Rouge says, "Yes. They came, but nothing has changed and they don't expect it to for a quite a while." He hates lying to his wife, but knows that telling her that Kysing's condition has already begun to deteriorate will not help matters.

"Why didn't you wake me, baby?" she asks.

He looks into her eyes and says, "Because you need all the rest you can get. I'm worried about you too, Yara. I'm waking you now to let you know that I must leave the hospital."

"But why? Is your job giving you problems?"

"No, sweetheart. My boss understands completely. He sends his loving condolences, and he's giving me paid vacation time. He's a rare man, that one."

"Thank Mr. Gannett for me when next you speak."

"He and his wife sent those flowers in the corner."

She looks at the arrangement and smiles. "They're very beautiful."

"Yes, they are. I woke you because I need to see to the final arrangements for Kilarin. It is something that must be done sooner rather than later. You stay here with Kysing and I'll attend it. I will go to the house and get you a few changes of clothing so you can shower here. Don't worry, I won't forget your underwear or toothbrush." He smiles, as does she.

Even in her worn condition, Yara senses something unmentioned. "Banja, I love you so much. I couldn't get through this ordeal without you." When he reciprocates her love, she searches his eyes and asks, "What aren't you telling me, honey?"

Surprised by her intuition, he looks to their comatose daughter and bows his head with a deep and sorrowful sob. She caresses his cheek, gently cupping his face in her hands until their eyes align.

"It is most important now that I converse with my father. I fear that I must seek his counsel if there is to be any real hope for our daughter."

"But he's thousands of miles away, Banja. What can he do from Haiti? Can't you just call him from here?"

"No, dear. A simple phone call will not do in this case. I must seek a much deeper connection." Tears begin to fall from Banja's eyes before confessing, "Forgive me, but I have been less than honest with you. The truth is the doctors fear that our baby is slowly slipping away. Her condition is slowly worsening, so I must do everything within my power to save her. I must venture into a place that we know as the Realm of Dark Lights to seek counsel for Kysing's sake. I need you to trust me, Yara. Can you do that for me? For her?"

Yara now realizes her husband's enormous pain, feeling a sense of shame because she has only shown concern for Kysing's plight without considering that her strong husband may be withering inside, too. She nods her head and hugs him tenderly.

"Be safe," she whispers. "I love you so much, Banja."

"Our children grew up somewhat afraid of their grandfather because of that peculiar scarring on his body. They do not know what it means, and I have never fully explained its significance to any of you. You see, long ago, my father risked his own life and very soul to rescue me from certain death. He became a seeker in the dim, probing for a flicker of hope and a remnant of the desire to live. I must now ask him if there is anything I can do to save my own child. You must hear me, and please mark these words well, Yara. Even if there is the slightest chance that I can procure the gods' permission to perform a blood ritual called the *Fire Bond*, nothing will ever be the same. Our lives, should I even survive this, may change in unimaginable ways. You may never look upon our child nor me the same way, again. Do you understand this at the very least, Yara? Nothing of our happy lives may ever be the same again. Even the love that you now have in your tearful eyes for me, may be swept away like grains of sand before a furious wind."

"That will never be, Banja. No matter what happens, I will always love you. Even though I am struggling to understand, I believe." She whispers with her forehead touching his, "I believe. I believe."

"Time is short for her, and she is our heart. Nothing is as important to me. When time permits, I promise to explain all that I have not told you of my past. I must go now. I do not wish to leave your side, but I will try to return before the morning sun has fully risen. Please contact me if there are any developments."

"Go. I will keep watch. Hurry, Banja. Hurry!" she says in desperate whispers. "Hurry."

Banja Rouge kisses his wife and then his daughter. While gently cradling Kysing's cheeks, he whispers, "Here me now, daughter. Let my voice be as a far-reaching echo, rippling like the peaceful waters of the ocean across the dim of time and darkened hollows to your damaged mind. The moment may soon come when I will whisper your name three times, and you must answer my call. Please, my child. No matter what it takes, even if it seems like a dream, you must answer my call. And you must choose life." He leaves with reluctance.

Chapter 13

The Box

When Banja arrives at the house, he takes the receipt of his father's plane ticket from the glove box of the truck. He has nothing more than a drink of water and goes into the laundry room. To the left of the hallway leading to the garage, opposite the washer and dryer, are shelves of preserved fruits and vegetables from Yara's garden or the farmer's market. While considering the many treats, the hunger in his belly growls its malcontent.

The first container, on the left side of the second shelf from the top, is a malignant looking mason's jar with a pickled calf's tongue. Banja Rouge carefully forces it into the wall when a small panel collapses inward until there is a click. He then moves to the lowest shelf and forces the last jar of pickled tongue until it clicks to release the shelf. He swings it outward to reveal a hidden red door. Banja considers the door, thinking of the warding sigils of invisibility that he never bothered to paint at its center and four corners. It is something he intends to remedy when time permits.

Banja Rouge takes a deep breath and turns the knob, pushing the door inward. As he fires the candlewicks at the top of the steps, the light reaches only so far down into the darkened well. He ascends two steps to close the door behind him.

Taking hold of the four foot galvanized pipe that hangs downward, he steps up. Overhead, bolted to a beam, this pipe serves as a lever. By pushing the lever toward the ceiling, a clever series of pulleys and sprockets draw taut a length of chain that pulls the shelf closed in the washroom. It locks into place as he forces the piping onto a metal bracket above to secure this private haven.

He moves carefully down into the murky depths, removing both shoes and socks before flexing his toes upon the cool clay floor. Now he lights two more candles at the bottom of the steps. The room is twelve feet by twelve feet and the concrete floor is covered by thirteen leveled inches of red, earthen clay. He moves about the essentially empty vault and lights the remaining eight candles on the walls. The twelve candles, though there is electrical lighting, are all he needs to illuminate this sequestered, but previously unused room.

A six-foot long altar, supported by three stacks of flat stones rests at the head of the room. This altar stands only two feet high. Its surface is a dark greenish slab of shale, discretely embedded with whitish and greying lines. In the corner of the room, stands a pointed stick and a round lid that is thirteen inches across. Strapped with a leather string that holds it to a peg on the wall, a small, sheathed dagger awaits his touch.

Banja takes the seven-inch dagger from the wall, holding it reverently before unsheathing the glistening blade. Without hesitation, he slits the palm of his left hand! Opening his clenched fist, he presses his bloody fingers and bleeding palm at the center of the stone slab.

He whispers, "Upon this cold altar—upon this sacred rouge clay floor—or even at the very gates of hell itself, Great Spirits, I will risk my soul for one that I love. Bless me with the reprieves of your infinite wisdom. Judge me a good man, a worthy man, and grant even my extreme desires for I am willing to hazard death to have them so. Hear me now, for I am Banjalanah Rouge, son of Kwaban Rouge, your most faithful ward."

Allowing his blood to drip onto the red clay surface, Banja takes a tape measure from a shelf to measure the floor from the outer wall at the foot of the stairs to the eastern wall, marking it dead center. After putting the tape away, Banja takes the thirteen-inch lid and runs its bottom edge through the blood of his left palm before placing it at the center of the room. The bloody side lies upon the clay floor. He lathers the pointed tip of the stick with his blood and uses it to trace the perimeter of the round lid. At the center of the lid lies a small hole. Here is where he forces the pointed stick to puncture the floor. He removes the lid and tosses it behind him. A discrete sizzling sound arises. When he looks down, the round tracing of the lid smolders, causing him to smile.

Now that all is prepared, Banja Rouge places the receipt for the airline ticket at the center of the circle. He stands with his fingers locked in prayer, directing his forefingers toward the ticket. When Banja hears a quiet whisper within a subtle breeze, he sits at the foot of the circle and folds his legs beneath him. Soon, all else fades from corporal existence. Neither sound nor scent intrudes upon his thoughts as he discerns a subtle pinpoint of light growing in the distance. He continues to whisper prayers as the increasingly brilliant light approaches.

* * *

Kwaban Rouge wakes in the quiet hours just before dawn creeps upon the Haitian horizon. His aged pupils boast blue-rimmed cataracts that have threatened his vision for several years. He yawns and stretches his long arms while still laying upon a bed that seems little more than a cot. The old man groans as he rises to the cock's crow. He smiles, for once again, he and that old speckled rooster have survived to greet a new day.

The bare floorboards are cool when his toes flex to prepare his feet for the scant weight they are about to support. He looks frail, this ninety-year-old man. His skin is dark and the short grey hairs of his head mimic the stubble of his chin. Though his ribcage is clearly visible, Kwaban Rouge is well fed, missing no meals unless by choice. The elder men and women of his village make sure that this man of spirits hungers for nothing, even in the leanest of times.

He separates the sheer curtains to peer up at the fading stars and prays; thanking all that is benevolent for the blessing of a new day. As he turns toward the sink across the room, a cold wind brushes his skin, causing the short hairs to bristle across his entire body. He glances back, searching the horizon before moving toward the basin that has nearly filled throughout the night, with one hesitant drip after another. He uses a match to light a candle and then relieves himself in the rust-stained toilet.

The old man takes a cup from the shelf and dips it into the pocked basin, drinking from the bitter water. The aluminum reflection of the old mirror above the dripping faucet has begun to recede from its outer edges as a sign of better times gone by.

Kwaban cups his hands in the basin, bending at the waist to wash his face when a terrible shiver courses his being. He freezes for an instant, sensing a disturbance in his world. The water seeps through his fingers, dripping back into the basin. The sound of each drop seems delayed, as if he is engulfed by a distorted version of time. He shivers when his eyes slowly open to a blinding light that becomes his mirror, as if a doorway has just opened to the sun. When Kwaban hears slow, heavy footsteps echoing from the wooden stairway, he looks back upon an entire world transformed into a vivid sheet of white nothingness.

He squints and falls to his knees. With his right hand, Kwaban Rouge clutches at his heart. As if in pain, he reaches toward the ceiling and utters, "Banja? My son, what has become?"

The old man begins to weep upon the floor as though his soul has torn asunder, for he knows what bodes unwell.

Less than an hour later, as the temperature slowly rises, Kwaban and Fassa travel up a hill to a thorny patch of briars where they chop at the iron weeds with machetes and begin to dig through the roots. Once Fassa receives a blessing of absolution from Kwaban Rouge, he forces open the rotting coffin. The old man sweats and strains to drag a dusty cist from between the black, skeletal legs of a young man in the coffin, stealing it away before drawing the attention of others. Fassa helps him to carry it up to his loft, and then leaves with a shiver of good riddance.

The old man uses his own tears to clean the slight grime away. The teakwood box is twenty-six inches long by thirteen-and-a half inches wide. Kwaban uses both hands, reaching for the scar that runs up the back of his neck, tracing it to his forehead and down the bridge of his nose. He follows the scar down his lips and chin to the middle of his chest where his thudding heart pounds out a message of impending doom.

He recalls the violent, bloody days of the Tonton Macoute. He relives the decisions of Banja's mortality and the feverish agony that followed. Finally, Kwaban Rouge reaches in to touch the curved blade. As if impervious to the elements, it gleams against a bed of dark red velvet. The rounded point of the scythe-like blade only requires that he wipe it to clear the thinnest film of dust. With great sadness, Kwaban caresses the haft of carved human bone. The face of every man he killed with this blade to save his son that night, and every person whose blood has ever sated its thirst long before then, flashes before his mind's eye. Yet, this revered instrument of ritual and death remains mythical among most of the island's inhabitants. Once called *La lame de l'ouragan rouge,* or Blade of the Red Hurricane, it is something many have heard of, but few have ever seen or handled.

A young woman named Arindia, Fassa's daughter, soon appears to help Kwaban prepare the box for immediate transport. Two hours later, her dusty jeep pulls into the parking lot of the FedEx terminal to arrange the box's immediate flight to America..

Chapter 14

Within the Flash

At the living heart of the dark lights, white brilliance surrounds both father and son. There are tears as Banja Rouge explains his plight in a place where he is merely a child and his father a much younger man.

With a voice that defies the body of the child from which it is spoken, Banja says with mounting sadness, "Kilarin has passed beyond the thinning veil, fallen to a crushing demise before our eyes. Too far away. Too far. I was not strong enough to help him, father!"

Kwaban Rouge whispers, "My grandson is dead? Oh, my dear son. Heavy is the heart at such terrible news."

"As I stood upon the riverbank and watched a man of power all but assure my son's death, Kilarin's wounded body dangled as his own son was rescued only seconds before my blood came crashing down. Of the two, my son was clearly more at risk!"

As pale, swift shadows pass over them, Kwaban reaches for Banja's river of tears, touching his cheeks as his own eyes well. Dressed in white linen, sitting with their legs crossed, they place their foreheads together to weep.

"I am sorry, Banja. So sorry."

"Now, Kysing hangs on to life by a fractured, unraveling thread. The loss of my son has torn us to pieces, but to face the loss of them both will surely destroy us. My wife now holds vigil, sitting at her bedside alone and afraid she will be engulfed by the specter of death."

"How can such tragedy befall the good of heart?" Kwaban asks. Banja's father pats his right hand over his heart three times and reaches toward the northwest with his left hand searching the *Reach*. "Yes, Banja. I can feel her spirit reeling. Oh, my son, the fear of uncertainty looms like a fading aura about her. Her body is ravaged by a mind in turmoil."

"I cannot fail her, too. I will not lose her as the man who imperiled both my children breathes in mockery of us all. I would rip out my own heart if that will save her. I would shatter this world in two if vengeance will be served, father."

Sadly nodding his head, Kwaban allows his tears to flow freely because he knows his son's pain. The last vestige of Banja's peace teeters on the edge, coupled with his daughter's fate.

"I know well of what you speak, Banja. I know what you ask of me, but it is a most perilous journey that you now seek." Kwaban Rouge opens his linen shirt to expose his chest and the ugly scar from years gone by.

Banja looks to his hands against the pillar of white upon which they sit before raising his beseeching eyes to his father to say, "I will it so, for I know that which I ask. I would render my soul and all of life's vitality to save my child from passing beyond the thinning veil. If the gods demand my wretched husk skewered upon the shores of the crumbling shale of the bereft, then I must will it so. What good am I if I am not willing to risk all for my own heartstring?"

As Banja watches a younger version of his father rise to his feet to remove his shirt completely. Turning slowly with outstretched arms, Kwaban Rouge asks, "Are you certain, Banja? Are you as sure as life eventually leads to death for all things?"

"Yes, father. I am certain!"

With gloomy acquiescence in his eyes, Kwaban looks down upon his son. Now he turns his eyes upward and shouts, "I am Kwaban Rouge. Rouge am I, and this is my seed, whose lifeline threatens to break away like a leaf from the limb of a tree in winter. We have striven our entire lives to be good men of family and worth. Hear me now in the dour of our time, for I must pass my knowledge of unspoken things unto him so that he may please you in this attempt to revive the vitality of his dying child—my child. Here me now, great Harbingers of the Divide, I am Kwaban and he is Banjalanah. Harken unto our cries as was sworn to my family long ago. Rouge are we, and none shall fear the pain of wrongful destruction. Harken my voice. Here my plea!"

As Kwaban's pleads echoes among the quickened shadows, the white plain seizes and quakes like the deepest of heartbeats.

Kwaban looks upon his son and warns, "You must perform *Feu de sang*, the Blood Fire ritual without waver. From quiver to quill, you must lacerate your own flesh with *La lame de l'ouragan rouge*. Utter no sound of pain nor weakness, but you must roar defiantly when the blade breaches the tip of your manhood." Having said these words, Kwaban looks into his son's eyes. "Banja, my son, do you still wish it, though death is promised to us all?" He reaches for Banja's hand and traces the scar down his chest.

"Without waver, father. I wish it, unflinchingly!"

Kwaban says, "To gain permission to even attempt the Fire Bonding ritual, you must first win the Harbingers' favors by performing the dragon's dance of light and dark. You must please them. Only then can you use the Blade of the Red Hurricane. Procure the items you will need, Banja. In my time, strands of hair or blood sufficed. However, in this day and this age, an image is an even more powerful talisman. Command the wind, the rain, the earth, the fire, and you shall have what you seek. Nevertheless, know this without fail, my son, nothing of your lives may ever be the same."

"Yes, father. It shall be done."

"Now, I must teach you to perform the Harbingers' Dance. Sear all that you see into memory, as if branding your flesh. Watch and learn."

After being in a realm that distorts time, whether by minutes or hours, Banja Rouge wakes on his back. His sweaty head lies within the circle on the red clay floor. His drumming heart and heavy breathing are the only discernable sounds as his chest heaves up and down.

**

Her heart beats at rest in a quiet moment, until Pauline Mecklenburg awakens to a sudden flash. She rises and looks to her sleeping son's bed. Assured that nothing is amiss, she relaxes into slumber. A moment later, her husband experiences the same thing, as if a bright light has just penetrated his closed eyelids. The door squeaks shut, but no one is there. Dawn is upon the horizon. Stacie begins to stir.

Banja Rouge steps out of the elevator on the ICU ward, with a gym bag of Yara's clothing and undergarments. His hand is bandaged.

When he walks into the room, she rises to hug her husband. Her eyes are red from reoccurring periods of utter sadness. She looks tired and unkempt, as any worried mother would in such circumstances.

As Yara showers and changes, Banja Rouge whispers into Kysing's ear. In the dim lighting, he says, "When you hear me calling, you must come. Although this place will be unfamiliar and very intimidating, just follow my voice. You must come. I love you, baby. Please hold on."

Banja backs away, taking his cell phone to look at the two images he has recently captured.

Chapter 15

The Circle of Life

After sending the blade to the United States, Kwaban Rouge remains in Haiti for two days of sad goodbyes and celebrating with his friends. This celebration commemorates their lifelong love for a man they consider a reverent emissary of the spirits. It is forbidden to speak of the massive earthquake that nearly destroyed them all as a result of Kwaban's spiritual battle with the dark forces wielded by those who once served Francois Duvalier. Long have vengeful members of the Vodou harbored contempt for the man who almost singlehandedly removed them all from the power structure of Haiti while in the service of a madman called Papa Doc.

Tonight, they sit at tables covered with fried dried beef, plantains, fried cod fish cakes, and drinks, while taking turns recanting Kwaban's many acts of kindness and service to the spiritual needs of this community and surrounding villages.

Though he sits among his people, his extended family, Kwaban is most concerned for the plight of Kysing Rouge. Nevertheless, he owes his people this moment because he will never see them again. He trusts his son to know when it is time to perform the two-part ritual known as *Blood Fire* and the *Fire Bond*.

Kwaban Rouge has been a healer and advisor throughout his life, imparting lasting wisdom through all manners of things. Many sob and moan to sad laments, knowing that he will never return, but they are also happy that he is finally going to join his family in the twilight of all things. The family of Banja Rouge visited Haiti years ago, and these humble people treated them all like the heirs of royalty.

Banja's children wanted for nothing, learning and experiencing new and wonderful things each day. The entire village came to love and honor the family of Kwaban Rouge. Each day or night, they would sit about a fire and tell stories and legends that enthralled the children. Over all, it was a delightful experience.

Still, Kilarin and Kysing Rouge preferred to spend most of their time among the people than with their curiously scarred grandfather. He often seemed so aloof and unapproachable, but nothing could be further from the truth. Content to watch them running, playing, and discovering new things, Kwaban Rouge never forced himself upon them. That is not to say there were not tender, more intimate moments shared. The wise old man sensed their slight distress in his presence, loving Banja's children no less for it. The kids' intimidation, however, came from much more than his appearance. Banja's father was a tall, lean man, but they discerned something potent in Kwaban that made him seem like a towering giant among other men. His close proximity always brought about a slight tingling sensation to their scalps and skin. While whispering late one night under a makeshift tent with flashlights, the children discovered they shared the annoying discomfort in Kwaban's presence.

Fassa, whose daughter will assume Kwaban's position as a daughter of spirits, stifles his tears for a man who practically raised him after hooded assassins murdered his parents as enemies of a disheveled state. That seems so very long ago, now.

Fassa recalls sitting before a mesmerizing fire many years in the turbulent past. That night, beneath the hunter's moon, Kwaban Rouge disseminated powerful and meaningful words of wisdom to Fassa, who was a lost teenager in need of positive direction.

That night, while trying to curb the tendencies of a young man's intense anger, Kwaban Rouge calmly declared, "Life is about change, boy. If we are not changing and evolving as children of this world, we merely exist upon the earth to consume the air. Our most dismal and painful vicissitudes are not always of our making. Rather, they are subsequent of simple circumstance, or the immorally and often ill-conceived decisions of other men. At times, change comes as the weeping winds of a most barren land—full of upheaval—wroth with turrets of pain and the rigors of ruin . . . such that we may wish to simply lie down and die. Sadly, many of those still walking and breathing are just as dead inside. This has always been true for the likes of humanity. Ever shall it be as the sun brightens the mother earth, my dear young friend. I see such might in you, Fassa. I see the strength of your beautiful mother and the fearlessness of your father, but the only thing you need prove here and now is that you are willing to learn to contain your anger because the day soon comes—soon comes—when you will suddenly realize that not every battle is worth waging. The ever-present threat is that this realization usually comes one second too late, when the blade seeks to shave bone and cleave flesh. You must learn to calm your heart and shed the uselessness of constant rage and anger, lest you cannot remain among the living because all that is truly life is already dead inside of you. I know your pain and sorrows . . . your hopelessness. I know you have been sneaking about, stealing, drinking, and constantly fighting to prove yourself to other boys who only pretend to be your friends—until the day comes when you are not. Upon this present path, you are doomed to drift through the rest of your life feeling as if you are alone. Therefore, rather than enduring the loneliness, you would choose to be as dung under the heels of troublemakers instead of tilling your own path. I am here only to say that you are welcome at my side until the day I part this land because we are all family, even if no blood passes between us. I had my doubts, but what sort of man would I be if I remain content to watch you continue to wither and die because your broken heart has been given no reason to mend? What sort of man would I be if I watched as you continued to defile your ancestry because you have lost sight of the faces of your brave mother and father?"

After consuming the meal Kwaban chose to share like a starving dog, young Fassa tried to stand and walk away in defiance. However, he fell to his knees and leaned on Kwaban Rouge's leg where he sat before the fire, weeping like a baby. Fassa's life changed for the better that very night. That memorable turning point is deeply rooted in the hearts of both men.

Kwaban is early to bed on the night of his 2:00 AM departure. He wonders of his son's dilemma, feeling no new disturbances in the lifelines of his lineage. That, however, may soon change like those weeping winds.

* * *

Banja Rouge kneels at his sleeping wife's side, wearing a surgical mask. With loving care in his eyes, he caresses her smooth cheek with the back of his right hand. She stirs just as he slips a nickel-plated revolver and a note into her purse on the floor. Hopefully, without need, she will probably find them later.

Yara wakes with dread, feeling his presence in close proximity. She now smiles at her husband, knowing without doubt that the caress was no ominous dream. After all, the soft brush in her dream had been the robe of the grim reaper coming to harvest. She looks to her daughter. The thought prompts her to remove the surgical mask so that she might kiss her husband, who does the same. The embrace is lasting and much needed by both husband and wife.

She rubs his hairless chin and head with wonder. "Baby, you're clean shaven. What made you decide to change your appearance? Don't get me wrong. It's a nice look on you, but I prefer you with hair."

He smiles and says, "It is necessary. The hour has come, so I must leave you for a time. I must go to the safe room while Kysing rests peacefully. If this works, others will probably question you about my whereabouts. You must say nothing, no matter what they tell you. Understand?"

Though confused and frightened, she nods in agreement. "Please be careful, honey. Come back to us safely."

"I love you, Yara. Our marriage and raising a family with you have been the highlights of my life. What would have become of me if we had never met? You have blessed my life and soul beyond conveyance. Now, sweetheart, I must go."

"Baby, can't you . . . can't you tell me just a little more about what you plan to do to save her?" Yara asks with mounting unease. She whispers, "Please."

"I'm sorry, Yara. I cannot, for these are ancient and secretive things. I do not know if I even possess the strength to endure what must be done, though I will it so. I would gladly give even my life to see our daughter live in any form. I can no longer bear to see the pain in your eyes while adrift in the shadow of impending doom. What I must do now may save not only her but you, too. I see you drowning in sorrowful despair, and . . . and it is killing me inside, Yara." The near whisper now reflects Banja's own fear and anxieties when his voice cracks. "It is killing me."

Tears fall from her eyes as he kisses her lips and cheeks. She holds him tight when he informs, Kilarin's funeral is set for five days from now. Ella, has had the baby and will be arriving from New York with her husband in four days. You twin brother also left a message. He just got back into the states and will be driving up from Georgia as soon as possible. They want to be here for the family in any capacity necessary. Honey, you must turn on your cellphone so they can reach you. Put it on vibrate and let them reach out to you."

"You're right, baby. I shouldn't shut them out."

"Good girl."

He goes to Kysing's bed with the mask replaced. Again, he whispers to her, "Remember, my love. Answer my call that you may live again, as have I. Please hear me, and remember." He caresses her warm, puffy skin and leaves the ICU with a dreadful purpose.

* * *

Two floors down, Pauline Mecklenburg stops her husband from entering Stacie's room. Larkin does not understand until she joins him in the hallway.

"What the hell is going on, Paula? Why won't you let me in? Has that man come back?"

Pauline places her fingers to his lips while looking about to see if anyone is within earshot when she discretely explains.

"No, Larkin. It's nothing like that. Just give her a moment and then you can go in. Look, husband, you know how daughters are with their father's when . . . you know."

"Know what?" he asks.

Pauline smiles as his ignorance forces her to say, "You know. She just started her period and needs a moment, okay. Stacie always flows heavily at the beginning of her cycle. While she's dealing with some slight cramping, she just needs a few moments."

"Oh. I see." He looks to the floor, placing his hands in his pockets, and nods.

Pauline could have simply explained by saying that it is a female thing, but she cannot resist chuckling at his manly embarrassment. "God, for such a very smart person, you sure can be quite daft at times. This truly is a Kodak moment." She grins because he is still uncomfortable with the subject, even after years of marriage.

"I tend to agree, my sweet. Tell you what. Why don't I come back a wee bit later, okay? Give her my love. Tell her to get some rest." He hurries out of the menstrual zone where most men learn to tread lightly.

As he leaves, his wife says to herself with a grin, "God, he is such a man."

Before the elevator slides open with a quiet ping, Banja takes two of the five locks of Kysing's shaved hair from his left pocket. From the other, he removes a small bag that contains strands and shavings of his now hairless body, even those from the pubic area. He dumps some of the contents into his hand and puts the bag back into his pocket. Despite the fresh wound, Banja rolls them between his palms to mingle the hair samples. He quickly ties each lock of braided hair into tight knots. He rounds the corner and leisurely heads toward Stacie Mecklenburg's room, where he pauses for only a few seconds.

Soon, he discretely slips the second knotted braid behind the nameplate outside of Robert Mecklenburg's room, as he has just done at the sister's door. Raising his open palms, Banja bows his head while whispering some small incantation.

Just before he walks away, a nurse opens the door, startled to see him there. He looks like a man who was just praying, so she asks, "Hello, sir. May I help you?"

The seemingly harmless man looks at the room number and says, "No thank you, ma'am. I seem to have gotten off on the wrong floor. Please excuse me."

"Okay," she says with a smile. "That seems to happen all the time. Can I help you find your floor?"

"Thank you, but that won't be necessary. I've got it straightened out now. Thanks again." He heads for the elevators, but not before Mayor Mecklenburg comes out after recognizing Banja's distinctive voice. He is concerned that his children are in danger. As if Banja feels him watching, he resists the urge to look back before rounding the corner.

"Nurse, what was that man doing here?" Larkin demands.

"Oh, I believe he was praying. He's just a little lost."

When the nurse repeats Banja's words, Larkin warns, "Do not trust him near my kids' rooms, again. If he returns, call security at once because he made threats right after attacking me in the chapel.

He may be dangerous. Is that understood?"

"I heard a rumor about an incident in the chapel. Was that him?"

"I'm sure of it. Do you understand now?"

"Yes, of course. Would you like me to call security now, Mr. Mecklenburg?" she asks, drawing the attention of the other nurses.

"Since he's leaving without incident, let him go. But that fucking... I'm sorry." Larkin inhales deeply, wisely taking a pause before using a racial slur he would sure regret making to a woman with interracial parentage. "Please be diligent."

"Yes, of course," she says with a smile. However, when she turns and walks away, a curious scowl crosses her face.

He returns to Robbie's room and calls his wife, afraid to leave his son alone.

Ten minutes later, one minute past midnight, the phone at the home of Chief Archibald Mecklenburg rings. He sleeps alone, missing a wife who died from the malignancy of breast cancer after it metastasized to ravage her body. Four years later, he is dreaming of her when awakened in the dead of night.

"Yeah," he says gruffly into the phone. The smell of stale bourbon wafts into his flaring nostrils from his whitish mustache and the glass on the nightstand. "What is it?" he asks, anticipating an unwelcomed call from the precinct.

The voice on the other end says, "I'm sorry to wake you this time of night."

"Larkin? Why are you calling so late? Something wrong with one of the kids, or is this about Mac's death?" He ruffles his white hair, and rubs those tired eyes as he sits up on the bed.

His brother says, "Neither. The doctors think they can release them both in a day or two at the most. I'm worried about them though."

The chief replies, "That's good news, so what's there to worry about?"

"The man that attacked me in the chapel was outside my son's hospital room just a few minutes ago. I saw him with my own two eyes, and I think he's up to something."

With concern, Archie asks, "What happened, did he confront or threaten you and Robbie in any way?"

Larkin says, "No. I don't know what he was doing, but the nurse surprised him just before he entered the room. She said he was praying when she opened the door, but he lied about being on the wrong floor and walked away. I recognized that voice so I got up and went to the door. I watched him as he walked toward the elevators. He knows that I saw him. He has this wicked little way about him that I just don't trust."

"This guy has you rattled, and now you want me to send someone to teach him a lesson. Is that it, Larkin?"

"Well, the thought hasn't occurred to me. But now that you've mentioned it, that would be mighty brotherly of you."

Chief Mecklenburg, who has gained new insights since the chapel incident, bulks a little. After sighing unapprovingly, he says, "Larkin, goddamn it, now you're going listen to me. I am sorry that you are stressing over the issues of safety with a distraught father that you got all riled up with your intemperate tongue. Yes, we are family and you know I love those kids to death, but I am gonna tell you right now that there is no way I'm sending a couple of goons to bust his chops. You're calling in the middle of the night because he gives you the heebie-jeebies. I swear to God, sometimes I wonder if you have ever felt guilty enough to apologize to anyone for anything. Man to man, Larkin, sometimes—that's all it takes to end a potential skirmish. Look, even though you are all outside of my jurisdiction, I had this guy checked out from top to bottom."

"Well, what did you find out?"

"He has no prior police record, other than two speeding tickets over an entire lifetime. Our cousin, Timothy Gannett, says he is a model employee at Gannett Lumbar. In fact, he just gave Rouge a raise and a promotion as his lead supervisor at the yard. Furthermore, on his very honor, Tim attests that the man is unbelievably patient with extreme assholes, like the mean-spirited racist bastard he had to fire just before giving Mr. Rouge his job. In his own words, Tim said 'if Mr. Rouge attacked Larkin, he must have had God's own wrath of a reason to do so.'"

Larkin grows angrier at each word. "You act as if that Black bastard is some kind of saint, Arch. How can you say such things to me? We're brothers and these are my kids for Christ sake!"

"Larkin, will you ever realize that you cannot continue treating common folks like shit running downhill before it grows legs just so it can climb back up that hill to get at you? I am saying this for several reasons. Must I itemize them for you?"

"But. . . ."

"I see that I do, so just keep your yap shut and listen to me. For one thing, I am dead dog ass tired. This is the first chance I've had to get some rest since Mac went postal on that damned bridge the other day. I've been in a constant scuffle with the feds over the disposition of Mac's body and making his final arrangements. To make things worse, the Feds are even calling my allegiance with law and order into question. I'm disturbed by the fact that you have forgotten that you are the frigging mayor of an entire township—two towns—actually. Mr. Rouge lives within your jurisdiction, so handle it as any mayor would. Call your own Chief of Police and have him assign someone to give Rouge a stern warning to stay away from your family. I said give warning, not a mauling. Get a freaking restraining order if necessary. Have Judge Baker push it through without the formalities. If he worries you this much, call the Chief in Tega Cay and have a deputy or two assigned to guard the kids' rooms. Damn, son, how is this not painfully clear to you? On the other hand, maybe you are just capable of fixing high school basketball games and paying off people to undermine Mayor Joe Riley's entire administration to guarantee it fails. Yeah I know about those things and it makes me wonder what else you're capable of. I really don't mean to seem so insensitive, but we both know every word I've said is true. I have been dealing with a slew of problems, brother, and I am plum worn out. You have the means, Larkin. I shouldn't have to be awakened in the middle of the night to remind you of that. So handle it. I have got to get some rest, and I'll check on you guys tomorrow. Okay?"

Larkin's sunburned skin cools with the painful realization that his brother is right. He is embarrassed by what must seem cowardly.

"Yes, of course you are right about everything. I'm sorry I woke you up. Jeez Louise, I must be losing it completely. I know you have a lot on your plate, and here I am—acting like a foolish kid—scared of a bully when I'm the bigger of the two. I'm sorry, Arch. Get some rest and we'll see how I can assist you with the feds when we talk tomorrow."

With a deep sigh, Chief Mecklenburg says, "You let me deal with the Feds. You have to worry about your own ass. Goodnight, Larkin. Give Pauline and the kids my love."

***

Fassa and Arindia accompany Kwaban Rouge to concourse 'D', waiting until an attendant allows passengers to begin boarding the two-hour trip on American Airlines' Flight 111 from Port-au-

Prince to Miami, Florida. Once there, he will have to endure a two-hour layover before taking a connecting flight directly to Douglas Airport in Charlotte, North Carolina.

Before approaching the gate with his credentials in hand, Kwaban receives a traditional blessing for travelers by both Arindia and her father. As they pray, even with discretion, they draw the attention of some giggling teenagers and insensitive young adults.

Although unfamiliar with these three people, a few traveling natives take silent offense at what they consider disrespectful behavior. Because of their sharp, reproachful glares, the giggling halts abruptly.

The Boeing Dreamliner 787 variant is a long-range, midsized, wide-bodied twin-engine jetliner, with a seating capacity of up to 330 passengers. With the outflow of American college students winding up their Caribbean spring break of island hopping, missionaries of charitable disaster relief, and the eclectic vacationers retuning home, Flight 111 has 240 souls aboard.

With the plane secured and passengers settling down, Captain Alvin Meeks looks at co-pilot Jon Blaine and smiles. "That completes our preflight checklist and everything is in the green. Do you concur with this assessment, Jon?"

"Check. We are five-by-five, Captain Meeks."

Meeks contacts Flight Control with his flight plan locked in as he taxis toward his designated runway for takeoff. He addresses the passengers with a smooth, even-toned, safe-flight speech that gives a soothing assurance of complete confidence and control.

For no apparent reason, Kwaban Rouge shivers as if seized by sudden, chilling panic on a wintry day.

As Flight 111 begins to build speed for takeoff, Captain Meeks says to the St. Croix native, "Jon, let's go home. Well, my home anyway."

"Roger that, Captain Meeks."

Meeks yanks his chain by saying, "Thank God we are booked to near capacity so we won't have to divert into the "Crosshairs" to pick up more passengers to validate the need for this flight. Do you know this is the first night flight from Haiti in years? It's a good sign that the economy is rebounding all around the world."

The co-pilot asks, "Crosshairs? I have heard that term before. What does it mean, sir?"

Meeks smiles at him and says, "Call me Meeks, Jon. There is no need for formalities right now. Anyway, you have to know about the crosshairs and the curse of one."

The flight's engineer looks over his shoulder at the captain, knowing where this is heading because he once fell for it himself.

"The what?" asks Jon Blaine.

Captain Meeks wipes the smile off his face to assume the look of serious disbelief when he asks, "What? Just how long have you been flying, son?"

Jon says, nervously, "Ah. This is my sixth trans-Caribbean flight, sir. I've never encountered a problem that couldn't be handled."

"Well, that should be experience enough," Captain Meeks says to the co-pilot. "You've been around long enough to know about the curse of one. Planes with three ones as flight designations have ended in disasters more times than airlines admit. The Bermuda Triangle has swallowed them completely over the last seventy years or so. True story. No shit."

Jon laughs. "Yeah right."

"On my life, this is no bullshit. What's even worse is the curse of flight thirty one eleven." He sees the confusion and further explains. "Thirteen flights—thirteen—designated thirty-one eleven have met with fatal disasters in the last twenty years, my friend. A handful of them was actually in or headed to the triangle or "crosshairs" when they crashed, exploded, decompressed, experienced total engine failure, or just simply disappeared. I swear," Captain Meeks lies with a straight face as the newbie flushes and loosens his collar.

Jon says, "No shit? You are just yanking my chain right?"

They liftoff and Captain Meeks says I guess aliens are still obsessed with how you get three without one plus two. Something is missing hey, Mon. It just don't add up. Spy plane, shoot it down!"

The bewildered look on the co-pilot's face is just too much. He and the flight engineer burst into wild laughter.

* * *

Banja Rouge turns on the wireless printer to download the images from his cellphone. He adjusts the sizes before printing them out on high-resolution, glossies. Rifling the desk drawer produces a pair of scissors. After cutting the images away, Banja places them on the parcel that came today and proceeds to the laundry room.

Downstairs, with the hidden door secured, he places the box on the altar to remove its contents. Banja puts the photographs on the right and left side of the aged shale slab. Now, he carefully removes the dark red velvet containing the blade without having gazed upon it yet. The wooden box slides neatly between the stone pillars on the floor and he places the velvet cloth at the center of the cold alter.

Banja closes his eyes and raises his open palms to say, "All that I am—all that can ever be—now lies broken, shattering like brittle bones on the brink of wreckage and ruination. The things that I now endeavor, I do so willfully. I am Banjalanah Rouge. I am borne of Kwaban Rouge, and I now wield *La lame de l'ouragan rouge*. I am Kilarin Rouge, whom has already passed beyond the *Reach* to breach the thinning veil of all things. Welcome and guard him well. I am yet Kysing Rouge, now adrift in the fallows on the cusp of destruction. Here me, Great Creator, for she is an innocent who endangered her own life to assure the continuance of another! Endorse my desire to please the Harbingers of the Dark Lights, the denizens of life and death, where souls may travel through the perilous dim. Bless me, your pitiful, humbled servant, with the strength to please those who bridge the void between existence and expiry . . . between heaven's embrace and the white-hot maw of hell. I beseech thee—not for myself—but for the better part of me."

Banja walks away to open a small cabinet where there are black and white candles. Four candle mounts are situated on the four walls to support brass candleholders made for two. The black candles are three inches shorter than the white ones. Each black candle is placed to the left side, while the taller white ones are seated on the right. He lights every set, praying immediately to the Harbingers of the Dark Lights until all are lit.

Now, Banja Rouge strips away the bandage to reopen the wound in his left palm. After lathering the tip of the pointed stick with his blood, he evenly dissects the thirteen-inch circle, leaving an inch or so where they would intersect untouched in the middle. After completing the three pie-shaped sections of the circle, Banja draws a straight, thirteen-inch line from the circle's edge toward the far wall. On the opposite side, he scores the red clay floor from the circle all the way to the center pillar of the shale altar. From his pocket, he takes what remains of his own hair shavings and dumps it into his right palm and blows it over the dissected circle.

He looks at everything he has done, satisfied with its accuracy. Now, he uses one of Kysing's locks of hair to bind the image of Robbie Mecklenburg. He does the same with that of his sister Stacie, placing each within one of the pie-shaped sections closest to the altar. Robbie's image is to the left, his sister to the right.

The tips of the final lock are loosened a bit and rebraided end-to-end to form a circle, which he scorches with the flames of both candles. He smells it, inhaling deeply. Then he kisses it and holds it high to whisper another prayer. This lock of hair will rest in the section farthest from the altar, where the thirteen-inch line gouges the clay.

Banja disrobes, completely, before taking the small dagger from the peg to slit deeper wounds into both his palms so that his blood flows freely. With six digits meshed together, his thumbs are crossed. The tips of his forefingers are touching. With the blood collecting between his palms, he prays, reciting ancient words as he points his forefingers downward so his blood runs copiously into the scored lines. He allows his blood to trace around and through the circle upon the red clay floor. The desperate but determined father now traces it to the foot of the altar.

Banja Rouge stands before the horizontal shale for a moment, contemplating the agony of this endeavor, but the pain of losing both his children to a single tragedy holds the promise of greater anguish than is known in this entire world.

Suddenly, he plants his palms down upon the cool slab of dark green shale, where he will leave bloody handprints on either side. With his head bowed, hands still upon the surface, he utters, "I'm he who must command the future life of one I love with the furies of wind, of water, of earth, and of living flame. I am unmovable from this path of wrath, of ravage, and even the probability of my own destruction. Into the affray, I shall gladly leap where the eye of the storm lies seething for retribution! I am Banjalanah Rouge! I am made of Kwaban Rouge, and I now wield the Blade of the Red Hurricane!" With both hands, he opens the flaps of velvet to expose the gleaming metal of *La lame de l'ouragan rouge*!

The candles flare. The earth seizes and quakes as if the world is sheering apart. Thunder pounds the air as lightning gouges the ground outside the house. Every mortared brick that forms this private domain, suddenly crack and fissure as if this home is about to crumble into shards and dust. His eyes turn completely white; no pupils will give him sight in the darkness that he seeks. The flame of each candle flares upward as if to set this abode on fire.

When he picks up the blade by the carved bone haft, a thousand images flash through his mind's eye. He sees the furious winds of twin funnels ripping away the west wing of the presidential palace, brick-by-brick, howling like airborne banshees of doom and obliteration. He recalls the roof and floors above flown away like smoke as he covered his ears and screamed for his mother. He remembers the vicious beating by the boy with the club, blood spilling from every swollen wound where broken bones protruded. His teeth and jawbones . . . crushed. His left eye was nearly swollen shut as the right one hung from its socket to rest upon his shattered cheek. He recalls his life force slowly ebbing unto the furthest boundaries of the *Reach*. Similar images of Kilarin's body after the fall, seals his resolve.

"Heed my call, for I demand a life to save a life. Grant me the transference of the *Fire-bonding* where my own blood will set to flames!"

As Banja gleans the blade with his bleeding hands, his blood absorbs into the bone carving and into the metal. After decades of hungering in a rotting wooden casket in Haiti, beneath a thriving briar patch where no one dared to venture, its thirst is great. The thorny briars never spread out of its circular pattern, but it had grown dense. Each malignant stalk was at least an inch thick.

On the day of the box's removal, Fassa encircled the thriving patch with a strong rope. He pulled as hard as he could to hold them back, circling a tree before handing the rope to Kwaban who gripped it tightly to lean backward as his friend used a machete to hack away at the stalks as closely to the ground as possible. It was hard work.

Thousands of miles from South Carolina, Kwaban sits midway. The window seat overlooks the starboard wing and engine. When he closes his eyes in the late hours, his chest seizes as if an invisible force draws the breath from him. He shivers again as Flight 111 reaches its altitude, leaving Haiti behind as it soars to America. He feels the disturbance within the *Reach*. As a tiny pinpoint of brilliant light begins to form in his mind, he says to himself, "It has begun."

Chapter 16

The Tempests of the Air

Banja Rouge is now drenched with sweat. As if moving through a dream in slow motion, he heaves oxygen from the air through his mouth and flaring nostrils, growing weary as he performs the Harbingers' dance. His body twists and turns, twirling in endless circles far and away from the etchings on the red clay floor. His eyes are ivory pearls as his feet carry him through the steps and melodic hand motions seared into his mind. His body is here, but his essence is also contained within the fluctuating boundaries of the Reach where he feels every cramping muscle.

His fluent movements range from harmonious vacillations and melodious sensuality, to threatening, warlike gestures that tell the unspoken story of the god's of his unique Haitian ancestry. However, it has been over an hour since he began this venture to win their favor and his body tires. He has only consumed water for the last three days and this seemingly unending dance drains him as sweat lathers his completely naked, hairless body. With every thrust, every gyration, his strength wanes where failure is not an acceptable option.

As his heart pounds within his chest, the candles flare in sets of twos and threes, as if demanding more and more. Banja Rouge reaches for his father among the sleeping passengers of Flight 111. Though seated over the starboard wing with his white eyes fixed, Kwaban is now with him. His hands are raised before him, fingers splayed. His quiet utterances urge his son on, imparting his own spirit to bolster Banja's strength.

Banja whispers into Kwaban's mind, "Father, I grow weary. My heart threatens to burst from my chest, and my breath is not breath enough. I am failing our family. Help me, father."

When Kwaban Rouge bares his teeth and clench his curled hands into fists, his long fingernails draw blood from his palms.

Some passengers wake to stare into those frightful, ivory eyes when he utters aloud, "Seek. Seek, my son. Seek—for we are Rouge—undaunted by the physical plane. Nothing made of flesh— not even our own—holds sway over us within the *Reach*. Seek that which you must have, even as the cloak of death overshadows this trial by blood and fire."

The world seizes with a boom when he unfurls his bleeding fists and casts them forward. An unnatural energy begins to charge the compressed air of Flight 111, causing the plane to shudder and dip while waking passengers shriek. Kwaban begins to utter low guttural sounds as lightning suddenly flashes across the cloudless night sky. Again, and in tandem with the flaring candles, the Dreamliner shudders and creaks as if highly stressed.

Captain Meeks and his co-pilot are bewildered as they look at the radar. Although there is nothing but clear skies ahead, Meeks cues the mike to address the frightened passengers.

"Sorry about that folks. It seems that we have run into a little turbulence from cross winds and a patch of heat lightning. Rest assured that we are fine and there is no need to worry. Pending getting through this rough patch, I ask that all passengers wear seatbelts until further notice."

He looks to the co-pilot, who shakes his head to the negative because there is still nothing to explain this sudden tempestuous malady.

When it happens again, Kwaban's window cover and several others slam open, sliding up so hard that they jam in their frames.

When an azure brilliance illuminates him, a startled woman finds it impossible to turn her eyes away, seeing wraiths circling Kwaban Rouge for a split second. When a flight attendant hurries toward the sounds of worry and fear to calm the passengers, she notices that most have trained their attention on that same frail old man some people laughed at in the terminal.

The woman, who screams loud enough to wake the dead, looks at the approaching flight attendant with her left palm across her lips as he she points her trembling right hand toward Kwaban. She is not the only one.

"I see something. They were like . . . like ghosts all around him. It seems like something evil. Look at him. What the hell is he doing?"

Kwaban does not abate his incantations, unconcerned by issues of the physical plane of existence. "Dance, Banja. I am with you, my son. Seek. Seek!"

The air marshal, one of them, loosens his seatbelt and locks onto the passenger in seat 132. He and the flight attendant are approaching Kwaban Rouge.

"Sir? Are you okay?" When lightning strikes all about, the airliner dips, spilling one to the floor and the other into the lap of another terrified passenger.

"I see them too," someone shouts. "It's him I tell you. Whatever is happening, it's got something to do with him!"

A distinguished, older woman from three rows up says, "Please, be calm everyone. I'm a doctor, and I think he's having a seizure of some sort. He needs medical attention."

The attendant asks her to take a look at him, helping her move safely in the midst of worsening turbulence.

At this time, Captain Meeks is calling Miami International Airport to advise them of the unusually hostile air currents, but there seems to be nothing on the radars or satellite imaging. Miami International contacts associative airport towers, but they all concur. There is simply nothing out there for them to see. The National Weather Service agrees, until the satellite's resonance is changed. Raising the resolution proves useless. When the tech lowers it, however, they see it. The military SATCOM is alerted that a flight may be in trouble over the Atlantic on approach to Miami International. The transponder signal is cued up. By training its attention on Flight 111's vector, adjusted telemetry shows some form of static energy, which seems to be moving with the Dreamliner instead of against it. Everyone is placed on high alert when Homeland Security becomes involved because this cannot be ruled out as an act of terrorism.

As the blade slices through the air, the atmosphere in the temple grows as thick as smoke. Until now, the flames have been equal in height as they flare toward the heavens. However, as Banja Rouge approaches the end of his strength, the white candles' flames grow even higher.

"Father," he cries in the turbulent brilliance of another plane. Kwaban answers, "Yes, Banja. The end is near, dance!"

The passengers can hear his words. One of which shouts, "Oh my God, his hands are bleeding."

Banja's arms crisscross his chest, twirling in place, faster and faster as the flames of the white candles' grow steadily higher!

After repeated attempts to communicate with the passenger in seat 132, the elderly doctor looks at the attendant and says, "I'm no longer certain that this is a seizure. It is more like some kind of fugue state or a trance. I can tell by his dialect and verbiage that he is probably a Haitian national, yes? What's his name?"

The attendant says, "His name is Kwa . . . Kwaban Rouge. We have to do something. He's upsetting the other passengers." She looks about and shouts, "We need everyone to please remain calm, and remain seated. We will handle this."

Captain Meeks is advised of the situation, but they are closing on their destination. Diverting from their course now isn't a palatable option. However, they are only fifty miles from Miami International.

The doctor calls his name, but Kwaban is moving deep within. His heaving chest seems to have a constant and steady rhythm that disturbs her greatly. "He may be having some kind of cardiopulmonary event. I need my stethoscope from my bag above my seat. Hurry. Please hurry."

The air marshal does not take his eyes off the old man, feeling within himself that this passenger could have something to do with what is happening to this airplane. It goes against all logic, but this former police officer has seen unexplainable occurrences in his lifetime.

In South Carolina, the hospital trembles. The ground quakes violently.

Kwaban says aloud, "Yes. Now, Banja. Do it now, son!"

The black candles now flare three times before merging with the flames of the others, continuing upward. The ceiling disappears. Like the coils of writhing snakes, a living greyish-black cloud of smoke roils with electrostatic energy. Its center is a black hole.

As Banja Rouge spins faster, Kwaban commands, "Yes, my son. You have gained their favor. The Harbingers are pleased. Now draw your hosts into. Draw them into!"

Before Banja twirls into a crouching position, the thick toenail of his trailing right foot scrapes the surface of the clay floor to form a perfect circle that barely touches the end of the thirteen-inch line before he halts. Banja's chest is heaving when the left hand comes to rest upon the floor, supporting most of his weight. With the blade raised high as if to strike and his muscular right leg stretched out, he now faces the circle before the altar. He bares those white teeth beneath white eyes that seem to pulsate. It is a frightful gaze, this opacity, which focuses on a singular purpose.

Water begins to rise up through the clay as if a small spring has suddenly formed in the section where Stacie Mecklenburg's bound image rests. A mound of sand granules grows, simultaneously, beneath Robbie's bound image. Banja's white eyes remain affixed on these sections, clearly seeing all. As if a tiny dust devil is wreaking mischief within the circle, the photographs slowly begin to turn. Loose strands of Kysing's hair move with subtlety.

Banja Rouge now stands before the thirteen-inch trench with his hands raised in amazement; his wounds have disappeared.

Now he spreads his arms to command, "Come . . ." He raises his eyes, reciting his thanks to the Harbingers of the *Reach*. ". . . with me—into!" He demands the same, repeatedly.

When Dr. Christian Labor reaches for Kwaban's shoulder to place the stethoscope to his chest, she shudders with a whimper. As if she has touched a livewire, her entire body tremors. She is powerless to remove her hands as her wide eyes see things of unnatural powers. She quakes and utters a muffled, shrieking cry for help. The violent air about the airplane threatens to sheer it to shreds. The cockpit instruments begin to spark and short out from a massive surge.

Alice Graham, the flight attendant seeing to this frightful matter, while the others go about calming the passengers, asks, "Ma'am? Doctor Labor, are you all right? What's happening, doctor?"

Doctor Labor cannot answer, but her wide stretched eyes and trembling lips reflect absolute terror. The air marshal reaches.

The flight attendant looks at him and says, "Something's wrong." When she makes the mistake of touching Dr. Labor, she feels it, too. She sees a flash of white, then a slideshow of fast moving images that horrify her. She tries to scream, only managing childlike sobs as creatures beyond myth swim through the air, circling. Each looks her directly in the eyes, whispering in her mind. These things, their eyes seem almost blasphemous.

* * *

At the hospital, the shockwaves grow in frequency. Stacie Mecklenburg screams as her mother tries to reach her bed and loses her footing at the same time Banja sweeps the air to the right. When Pauline tries to stand, she falls again, propelled toward the wall.

Stacie Mecklenburg passes out as her bewildered mother stares at the transparent image of that Black man now standing over her daughter's bed. His eyes are a fearsome gaze. His arms are curled before him as if holding a heavy burden. He is there, but she can see the wall through his phasing body. Suddenly, there is a static charge in the air, which brings lightning and wind-driven rain from the ceiling. This unnatural downpour drenches the room and its inhabitants.

Pauline Mecklenburg shouts at him as Stacie's limp, unconscious body rises from the bed into his intermittent arms.

An ominous voice in her mind states, "One life forsaken for one life safe. One life dims for one shimmering soul to take. Can you now cry for them all, mother? Can you cry for our children now?"

She watches in disbelief, but she can do nothing. Banja Rouge turns with her daughter in his arms to walk right through the wall.

The mother screams, "No . . . please!" She blacks out, lying face down in a foul pool of water.

The floor seizes and fissures with the sound of brittle, crackling tiles. The bristling, static-charged air begins to howl as a sandstorm blinds Larkin. His shoes slide backward against hurricane winds. His blazer tears away from his body to fly through the blown out window. The velocity of the windborne grains of sand crack both lenses of his reading glasses as the pages of a discarded newspaper swirl. There, Banja Rouge stands above his unmoving son. As Banja phases in and out, his loveless eyes clearly lock on to the subject of his malcontent. Mayor Mecklenburg struggles to save his boy, slipping on broken vials of blood. As building materials begin to strip away from the outer wall adjoining both rooms, he has to hold on to avoid joining the pages that fly through the gaping hole where the window used to be.

Blood samples and the shattered glass of once sterile vials blow across the sand strewn floor, drawing toward the opening at the mayor's feet. The screaming lab technician, who came to draw Robbie's blood just before this strange calamity began, clings to the closet door.

As Robbie's limp form begins to rise into the transparent arms of the mayor's sworn enemy, he shouts, "I'm sorry. Please, sir. Please don't take my son. I was wrong to use my authority in favor of my own. I know that now."

Upon his knees, Mayor Larkin Mecklenburg continues to shout his pleas over the airborne wolves, but his voice is muted in the presence of deaf ears where howls the air. The flying sand is thick, forcing Larkin to use his arms to shield his squinting, encrusted eyes. Static electricity blazes throughout the writhing fuselage, as terror-stricken passengers continue to panic.

The women, who seem locked within the currents of a power surge, are suddenly flung in different directions. Neither is conscious when they crash.

Silence fills the air of the sky and upon the earth.

The air marshal lies quaking from the reversed jolts of juice from the Taser he elected to discharge into Kwaban's chest instead of using lethal force. The old man pulls the leads from his body, before shutting his eyes to slip into a deep sleep.

When the turbulence suddenly ends, Captain Meeks calls for a report from the flight attendants concerning the condition of passenger 132, but he gets no answer. The co-pilot monitors the autopilot with his hands on the stick in case any sudden problems arise while Captain Meeks looks at the camera monitoring the cockpit door before unlocking it. When he steps out, there can be no doubt. Something is terribly wrong. It is too still, too quiet.

After coming through a rough ride like that, there should be the sound of stressful voices, but he hears nothing more than the squish of his own footsteps. He looks down at the galley's floor, where the carpeting is soaked as if a water sprinkler has activated to put out a fire. Every surface looks as though they were recently hosed down.

Captain Meeks moves toward first-class. Now standing in a half inch of water, what he sees there prompts him to hurry. He looks back, nervously, as he passes into another section.

His breath stops. In the dim quiet, every passenger and crew member is unconscious and soaking wet in his or her seat. A few, those who must have panicked, are lying in the aisles. He checks for pulses, relieved that each one is still alive. He looks around for anything that might explain this phenomenon, but nothing seems to be out of place other than the present condition of the passengers. He tries to wake the flight attendant by calling her name, only getting a response by lightly slapping her cheeks. She stirs, moaning her way back to screaming consciousness.

Once she quiets down and is able to sit up, Alice Graham tries to explain the inexplicable. Nothing she says makes any sense. Because she was rendered unconscious before the tempest peaked, she asks, "Why am I soaking wet?" Panic ensues. "Oh God, we crash-landed over the Atlantic. What are we going to do?"

"Calm down, Alice. Just listen for a second. Do you hear that?" Captain Meeks says, taking her arms firmly in his grasp. He looks into her harried eyes, and smiles. "There, you see. Our engines are still running at optimum capacity. Can you feel them purring along? We are still floating through the air. Now I need my best girl to pull herself together. We experienced some temporary equipment failure in the cockpit, but we are okay now and will be landing soon. I'm going to need you to rouse the

Federal Sky Marshals first, so they can help if there are any problems. I noticed that Cynthia and Robert are still unconscious so you have to try to get them up to check on the passengers. When they wake up, there is bound to be the same type of panic you just experienced. Do the best you can to keep them calm and in their seats. Once we are safely on the ground, initiate the emergency landing protocols to get these people off this bucket as quickly and orderly as possible. I'm sure that the camera footage will help us to sort this all out."

"Look around you, Captain Meeks!"

"Sh. Sh. Sh. I never called your assertion of things into question. I know you, Alice. You are as levelheaded as they come. So let's just try to do our jobs and get these people home safely. That is all I am saying at this point. Can you tell me anything else about what happened back here?"

She immediately looks at 132, a rush of fear threatening to overtake her. With cringing apprehension, Alice points at the sleeping old man, who could be dead for all she knows. She manages to whisper, "Dragons, they spoke to me. Him. Something, I can't explain." She feels sick, vomiting in the aisle despite herself. The pilot is patient and sympathetic as she purges on the spongy carpeting. With great shame, she tries to compose herself in the presence of her captain.

Ignoring the part about speaking dragons, he asks, "Him, this harmless looking old man? What could he do? How can he be responsible for all of this?" Her captain abandons her side with a small pat on the shoulder. Gratefully leaving the crouching position and the pressure it places on his knees, Captain Meeks approaches Kwaban Rouge to take a pulse as Alice shrieks a dire warning not to touch him.

"Sleeping, just like the rest of the passengers. Can you function, flight attendant Graham?"

She is shocked because nothing happens when the captain's fingers make contact with Kwaban's skin.

"I'm sorry, Captain Meeks. Of course, I'll get right on it. Where's Doctor Labor?"

"Who?"

"The passenger, who was trying to check the old man out when— there, that's her. She may be injured."

With her skirt hiked up to her midriff, the older woman lies askew the lap of two unconscious passengers a few seats away. Luckily for her, the armrests were in the upright position between them; otherwise, she would probably have a broken back. As they quickly approach, there is a ping as the co-pilot's voice summons the captain to report that they are only ten miles out. Meeks looks about the sloshing cabin, wondering how much water may have seeped into the lower compartments. She feels a bit heavier than before.

Meeks heads back to the cockpit, anxious to access the gauges for any weight differentials. Though certain that this smelly water is the product of some kind of malfunction in the fire suppression system, he thinks it prudent to check.

He strides forward and says to himself, "This is one hell of a ride. Lord, if you let me set this beast down safely, I will never yank another newbie's chain about aliens and curses. Never again. Seat 132. Fuck me stupid."

Air traffic control instructs all incoming aircraft to circle until Flight 111 is safely on the pad. Upon touchdown, amid the approach of wailing sirens, the passengers slide to the pavement where many wish to kiss the ground. The second sky marshal, Calvin McCoy, who remained anonymous during the rugged flight, waits at the bottom for Kwaban Rouge. The other follows Kwaban Rouge to the ground, where they cuff the old man and treat him like a potential terror threat. Once Kwaban Rouge is sequestered, someone notices that he and the cockpit crew are the only people who got off that flight completely dry. Flight 111 is grounded and her wet, disgruntled passengers will be questioned and rerouted to their destinations as quickly as possible.

They vigorously question Kwaban Rouge. Whether loudly and raging, or meekly spoken, their threats do not fluster the old man, who remains silent even during the humiliating strip search. A myriad of law enforcement officials will harass him for hours on end. Every now and then, someone will exit the secure room completely unnerved by the silent gaze of a horribly scarred old man. Some will mention Kwaban Rouge's creepy eyes, how they experience a disconcerting sensation of skin crawling proportions in his presence. Because he is uncooperative, they intend to carry out the threat of holding him, indefinitely.

Chapter 17

When In Darkness We Seek

Within the bowels of a darkened well, Robbie Mecklenburg awakes upon a gritty mound of sand. He trembles while attempting to sit up. Like the sands of the hourglass slipping out from beneath him, he slides upon his back with a groan. Staring up into the darkness, he finally rolls onto his stomach to get to his knees. He wipes his face clear of the annoying granules, shaking them free from his hair. The kid calls out only to hear his own echoes resounding throughout the black. There is nothing, no sounds other than the reverberation of his voice and the crunching, squeaking sand beneath his feet when he rises. There is no pinpoint of light to guide the boy's steps as he attempts to find the door or the walls of his hospital room.

He is yet to notice that there are no stitches, no swelling, no cast, nor pain from placing weight on the broken leg. With his hands stretched out before him, he moves cautiously across the cool, sandy surface beneath his bare feet. When Robbie hears something, he stops, turning his ear toward it like a blind man who knows someone is nearby and watching.

"Dad?" he shouts. "Mom, is that you?" Because no one answers, his intensified fear swells within. "Hello," he cries out, again. "Who's there? I can hear you breathing. Are you hurt? This bullshit isn't funny, asshole!"

He has already moved several yards away, finding no walls or the door to his hospital room. He is alone, lost in an unfamiliar world of utter nothingness. When the echoes subside, he clearly discerns the sound of breathing. When the echo of his own voice finally abates, it carries with it his false bravado for this is no mere dream.

Stacie Mecklenburg's firm, young, athletic body is no longer garbed in the unflattering hospital attire. She is wearing her favorite, blood red, satin nightgown. Half of which is much darker and heavier because she awakes lying on her right side in a pungent pool of water. After sitting up to gather and wring out her long hair, she quietly listens to the breathing in the background. She knows not where the constant sound originates. Now accompanied by a thudding heartbeat, Stacie is not sure if it is her own breathing or that of someone nearby.

Disoriented by her fears, the darkness, and the disconcerting noises, panic is but a drip away. Finally, she summons the courage to cry out in the living well of black that seems darker than a moonless night.

"Can anyone help me? Is someone there? Please help, I'm lost and I'm scared. What's happening?"

She begins to move in all directions, searching for some surface to guide her where there is none. While holding her arm out, flexing her fingers and wrist brings absolutely no pain.

Although she has been walking in water on trembling legs, she decides to sit until someone comes to rescue her from this terrible, dreamlike place. When she realizes that she is supporting herself with the broken arm, she flinches and marvels at its wholeness.

* * *

Yara Rouge calmly awakens to an extremely troubled world. There are anxious voices coming from everywhere. She opens the door upon a dreadful scene of devastation, venturing into the hallway to ask what has happened as people rush to-and-fro. There are nurses and doctors scrambling in and out of every room on the ICU. Firefighters, dressed in full gear with axes, are searching for any signs of fire because there seems to be the smell of smoke emanating from somewhere. The blaring alarm is frightening and ominous. Paper and medical equipment are scattered everywhere. When the alarm shuts off, Yara wonders why she never heard it.

When one of Kysing's nurses approaches, she asks, "Nurse Hardaway, what happened here? Is there a fire?"

The nurse looks at her in disbelief. "Ma'am? Are you telling me that you didn't feel that or hear anything, Mrs. Rouge? Were you injured and knocked unconscious?"

"What on earth are you talking about? I just woke up, but I wasn't unconscious."

"Let's check on your daughter. I must make sure that she wasn't harmed during the earthquake or tornado, or whatever the hell happened a few moments ago."

"The what? I didn't feel anything. How bad could it have been?" Yara asks, completely confused as they start to enter Kysing's room.

The nurse halts, suddenly speechless. They are standing just inside Kysing's room where nothing is disturbed or overturned. None of the equipment has been displaced or unplugged like the other rooms throughout each floor. There is only one thing in this misplaced serenity that seems amiss, something that was never there before.

Both women stare at the floor. Nurse Hardaway asks, "What in God's name is that?"

Yara drives her hand over her lips to quell a shriek. The nurse stares at the floor, where a black circle surrounds the hospital bed. With a gasp, Yara directs the nurse's attention to her comatose daughter, who is floating about two feet above her bed.

"Kysing, oh my God," she says in a near whisper. Nurse Hardaway's slack jaw works to speak or to scream, but she can say nothing. They both try to approach the bed, but an invisible barrier repels them. The women hit the floor after slamming into something unseen. Feeling as if they both ran face first into an immaculately clean plate-glass window, the stunned women help each other to regain their feet.

Reaching out with anxious caution, they feel a smooth, invisible shield. Tracing it all the way around the bed, a yellowish static surrounds their fingertips and palms. While in contact with the barrier, the static charge crackles as their hands move across its surface. Yara's floating daughter now slowly descends toward the mattress. The straps that secured Kysing's body are tattered, hanging from her like broken vines from a tree limb.

"Oh my God, what's going on here? Why can't we get to her?"

Yara looks at her teenage daughter, tempted to shout at nurse Hardaway to do something. She remains silent as the nurse runs out into the hallway for a firefighter. When the worried woman turns away and then back again, looking at her peaceful daughter, she grasps her arms and shudders.

Fluctuating lights startle Yara Rouge, when she whispers, "Banja?"

***

While the best civil engineers in the region arrive to inspect the hospital to make certain that it is still structurally sound, Detective Arnold Reeves is questioning the Mecklenburgs in the waiting room. His partner, Detective Peter Blake is elsewhere, questioning the other witness.

The police are keeping the media out of the hospital while they investigate the strange goings on, but someone takes a small bribe and sneaks a local camera team inside. The camera crews and reporters left outside are conducting interviews with people who have vacated the hospital. Others are speculating on two huge gouges in the earth and ripped out sections of the east side parking lot where a large portion of the wall is torn away just a few floors above. Two distinctly different paths are clearly marked by overturned or displaced automobiles.

Forensics specialists are collecting water samples and grains of sand from the hospital rooms of both Stacie and Robert Mecklenburg. Because kidnapping is a federal crime, FBI Agents are dispatched to the area. South Carolina State Governor Nikki Haley answers Fort Mill Police Chief Allen's plea for help with this strange case because, frankly, this is beyond the locals.

Fortunately, Mayor Mecklenburg was a generous contributor to her campaign so she is quick to assist in his time of need. When the governor's requisition is run up the ladder, two agents are rerouted to the region midstream their return to Quantico after successfully capturing a fugitive murder suspect and solving a case that led them to Atlanta.

Chief Archibald Mecklenburg shows up just as the investigating detective reiterates the unbelievable story told by Pauline while she shivers in her husband's arms.

An Amber Alert is not yet in effect.

As Chief Archibald Mecklenburg approaches, Detective Arnold Reeves repeats, "So let me get this straight, ma'am. You are saying, as a matter of record, that all of a sudden the floor and entire room begins to shake, waking you from your sleep. There is a weird gust of wind, but when you try to get to your daughter's bedside, something shoves you across the room. As if the sky opens up in your daughter's room, a heavy downpour comes from the ceiling. However, it isn't coming from the hospital's sprinkler system. You also claim that there are both lightning and thunder . . . inside the room?" "Yes," she says with a quiver in her voice.

"When you try, again, to get to your daughter, Stacie, you suddenly see a familiar African American male standing over her bed. You say that the suspect is there, but then he isn't. He seems transparent because you can actually see right through his body at times. Now, your daughter's unconscious body begins to float off the surface of her bed into the suspect's arms and he takes her—walking right through that wall without using the door next to him. The shock causes you to pass out. According to your recollection, is this an accurate account of Stacie's disappearance, Mrs. Mecklenburg? Are you certain that this is all you would like to say, ma'am? Did the intruder say anything to you? Anything at all?" the detective presses.

The distraught mother glares at the skeptical detective before shouting, "Don't you think I know how it sounds? I can hardly believe the words coming from my own lips, but it happened. I saw him. At first, he was there, but not completely solid. Like a ghost or something. He took my precious daughter and walked right through the freaking wall I tell you!" She shivers beneath the blanket, which does nothing to fight the bone chilling cold she is experiencing. Her eyes move far away. Now she buries her tears in her husband's tattered shirt.

"Okay, Mrs. Mecklenburg. I understand your distress, and I'm sorry for being so aggressive. It's just that this is an incredible accounting of events, and I'm just collecting any information that may be helpful in finding your children. Small things are known to be extremely helpful in legitimate matters of abduction. Something that the victims believe to be irrelevant often gives us clues to motive or even methodology."

"It happened the same way with my son, damn it! Except . . . except, it was like a desert sandstorm had come out of nowhere. I swear it to God in heaven. We are telling you the truth. Just ask the girl, the one from the blood lab. She will confirm my story. It was like a tornado just ripped the windows and the walls away as if this hospital is constructed of paper. Go on. Ask her. Ask her!"

"My partner is questioning the other witness as we speak. She is a little shaken up right now, as you can imagine."

"No, sir. I can tell by your smug attitude that it is you, who cannot imagine. It is easy to see the doubt in your eyes. I hear the cynicism in your voice, Detective Reeves. We are not lying about this so do your fucking job and find our children before that man does them harm!"

"Mayor Mecklenburg, sir. . . ."

"Motive," Pauline whispers as if the detective's words just echoed in her thoughts.

"What? I'm sorry, ma'am, but what did you just say?"

She sits up and looks at her husband. "He said. . . ."

"Go on," the detectives urges, as he gets closer to hear her words, if she even completes the statement. "Anything, just tell me. It's okay."

She swallows hard as her husband asks, "He spoke to you? Well, what did he say, honey. Go on. It may be important, just like Detective Reeves says."

She looks at the detective and says, "I believe he either said, 'one life taken, or forsaken, for one life safe.' Ah, also, he said . . . hmm. 'One life dims for a shimmering soul to take. Can you cry for them now, mother? Can you cry for our children?'" She places a palm across her mouth and cries, "Oh God. Oh my dear God in heaven, help us."

On bended knee, Detective Reeves attempts to prompt her on by asking, "Are you certain those were his exact words? Does it mean anything to either of you?"

Pauline glares at her husband with a measure of wrathful spite, as he looks to the floor in scolded shame.

"Larkin, it was you," she says to her husband. "He holds you responsible for everything that happened since the basketball game to the accident on the bridge!"

"Responsible for what, ma'am. Go on, please."

Mayor Larkin Mecklenburg interrupts the rest of what he knows is surely coming. He takes her in his arms, which she resists amid her scalding tears. "Obviously, that man is delusional. It's possible, he blames us because, well. . . ."

The detective asks, "Yes? Please go on."

". . . that accident on the bridge was clearly not our fault. We had nothing to do with it, and our own children were nearly lost to it."

Pauline Mecklenburg adds, "It's all your fault, Larkin. You had to be so cruel and insulting their grieving family. Our son lives while his is dead. His daughter saved Stacie's life in that bus, but you held up the ambulance that would have transported them both to the hospital."

Captain Mecklenburg moves in with bewildered concern.

"Larkin. Pauline. I got here as fast as I could."

They both rise to hug him. The mayor is relieved that his brother announced his presence when he did. Pauline's hair and clothing are drenched, while Larkin resembles a whitetail buck that has just forged its way through a briar thicket to elude the pack of hunting dogs hot on its trail. His slacks are shredded, shirt a tattered rag. The skin on his face and hands are pocked with small, red beads of clotted blood that will become tiny scabs. It looks like he took a face full of birdshot.

"I'm so sorry I wasn't here to protect you guys. I should have taken this threat more seriously. I brought some clothes. Paula, these are some of my wife's things. I hope they fit."

"I told you he was up to something, damn it! I told you, but you didn't listen to me, Archie. You wouldn't fucking listen because you were so busy enjoying a chance at browbeating me."

Captain Mecklenburg expected this reaction from his brother, and rightfully so. He is caught between sequestering his guilt and trying to be helpful.

Reeves says, "That's very helpful because we will need to examine your clothing for DNA evidence. Hello, Chief Mecklenburg, it is

nice to see you again after so many years."

"You two go on and get changed," Archie says, handing Mayor Mecklenburg a bag of clothing. He turns away from the embrace with a scowl.

His angry brother lashes out by saying, "Archie, what's going on here. For what reason do they want our clothes? Are we being accused of something?"

Detective Reeves seeks to defuse the mounting hostility by stating the obvious, "Mayor, Mrs. Mecklenburg, as the chief here knows, it is standard procedure. We will also be taking samples of your DNA, but you shouldn't think of this as anything more than police protocol. If anything, we seek only to eliminate you as suspects. We aren't accusing either of you of any wrongdoing, so please comply."

"So that's why that woman used a comb on my hair to collect sand and dandruff? Is that supposed to help find our abducted children? You should be out there combing the streets instead of playing Sherlock fucking Holmes."

Chief Mecklenburg sighs before saying, "He's right, Larkin. This is just a formality, so please don't assume that this is an accusation in any way. Just go into the restroom stall to change, shoes and all. An officer will be standing just outside. Do not place your clothing on any surfaces, just allow the officer to put them in the bags as you remove them. When you're done just hand it to them."

"They want our shoes, too?"

"I brought replacements for you both. They may not fit perfectly, but I believe they will do in a pinch."

"Several vials containing blood samples from different patients shattered in your son's room. Forensics will have to determine the sources and blood types. We have to take your shoes because there seems to be a greater concentration of blood evidence on them. You said the technician had just come in and was preparing to take Robert's blood. Since she never actually got the chance to do so, his blood shouldn't be present unless the suspect injured him first," explains Detective Reeves.

Detective Reeves sends a male and female officer with them. When they return, Detective Reeves' partner is saying, "Security has zip on the elevator cameras and stairwells. Although the cameras overlooking the east parking area seem to have suffered some sort of malfunction, they managed to capture footage of two massive funnels ripping through the parking lot at the exact time of the disappearances, but none of them captured the suspect's image. Coming nor going. I posted men at every possible exit in case the suspect is still on the premises. We have officers combing every room, empty or occupied. They are also searching the basement and subbasement. Some kind of extreme weirdness happened here. The third eyewitness to the events in Robert Mecklenburg's room is tremendously upset. However, as crazy as it sounds, the blood lab tech corroborates Mayor Mecklenburg's account. Because she collects blood from different floors, she has seen the suspect two floors up in the ICU where his daughter is in a coma. Name is Rouge."

"First name?"

"Ah, according to hospital records, the daughter's name is Kysing Rouge. Parent's names are Yara and Banja Rouge. Son, Kilarin Rouge died during the bridge episode when he was ejected from the bus. While firemen were in the process of rescuing Mayor Mecklenburg's son, the Rouge kid dislodged from the support cable and fell to his death right before his parent's eyes."

Lead Detective Reeves looks at his notes. He peruses Pauline's statement and says, "That's what he meant. Well, there's our motive." He instructs Detective Peter Blake to call dispatch for an address and a warrant to search the suspect's home. He wants a BOLO placed on the suspect and all registered vehicles, initiating a standard Amber Alert with descriptions of alleged suspect and both victims. Until the feds arrive, he intends pursue a resolution to the matter of Banja Rouge's involvement in the disappearances.

Chief Mecklenburg suggests, "Screw wading through the red tape. You should have someone discretely observe through the windows of his home for any signs of criminal activity while someone in plainclothes rings the doorbell. Get tactical to the location ASAP. Let the warrant meet you there."

"Do it," Reeves says to Blake. "Have Bruncher and Pace handle the sneak peek. Call in Langston and Briggs as backup in case he's there and tries to backdoor us." He places a hand on his hips and takes a hard blow, walking in a circle as he looks from floor to the ceiling. "They say there was an earthquake, but no one else in the city felt or heard a thing. Other than the people here, of course. Several visitors and hospital personnel concur, although the only structural damage occurred in Robert and Stacie Mecklenburg's room. There seems to be evidence of a thunderstorm in Stacie's hospital room, but the ceiling itself is bone-dry. What really happened here? And what is that god awful smell?"

Chief Mecklenburg says, "I noticed that, too. It reminds me of that old artesian spring we had on our property when we were growing up."

"It smells like rotting eggs."

"Yeah, that would be the odor all right. It's the combination of sulfur and various minerals," Chief Mecklenburg responds. "Is there anything else you can tell me, Detective Reeves?"

"Well, sir. . . ." As he looks at his notes, shaking his head, he leans back against the wall just outside Stacie's room. Suddenly, a subtle crackling sound comes from behind the detective. When he looks back and tries to move, his weight almost drives him completely through the dry-rotted wall near the nameplate.

"What the hell?" Chief Mecklenburg shouts, hurrying to help the detective before he can fall through. Larkin also tries to help pull the man free.

"What in the hell is going on here?" shouts Detective Reeves.

When Larkin and one of the forensic techs come to help Archibald pull him out, the detective is stuck. The cuff of his blazer snags on something. The forensics tech steps back inside and guides his arm through the wall from the inside to avoid injury by splintered wood.

With his hair and dark suit now a whitish mess, Detective Reeves realizes that he has also broken through the waist high wooden border that traces the entire hallway. After examining it to be certain it is actual wood, he grabs a handful of porous drywall, which crumbles into dust. They are all amazed when they step back to see the damage he has done just by leaning against the wall.

Wearing a clean white jumpsuit, boots, a mask, and safety goggles, the forensic specialist quickly takes a sample of the wall's materials. As she does so, the plaque falls from the wall and fractures into a thousand shards.

Pauline shrieks, "My God. That's it, that's exactly where he walked through the wall with my daughter. You can almost make out a complete outline!"

"What's this?" Larkin says as he bends over to retrieve something that seems out of place.

"Stop, don't touch anything. That could be evidence!" Reeves warns. He uses his cell phone to take photos of the disintegrated area and that black thing on the floor before using his gloved hand to place the knotted, singed lock of hair into a plastic evidence bag.

"Oh Christ," Mayor Mecklenburg says. "Come with me. Hurry!" The others follow him one door down the hall to Robbie's hospital room, where he points. "This is where he passed through the wall with Robbie. Check it, detective. See if they're the same."

Exercising a little caution this time, Detective Reeves places his hand on the wall and pushes. Nothing happens. When he moves a little to the left and pushes, his hand drives through to his elbow. When he pulls it free, the plaque comes off and shatters within a cloud of powdered drywall. There it is, another knotted lock of braided black hair.

He muses, holding it up to the light with a pen before dropping it into a separate bag. "This is braided human hair. A solid lead." He hands it to a forensic technician and says, "This is probably our best DNA lead. Put a rush on it for me."

They all back away, gawking at what almost looks like a nearly perfect outline of someone's body and the one that was carried away. In total dismay, Pauline buries her eyes in Larkin's chest. As if this is not enough to shut down the mind completely, there comes a cry for help from the other room. As they approach, one of the forensic technicians helps her co-worker out of the room before she collapses to the floor.

The woman begins to wheeze, and her skin blushes with hives. A nurse comes to her aide, and shouts, "Help. I need a doctor here!"

As her throat begins to swell shut, she manages to tell the nurse, "Sulfur—allergic! Must have. . . ."

When a doctor arrives, she is greying out, chest heaving to draw in even the smallest breath. The nurse says, "She's allergic to sulfur. Look, she's wearing a RX alert bracelet."

Dr. Phillips says, "I need fifteen milligrams of epi. Quick!" She rushes off to get epinephrine as the doctor taps on the woman's face and says, "I'm Doctor Phillips. Can you hear me? Are you acutely allergic to sulfur?" She nods just before graying out.

He places a hand beneath her neck to raise her head, pinching her nose as he inhales deeply to blow into her mouth. Her chest is not rising as he wishes; she is deadlocked. The nurse runs back and he plunges the needle into her.

The hospital administrators are forced to agree when several doctors suggest that this floor may not be safe. They should evacuate everyone.

Detective Blake returns and whispers into his partner's ear. Reeves looks at him. Blake nods and says, "She's waiting for us. Let's go."

They head for the elevator. When it opens two floors up, someone is waiting to guide them to Irish Feeson, and both Doctor Connors, who are greatly concerned for their patient.

Mrs. Feeson approaches the officers to say, "This is absolutely incredible. I have never seen anything like it in all my years. Come quickly!"

Extremely loud metal-to-metal banging noises are coming from the room. Both detectives place their hands on their weapons until they see what is happening. Yara Rouge is standing in the corner of the room, watching as two firefighters hammer away at the invisible wall that keeps them separated from Kysing Rouge. Both men finally quit, leaning on the handles of heavy sledgehammers to catch a breath. A bent, broken axe head and handle lay on the floor.

"What the hell," the farthest one says, breathlessly, his face lathered with sweat. "Shit!"

The other man just lets the handle fall to the floor as he grasps his knees to catch his breath. He raises his visor to get more air. "We must have pounded at that thing a hundred times each. It will not budge."

Moments later, two of their comrades walk in with the heavy acetylene tank. They unravel the hoses used to combine the mixture of ethyne and oxygen through the torch's tip. With the valves open, the striker ignites the flame. Everyone is asked to leave the room. Because Kysing is being oxygenated, the danger of explosion is obvious. Yara Rouge refuses to go so they have to force her into the hall for her own safety.

Once adjusted, the firefighter applies that blustering flame to the invisible barrier, raising its temperature to 6300 degrees Fahrenheit in a matter of moments. The concentrated flame splurges against a wall of nothingness for ten minutes without any results. One firefighter has an idea so he grabs the unused basin and fills it with cold water. After five more minutes, the man with the torch gives the thumbs up and suddenly slides to the left to turn away. The other fire fighter dashes the hotspot with cold water, trying to cause a violent reaction, but the water just boils in midair and evaporates before their very eyes.

Moments later, the sparks are flying in one direction as the heavy saw, with a diamond-cutter blade, screams. The heavy circular saw is heating up, steadily wearing the cutting blade down until it has to be changed. While a firefighter exchanges the expensive blade with a new one, they reapply the torch where he will attack it in another demoralizingly futile attempt.

As if the effort has angered whatever force is responsible for this unprecedented phenomenon, the floor . . . the air . . . the world seizes. The floored firefighters gather themselves. The reporter in the hall with the discreet headset camera shrieks as

Kysing Rouge, again, floats above her bed. She is recording an impossible scene through the open door. As if it is a warning of God's annoyance, a sulfurous breeze rises within the room. The overwhelming odor causes some to gag and vomit until they have to crawl into the hallway to catch their breath.

Seemingly impervious to the smell, Yara Rouge re-enters her daughter's room and reaches for the invisible barrier. During her slow approach, the others scream warnings of the extremely hot surface. Despite the wisdom of their words of warning, she touches the cool partition and wraps her arms around it. Those who are watching, gasp as she presses her body against it without a painful reaction.

With tears in her eyes, possibly of joyous hope, she whispers, "Please, baby. Please fight to come back to us, Kysing. Be at peace and heal. Do it for mommy, Kiss-kiss. Do it for us, please. We need you so much." She weeps infectious tears, looking to the sky in silent prayer.

Kysing, who has been slightly bobbing up and down, begins to descend. Slowly, her unresponsive body finally comes to rest on the hospital bed.

* * *

Ever so slightly, the blade seems to vibrate in his hands. Banja is now empowered to do this horrid thing. It is the only way to complete this task. When Banja Rouge takes deep breaths to steel his will and forge onward, the flames dance, flaring three times as the static tempest discharges into the thickening air down in this temple.

"Father, it is time for the blood fire to burn."

"Proceed, my son. I am with you always. Gather your strength for the horror that ensues. Fear it not for we are Rouge,

Banjalanah. The Great Creator, and the Harbingers of Life and Death have blessed you. Utter no sound until you reach the ends of your manhood, then let the blood fire loose upon the blood-soaked earth. Seek, my son. Seek!" They both see a small pinpoint of light in the distance.

The Customs and Border Patrol security officer, who is actively watching the monitor, sees a flash in the room where Kwaban is captive. He asks the other. "What the hell was that? Did you just see a burst of light? It was there for just a second, but I swear I saw something."

The other CBP representative looks away from his newspaper to say, "No, but it looks like he's talking to himself. I swear to God, I don't want to go back in there because that old man creeps me out."

"Tell me about it." Looking away from the monitor, the CBP rep peruses the cursory incident report. He sits up and quotes, "Says here that the old timer was peaceful, but suddenly became agitated during Flight 111 from Haiti for no apparent reason. According to a passenger, named Dr. Christian Labor, passenger 132 began to chant something as his eyes rolled back into his head. Initially, she was certain that he was having some kind of seizure. After further observations, the doctor believed 132 to have entered some form of fugue state of a supernatural nature. What? This doctor needs to lay off her stock of meds. According to the reports given by Captain Meeks, the crew members, and several passengers, Mr. Kwaban Rouge's sudden outburst seemed to coincide, exactly, with the atmospheric anomaly for which no one can adequately account because weather control does not confirm. First, it was smooth sailing, and then all hell just broke loose. Even with their reputations on the line, they are convinced that passenger 132 was somehow responsible for the sudden and inexplicably violent electrical storm. Apparently, he used some form of electrical charge to incapacitate Dr. Christian Labor, a veteran flight attendant named Alice Graham, and even the primary Federal Sky Marshal. After the bad weather passed, Captain Meeks engaged the autopilot and left the cabin because no one responded to his hails to the crew. He reported a foul odor and the floor was sopping wet, as were all of the unconscious passengers and crew members. No one was hurt. He found this old geezer soundly asleep in seat 132. Somehow, even though everyone else was soaked, his clothing was dry. There is no evidence of bleeding wounds reported on both his palms. No chemical agents or toxins were found on Mr. Rouge's person when he was thoroughly searched, but they brought the creepy old-timer here anyway."

Brenner says to Kauffman, "Jesus. What would prompt rational, professional people to make such incredible claims against one frail old man? Still, he gives me the willies. Why don't we elevate the volume and record the audio feed in interrogation room one. If he is actually talking to himself, what he says may help solve this madness. When the audio feed is raised, both men sit at attention when they hear the electrical maelstrom across the speaker.

"Seek, Banjalanah! Seek to the end your manhood! Seek!"

"What the hell is that sound, and who is he talking to?"

Kauffman detects a shimmering light on his monitor and nearly falls from his seat. "There. There it is again. Heebie-jeebies or not, I'm going in to check it out. That sound and the light have to be coming from somewhere. You coming?"

Brenner does not want to get up, but he cannot endure Kauffman standing over him with that disapproving gaze. Together, they approach the locked door. Going on the count of three, Kauffman swipes the keycard and Brenner forces the door open. They enter, quickly. Brenner is taken aback while Kauffman, instinctively, reaches for a weapon that never clears the holster.

What they see is not meant to be witnessed by their eyes. The screams of two grown veterans of their field resonate with madness. They resonate with utter pain. Their horror resonates with the terror of sudden blindness.

* * *

At the very bottom of the bone haft is a carved out slot. He uses his fingernails to dislodge a small curved piece of metal that is open on both ends, wide and small. He slips the wider end over the tip of the blade and forces it as far as it will go. Only a sixteenth of the razor sharp tip sticks out of the modified sheath.

He prays for strength. With both hands on the hilt, Banja turns the curved tip toward himself and reaches over his head. With determination, he resists the urge to flinch when the cold blade touches the cleft of his buttocks. With little effort, the blade parts his skin. As he draws it upward, the flames rise. He must not waver, slicing his own flesh in as straight a line as possible. Teeth tightly clenched, Banja Rouge quivers and quakes, but makes no sound in the midst of immense self-inflicted pain.

Sweat rolls from the dark brown skin as Banja slits it open as deeply as the shunt allows. Straining to bring it between the shoulder blades to the nape of his neck, Banja pauses to compose himself. His blood runs freely, dripping from his body. He continues now, slicing straight up his neck. Somehow, he draws the blade over and across the newly bald scalp, down the forehead to the bridge of his nose. Although Banja's skin parts like tepid butter beneath a blunted blade, he refuses to utter a sound as he splits his lips to proceed down his chin. The blade seems to be alive now, whispering his name.

As Banja Rouge carefully cuts down his throat and proceeds to perforate his heaving muscular chest, he has to adjust his grip without the blade ever losing contact with his body or all is for naught. Nearly at the end of this agonizing journey through a private hell, he splits his navel, pausing at his clean-shaven pubic area.

Kwaban urges Banja on with his palms together before him, quivering as if he wields the knife. "Seek, Banja. Seek to the end your manhood. Seek!"

When Banja forces the blade to slice down his penis, he is rocked! His teeth are clenched so tightly, they threaten to shatter in his gums.

"Seeeeeek!"

Banja makes the final cut without pausing again. When the Blade of the Red Hurricane splits through the head of his penis, he roils. Banja rages with a shrieking growl, rattling the ceiling and the seizing earth!

The world quakes as the flames and smoke of the candles slowly begin to circle overhead, coming together to form an ominous, but beautiful, living, circular vortex. With both hands raised to the side, his white eyes seek the heavens as the voices of a thousand horrors roar from his bloody lips before the thirteen-inch trench where his blood drains.

He howls as the world compresses and expands, and then his blood ignites from his buttocks to the tip of his manhood!

Banjalanah Rouge, literally, pisses fire, igniting the trench and the circle etched upon the floor all the way to the altar. With his skin still aflame, he tosses the bloody blade, which lands perfectly at the center of the altar.

Again, the ground quakes as he steps painfully forward. With his eyes affixed upon the circular braided lock of Kysing's hair, he calls her name. Then he calls her name, again.

"Kysing, come to me, baby. Come to your father, Kiss-kiss."

Chapter 18

Into!

K ysing Rouge, who knows that her vision had been impaired by her injuries and subsequent operations, thinks that she simply cannot see. However, the density of darkness encompassing her is truly the reason for her blindness within the *Reach*. The utter, complete, darkness, now surrounding three displaced souls is no longer a paradox of peaceful disquiet.

This fearful, otherworldly, place becomes more disconcerting because multiple heartbeats are nearly indistinguishable from one another. There are fiendish sounds from fleet, whispering spirits all around her. Even so, she is given to hope when a familiar voice calls from the distance.

"Dad, is that you? I came just like you said," she shouts. "Hello. Is anyone out there?" Her echoing voice seems to go on forever.

According to Kysing's left foot, she seems to be standing upon sand. Meanwhile, her right foot is in water. No matter how far she steps to the right, her left foot always comes down on sand. When she turns around, her left foot sets on gritty sand and her right foot splashes.

After running in all directions, Robbie Mecklenburg breathes hard, finally noticing that his broken leg no longer hurts when he bends over to place his sweating hands upon his knees. The entire time, he expected to run into a wall or to fall to his death, but he is surrounded by near complete nothingness. There is only the crackle and feel of gritty sand on the smooth, glasslike surface beneath his bare feet. He also hears the same disturbing heartbeats, discerning that his is the racing one when it finally slows with his breathing.

Banja's eyes are ivory, polished whites, as he sits at the head of the circle with his legs crossed beneath him.

"Can you hear me, Kysing? Kiss-kiss, can you hear me? Be not afraid because my voice is the fire!"

Stacie Mecklenburg and Robbie both hear a searing sound as distant lights on the floor quickly approach. It is fire, coming fast!

Each tries to outrun it, but it moves too quickly, meeting them at every turn until they finally stop.

Kysing sees it too, looking at her hands and flexing fingers to be sure her vision has returned. Her father's voice assures that she has nothing to fear. Following his voice, as instructed, she reaches a circular wall of flames.

Banja says, "You are anchored safely within the *Reach*, my child, and I am here with you. This is a place of many wonders. Sometimes of light. Sometimes of utter darkness."

"But it scares me, dad. What's happening to me? Why are we here?"

"The ritual to come is known as Collage au feu, the Fire-bonding, sweetheart. You have no cause for alarm because I was also reborn herein."

As Banja Rouge speaks to his daughter, four circling lights suddenly appear above in the distance, drawing both of Mayor Mecklenburg's children toward them. There are two lights for each, playfully circling one another. A low flame guides their footsteps without impeding their movement so long as they follow its path. When they reach the area where the overhead lights become one, fire encircles them. When they stop shouting for rescue from waist-high walls of flames that hold no heat, they feel compelled to sit. The dim suddenly returns, but now neither can stand. They panic and struggle. Magnetized, they can no longer move freely through the darkness beyond the rings of fire.

"Am I dead?" Kysing Rouge finally asks of her father.

"No, Kysing. You have not yet passed beyond the thinning veil. However, I have brought you here . . . I have brought you here because you are dying, my love. This is the only way to save you from sharing your brother's fate."

"Kilarin," Kysing whispers, sadly. "Why? Why did you have to leave us?" she whimpers with absolute sorrow. Kysing clutches her chest where a hole has taken her brother's place. She loved him very much, but Kilarin is gone now.

Both Mecklenburg children can hear the conversation between father and daughter, but they are deaf to one another's inquiring voices.

"Kilarin died because someone interfered with his rescue, and the same man delayed your transport to the hospital. That is why we are here, Kysing. In times of enormous despair, when the agony of total loss looms, the Great Creator has the power to grant the request for retribution or liberation. Either way, the children of the enemy are always the vessels used for this purpose. That is the only way. Your life is imperiled, hanging by a strand as thin as the spider's web. You have choices to make, even to die if you so wish. However, I am begging you to choose life because, at this very moment, your mother reels at your bedside where she feels helpless and hopelessly lost. Yara dreads that she will lose her sanity and even the will to go on living, should you pass beyond the boundary of the *Reach*. We are both afraid, so I have gone through great struggles to give you this one chance to live again."

"Mom is so broken, dad. I don't know how, but I can sense her pain. I can hear her weeping in the dark. Each burning teardrop widens the hole in my heart. What can I do, dad?" She bows her head, quietly sobbing as she repeats, "What can I do?"

"You can choose to live outside of the broken body that bore you unto this world, my sweet child. Your damaged brain causes your nervous system to wreak havoc on your struggling physique with violent, convulsive fits."

When Kysing raises her fists to the black sky to sob, "Why is this happening to me? What have I done to deserve this, when all I want is to live!" this dim world seizes, as if moaning its sadness. "What must I do? What can I do, dad?"

When the ring of fire flares upward, her father is standing behind her. "You must choose." Banja advises.

Kysing's scalp begins to tingle as static crawls along her skin. Banja's touch startles the girl, who flinches and turns to defend herself from whatever has come out of the darkness. She smiles when she sees her unscathed father, whom she hugs immediately. He holds his daughter as if it may be the last time.

He finally lets go, and turns her around. "You are still willing to fight. That is good. Sit," he says. When she does as directed, he points and says, "Let the blood fire subside so that she may choose her own fate."

The fire obeys the command. There are now three rings of fire, burning about ankle high. Where they intersect, the flame vanishes. When dim lights illuminate the people at the center of the other rings, Kysing can see them. When she recognizes the Mecklenburg siblings, Kysing Rouge remembers their father's indignation toward her.

When she was clearly hurt, with her only brother lying dead upon the ground, Mayor Mecklenburg could not have been more indifferent. Even after Stacie told her parents of Kysing's selfless act, Mayor Larkin Mecklenburg all but spat in her face. Now, understanding her father's mention of an enemy, she gets angry. Her ire seems to affect the surroundings, which rumbles with violent quakes. When her rage abates, so does the upheaval of this place.

She feels compelled to ask, "What have you done, dad? What is expected of me?" She looks over her shoulder and sees his white eyes as his right hand points toward them.

"One life lost, while the other wanes. You must take one of them as a host. You may completely cast one of them out and take his or her place. That soul and its consciousness will transfer into your dying body where it will be absorbed as the life-force used to nurture and heal your body."

"No," Kysing whispers. "No, dad. I can't do that."

"However, there is an alternative. You can share one mind and body by binding with the soul you choose until your own heals. If your badly injured body passes beyond the mortal plane, you may live out that existence, as I have since long ago when my father displayed his willingness to die to save my innocent life. Through the agony of blood and fire, as I lay upon the cusp of death's door, he offered me these very same choices. I was all that remained of our butchered family. Reeling in the wake of such pain and heartache, he begged me to live. When I chose life, he drew me into."

The world seizes again and the flames flare three times. Now Robbie and Stacie can see each other. They have heard the entire conversation, understanding that this is no mere dream after associating the voices with the faces of those concerned. They can see Kysing Rouge and her father. Although they cannot move, they are happy to be alone no longer.

Kysing looks at them both, tormented by the choice she now must make. She bows her head and sobs quietly because this goes against the natural order of things in her heart, but she cannot ignore the constant brush of her mother's overwhelming grief.

"Choose!" Banja's heavy voice demands as the flame flares, again.

Kysing Rouge continues to sob with her eyes shut. She holds herself, slowly shaking her head to display her reluctance to do so.

When the living flames flare again, the force holding Robbie and Stacie Mecklenburg releases them so they may stand if they wish.

Standing behind his distressed daughter, Banja looks at Kysing's choices with those white eyes glistening. When the dark world seizes, he says, "Seek!" placing his huge hands on Kysing's right and left temples.

Suddenly, the faces of all four turn upward to the dim, with their eyes gleaming white as a myriad of images course through their souls. They equally share all of the pain and emotions that have led to this very moment. They quiver and quake, made to witness the time of the wicked Tonton Macoute and Banja's capture in Haiti. After their minds are invaded by the horrific vision of Banja Rouge's vicious beating, and the utter pain before and during his transference as a young boy, they relive the violent rampage on the bridge that brought about Kilarin's death. No one is spared the exhaustive dance to please the Harbingers nor the cut from quiver to quill. The sting of sweat upon open wounds.

"Seek!" he commands. "Choose life, daughter. Choose life!"

Now they can all see Yara Rouge sitting before three coffins on a dreary, rainy day. Her husband is nowhere in sight. Although surrounded by friends and family, Yara is all alone. An expression of frozen pain— abject and absolute grief— replace her tears. Her hair has greyed, aging her twenty years. She is but a withering rose surrounded by well-wishers, whose words of comfort hold no solace as she wilts to her knees before the coffins.

On the other side of the graves, the Mecklenburg family stands intact beneath black umbrellas. Their backs are turned. Yara Rouge looks upon them before reaching into her black purse for a handkerchief, drawing the gun instead. She shrugs the hands of bystanders from her shoulders and struggles to her feet. She cocks the hammer while approaching the three coffins as people beg her to stop. Stacie Mecklenburg is the only one to glance back with teary eyes.

Slowly, ever so slowly, Yara Rouge looks at the Mecklenburgs and raises the trembling gun to her temple!

Kysing Rouge screams.

When Banja removes his hands, the trance ends for all. Kysing Rouge and both the mayor's children are shivering. Stacie holds herself, sweating steam while groaning with agonizing remorse.

Robbie wilts to the floor, scooting a few feet backward. Cowardice allows him to abandon his sister to her fate, but he can go no farther than the blazing flame that suddenly holds heat when he turns to run away.

Kwaban Rouge, now shackled and locked in a maximum security holding cell somewhere in Miami, says, "Choose life, granddaughter. You must choose life!"

Kysing Rouge whispers, "Grandfather, I'm so sorry for how we greeted you with such fear. I understand now."

With her head bowed and her hair encompassing her tears, she slowly raises her finger in Robbie Mecklenburg's direction.

Looking to the sister, he just tried to maroon, he cries, "No!" His desperate attempt to run away is thwarted by fire. The world seizes, again, as her finger slowly rises in his direction.

"I'm sorry," she murmurs.

Shocked and truly disheartened by a sad realization that her brother would so easily abandon her, Stacie Mecklenburg's meek, whispering voice calls, "Kysing, please don't." With frightfully gleaming, ivory eyes, both Banja and his daughter look to the right, where Stacie Mecklenburg now approaches the boundary to kneel before the flames. She taps her chest with her trembling white knuckles.

"Me. Choose me," she pleads repeatedly through tears.

Banja stares at her, asking, "You would do this . . . willingly?"

"Yes, because she is my friend. She saved my life, risking her own when I could not save myself. Because . . . I love my cowardly brother as much as she loved your brave son, I choose to take his place regardless of what happens to me. I will volunteer because . . . because I now realize just how much my father has wounded your family with his arrogant lack of compassion. My answer is yes because I also choose life."

The world seizes and the flames flare three times. As her father is about to speak, Kysing Rouge says in a voice other than her own, "There will be pain."

Banja Rouge looks to his daughter, realizing that the Harbingers are speaking through her tongue.

Stacie nods, clasping her hands between her knees. "After all I've seen and experienced, I expect nothing less."

"Your words are honorable and bravely spoken, child. Heed us carefully now. You must not fight her for control because such struggle will only seal your fate," Kysing's slow, deep voice warns.

"I promise, I will not fight her," Stacie says, comprehending that Kysing has just referred to herself in the third person. "I only ask that

you free my brother, unharmed. Please."

"He is no longer of consequence," Kysing replies.

"He is to me and my family," Stacie says.

As if Stacie's plea is ignored, Kysing says, "There will be pain. Maybe not so much as you would expect at first, but it will come. It will grow."

When Robbie Mecklenburg shouts, "No, Stacie, you can't do this!" an angry heartbeat grumbles throughout this darkened expanse, shaking and rattling the surface beneath his feet.

"Shut up, Robbie. Please, stay out of this. She needs my help, and I cannot bare it if she dies after saving me. I have to give her a chance to stay alive for all our sakes."

"There will be pain."

Stacie looks at Kysing and her father before saying, "Yes. I know. Nevertheless, where there is pain, there must also be life. Isn't that also true?"

"Wisely spoken are the words of this child, in whom we discern no deception. So much wiser than even she knows. She is a most worthy vessel. Choose!"

Kysing points her finger at Stacie Mecklenburg. In her own voice, she says, "I choose you. Let it be known that your charity will never be forgotten. You are my friend, and I am yours, Stacie Mecklenburg. Therefore, I choose not to take your life but to share your body."

Stacie nods her head as the tears flow. She stands and approaches her brother. Robbie comes when she beckons. The flames abate where they face one another. With great apprehension, he hugs Stacie, begging her not to do whatever they are proposing. Yet Stacie is resolute.

With a last ditch effort, he takes her hand and says, "I'm sorry for trying to run away and leave you. I'm sorry. Please, Stacie, let's just go!"

"I must stay, Robbie. This may be the only way that all three of us can leave here alive. Look at her father, Robert. Look at him. He has not undergone such trials just to walk away without satisfaction. Look into your heart. Even you protested being rescued first when it was clear that Kilarin Rouge was in mortal crisis and in need of more immediate help. For the first time in your life, you displayed the capacity for selfless compassion when dad's influence all but assured his son's death. That is why I am willing to share my consciousness with her. If it is not too late, her body may mend and he can probably reverse the spell. Or whatever this is. I have to give her this opportunity, but you must promise to keep quiet about it. Promise me, not a word. Promise that you will not betray us, Robert!"

When he finally agrees, she hugs him, again, thanking him for a promise that she knows he will probably break.

The Harbingers speak through Kysing, again. "Because young Rouge chooses not your destruction, there can be great pain, but you must not try to contain it. When the anguish builds within, so too shall the raging storm without. When the tempest comes, freely give all agony to the lightning. Share what you can with the light to ease your suffering."

Stacie asks, "How will we know? How will we know how to release the pain?"

"Just as the sun will surely rise, you will know. Just as darkness follows the light across the horizon, you will know."

She looks to her brother, again. "Promise me, Robbie. Say nothing please."

Robbie Mecklenburg nods, reluctantly. When she lets go and faces Kysing, Banja Rouge sweeps his left hand in a semi-circular motion and says, "Sleep."

Robby is rendered unconscious, slipping to the floor where he slumbers, quietly. The flame completely surrounds him, shielding him while widens the divide between Kysing and Stacie within a nearly perfect figure eight.

Stacie faces Banja and Kysing Rouge to ask, "If this works and she lives, will you release me? Will I go on to live a normal life, get married, and have children someday?"

The flames flare. Kysing stands next to her father, who says, "As long as nothing interrupts the force that binds you together, you will enjoy a long and prosperous life. I will share any pain that you may both experience to lessen the discomfort to come." He steps forward with his hands and eyes raised in prayer before cupping her cheeks. "I thank you for willingly making this sacrifice, which proves that you are good of heart. I now realize that my daughter would only have chosen your brother because she considers you a friend. Are you ready, young one?"

Stacie Mecklenburg bravely stands tall to say, "I'm afraid, but I think so."

"Dad, will she be safe?" Kysing asks. "Will you watch over us?"

Banja Rouge looks to both girls to state, "I will remain in contact with you once the Fire-bonding merges your consciousness. If removing your spirit from your damaged body does not help it to heal, it will be up to you to decide your own fate. All that we have discussed herein binds us to that end. We must hope that you will heal quickly because madness may ensue upon sharing one mind for too long. There will be no secrets left between you. As if there is no barrier to separate your adjoining souls, even your fears and fondest memories will pass between. However, you may speak and act as one at all times, or you can elect to exchange total control. In trance-like voices, both teenagers will say, "Yes, father."

Banja smiles and says, "It has already begun. Do not struggle for control, daughters. Share what a willing host freely offers, so that in the end, we hope to return to normalcy with both minds and souls intact. Know this, once touched by the Harbingers, nothing will truly be the same for either of you. I want to thank you both for choosing life." With the tenderness of a loving father, he hugs them, kissing each upon the forehead.

Banja fades into the darkness, backing away just as the two girls reach for each other's hands. The lights overhead pulsate, drawing their attention skyward as their heels rise inches above the surface. Soon, they leave the ground, rising upward where they hover in anxious anticipation. Slowly, they revolve in the air. The nearer they come, the closer the lights are to rejoining. A frightening searing sound ensues as their garments suddenly burn away.

"Into!" commands a voice from the surrounding darkness. Facing one another, the two souls begin to converge, sharing the same space. As their opaque bodies merge, a tingling sensation builds into the uniquely exquisite pain of complete convergence. Finally, the girls are one, screaming as serpentine flames engulf this reeling representation of their conjoined souls.

When it is over, a limp, silent form slowly descends into the arms of Banja Rouge. He looks lovingly at the sleeping girl in his arms, hoping that she is the answer.

Chapter 19

Out of Thin Air

Banja Rouge looks up mere seconds before the tactical team initiates the full breech of his home. There are crashes as battering rams give them entrance through both front and back doors. He hears frantic, muffled voices overhead. Hurried footsteps move throughout both levels, searching room to room as tactical clears the home so detectives can search for evidence of the missing children.

Nevertheless, Banja is safe below the intruders, hidden from prying eyes while praying for his daughter's swift recovery.

Because Banja Rouge anticipated the eventual invasion, he left all of the doors unlocked to avoid unnecessary damage to his home. Still, they break them down without trying the unlocked doorknobs. Moments later, they are kicking in doors upstairs. Every now and then, something crashes to the floor. The police officers seem to enjoy trashing the home.

Welling from his eyes, tears cascade down Banja's cheek. The tears do not fall for the poor treatment of mere possessions; he now imagines Yara's reaction when she walks through the once decorative French door to find her home in shambles. With Banja's ire rising, the floors begin to quake beneath the feet of the unsettled officers.

After the sudden disturbance ceases, they exit the seemingly empty home of a suspected kidnaper with Mayor Mecklenburg's secret bounty still on his head. If he harms the children, in any way, a dead Banja Rouge will earn someone double the fifty-thousand dollar bounty. The quiet reward for information leading to his capture and the recovery of the children holds a more nefarious meaning to loyal police officers privy to Mayor Mecklenburg's true intentions.

Kysing's father is holding vigil at the center of the room, sweating profusely. Even though the cauterized scar hampers the movement of his aching body, he gathers samples of fine, powdery clay from each section of the scorched circle. He covers the cupped right hand with his left and whispers a prayer. When a wisp of smoke escapes his fingers, Banja Rouge places the cupped right hand before his split, chapping lips and gently blows.

Exhausted by his strenuous toils, Banja Rouge drinks two bottles of water. Crawling onto a small cot taken from the closet, he curls into the fetal position. After covering his naked body with a clean sheet, he jerks and shivers as the high fever runs its course. He whispers, "Father," before passing into oblivion.

* * *

Again, the firefighter prepares to attack the invisible barrier around Kysing Rouge's hospital bed with the heavy circular saw now endowed by a new diamond-encrusted blade. Thus far, each attempt has ended in miserably exhaustive failure. Primed to go at it from a different spot, he starts the loud saw, bracing himself to apply pressure once he makes contact.

The rescue worker drives the saw forward, sheering three-inches from the foot of the bed. He nearly slices off the girl's toes as the saw gets away from him!

It slams into the wall, skittering across the floor before whirring to a halt. Everyone present stares in amazement, relieved that no one was standing in the path of the runaway piece of equipment that was sure to ruin someone's day. They reach out to touch what is no longer there. Even the black scorched circle on the floor surrounding the bed has disappeared.

Yara Rouge and the nurse rush from the waiting room to Kysing's bedside when called. As Yara caresses her daughter's swollen face in tears, the nurse times her heart rate in case the machinery is no longer accurate. She clips the oxygen saturation sensor back onto Kysing's left forefinger. The duty nurse calls Kysing's doctors. Soon, they begin prepping the equipment and the bed to evacuate the room should the strange barrier return.

* * *

Thirty minutes later, Santana "Sandy" Danes interviews the contractor, who is supervising the temporary hospital repairs, as WBTV shows exclusive footage of the damage. As the network broadcasts her eyeglass camera's footage of the most disturbing occurrences at the hospital, including the floating, comatose patient and the utter disarray of the ICU, Santana Danes asks, "In your own words, can you explain what happened here?"

Martin Kerns removes his white hardhat and clears his throat. "Well, members of my crew have been repairing the damage done to the light fixtures of the ICU while rescue workers, engineers and some kind of government scientists were still puzzling over a way to get to a patient when the lights began to fluctuate. They had the room of the young African American girl cordoned off, consulting with me to see if I had any ideas on how to breach an invisible barrier that defeated sledgehammers, torches, and a diamond cutter. They even tried penetrating the perimeter from the floor below to no avail. Other than using high explosive, which can only do more harm than good, nothing came to mind because I've never seen anything like it. The electricians thought that the power fluctuations were an overload of some form, immediately checking the systems for signs of broken connections that could be fire hazards. However, nothing seemed out of place. Every electricity generating conduit is running at optimum output capacity."

The WBTV reporter says, "Ah huh, that's good to know. Please go on, Mr. Kerns."

Kerns continues by saying, "At the same time, other members of my crew were engaged in repairing the inner and outer walls of the damaged hallway, while a crane attempted to reinsert the vacated windows of the repaired outer walls of the hospital rooms where the mayor's children first went missing. Understandably, my men inside were a little spooked when the lights went out. For some inexplicable reason, the crane holding the window aloft also suffered an undetermined malfunction. Then, of course, the sudden tremors came. I immediately radioed my people, ordering them to vacate the area for their own safety."

"What happened next, Mr. Kerns?" Santana Danes asks, hungrily.

"Two of my oldest and most trusted employees, honest men I have known for many years, claimed that when they ran into the hallway heading for the stairs . . . nothing. Ma'am, they told me that there were no power fluctuations and that all of the hallway lights seemed fine. The floor was not shaking at all. It was as if they had just walked into another world, somehow. A normal world. The crane restarted and the hydraulic lift worked just fine at the exact moment the lights in the rooms came back on. I've seen strange things happen on a site before, but nothing like the goings-on in and around this hospital."

"So the lights came back on and the trembling suddenly stopped. Then what happened?"

Kerns rubs his raspy chin where the expensive razor must have failed him. He sighs before saying, "Well, my employees, who asked not to be named at the moment, decided to follow my orders anyway. As they resumed heading for the stairway, they heard a moan coming from the missing girl's room and loud snoring from the missing boy's room. They didn't know whether to haul tail or hide. When the distressful moment passed, they each thought that maybe they had left wounded workers behind, so they had to go back to check. As they attest, there they were. Both of the missing children had simply reappeared out of thin air. Both were sleeping like babies, as if nothing had ever happened. It's like we are living in an episode of the Twilight Zone or something."

After thanking Mr. Kerns, Santana Danes looks into the camera to say, "Even though the police and hospital administrators are yet to comment on the uncanny reappearance of the Mecklenburg children, we have been able to ascertain that Mayor Mecklenburg's son, Robert, has been moved to another room with his broken leg still healing. Likewise, the daughter of Pauline and Mayor Larkin Mecklenburg, Stacie has also been moved into another part of the hospital. Like her older brother, she will remain under guard at the insistence of her father. A reliable source has shared a bit of very interesting information with this reporter during our coverage of this bizarre case. It would seem that the Tega Cay basketball star, Stacie Mecklenburg, known to many of her fans and opponents as the Mech, has reappeared with one distinct difference from her brother Robert.

As our viewers recall the horrendous bus accident on the new Catawba bridge just days ago, when the rampaging eighteen-wheeler left a trail of devastation in its wake, you may also remember that it was reported that the mayor's daughter was brought in with a badly broken arm and several lacerations. Miraculously, Stacie Mecklenburg's professionally documented injuries have completely healed. Because the young woman's more minor injuries disappeared as if they never existed, doctors were prompted to X-ray the broken arm in its cast to be sure that nothing had been displaced. They were stunned to find that her bones have completely healed in a matter of days. As you can tell by the many well-wishers and schoolmates gathered behind me, everyone here is relieved and happy to know that both teenagers have somehow returned unharmed. Nevertheless, what of the prime suspect in their alleged kidnaping? Because eyewitness accounts place Mr. Rouge at the scene, authorities are anxiously searching for the suspect because there are many unanswered questions surrounding the inexplicable happenings here at the Carolina Medical Network Facility."

Santana Danes glances back at the large group of people, allowing her camera operator to sweep the crowd, which expresses joy with exaggerated whoops and handclaps when they realize that the news crew is filming them.

WBTV reporter Danes assumes a more concerned demeanor when she clears her throat to say, "Although this case is far from over, someone has to ask the hard questions. When you recall my exclusive film footage of the well-known, but badly injured coma patient, Kysing "the Stinger" Rouge, floating above her hospital bed behind an impenetrable invisible barrier as this hospital experienced what many are calling supernatural or paranormal phenomena, we must all ask ourselves what really happened here? How does the apparent earthquake or tornadoes, the kidnappings, and Kysing Rouge, whose brother Kilarin Rouge died because of the tragic Catawba bridge incident, and their missing father, tie into these unprecedented events? This investigative journalist promises that you will all know the moment we do. Thank you. This is Santana Danes of WBTV News Charlotte."

* * *

Preceded by Detective Reeves, FBI Agent Michael Sievert walks into the Rouge home. Because the weather is a bit brisk, Sievert is wearing a black trench coat, which rustles when he places his gloved hands upon his hips. He looks dubiously at the complete mess and then at Detective Reeves with reproach.

"Is this how you normally handle potential crime scenes around here, Detective Reeves? I want the names of everyone involved in trashing this home."

Reeves takes exception and says, "I admit that our men were a bit passionate about finding the perp and the kidnapped children, but we breached the home from every entrance knowing that the suspect owns a registered .357 revolver. He attacked Mayor Mecklenburg in front of witnesses in the hospital's chapel and made threats toward the family before the children disappeared. So yes, there may have been a lack of decorum. There always is when one of our own is involved."

Agent Sievert looks down at the paper-strewn floor before saying, "On the way here, you asked me if I and Agent Seward were pulled off another case and rushed into this one when the FBI was asked to investigate. Why did you ask me that, Detective Reeves?"

"Well, because I came looking for you and both you and your partner were in the locker rooms in plain clothes. Most people mistook you for detectives or new transfers."

"I'll tell you why we were there, Detective Reeves. Our investigation started there, getting the feel of things by simply listening to idle chitchat in a place where police officers feel the safest. Now, while I overheard nothing unusual, my partner did. The condition of this crime scene confirms what she overheard."

"Wait one minute!" Detective Reeves interrupts with hostility. "You came here and spied on us when there was a maniac out there with two innocent kids? What the fuck kind of technique is that?"

"Take a look around, detective. Take a good look."

"Yeah, so what?"

Agent Sievert says, "This wasn't just a hot breach of a suspect's home, but it has all the earmarks and warning signs of a manhunt for blood money. As lead investigators, I assume that you and your partner were present when the perimeter breach occurred."

"Of course," Reeves says, defensively. "Where else would we be?"

"So you were present while Tactical cleared the premises, which suggests your continued presence as officers happily made a shambles of this alleged crime scene and did absolutely nothing to stop it. Perhaps you were too busy trying to collect on the fifty thousand dollar bounty

Mayor Mecklenburg recently placed on the suspect's head." Detective Reeves is obviously shocked, caught completely off-guard. Reeves' silence is a sign of perplexion; his thoughts are scattered, wide-ranging images and secret imperatives.

"That's why we often start our investigations by sitting around for ten minutes or so in the police locker rooms before visiting the scene. Police officers are supposed to be professional peacekeepers, not a wild pack of marauding mercenaries. It's a good thing they didn't find Rouge here because the abductees probably would have ended up as casualties in the line of fire. But I'm convinced even that would have been blamed on the suspect along with coinciding ballistic evidence."

"How dare you accuse us of a potential cover-up? Our men are good officers, and they would each have gladly lain down their lives to protect those kids so don't you come here accusing us of wrongdoing when we were all acting in the best interest of the victims. Instead of trying to place our heads on the chopping block for simply doing our jobs, maybe you should reprioritize your reason for being here in the first place, Agent Sievert."

"Undoubtedly, detective, anything involving the best interest of the victims would involve leaving as much of a potential crime scene as intact as humanly possible. Until further notice, you are dismissed Detective Reeves. I want that list by the end of the day, each person involved. I'd hate to have to bring your chief into this, so please honor my request. Just to get the record straight, we aren't here to bust your chops. I just don't want any of those men to have further involvement in this investigation because their motives are now corrupted and tainted by the possibility of personal gain."

At that moment, the good looking spy, but a spy nonetheless in Detective Reeves eyes, walks in with the crunch of glass beneath her feet as she snaps on her latex gloves.

"Wow," Agent Lee Anne Seward says, preceding a sigh. "The locals really did a number on this place, never mind the fact that the girl's bereft mother will come here to find that her home has been vandalized by the cops. Conveniently, that can always be blamed on the deviance of this upper-middle-class neighborhood's criminal element."

She turns on the glowering Detective Reeves across the room, who does not think she saw him because she never looked in his direction.

"Agent Seward, what have you found out?"

Agent Seward notices that the deadbolt on the front door is not sticking out. She bends over slightly to test the knob, finding that it, too, is unlocked. She glances at the detective and her partner, who knows she is about to ask, "Did anyone find a set of keys, Detective Reeves?"

"Yes, why do you ask? They're right there on the table by the door in plain sight. The suspect's work truck is in the driveway and a second car is the garage. She hasn't left the hospital since the incident with her daughter."

"With a full set of keys clearly in sight from the front door, did anyone bother to test the doorknob to see if it was locked before battering them down? No, of course not."

"No. We used standard procedures to penetrate the home. Since both vehicles were unlocked, both engines were stone cold but our forensic team vacuumed both for hair and fibers. So far nothing links either vehicle as the mode of transport."

"I believe it is more standard than procedure to quietly test the locks of a door before bashing it in. This indicates that the suspect deliberately left all the doors open to avoid having his home ransacked. Had you bothered to check, this unnecessary damage could have been avoided—no matter what you thought."

She turns to her partner and removes the file under her left arm. She opens it and reports, "They are holding the grandfather, confirming that the time of the disturbance at the hospital coincides with an event on his flight that is presently and officially categorized as "anomalous/unexplained." The aircraft remains grounded even though it passed inspection from nose to tail, but nothing mechanical explains the condition of the passengers when a Captain Alvin Meeks walked through the fuselage. The grandfather, Kwaban Rouge, was reported to be in a trancelike state while repeating incantations. No photos came with this file. The atmospheric disturbance plaguing flight 111 during the journey from Haiti to Miami bears an uncanny resemblance to the events taking place here. Ceasing seconds after the disappearances. Several witnesses aboard Flight 111, including a veteran flight attendant, two highly seasoned Federal Sky Marshals, and the doctor who attempted to examine passenger 132 have all given corresponding statements. An unspecified arm of Homeland Security is holding the old man, but from a legal standpoint, they really can't prove that he actually did any physical damage to the plane or its passengers. They may hold him for a few days, but they have to let him go, eventually. By what was alluded to, he has them spooked. His demands for release to visit his failing granddaughter cannot be ignored, not without the possibility of nasty legal repercussions. The suspect's surname went hot in the database, so I pulled the file. So far, however, his son has gone off the grid."

As Agent Seward prompts her laptop for any updates, the forgotten Detective Reeves ridicules, "Get the fuck out of here. You mean to tell me that they sent us a pair of newfangled, modern-day versions of Scully and fucking Mulder. Jesus H. Christ. You've got to be freaking kidding me."

Agent Sievert stands erect, looking away from the file to say, "Get me that list, detective. Since we are on the same side of the law, Detective Reeves, I will exercise as much patience as I can in reference to your snide, profane remarks because, like it or not, believe it or not, there are things in this world that aren't always so easily defined. You, yourself, just fell through a wall in a hospital building not yet twenty years old."

Detective Reeves glares at them, defiantly. He is less intimidated because he feels he has countermeasures for any accusations of misconduct by these high and mighty feds.

This cocky detective will take breaking, but the formidable FBI team doesn't want to waste time on the spike of enlightenment that he obviously needs driven into the heart of his inflated ego. Reeves has a reckoning with that lightning bolt, whether he knows it or not.

"Are you kidding me?"

They ignore the attempt to rile them. Agent Sieverts says, "Why don't you start with upstairs, Agent Seward. I'll search downstairs and the garage area."

Agent Seward heads for the stairs.

As the slighted detective approaches the busted door, Agent Sievert says, "Ah, Detective Reeves, a moment please."

"Yeah. Yeah. The list, I got it."

"Wait, detective. Can you join me over here, please." When Reeves joins Agent Sievert at the desk, he says, "The homeowners don't seem to be slovenly. The kitchen, despite a few broken dishes, is immaculate. Notwithstanding, the complete trashing of this scene, every home collects airborne particles even when someone dusts regularly. It just can't be helped. The slight impressions here, there, and there, lacking dust film suggest that several items have been removed from this desk. A computer, perhaps. Is it listed with any items removed from the home?"

"Let me see," Reeves says. He looks at the list while Agent Sievert takes crumpled remnants of cut out photographs from the wastebasket next to the desk. As he carefully unravels the balled up printer paper, Detective Reeves calls the evidence locker to inquire about any items not listed from the Rouge case. The negative answer makes him anxious, knowing that the truth will only serve as proof of incompetence.

Agent Sievert can tell by Reeves' expression that they have no such items listed.

Agent Sievert carefully unravels the paper cutouts and flattens them on the desk. Taking the magnifying glass from a coffee cup used for easy access to pens and pencils, he looks at the paper for anything unusual. After examining the paper, he places them in evidence bags.

Sighing with disappointment, he walks past Detective Reeves to inspect the yellow police tape crisscrossing the kitchen door. After careful examination, he asks, "Detective, do you see the crimped end of the tape here and here?"

"Yeah, so what of it?"

Agent Sievert grows weary of Detective Reeve's attitude and his ignorance. "Look at these areas. Look here and down there. The end of the tape is crinkled because it was removed. The clean areas on the wood represent areas where the tape used to be before removal. Because of the damage to the ends, they were repositioned to accommodate the shorter length. Someone has been in here."

"But that's not possible. We have a man posted on Wisteria to watch the front of the home and garage entrances, while one is posted on Bella Street to watch the rear."

Agent Seward, stalling in the middle of the staircase to listen in, says, "It means that one of your men, probably one of them on the rear watch, has broken in and removed possible evidence. On the other hand, if someone dozed off, it could mean that our person of interest has been here."

"Bullshit!" balks Detective Reeves. "If you're suggesting that one of my men was sleeping on the job or is a thief, you're seriously off your rocker, lady."

"How long are the shifts, and how many have been deployed throughout the night, Detective Reeves? Please, no more of this sanctimonious crap. Just answer the question?"

Reeves looks at his watch. "Two officers. Two eight hour shifts since we breeched. First shift change occurred at zero three hundred hours—three o'clock this morning. It's approximately ten hundred hour now, so the next shift change will take place within the hour. I've already requested that shifts be broken down to 6 hours."

"Let's go, right now." Agent Sievert demands. "Where are they positioned on Bella Street?"

"Halfway down the block in the dark green sedan, but you don't really think one of them did it, do you?" The agent's harsh glance advises caution. "Okay, but you're wasting your time because this isn't our first rodeo together. I can personally vouch for every one of these men, which I hand-picked."

They exit the home and get into Detective Reeves' car. As they turn the block, Agent Seward quickly circles in the opposite direction. As Sievert and Reeves approach the dark green sedan, Agent Seward rounds the corner and pulls up behind the yawning officer. He snaps to when they slam their doors shut.

Officer Plant notices the car pulling up his rear, hoping he is being relieved early. He lowers the heavily tinted window to say, jokingly, "What's up, Detective Reeves? Are you here to spell me? Oh wait, that would mean that you either suspect the perpetrator to return or you got yourself demoted to house-sitting division."

Detective Reeves leans on the car, perusing the back seat and floor. "Yeah, well you never can tell, Charlie."

"Who's the suit and the looker pulling up the rear?"
"Ah, Charlie, I'm gonna have to ask you a few routine questions."

"Okay. Shoot, detective."

"Has there been any activity on the premises since you took your post? Have you seen anyone approaching the house at all?"

Officer Plant stretches with an exaggerated yawn. "No. There has been nothing to report."

"Did you doze off, even for a little while? I know how these long solos can take a toll. That's why I' breaking them down to six."

"Negative. You know I never sleep on the clock and that is why you assign me to these home sitting jobs. What's going on? Why am I getting the third-degree, Reeves?"

"It's probably nothing, but I'm gonna have to have to ask you to pop the trunk, Charlie." "What?"

"You heard me. Don't give me any grief about it, just do as I ask. Please, just open the trunk right now."

In protest, Officer Plant cusses under his breath and mumbles his discontent as he exits the car with the keys. "Glove box button doesn't work. Gotta use the keys. I want you people to know that I'm beginning to feel unloved here, and I take great offense. Whatever this asshole is looking for in my trunk, you won't find." He fumbles with the keys, dropping them; a possible sign of nervousness.

He pops the trunk where they find nothing out of place. Detective Reeves asks Agent Sievert, "There, are you fucking happy now? I don't appreciate you accusing one of my assignees of being a thief. And furthermore, you dick...."

Agent Seward interrupts, "Furthermore, Detective Reeves, I think I can speak for my partner when I say—shut the fuck up—you slouch. Watch and learn!"

Officer Plant defends his fellow law enforcement officer by saying, "Hey, cunt, just who the fuck are you to talk to us like you just scraped us off the bottom of your cutesy little shoes? Bitch you must not know who the fuck you are...."

Agent Sievert, the strong silent type, is no longer silent. He grabs Officer Plant by the throat, cutting off his air. He slams his back against the car before Detective Reeves can protest.

"You see it?" Agent Sievert asks her without taking his eyes from Officer Plant.

She smiles and says, "Yeah, I got it. The good officer here just couldn't resist looking at his stash when he pretended to drop the keys. Normally, a bag of garbage behind a leafless tree isn't so conspicuous. Look around you and tell me what you see, Detective Reeves. This seems to be a nice neighborhood, no trash in sight. Add two brand new bags behind a naked tree in a nice upper-middle-class neighborhood and bingo! You either have two dollars' worth of aluminum cans that fell off the back of someone's truck, a bundle of tortured dead animals, or booty."

"What the hell are you two doing?" shouts Detective Reeves. "Let him go right now!"

Officer Plant goes for his weapon, but Agent Sievert clamps down on his throat and locks his hand in place on the gun while strapped in its holster.

Agent Seward emerges from the shrubbery with a pair of black, heavy-duty garbage bags. She carefully hoists them onto the closed trunk one at a time.

With her gloved hand, she carefully opens one bag and sniffs. "Doesn't smell like dead kittens. No rancid beer or molded soft drink cans rattling about."

She proceeds to remove the twenty-inch Hewlett Packard touch screen. At this point, Officer Charlie Plant stops struggling.

Agent Sievert yanks Officer Plant's hand from the weapon, which he removes from the holster himself. Holding it by the barrel, he jams it into the chest of the extremely embarrassed detective Reeves.

He looks Reeves in the eyes with disdain and growls, "Now you deal with this, asshole!" He releases the officer and joins his partner to remove the desktop's CPU and matching laptops from the other bag.

Detective Reeves takes hold of his handcuffs and forces the thief to face the car with his hands behind his back. "Officer Plant, you are under arrest for allegedly removing personal items from the residence of a suspect that possibly contain evidence vital to this kidnaping investigation. You have the right to remain silent. Anything that you say can and will be used against you in a court of law. If you cannot afford legal counsel, a union representative will provide you one. Do you understand these rights?"

Officer Plant begs, "Please don't do this to me, Detective Reeves. Please think about my family."

Detective Reeves looks at Agents Sievert and Seward, dropping his eyes in shame. "I'm sorry, Charlie, but there is nothing I can do for you at this point. As far as your family goes, you should have been thinking about them before you decided to steal from an alleged crime scene."

"It's just a bunch of fucking junk, for Christ sake. I mean, what's the harm if you just put it all back? Please, just put it all back before I lose my pension."

Agent Seward looks at the setup and replies, "This is high-end stuff. I know because I have the same system at home for personal use. This desktop's combination CPU and monitor are worth a couple of grand by themselves. This laptop is brand new and worth nearly three-thousand dollars. I'd say it's probably less than a year old. The other one is comparable. Only thing missing is the printer. I suspect it's a wireless printer, copier, fax machine and scanner combination. A bit bulky for a fast exit. Officer Plant, a very pretty penny went into these electronics, but this one would have landed you, or anyone you sold it to, in jail because it is Wells Fargo property. The wife, whom I just interviewed, is a mortgage loan officer for that bank. They would track you down the minute you turned it on without their revolving passkey. You probably didn't have time to actually take a good look at it. In fact, each one of these devices are equipped with GPS anti-theft applications. At a minimum, for any one of these objects, you're looking at grand larceny."

"Christ!" Officer Plant cries. "Oh Christ!"

"Let's retrieve the printer from the house and cart all of this stuff back. Tech-support should crack the personal passwords in minutes. I found two glossy photocopy cutouts, which may be physical evidence tying Rouge to the kidnapping. A part of one cutout looks like the material used on hospital gowns. It's a longshot, but still a possibility. According to the list, one cell phone was recovered from the home."

"Are you telling me you already knew what was entered into evidence, but still had me call in to ask?"

Agent Sievert replies, "I need to know which side you are on. Besides, this is a very teachable moment, Detective Reeves. Did you learn anything so far?"

Detective Reeves approaches and clears his throat. He says, "We don't really know if there is anything here that will impact this investigation. Since this case was handed over to you feds, no one cracked the phone's password to see what was in it. Even if there is something, the kids are safe. I guess what I mean to say is ... what I mean to ask is ... is any of this worth ruining his entire career? Officer Plant is a god-fearing man, a faithful husband, and a great father to his kids. He just had a momentary lapse in judgment."

"Your devout Christian, your faithful husband, who is such a great father to his children, is a stinking thief and a liar who compromises the integrity of crime scenes by pillaging on his watch. He is exactly the type of cop that gives law enforcement a bad name. This kind of misconduct will serve to cast doubt on every case he's ever worked for you." She approaches the apologetic Officer Plant, who is whimpering like a baby. Because Agent Seward is taller than he is, she lifts him off the ground when she plants a knee squarely in his balls. Officer Plant curls up on the ground at her feet coughing and puking his guts out when she says, "Who's the cunt now, bitch? I hate that fucking word, and I hate it even more when it's being used in reference to me by a sniveling, short-stroking prick like you."

She grabs a bag of the stolen electrical equipment. Agent Sievert takes the other. He looks at Detective Reeves and says, "He tried to draw down on me. I could have blown his brains out, remember that. Do what you like with him, Detective Reeves.

Vote your own conscience on this jerk. After all, assholes always seem to protect their own pieces of shit wherever we go. Let's consider a vicious knee to the balls a reward for being naughty and disrespectful."

They return to the house, retrieving the wireless printer and any USB or HDMI cords Officer Plant may have left behind in haste. When thieves are in a hurry, they usually leave cords and remotes to electronic equipment behind.

Before leaving, the agents do a quick onceover of the home. Agent Seward searches upstairs, while Agent Sievert scans downstairs with those discerning eyes. The photos and awards tell a story of a once happy, industrious family. Only the disarray and broken possessions speak of any recent upheavals.

Agent Sievert walks into the washroom just off the hallway to the garage. Here, he opens the dryer and washing machine. Both are empty. He now inspects the shelves of jarred food, flinching at the sight of the cow's tongue in vinegar. As he reaches for further a closer look, he hears and feels a low, almost guttural sound that reminds him of the tremors from his youth in Sacramento, California. He experiences an intense, gnawing feeling of eyes watching him. It builds like the serpentine coils of a rattler about to strike. He feels slightly nauseous. The agent looks about, suddenly drawing his weapon when he hears granular shards of glass beneath his partner's feet!

Agent Sievert takes a deep breath and quickly apologizes, though both agents are disturbed by the fact that he did not sense Agent Seward's approach. They leave because of the remote chance that Banja Rouge may be the area.

Down below, the stable vortex slowly swirls. There are clear connections to this world and the souls touched by it. Behind the stare of those white eyes, he listens to the voices that advise, "You are cleansed, but weak, Banjalanah Rouge. You must eat of nature or eat of the flesh, but you must feed soon."

Chapter 20

A Stranger Calls

Stacie Mecklenburg's doctor releases her. Although greatly concerned, there is no viable excuse to keep her in the hospital because her wounds have up and disappeared. His desire to study her is met with staunch resistance.

The driver resists forcing his way through a throng of muffled questions and intense lights. The strangers will receive no satisfaction as police officers, serving as barriers, warn that this is private property. The newshounds, these invaders of privacy, remind Stacie of a documentary she once saw of an enormous school of circling hammerhead sharks. From the family Sphyrnidae, they slowly circled lower and lower into a deep oceanic abyss.

Since the dreamlike transformation, she sees things much differently. At times, it is like moving in digital fast forward or reverse.

Every sound, every sensation seems to have developed its own form of reverberation. Even taste and the textures of food have developed their own kinds of echo.

Paula Mecklenburg's voice has become one of those echoes. She now stands in the doorway with the housekeeper, who has rushed to the door to greet them both. The mother's smile fades as she realizes that her daughter is not standing next to her while Neara Jones stretches her arms wide to embrace the young woman she practically raised.

Time shifts backward amidst the clamoring voices and intrusive flashing lights. The driver slowly works his way through the crowd of reporters as Paula Mecklenburg says, "Just look at them. These people are like hungry animals, chomping at the bit for some bone to chew on. Your father thinks we may have to get a bigger house, live completely fenced off from these vultures. But don't you worry about that, sweetheart. You don't ever have to talk to anyone unless you choose to. Stace? Sweetheart, what's the matter?"

For a few seconds, there is a disturbing expression on her daughter's face. It is not quite a smile, not quite a grimace. Standing before the threshold of an open door and Neara's open arms, as if both are closed, Stacie presses the doorbell. Like an unexpected visitor, Stacie Mecklenburg smiles as if hearing that pristine chime for the very first time in her life.

"Stacie? What's the matter, sweetheart?" her mother asks. She looks at her daughter's expression, slowly raising her eyes to the cameras at the perimeter. Stacie had the same look on her face when they turned onto the property, a quiet awe and withdrawn fear.

Before Paula Mecklenburg utters another word, Neara Jones steps out and drags Stacie in by the hands. With tears in her smiling eyes, she says, "Girl, come on in here, ringing that doorbell like some lost stranger. You still got jokes. Lord only knows, it is so good to see you in one piece, child." She hugs Stacie with a fleeting sense of relief.

While Neara Jones is too close to see it, Paula Mecklenburg notices the genuine smile on her daughter's face. With closed eyes, she hugs the warm and loving Black woman. The sight of their fond closeness once bothered Pauline Mecklenburg.

There was once a fierce envy deep in her heart, but dealing with it openly helped her to become a better mother to her daughter and a better employer of the woman who taught her to embrace those who embrace her children without hidden agendas. The reckoning between them came when Neara Jones threatened to quit because a few unnecessarily nasty incidents that Paula Mecklenburg instigated when the She-Alpha asserted herself with the wrong person at the wrong time.

The housekeeper recognized her jealousy and called her employer on it, raking the uppity mayor over the coals while she was at it. She did not back down when insulted or felt mistreated, boldly declaring that they needed her much more than she needed them.

As far as Mayor Mecklenburg was concerned, Neara's words were, "You may think it, but you had better never say it to my face. Your eyes always tell me that you are just one blinking squint away from using the word nigger!"

Ten years have passed since that ugly business, when young Stacie wrapped her legs around Neara Jones' legs and begged her not to go. Of course, the seven-year-old girl's distress added to the guilt and tears after causing the nasty spill that fractured Neara's wrist. From the floor of their previous home, with both Stacie and Robbie weeping at her side, Neara tearfully reminded Paula that they used to clean homes and toilets together. Neara Jones reminded the woman of the house where she had come from, and how she took Pauline Caster under her wing to teach her the ropes. Neara Jones' final words on the matter before granting her Christianly forgiveness were, "It often takes a village to raise a child, Pauline, but only one person to mess them up for life. If you think that loving your children as if they are my own is messing them up, then I will never darken your doorstep again. I swear this by God Almighty, himself."

However used to seeing their warm greetings since that dark day, Paula soon realizes that this is something different when Stacie opens her eyes and backs away. She is no longer smiling. There is a chilling moment when Stacie recedes and says, "You're not my mom."

"I know, but she is," Neara says, jokingly, as if she doesn't notice the slight disconnect. "You still have that twisted sense of humor."

"Neara, hi, how are you?" Stacie says, seeing her at this very moment for the first time since the accident. She hugs the old woman, again.

Now she hugs her mom. "Mother, I'm so glad to be home." She looks at the ceiling, the walls, and the intricate pattern of the flooring. She recalls a kind of swirling, but easy-going vertigo when she stares down at the floor from the second floor.

Paula hugs her back, smiling while convincing herself that the stress of the past few days has affected her own imagination. She is content to attribute Stacie's quiet disconnection to the drugs in her system and recent traumatic events. If it were anything more, she would have to pop a pill herself.

* * *

With folder in hand, Agent Sievert enters room 414 with Mayor Mecklenburg. Robby raises his bed, sitting up to endure the questioning.

Larkin Mecklenburg invites the Federal Investigator to sit closer to the boy's bed. He says, "Robbie, this is FBI Agent Sievert. He is here to ask you some questions regarding the abductions. Son, you have nothing to fear. You're not in any kind of trouble, but we need you to answer his questions as best you can. Okay, son?" "Yes, dad," Robbie complies, taking a hard swallow.

The investigator does not reach out to shake Robbie's hand during the introduction. He only smiles while evaluating the young man's demeanor, which begins from the outset and never really ends during such interviews.

Sievert opens the file and peruses some minor details, discretely noticing the young man's growing uneasiness with every turn of the pages. "Robert, you can relax. Relax. Are you aware of the details surrounding what happened here?"

"Yes. My parents told me."

"No, maybe you didn't understand my question," Agent Sievert calmly plies. "What I want from you, Robert, isn't what others have told you or advised you to say. What I need from you is the most accurate accounting you can give me from your very own point of view and experiences before, during, and after you were held in captivity. Do you understand?"

"Yes, sir. I think so."

"Mayor Mecklenburg, can you assist me by dimming most of the lights please?" As the anxious father hurries to comply, Agent Sievert adds. "I usually ask that I be left alone with the victims, but I will allow you to stay as long as you agree to say nothing. A parent's presence usually produces one of two results during such proceedings. Your being here can give the young man a sense of security so he feels free to discuss this matter without fear or it can hinder him from expressing vital information, as with the case of a young rape victim sitting before her parents. This kind of psycho-regressive interview can have delicate, but profoundly important effects on any investigation. Is that understood, sir?"

Mayor Mecklenburg nods his head and moves to a more distant seat. "Good. Robert. Robbie, may I call you Robbie?" The kid nods the okay.

"Robbie, I would like you to listen to my voice and simply relax. I need to hear your point of view from the very beginning. No detail is too small or unimportant. Just relax, son. Close your eyes. Yes. That's it. Now, I would like you to describe what you can remember from whatever point you see as the beginning of this incident. I'm interested in your beginning, wherever and whenever you became a part of this story even if you begin with what you had for breakfast or dinner." The kid smiles. "Tell me. Who or what did you feel, hear, or see?"

Robbie says, "Okay." He opens his eyes, glancing at his father before closing them again.

Sievert watches his pulsing jugular and flexing neck tendons, already detecting the boy's reluctance to disclose the full story before he even begins. The investigator is almost certain it is only partially due to the father's presence. The agent sits quietly, giving Robbie a chance to gather his thoughts before speaking.

"Breathe deeply, in and out. Relax. In and out. In and out. That's good."

"I was hanging from the bridge...." he says before clearing his throat to begin again. "I was sleeping in my other hospital room, maybe dreaming. I heard noises, voices. I think it was my dad and a woman screaming. I was cold when I woke up with grains of sand stinging my skin and eyes. Sand was on my bed. There was a breeze—no—there was a strong, angry wind. It was blowing like crazy, as if I was outside. I tried to get up, but something seemed to be weighing me down. I heard this sort of creepy crackling, grating sound, as if wood was splintering. Then, for a little while at least, I seemed weightless. There was just nothing. Soon I could hear voices and heartbeats in the darkness, but I didn't feel as if I were in any danger until. . . ."

Robbie goes silent at this point. Sievert sees it as a conscious shutdown, something he can normally work through without difficulty.

However, he has doubt in this case.

"Robbie, are you okay, son?" asks his father.

Sievert shakes his head in frustration. With two fingers over his lips, Agent Sievert quietly shushes the mayor and suggests the door with the same. Mayor Mecklenburg, however, refuses to go. This is actually fine with Sievert, since he senses that the kid is going to hold back no matter what. Starting with the bridge and readjusting his point of entry is certainly evidence of that, but he may yet garner something of use.

"I'm surrounded by total darkness when I wake on a mound of beach sand. I can still almost smell the salt or something else."

"Did you hear the sound of sea birds, gulls, or waves perhaps, Robbie?" asks Sievert.

"No. We were nowhere near the ocean or the river, just in this huge black place with a thin layer of sand covering the smooth floor that felt like glass. The sand squeaked under my feet as I stood. I could hear voices and heartbeats all around, so I yelled for help. I ran in all directions, but I never hit a wall or stumbled across anything on the floor. It seemed as if this place just went on forever. When I finally stopped to catch my breath that is when I realized that my leg didn't hurt anymore. There was no cast on it, no pain at all. No stitches anywhere."

Agent Sievert's calculating mind prompts a glance at the cast on the boy's leg, considering the possible use of hallucinogenic drugs to subdue the captives. He looks at the stitched and bandaged cut on Robbie's ankle below the cast. There were no unnaturally occurring chemical compounds found in the toxicology reports of either victim. Still, his sister reemerged unscathed, completely healed of wounds that were previously documented and x-rayed. What could catalyze such a recovery? What makes them different in this regard? What makes them different?

Mayor Mecklenburg interjects, "Drugs. He must have used drugs on them. Robbie, you couldn't have been running, your leg is broken. You were dreaming, son."

Taking offense, Robbie says, "I was wide awake, dad. This was no dream. It couldn't have been."

At this point, Agent Sievert runs his fingers through his sandy brown hair. He faces the father, leaving his seat to whisper, "One more word from you, mayor, and I will walk out. Understood? I will not ask you again because any interruption in Robbie's stream of thought may cause him to omit important details that could lead to solving this case. Now, is that what you really want? He already has his guard up. Your interference has probably compromised this interview already. That's all it takes. Maybe he was dreaming or given some psychotropic drug that metabolizes and dissipates quickly, but he wasn't dreaming in his hospital bed in a room where the window was ripped away. Please remember that he reappeared much the same as he disappeared. Meanwhile, your daughter was returned without lacerations, contusions, or broken bones. That, subsequently, remains a mystery in itself."

Mayor Mecklenburg's bruised pride shows on his face, but Agent Sievert's serious stare forces him to acquiesce.

"I know it makes no sense," Robbie says. "But I swear it's true. I was not dreaming. I wasn't drugged, but it was like being trapped in a place unlike anywhere else on earth." Both men return to their seats.

"That's okay, Robbie. Please continue. You caught your breath and then what?"

"Fire," he says. "Living fire spoke to me. To us."

Agent Sievert sits at attention now. "You referenced 'we' or 'us' for the second time. What do you mean by that?"

"The circling lights and fire brought us together, my sister and me. I couldn't even see her at first, not until he told the fire to subside. Stacie was standing in water—I heard it with her footsteps. But the sand on my side of the flames was still dry. Completely separated and dry."

"Go on, Robbie. I'm listening."

"There were creatures, some moving almost too fast to see or sense. His voice was the fire, directing us to the. . . ." The boy recalls his fear and the shame he felt at trying to leave his sister at the mercy of an angry man, who wanted vengeance. He would have left her there, alone, if he could. Instead, Stacie saved him from whatever fate she is now enduring. Tears of shame fall from his shut eyes.

Robbie grips the bedsheet with white knuckles. His heartbeat elevates.

"Do you know why you are still injured while your sister is completely healed? What about the man who took you, Robbie? Was he there? Can you remember him? Was he alone in your abduction or was there anyone else involved?"

"She didn't take us from this hospital, but she was there when the fire brought us to them both. His eyes were gleaming—white—like pearls."

"Who was there?"

Robbie licks his dry lips and swallows hard. "His daughter, the Stinger. Kysing Rouge. Her father wanted revenge for his son's death and his daughter's medical condition. His eyes were . . . god!"

"What about his eyes, Robert?" Sievert says as he approaches the bed.

"He had no pupils. Neither did the Stinger. I was so afraid. I tried to run, but the flames kept me from escaping no matter which direction I tried. It would not allow me to run away. Stacie traded herself for me. I begged her not to do it. I begged her to run!"

"What about your sister? What did he do to her, Robbie?" Sievert asks, watching the young boy clamp down on the sheets and mattress. His thoughts and allegiance are waging war.

"No, I can't!"

At the height of Robert's distress, when he would go no further, Agent Sievert takes the boy's hand and tightens his grip as if feeling for a pulse. "Tell me everything."

Darkness surrounds him. Swift, screeching banshees are whisking by on all sides. When Sievert opens his eyes, some horned creature stares back at him, floating effortlessly in the air.

The bioluminescence of its eyes is all that is needed to cast an eerie light about this place.

This dragon like serpent's massive tail and body seem to swim in the motionless air, slightly bobbing up and down. Without its lips ever moving, Sievert feels and smells the hot, sulfurous breath upon his skin. He hears its gruffly whispered words of warning. "You are one of the touched, a seer of things most men fear as madness. Do not transgress upon this realm, again, for all you will invite here is madness and, most certainly, death!"

The hairs on the nape of Agent Sievert's neck stand on end. His skin prickles. The second Harbinger to this realm snorts behind Sievert, who turns to discover that this one has a crown of circling black wraiths. Its pupils are reddish and black, different from the yellowish-green of the other. He is nearly overwhelmed by the seething anger from this one. Its contempt washes over the man's entire body.

The one with the circling shadows squints harshly when it speaks, "You have been warned. Do not intrude upon this realm again, for all other interlopers only invite destruction. What he has done here is not to be undone until it is time. You have been warned!" It opens its gaping mouthful of daggers, lunging.

Agent Sievert wakes on the floor in a panic. The mayor is patting his hands, shouting his name. Robbie Mecklenburg is watching from his bed with no particular surprise in his eyes. He seems unconcerned, a bit too detached for the moment at hand. When Robbie quietly turns away, he never realizes that he is holding the call button.

When a nurse at the desk opens the intercom, Mayor Mecklenburg shouts, "We need help in here!"

"Someone will be there shortly," reassures the nurse

When someone rushes in, Mayor Mecklenburg explains, "All of a sudden he began to tremble. It was as if he had somehow touched a livewire. I swear it. He went to his knees and began to convulse like an epileptic. Agent Sievert, are you okay?"

The nurse rushes out to find a doctor for the disoriented agent, who is still lying on the floor, trying to regain his bearings. The skin prickles over his entire body, a tingling madness that yet grows in intensity. He writhes upon the floor, scratching and clawing at himself. Being engulfed by a cloud of angry wasps seems the only comparison for Agent Sievert.

* * *

Agent Seward carefully places the fragile evidence in a box inside her trunk. She then hurries into the hospital to check on her partner. He sits up with his legs hanging off the bed in the trauma unit. A technician removes the sticky leads and wires while he patiently waits for her to finish.

As the technician leaves, Agent Seward enters, rushing to his side. She can hardly contain her emotions, but he stops her embrace. He keeps her at bay, not only for professional appearances, but also as a means of precaution.

"Please, you shouldn't touch me right now," Agent Sievert warns.

Feeling somewhat slighted, Agent Seward looks to the floor and swipes a wad of hair behind her right ear.

"Are you okay, Michael? Is there anything I can do?"

He recognizes her anxieties, so he explains, "It's not what you think. Look at me. It's not what you think. I just don't feel it's safe yet. I'll try to explain it when you get me the hell out of here."

As he buttons his shirt, Agent Seward asks, "I was told you collapsed and had some kind of seizure. What the hell is going on? Say something."

"Not here, okay. Please, just not right now."

She asks, "Well, the doctor says you can go. Your vitals may have returned to normal, but she would like more time to determine the cause of the episode. However, you are refusing to stay overnight. Have you eaten anything since breakfast?"

"No I haven't, actually," Sievert replies. "It's strange. I'm absolutely starving, but I don't want anything to eat. All I want to do is go back to the hotel and shower in some really cold water. Maybe I'll take a short nap afterward."

"Okay, partner. Why don't I drop you off at the hotel so you can pull it together? You shower and take a nap. Meanwhile, I'll pick up a couple of fat burgers and beer battered mushrooms from a place called McCall's Bar and Grille that I mentioned before. We can eat dinner before going over the evidence and events of the day for our report. Are you feeling up to it?"

"Yes. Yeah, that sounds like a plan." Sievert says as he slips on his shoes and blazer at the same time.

As soon as they leave the hospital, their section chief, Assistant Director Majors, calls. Agent Sievert places the phone on speaker between them.

"Is Agent Seward with you Agent Sievert?"

"I'm right here, sir," she answers. "What can we do for you?"

Their superior warns, "In the interest of cooperation, you should know that I have Tega Cay's Chief of Police John Cramer on the line, so please be mindful of your language agents."

"Not a problem, sir."

"Has there been any progress in breaking this case, agents?"

"We are still gathering evidence, sir. We hit some snags, to say the least," informs Agent Sievert.

Agent Lee Anne Seward interjects, "Not only that." She glances, abruptly, at her partner and resets her statement by saying, "Now that we have time, we will examine the evidence we have collected for a formal report by noon tomorrow, Assistant Director Majors." The polished, calculating voice of an older southern gentleman comes across the speaker. From the outset of clearing his throat, it is obvious that he wants to discuss delicate matters.

"Agents Seward and Sievert, this is Chief John Cramer here. I was told that Agent Sievert collapsed during an interview of the Mecklenburg boy. Is there any truth to this? Are you fit to continue this investigation?"

Agent Sievert sighs before admitting, "Yes, sir. That is correct, but I'm perfectly fine now. There is no need for concern about my ability to perform my duties, Chief Cramer."

"Yes, your superior assures me of the same. I'm wondering if your continued investigation into the matter is still warranted, since the children have been returned safely. Clearly, our suspect has gone to ground after having a change of heart, which is indicated by the return of abductees unharmed. I believe that Mr. Rouge will surface, eventually. Both the local and federal branches of law enforcement are monitoring for any financial activities from the suspect, whom I feel must come up for air sooner than later. Technically, is this still considered an active case of abduction?"

"Are we being recalled, Assistant Director Majors? Or is this really about ruffling a few feathers in a town where blatant investigative mistakes have surfaced, and inexplicably extraordinary phenomena have been publically recorded? Is this simply about protecting the tarnishing reputation of the thin blue line, sir?"

Again, Chief Cramer clears his throat. "Son, maybe the stress of this case is getting to you."

Agent Seward cuts him off by saying, "Assistant Director Majors, sir. It's painfully clear where this little tete-a-tete is headed, but we've been met with nothing but incompetence since we arrived to assume the lead in this case, which I remind you all is hardly the average situation because there are aspects surrounding this investigation that no one can explain."

Chief Cramer assumes a condescending attitude, trying to disguise it with some old fashioned southern charm that both Agent Seward's colleagues know to be a wrong turn with the Brooklyn bred investigator.

"Well, Assistant Director Majors, I can see that your little filly here is quite the passionate one. I declare."

As can be expected, his words only serve to further incense Agent Seward, but she is reigned in before she can let loose her utter disdain at being referred to as a young horse. Agent Sievert raises a hand to abate the ensuing verbal assault before she is able to launch.

Likewise, though many miles away, Assistant Director Majors intervenes by saying, "I must respectfully inform Chief Cramer that the Bureau frowns on such sexist references to both our seasoned or novice female agents. As far as this case goes, I will now ask Agent Sievert for his opinion. Agent, what is you cursory assessment?"

Agent Sievert answers, "Frankly, sir, my gut tells me that there is definitely more than meets the eye with this particular case. My own experience today is proof of that. However, I'm not willing to discuss it openly at this point. If you can give us a little more time, I believe we may be able to shed some light on things. Respectfully, I must admit that I do not agree with Chief Cramer's belief that the suspect has left the area. He is here, somewhere, watching us somehow. We intend to find this man before any harm comes to him."

"If I may," Agent Seward says, "Good family men don't usually go from getting a promotion while both his kids are primed for early graduation, with full-athletic scholarships, to kidnapping without an extreme stressor. Hence, the two victims the suspect allegedly chose to abduct is no accident but a pointed and calculated statement. Taking this brother and sister was no random act, but there, again, we come back to the true reason for this conference call. Mayor Mecklenburg used the influence of his position in his town to save his son, while that of the suspect barely clung to life on the bridge's support cable. The same support cable. The suspect's son, Kilarin Rouge, died before his parents' eyes, the terrified onlookers on either riverbank, and those watching the breaking news report. Meanwhile, inside of the dangling bus, the twin sister, who was obviously badly hurt, took it upon herself to rescue the mayor's daughter at her own peril. From what we've ascertained by interviewing the grieving mother of a very heroic young lady, and various witnesses, the mayor's actions even interfered with Kysing Rouge's transport to the hospital. The severity of her head injury may have gone unattended because of it. Isn't that really what this call is about, Chief Cramer? Let alone the miscreant behavior of your officers, many of which are really out to collect Mayor Mecklenburg's blood money. Yes, gentlemen, I fucking said it instead of pussyfooting around the bullshit."

In his dimly lit office, Chief Cramer and Mayor Mecklenburg suddenly flush, wincing in silence because this uppity bitch just hit the proverbial nail on the head. She killed the elephant in the room with a blind shot.

"Agent Seward, I would like to caution you at this time. Please contain your fervor. Try to remember that we are all on the same side and everyone involved would like to see a quick and decisive conclusion to this case."

Agent Sievert remains silent but supportive, which Agent Seward already knows. Agent Sievert merely looks at her with that "calm down" expression on his face, so she yields in light of her superior's words of warning.

Assistant Director Majors says, "Now, I believe a simple apology will suffice here. We all make mistakes from time to time."

When Agent Seward bites her lips and says, "I apologize for my overzealous outburst, sirs," she grimaces, brimming with contempt.

"Well, no harm done, Agent Seward. Your apology is accepted," Chief Cramer replies.

Majors says, "Thank you, Agent Seward. However, I wasn't talking to you."

"What?" Chief Cramer blurts out. "You mean you expect me. . . ."

"You heard me, Chief Cramer. I demand that you extend the utmost courtesy to my investigators, in which I have the greatest respect and confidence. I suspect that Mayor Mecklenburg is standing right next to you so hear me loudly and clearly, gentlemen, because I will not say this again. You asked for our help in this matter because, frankly, it is over your heads. I assigned this particular team because they have uncanny abilities that bring special insights to bear in bizarre cases, so I will give them a few more days to gather as much pertinent information as they can. Now that I am aware of the alleged bounty that the good mayor has foolishly placed on the suspect's head, and it has already disrupted our investigative protocols. I'm equally aware of the distasteful facts surrounding one of your own personnel's malfeasances unbecoming an officer of the law. Given the circumstances, I realize how these issues may negatively reflect upon public opinions for Mayor Mecklenburg, whose own brother caused the death of several of your citizens and serious injuries to many more. There has been unprecedented recklessness in the handling of this case, with the future of a veteran officer and comrade hanging in the balance. You simply wish to sweep it all under the rug now that the victims have resurfaced, but I trust the gut instincts of my agents over the good old boy system of doing things. I caution you both, since you haven't denied the mayor's presence, do not impede my agents any further. Do not interfere or you may both find yourselves on the hot seat. In the end, I'm certain that my agents can benefit from your assistance in clearing up the mysteries of this matter as long as we are all working together. Otherwise, stop mucking about! They have inimitable skillsets, which can only be beneficial in resolving this matter. If there is any chance to solve this case, they are it. Have I made myself abundantly clear Chief Cramer? Mayor Mecklenburg called the governor for a favor when he was under attack and at his wit's end. She, in turn, called us. We answered, posthaste. Not with a pair of fumble rookies, but with the best of the best. Now kindly allow us to do our freaking jobs."

The agents smile at one another as they turn into the hotel's parking lot. Seward displays a full-fledged grin when the police chief clears his throat in preparation to eat crow, which he accomplishes with grace and a renewed sense of Southern charm. She accepts without further bristling.

Once satisfied, Assistant Director Majors adds, "Thank you, Chief Cramer. As far as the recovered items and the disposition of Officer Plant goes, you can feel free to vote your own conscience. It is your house and your mess to clean up. We will not enter this issue into any official reports because we recovered evidence that possibly links Rouge to the case. We have enough to do without weighing in on the inner workings of your precinct as long as they do not become a hindrance to this federal investigation. Any other course of action will only serve to drag you all under a microscope, probing into the validity of your arrest records, evidentiary accountability, and so forth. That is a long, muddy, downhill rut, no one wants to travel. Thank you and good evening, gentlemen."

Agent Sievert remains quiet when the connection with the police chief is severed. His partner says, "Thank you, sir. I appreciate you having our back."

"Don't get too cocky, Agent Seward. I need you to control your temper and focus on the case. Understood? I believe that you are right about the bounty on the suspect's head, which makes for a dangerous scenario when it comes to working with the locals. I would like an updated progress report as soon as possible. You should know that you might be there until it is necessary to pull you out. You should also know that I'm looking into the whereabouts of the grandfather, but I'm met with considerable resistance. I've confirmed the exactitude of the events at the hospital and flight 111. I cannot see the timing as strictly coincidental. In fact, I got a friendly shot across my bow in that regard. But I will keep digging."

Agent Sievert asks, "What's going on, sir?"

"Certain occurrences coinciding with your provisional reports have come into play. Special Departments of Homeland Security are taking an interest. I'm told that video footage of the occurrences on the grandfather's flight is causing quite the stir, clamoring of next level paranormal events and the like. Now, tell me what happened to you at the hospital, Agent Sievert."

"I was using a regressive interviewing technique with the Mecklenburg boy, enduring constant interference by the father. However, I continued to guide the victim through his recollections, but it was becoming more difficult. When I realized that the kid was about to shut down on me, I made physical contact. The experience was disturbingly unique, to say the least."

"I see," says Majors. "I managed to get a whiff so I inhaled deeply and blew you two a kiss. Now I have to take a meeting. We will talk soon." He hangs up.

Seward asks, "What do you suppose that was all about, Michael?"

"I don't know, but if I had to hazard a guess, I'd say he got his hands on the film footage of the Haitian grandfather. During my routine investigation into Banja Rouge's possible mode of escape, though flying was highly unlikely, I stumbled across a one-way plane ticket that he recently purchased before the accident. The ticket is for his father to come to America. Digging a bit deeper, it looks like he was coming to join his family for good."

As they open the trunk to remove boxes of evidence to be analyzed and categorized, Agent Lee Anne Seward says to her partner, "How tragic for them all. It is our duty to solve this case, if at all possible, but I can't help feeling for this once happy family. Member by member, they are being ripped apart."

When they enter his hotel room, they place the boxes on the desk. Agent Sievert is aching for that shower. Agent Seward follows her partner and lover to the bathroom where he pauses to look at her. With longing in both their eyes, she slowly approaches, taking shallow breaths.

She reaches for Agent Sievert, wanting to touch him so badly that it pains her. He backs away, knowing that it will only sting.

Mimicking her mood by changing more to hazel than the piercing blue, her eyes seek the floor, as she asks, "So is it over between us, Michael? Can we no longer enjoy feeling desires like normal human beings? Please don't shut me out, completely."

"No, Lee, that's not it at all. In fact, I feel just the opposite. I miss you, your touch, and your whispers in my ears as you are lying in my arms."

"Then tell me, what's the problem?" she asks. "Please, Michael, I really need to know what is going on with you, with us."

He sighs before saying, "As I told Majors, something happened today that is still a bit overwhelming. I am having trouble processing it all because of this strange energy that is still causing my skin to crawl. Touch me now, and you will surely experience the same unsettling energy that has finally begun to defuse."

"An experience that caused you to be transported to the ER at the hospital?"

"Yes, every bit of it. Believe me. I want to be close to you, too, especially after what happened today. I just don't think it is safe yet. I'm trying to protect you from this indescribably unsettling feeling." As if he has just been shocked or burned, Agent Sievert shakes both hands before him, shivering as if cold. "I need to get into the shower, right now. I just can't stand it any longer. This is like having wave after wave of my skin crawling all over my body. This is maddening. Please, Lee Anne, just let me take a shower and get some rest before dinner. I think I'll be okay then. We'll be okay." He tosses his cell and wallet on the bed and gets into the shower fully clothed.

Seeing this, she concedes, respecting his space with an assurance that their hidden love affair is secure. What they share in moments of intimacy surpasses mere sex. Neither agent has found such a fluid ability to bond with others from their respective pasts.

Chapter 21

Touched

McCall's Bar and Grille is known for good food and a safe, quiet atmosphere, as noted on social media pages for those planning to visit the upstate area. Agent Seward looked it up before arriving, liking the reviews. However, her phone application neglected to inform her that both McCall's Diner and McCall's Bar and Grille are the hubs of law enforcement hangouts in the Tega Cay and Fort Mill areas.

The place is clean and quiet enough, though hardly lacking steady patronage. She has no interest in the second bar in the back where the dimly lit pool tables reside. Most beautiful, well-dressed women, such as she, are used to the silence that often comes upon walking into an unfamiliar establishment. The same holds true here when she approaches the primary bar to ask for a menu and a shot, but she senses subtle differences without making eye contact with anyone other than the busty barkeep.

The nagging eyes crawling along her back are unmistakably turbulent mixtures of lust, curiosity, and even malignant suspicions from the few who are aware of Agent Seward's identity. When she sees the encased police badge behind the bar and the photos of uniformed men and women along a dim wall leading to the restrooms, she knows all.

The door she just entered suddenly slams shut as someone leaves, carrying a twisted taint of anger and a familiar touch of shameful humiliation. Agent Lee Anne Seward's sensitivity to those around her is a burden that she never asked for. Her gift—her curse—is a plus in her line of work. Still, she wishes that it were possible to turn it off whenever she desires the quiet solitude of her own thoughts.

Agent Seward downs the shot and taps the bar with the glass twice. As the bartender approaches to refill her shot glass, Agent Seward suddenly turns to lean back on her elbows, looking at those who mostly avert their eyes after being caught staring. This is not a matter of trying to intimidate them, rather a show of confidence to deny their intimidation of her. At the very least, she knows by their eyes where each type of thought originates.

The contemplations of the smiling rookie, with the draft in his hand, are easily discernible. He nods the heads-up at the cop in civvies, trying to draw his attention to her. The one with his back to her is sitting alone right where the dim to dimmer lights converge. The rookie has no idea of the recent history between Detective Reeves and Agent Seward. Had he known, he would have kept his mouth shut and his adolescent thoughts to himself.

Detective Reeves quickly knocks two shots back, following them with a beer chaser. He winces and cracks his neck in an obvious attempt to get drunk in peace, while trying to ignore the rookie's tiresome insistence that he look back at some hot looking broad that just walked in. His identity, though never an active inquiry in Agent Seward's mind, is painfully clear now.

Before looking over the menu, Agent Seward uses a buck to select three of her favorite songs on the jukebox. She takes a seat in an empty booth at the far end of the line with her back turned, trying to avoid a scene. Just as Don Henley begins to sing "Heart of the Matter," she feels his slow, uneasy approach.

That damned rookie finally succeeded in bringing her to Detective Reeves' unwanted attention. His glass dragging across the surface of each table that lines the wall across from the long bar, reminds her of car tires hitting the reflectors when a driver is straddling the line. Yet, even as he approaches from behind, she senses no malice. There is only this vaguely muddled impression of guilt, self-pity, and maybe a hint of self-loathing. She allows herself to relax, but not too much because all those emotions, mixed with liquor, can easily become a sudden blast of negative energy directed toward her.

He pauses above her right shoulder, which she hates.

Without looking up from the menu, Agent Seward says, "Good evening, Detective Reeves. How are you?"

The short hairs on the nape of her neck are standing on end. Finally, he clears his throat to say, "Fine thanks. May I join you, Agent Seward?"

Yet to look him in the eyes, she says, "Lee Anne. Sure take a load off."

"Excuse me, what?" he asks with slightly squinted eyes.

Agent Seward rotates her right shoulder to loosen the sensitivity to his close proximity. She closes the menu and finally looks up at him to say, "Lee Anne. My name is Lee Anne. Have a seat Detective Reeves. What can I do you for?"

"Oh, thanks," he says as he finally moves into peripheral view. When Reeves sits, he says, "Nice to meet you, Lee Anne. You can just call me Arnold or Arnie, either or. By the way, the food is great here. Personally, I love everything on the menu."

By the time the Eagles version of "I Can't Tell You Why" comes on, the server takes her order, approximating a wait time. She asks if they would like anything to drink while waiting on their meal. The assumption is overlooked as common courtesy. They both order drinks, even though Detective Reeves is already feeling quite toasty.

They actually have a couple of laughs by the third drink and another set of songs. When he says, "Boy, you can really put them away," she looks away with a slightly self-conscious smile.

"Yeah, well sometimes it helps to drown out all the loud voices in my head. I avoid crowds because of it."

"You're pulling my leg." He looks around and says, "It's practically a graveyard in here during shifts. Now tomorrow night, Fridays are helter-skelter in this place. You know, I never would have mistaken you for the shy type."

She grows quiet because he obviously does not understand what she truly meant. Just as "Here Comes the Rain Again" starts, a few droplets tap against the bar's thick partition glass windows. He is completely oblivious to it, while she is acutely aware.

"Oh wait," Detective Reeves says. "It all makes perfect sense now."

She looks at him, dubiously. "What are you talking about?"

"Why he left so suddenly. It must have been when you walked in."

"I'm sorry, Arnold, but you just lost me at perfect sense."

"Charlie Plant. He was over there talking to me a few minutes ago and then he just left. Yeah. It makes perfect sense now," Detective Reeves says, eyes assuming this bemused look of remorse.

"I didn't notice. I was aware that someone left, but I wasn't paying attention."

He continues to look away and says, "Agent Seward, I really owe you and your partner a sincere apology for my attitude. I truly regret that we got off on the wrong foot, for which I must take full responsibility. The unwarranted negativity was very unprofessional of me, and anti-productive to boot. Please accept my apology."

She simply waves a hand to dismiss the need for apologies, though it is appreciated. Agent Seward can feel Detective Reeves' inebriated guilt sloughing off him like layers of dead skin and coagulating blood.

No longer looking away in shame, the detective admits, "I guess you've probably heard that I reported Charlie's actions to the brass. I really felt like a piece of shit, but he came in to say that he understands. Can you believe that? He says to me, 'I forgive you, Arnie.'" Detective Reeves considers the drink in his hands and looks her in the eyes to say, "That made me feel even worse. I mean, what else could I do? It was probably going to come out anyway and the brass would be up my ass. Internal affairs would have ripped all my people, including me, new ones. You feds, no offense, show up and instantly see things that were right there—right frigging there—before my eyes. I must admit that I felt deeply insulted, and disrespected, blindly going to bat for a fellow officer that I have known for years. Went full tilt without question at all. But right now, even my partner isn't speaking to me because of it."

She interjects, "It's all over now, so don't beat yourself up about it. You had his back, as anyone would. Being fiercely loyal is neither a crime nor sin, Detective Reeves. When your partner takes a moment to give this some serious thought, he'll come around."

"Well I appreciate the absolution, but I don't deserve it. Ah, yeah, there is one more thing. I am really sorry about the Mulder and Scully wisecrack. I was being indignant and way out of line. I replayed the mental tapes time and again. With each revolution, I felt more like a crumpled piece of paper that I just wanted to toss in the trash."

She grunts and says, "Actually, you weren't that far off there, detective."

"What? Get out of here. Still, I regret things. I'd like you to know that I'm considering asking for reassignment since I can't seem to see the forest for the trees. I feel as if the answers are staring me right in the face, but somewhere along the line, I have lost my professional objectivity. Maybe I lost it when I saw that young girl floating in midair, or when I fell through the wall in the hospital. Shit threw me for a couple of fucking loops, it did."

When her order finally comes, she gives the waitress her credit card. She pays for the drinks with cash. His included. She quickly realizes that Detective Reeves' machismo is taking a hit because she paid for the drinks. With his insistence, Agent Seward agrees to let him reciprocate the next time around.

While waiting on her card and receipts, Agent Seward moves in close to say, "As far as asking for reassignment goes, there really is no call for that. We need all the help we can get to solve this bizarre case. Listen, Detective Reeves, Arnie, you are a good cop. Your precinct has need of men like you. Don't punk out under the peer pressure that we both know allows too many bad cops to get away with murder. Do not drop out of the race just because you trusted the wrong person. We all make mistakes from time to time, but the point is to learn from them. Question everything when necessary, but learn how to step back and you will see all things more clearly." She smiles, thinking about the day her partner said those very words to her. The thought brings about a feminine softness to those piercing eyes as she says, "You don't have to feel guilty about how you handled Officer Plant. We never intended to enter the incident into our reports. When my partner left it in your hands, he meant it. Nevertheless, you still did the right thing—the hard thing—and that makes you a good man and a good law enforcement officer. The people that we serve and protect need more cops like you. As far as Officer Plant's saintly forgiveness is concerned, you should know that it is easy to offer because he already knows that the matter is squashed. Do not allow him to hold it over your head because that is exactly what he intended by offering you clemency. I have no way of knowing how many times you have used him in situations like this, but he's probably been stealing from crime scenes from the get-go. He only left when I came in because I am the unholy bitch who kicked his ass. It was plain and simple embarrassment, nothing more. The brass, which does not want to open that particular can of worms, has decided that dropping the matter is in everyone's best interest. So let it go, leave the guilt on a shelf for a time when you really fuck up. Doing the right thing serves notice to all who work with you in the future that you simply will not tolerate anyone tarnishing the sanctity of the shield. Now, Arnie, I have got to get back on the clock. I'm glad we had this time to really talk." She polishes off her last drink.

He marvels at her words. "Thank you, Lee Anne. I think I probably needed to hear those things. Are you okay to drive?"

She smiles at him. "Thanks, but I'm good. I can't seem to get too drunk to drive. However, I will extend the same offer to you."

He chuckles. "No thanks, I'm good. I can drive these streets blindfolded."

She pops a breath mint in her mouth and walks out, knowing that the rookie can't wait to question Detective Reeves about their conversation. She winks and smiles at the blushing rookie on the way out.

After considering Agent Seward's words, he pays the tab he racked up before she walked in. Five minutes later, after giving the nosy rookie the brushoff, Detective Reeves decides to revisit the suspect's home.

With light rain pelting the roof of the black car, he stops by the officer on watch to chat for a few seconds. There has been no activity in the vicinity.

When Detective Reeves pulls into the driveway and grabs a flashlight, his colleague down the street says to himself, "First he blows my cover and now this bullshit—stupid rat bastard. This ass wipe actually makes detective. Jeez, what is this world coming to?"

Moments later, Detective Reeves speeds away from the Rouge home. He waives as he races by the surveillance vehicle on Bella Street as if all is well.

His partner calls to apologize for an earlier disagreement concerning his betrayal of Officer Plant. During that heated conversation, the words 'rat' and 'snitch' came out several times. Without looking at the phone to see who is calling, Detective Arnold Reeves simply tosses it from the passenger side window. His red eyes are fixed as he drives recklessly through the streets, running traffic lights without sirens or lights.

Chapter 22

The First Storm

Stacie Mecklenburg shivers in her bed, holding herself as the agony builds. She writhes within its growing severity, turning from side to side without finding any measure of comfort in shifting positions. Her clenched teeth hold back the urge to cry out. Now she hears it, distant, but coming like a fever rising from her innards to the crown of her head. She feels it, like walking barefooted across shattering bones!

Within the reeling mind of a teenager, two souls desperately struggle to hold on to one another.

While the mayor attends to a backlog of paperwork in his study, Paula Mecklenburg and Neara Jones sit in the housekeeper's comfortable quarters, sipping top shelf brandy. The uncommon quiet between them is the proverbial elephant in the room. It is sucking the air out of all things joyous.

Finally, Neara Jones reaches out and gently touches Paula's hand. With a kind melancholy in her eyes, she says, "I know, Pauline. I saw it, too." The wise woman sighs. "I have been here for many years, and you know I love that child like my very own.

But she's been touched, didn't know me from Santa Claus when she rung that doorbell. It seemed as if she was looking at me through the eyes of a total stranger for the very first time."

A tear rolls from Pauline Mecklenburg's eye. "Why would you say that to me at this exact moment, Neara?"

"Because you wouldn't say it yourself. You have spent most of this time just thinking about it, though."

"When Stacie was younger, I remember her ringing the doorbell just so you would be the first face she'd see, even though she had a key. It was one of your inside jokes, with no malicious intent. But this . . . Neara . . . this was something much different. When you brought her inside for a hug, I didn't think you saw it."

"Oh, I realized alright. Just didn't let on is all. She has been through quite a lot these past few days. Pauline. . . ."

"Yes, old friend."

Neara Jones takes a deeply troublesome breath to ask, "Lord knows I hate to even think it, but are you sure nothing of a sexual nature took place while that man held them captive?" Neara Jones heathers, as she calls it, to stifle tears from crashing down her cheeks.

Pauline Mecklenburg shudders at the thought. She takes a sip of brandy and says, "God. Jesus. I was so afraid that it might be the reason for her strange behavior. Though she claims to remember nothing about the abduction, the examinations proved that nothing of the sort happened."

"Are you certain?" asks Neara.

"As certain as I'll ever be, Neara," she says with a redeeming smile. "It would seem that my daughter is still a virgin."

"Oh thank God in heaven."

"You simply wouldn't believe the way that angry man took them from us. It was like nothing I have ever imagined in my entire lifetime. I was certain I would never see my children again, not alive anyway. That man's lips never moved. Yet, he spoke such harsh words inside of my mind that my heart nearly froze over. With those unfeeling, cold, white eyes, he stared down at me as I struggled to get up from the floor. My God, it was as if he were the devil in the flesh. I was completely powerless. I don't know who or what he really is, but his trespass seemed utterly effortless." She places her free hand over her eyes to fight back the tears.

Neara Jones feels for her anxieties. "Lord Jesus, help us all."

Continuing on, Pauline says, "A freaking storm formed right there in my daughter's hospital room. At first, I was convinced that the sprinkler system had come on, but that would have caused the fire alarm to engage, also. I thought it was the end of the freaking world." "Sounds like some wicked hoodoo to me. For whatever reason, I am thankful that he decided to return Stacie and Robert unharmed. Maybe he had some sort of reckoning that changed his mind after the good Lord touched his heart. Either way, we must be thankful."

"I can't help thinking that this never would have happened if Larkin hadn't been so abrasive and selfish. He displayed such a cruel, callous, heartlessness, toward that family. Because my husband showed such degrees of indifference to their plight, one could not help feeling an overwhelming sense of shame. It's the type of humiliation that weighs you down. With every step you try to take away from it, the more burdensome it becomes. Sometimes, I swear to you, I don't even know who he is."

"Yes, I think I know what you mean. These days, we both have to take the good with the bad, and pray for the best."

Pauline Mecklenburg grasps the Black woman's hand and smiles, tears streaming freely, to say, "Thank you, my dear friend. Thank God this part is all over, at least."

Neara asks, "What do you mean?"

"My daughter's arm was broken, Neara. A part of the bone had splintered off and the surgeon had to fuse it together with metal. I saw the x-rays with my own two eyes, but when we got her back, even the incision had disappeared. Healed as if it was never there. How?"

"I see. You fear that such things must come at a price yet to be paid."

Pauline Mecklenburg squeezes Neara's hand and nods an affirmation.

Just as the sound of thunder rolls toward Tega Cay, a shrill scream shatters the relative peace!

* * *

Banja Rouge, starving and dehydrated, gorges handfuls of preserved pears from a shelf in the laundry room. The moaning thunder serves warning that he must heed the Harbingers' decree that he bolster his physical strength for the tests to come. Like a cannibal, driven mad by hunger, he takes no care for the etiquette of civilized eating. Alone in the dark, with two sealed Mason jars tucked in the crux of his left arm and an open one in his left hand, he digs into the contents with his long fingers.

The half-emptied jar tilts upward, allowing him to drink the sweet nectar before devouring the rest of the preserved pears. At the ending rumble in the sky, the thud of a car door slamming shut causes his heart to flutter. He moves toward the hidden door, but it is too late. When the flashlight pierces the darkness, Banja Rouge freezes and slowly backs into the shadows.

Cautious footsteps on crunching glass tell him that only one person approaches.

When the light pauses on the hidden door, the footsteps cease, momentarily. Now Detective Reeves moves into sight. "Damn," Reeves whispers to himself. "He's been here all along."

Like a shot, Banja Rouge moves on the distracted detective, closing from the shadows with but one purpose. Just as one jar falls to the tile floor, Detective Reeves senses that he is not alone. When he pivots to the left, reaching for the weapon that he left in the glove box, Banja clamps down on the detective's right wrist! Before Reeves can launch a blow with his left fist, Banja raises his hand to drive his inverted right thumb to the center of the intruder's forehead!

Detective Reeves freezes, staring into that white glare that causes his pounding heart to stutter. His mind burns, wishing to cry out as warped visions invade the sanctity of all things living in the realm of congenial normalcy. He simply whimpers as his eyes cross.

Banja's sweet, warm breath brushes Detective Reeves' tingling skin all the way down to his disturbed soul when he says, "Seek!"

Moments later, his car fishtails on the wet street. Heading for Interstate-77 at breakneck speeds, Detective Reeves draws the attention of a deputy sheriff, who lights him up. Detective Reeves ends the pursuit by simply hitting the switch to his own electric blues.

Recognizing the unfamiliar speeder as a brother in blue, the deputy assumes he is rushing to the scene of a crime.

*　*　*

Showered and rested, Agent Sievert answers the knock at the door. He smiles when Agent Seward asks, "Hungry?"

"Ravenous. Come on in," he says.

Agent Sievert moves his laptop, photos, and notes from the dining table to the modest desk. After taking the food containers from the bags and placing them on the table, she prepares to remove her trench coat.

He approaches from the rear, caressing her shoulders with a gentleness that causes her to smile. Agent Sievert helps her to remove the coat and tosses it on the small loveseat that doubles as a foldout bed when necessary.

She turns to face her partner, caressing his cheeks while peering into his deep, brown eyes. She asks, "I've missed you. Are you okay? Are we okay, Michael?"

He smiles, as if looking into her oceanic eyes drugs him, soothes him into a euphoric state of consciousness. His kiss answers all, dissolving her fears and doubts.

He inhales the scent of her wet hair as they embrace. Agent Seward asks, "Michael, are we going to make love or eat?"

When he greets her with a wicked little grin and replies, "That really sounds like one of your trick questions," they burst into laughter at the naughty implication.

She backs away, patting his chest with both hands. She grimaces before saying, "Come on. Let's get some food in us while it's still warm. Then, either we'll get some work done, or we'll get to work." When he sits, she removes his plastic fork and knife from the packaging, placing it on the napkins next to the takeout box. He smiles, and she glances at him with her head slightly tilted.

She asks, "What? I heard something, but didn't quite catch that last thought."

Agent Sievert says, "Mm. This smells great. What did you get me?"

She stands across from the table and says, "Don't change the subject."

He chuckles, and confesses, "Well, I was just thinking that you are acting just like a wife. A very good wife, that is."

She rounds the table and sits in his lap with her arms about his neck. Looking into his eyes, Lee Anne says, "Just because you are the only man that ever touched me without me hearing the names of other women in your head, don't get cocky, mister." "Is that right?" he teases.

With a measure of sadness, Agent Seward looks deeply into his eyes. "You know they are going to find out about us sooner or later. Then, we will be done in for simply resembling the rest of humanity."

"I think that you are incredibly beautiful when you allow yourself to show any hint of vulnerability, Lee Anne. Come to think of it, you're pretty hot when you're in kick balls mode, too."

"Can you just be serious and a little less cavalier for a moment? I have real concerns, and this is an important issue for us both, Michael. Isn't it? Please don't treat our incredible connection as if it is as meaningful as a disposable cup. Especially when you are deliberately guarding your thoughts from me."

Agent Michael Sievert wants nothing more than to assuage her deep-rooted anxieties, which has been growing to a crescendo in her heart for weeks now. After nearly four years of working together as partners, the last eight months have forced them to admit what they have come to mean to one another.

He searches her eyes and says, "Whenever I was worried about something, my grandmother always seemed to know. She would say, 'Michael, ease your mind. There is never the need to borrow trouble.'"

Both agents have endured a number of disastrous dating experiences over the years, until that one night when they looked up to find that they had both chosen to dine at the same street side café in Richmond, Virginia. Whether it was by simple coincidence or dictated by fate, they had chosen the same place to end casual relationships that just left them feeling sort of empty and unfulfilled. With their jilted dates gone, sitting across the court with the same look of hunger versus futility etched upon their faces, Agents Seward and Sievert finally looked up to see and feel a sort of sadness in one another. Though hidden from each other, until that undeniable moment, this feeling was something they had in common. Fate, it would seem, drew them to the same place at the same time to end something that actually brought them together for the second time.

"Lee Anne, we both know the bureau's stance on how relationships between agents tend to hinder their decision-making process when one or the other is in danger of being harmed." As tears begin to well in the eyes of the no-nonsense, Brooklyn bred woman, Agent Sievert smiles and brushes away the one that cascades down her left cheek. Ever so softly, he says, "We haven't been a secret to Assistant Director Majors for quite some time now, Agent Seward. You see, every partner we've ever worked with has classified us as certified spooks. The thing that seems like a curse upon our lives is a blessing to the FBI, to Assistant Director Majors especially. He understands our particular predicament. He and I discussed it at length months ago because he wanted to be certain that it never interferes with our proficiency. It sounds a little self-serving when I say it aloud. Nevertheless, the point is, you have nothing to worry about because we have nothing to worry about. As long as our relationship doesn't interfere with our duties, and we continue to exercise discretion, we have his unofficial blessing."

Before she has to decide whether to slap him for holding out on her or not, he caresses Lee Anne's back and cheek. Recognizing that she is truly speechless for the first time since they met, he kisses her, passionately. Dinner will get cold, but there is a microwave oven in his suite.

* * *

The WBTV News van is getting stuffy and a bit constrictive. With nothing to report and the weather turning nasty, Santana Danes flinches when the lightning crackles overhead. She looks at her operator and says, "That's it, Woody. Pack it in. Lower the boom, and let's get the hell out of here. The scent has gone cold."

Woodrow Drummer rotates the toggle for one last 180-degree sweep of the Mecklenburg property through the driven rain, and sits back in his chair to say, "And it took you this long to finally decide that?"

"Yeah. Yeah. I hear you, Mr. Wise Guy. Mess with me, and we'll stay to do the weather report." He laughs as she smiles, each knowing that she will always be an indoors type. Sandy has been bucking for a seat at one of the bigger tables for years now. Life in the studio, sitting before the cameras, that is her dream. If capturing Kysing

"the Stinger" Rouge floating in midair, without wires or harnesses attached, hasn't clinched her upward mobility, what will it take? Snatching one more good shot from the air, one more sensational story, could clinch the liftoff she desires. After sitting here for hours, Santana Danes is ready to cry uncle.

Meanwhile, inside of the home, Pauline, Neara Jones, and Mayor Mecklenburg, all converge on Stacie's room. When she screams again, they burst through the door only to find that Stacie is not there.

They check every corner and closet before scattering in different directions to search the house. Suddenly, a blast of wind slams the front door against the stopper.

Woody says, "Oh my God. Look. Look there, on the lawn!"

A shrill cry pierces the violent night as they watch Stacie Mecklenburg on the monitor. Stacie is kneeling on the wet grass, shivering in pain. Her soaked nightgown coheres to her firm, young body. Her long blonde hair is darker when wet, sticking to the contours of her skin. Each time the thunder claps overhead and the lightning crackles, she seizes and quivers before another heartrending scream.

Although coherent thought is difficult to process through the agony, Kysing Rouge whispers, "Remember what they said. We must give it to the light. Give it to the light. Get up now, we must stand because the heart of the tempest is nearly upon us!" "I can't," Stacie cries.

"We must!"

She struggles to her feet as the compressive static builds. In anticipation of the booming thunder coming overhead, she holds her arms out to the side. Stacie waits for the next strike with her eyes white and face upturned.

While the lightning sizzles, she opens her mouth and releases a scream that should shatter glass. Several deadly tendrils of electric blue are striking at the ground as she roars to release the agony within. Electric tendrils dance around her, as if she is the living center of a plasma globe. Her chest seizes to release a bluish glow, an aura that fully encompasses her body. When it comes again, she lets loose a shriek that rips at the hearts of those who love her.

Her parents and the housekeeper are now standing in the doorway, witnessing an unbelievable sight, just as the reporters watch in amazement. A tangible blast of energy, this bluish aura pulsates outwardly, and then it is gone. Only the howling wind and rain remains as Stacie Mecklenburg, who should be dead, places her palms together as if to thank God for her life. She crumples to her knees, breathing hard but smiling as she rolls to her side on the soaked ground. It feels so good to be wet and cool.

"We did it, Kysing. It really worked," Stacie says.

"Yes, sister," Kysing agrees. "It worked, and we are still alive."

"Thank you, sister. I don't think I could have done it alone."

Kysing says, "We will do what we must."

The voice of Banja Rouge joins this private conversation, saying, "You did well, my children. You should rest now, and sleep."

Pauline Mecklenburg is too afraid to join her husband when he races to their daughter. Neara uses the phone to call for medical assistance.

Meanwhile, in the van, Santana Danes asks Woody, "Did we get that? Please, for the love of God, tell me we got it!"

Woody watches as the girl's father runs out to collect her from where she now lies upon the steaming lawn. "Jesus, I can't believe it. She survived. Look, she's moving around."

Santana Danes stops sprucing up her makeup to look at the monitor in total disbelief. "My God, this is incredible. Are we still filming?" "We got it all, but it may be like looking into a flashbulb. I'll see what we actually have on playback while you prepare an underscore of this event. First, there was the floating girl in the hospital, and now this. Looks like your instincts were right after all."

With her makeup reapplied, she puts on her jacket to the sound of approaching sirens. "Okay, how do I look?"

When he gives her the onceover and the thumbs up, she gives him a big fat kiss. "Wow!" Woody says. "I like it when you're like this. Are we officially dating now?"

With her breasts and bra adjusted for maximum effect, Santana Danes caresses his hairy chin and whispers, "In your dreams, pal. Hurry, they're coming. I want a shot of the fire and rescue vehicles showing up, and then we'll take it from there. Got it."

"You know it. My camera is already primed with rain gear and ready to go. Just let me take a quick look at the footage. Between that blue pulse and the lightning strikes, there may be little to see."

She crosses her fingers before uttering, "Please god."

The rain stops tapping on the roof. When the fussy wind gusts once more before going to sleep, an eerie calm fills the world.

While the sirens are still distant, Santana Danes calls her network to request a live uplink. Meanwhile, Woody swears aloud, adjusting the playback resolution to prompt a clearer picture. It does not clear up until he lowers the resolution to find Stacie Mecklenburg rising to her feet with her arms outstretched at her side. He figures that her white eyes are just the result of reflecting light. When she screams and the lightning strands come down from the sky to dance all around her, something ominous and black comes toward the screen. Woody's heart stops as he shrieks and falls backward.

"Jesus Christ! What the fuck was that? Did you see that shit?"

She asks, "What? See what?"

"It came right at the camera with glowing eyes!"

"Woody, what exactly did you see?"

Still on the floor with his back against a wall of equipment, he points at the monitor and says, "That thing. It was alive!"

She helps him to his feet to rewind the recording, but the image is gone. There was nothing to see beyond the blue pulse. The ambulance and fire engine are close. She hurries him out of the door with microphone in hand.

Chapter 23

Reeves Undone

With their clothes back on, his shirt is open, while her blouse remains unbuttoned just enough to show just a bit of cleavage. Agents Michael Sievert and Lee Anne Seward have eaten before covering every surface of the hotel room with photos and various items from the scenes involved in this case. Both beds are lined with photographs, also.

Evidence bags containing samples, chemical compounds, and DNA analyses from each scene, now cover the surface of the table and desk. They contain sulfurous water from Stacie's room: sand from Robbie's room. The boxes also contain glasslike objects from the lawns of the Rouge home and the hospital where the anomalous weather shredded a section of the parking lot and ripped away parts of the hospital's wall.

While wearing two latex gloves on each hand, the agents place photos downloaded from their own cell phones, from the recovered family computers, and Banja Rouge's abandoned cellphone, among others on the floor. All are facedown, arranged in four rows of ten, with at least two feet between each row so they can walk amid them. Also lying among them are photos of the Rouge home, the hospital after the tumult, a comatose Kysing Rouge floating above her bed, the firefighters banging away at the invisible barrier. There are the photos of Stacie and Robert Mecklenburg asleep in their hospital beds, and the cutouts of the same. There are photos of the ransacked home after the police charged in only to find no one there. Unknown to Agent Seward, there is one photo among the grid she has never seen.

The agents are walking in the same direction between the photos on the floor, each looking at the backs of adjacent pictures to the left and right of them. When they reach the far end nearest the window, they trade rows to repeat the same slow pace toward the door, looking at each as if a part of an invisible puzzle with hidden patterns, though they are facedown. .

Now Agent Seward stands by the window, while he is nearer to the door. They begin moving toward each other amidst the photographic grid. He stops, eyeing a picture to his left at the foot of the first bed. Two feet away, she looks at a picture to her right. Without saying a word, they reach for one another's hands. The photos, like those of the Rouge home and the photo cutouts of the Mecklenburg children sleeping in their hospital beds flutter, subtly. These are taken from the carpet, with the latex gloves serving as insulation for their skin.

They place those twelve photos aside before approaching the bed closest to the glass doors of the balcony. Agent Sievert is in between, while she searches the maze from the side nearest the balcony. They repeat the ritual of trading places. Agent Seward stops, doubting her instincts. With eyes shut, he reaches for her hand and nearly touches the photo she contemplates with his right index finger.

By the time they are done, the agents a have selected eighteen photos, but they do not look through them. They are simply set aside for the moment. This technique, a ritual uniquely their own is done in complete silence; no words are spoken aloud. Their slow and deliberate movement, is not all together voluntary. It is more like wading through warm water; like walking through a fog with the thickness of oil. Although they walk the maze of photographs, with their hands moving across each one, there is no physical contact until their minds have searched among them for some intangible connection to the case. The subtle flutter of a photograph, as they have grown to agree, represents its call to the minds that reach out to touch it. The true connection of those that call is not always apparent nor easily discerned. However, they always speak in the end.

Now they approach the table and samples, handling each with a delicate touch. Finally, Agent

Sievert picks up two bags and says, "Exhibit one-twelve and two-thirteen are the same black, hardened, glasslike materials. As I suspected, this is obsidian, but I took this from the front lawn of the Rouge home. There were two different pieces embedded in the grass, but I only took a sample from one. Obviously, the lab took a small sample for analysis, but I don't remember it being this long." He takes a closer look at one of the tags, which has his file identification number on it.

Agent Seward says, "Look at the file ID for the second sample. I sent that one in for analysis after it broke off from the much longer piece I found at the hospital. They were right where the tornados struck. But if I recall correctly, obsidian is actually supposed to be molten lava that cools quite rapidly. What would it be doing here, and at both scenes? I'm quite certain that we would all know by now if this region is sitting on a volcanic event horizon."

"I'm sure that's not the case. You are right about the obsidian being out of place here. However, if you think that is weird," says Agent Sievert. "Look at this." He removes both samples and places them end to end.

She says, "I don't believe it. They fit together, perfectly. How can that be when they came from different places?"

The jagged edge of the black glass slits effortlessly through the rubber gloves, allowing a single drop of blood through the incision to settle on the sample. He quickly places them on the surface of the table to remove the latex.

Agent Seward rounds the table to examine his wound. "You should wash and disinfect that. I have alcohol pads and a few bandages in my luggage. Be right back"

While Agent Sievert washes the bleeding cut in the bathroom, she grabs her first aid kit from her luggage so she can disinfect the slight wound. The cool water stings his injured finger, but not for long. He grabs a napkin and applies pressure as she rips open the aluminum cover to remove the alcohol pad. As they approach one another, he removes the bloody napkin.

She stops, noticing the look of awe on his face while examining the wound. He flexes his finger and shows her the open palm where there is no blood, no wound.

She grabs his hand for further inspection, but there is nothing to see. She gasps, looking back at the table. The two-inch thick obsidian shards have fused; they are no longer separate pieces.

They sit at the table, speechlessly, looking at it. Each is hesitant to touch.

"What the hell is going on here, Michael? Fresh flesh wounds don't just spontaneously heal like that. Even when you nick yourself while shaving, it doesn't just stop bleeding. Not without clotting to form a small scab, at the very least."

"Nor do broken bones simply heal," Sievert replies in a mere whisper.

"No shit."

When the apprehension abates, Agent Sievert, gingerly, handles another sample. "I believe this is fulgurite, sand exposed to the intense heat of a lightning strike that turns it to glass."

She reads from the accompanying analytical sheet, "It was taken from the floor of Robert Mecklenburg's hospital room by forensics after the anomalous weather."

"Notice how flat and smooth it is. If you found it on the ground, it would have spiked formations on the underside, which indicate the dispersal of electric energy seeking the paths of least resistance. The widest point is where the strike first touches down and follows a thinning path of the lightning before dissipation."

"Maybe there really was an electrical discharge in that boy's room. A sandstorm, according to his father. Michael, what are your thoughts on this whole incident. I have my own theories, but the pieces that you are holding back from me are important in forming a working hypothesis." She looks into his eyes, seeking his thoughts to the very core of his soul with a pleading desire to know what he chooses to hold back.

"You will think I've gone completely mad, Lee Anne, totally off my rocker," Agent Sievert warns. He sits back in his seat with a sigh.

She grunts, trying to keep the smile from curling the corner of her lips. "So what else is new? For that matter, what have you ever found in our entire universe that doesn't make us both insane in comparison to most normal people?"

"As we both know, the Federal Bureau of Investigation never officially deems open or unsolved cases as paranormal in nature. Everything is supposed to have an explanation, whether through deductive reasoning or scientific categorization or the scientific process of elimination. As we also know, some things simply defy definitions that satisfy the prideful government entity for which we work. I want to show you something," he says, reaching for his laptop. "While you were out, Assistant Director Majors called and he uploaded this file to my unit. He isn't certain that it has anything to do with this case. As a favor from a friend in some specialized branch of Homeland Security, this was secretly sent to him. What you are about to witness cannot be mere coincidence."

She watches the footage from discretely positioned security cameras on the ceiling of Flight 111 from Haiti to Miami International. The old man gleaming eyes as he thrusts his hands forward, unfurling fingers that have drawn his own blood is a shock. The plane bounces and yawns in midair. Dr. Labor—paralyzed. Flight Attendant Alice Graham approaches with the Sky Marshal zooming in on seat 132 as he draws his Taser. Chaos ensues. The two woman and the Sky Marshal are practically repulsed by the blue. Rain? Next, she watches the higher and lower resolution satellite images of the flight over the Atlantic during its approach within the same time index. Lastly, Agent Seward looks at the surveillance footage of the sequestered passenger of seat 132.

Upon its conclusion, she takes a breath and asks, "The grandfather's eerie eyes and that wicked scar are even more disturbing while he is in motion or looks right into the camera. And what is causing that eerie flash?" Agent Sievert tries to warn Agent Seward as she reaches out to touch the paused image on the screen, tracing the old wound on Kwaban Rouge's bald head and face. When a static spark brings about a very painful shock, she withdraws quickly. "Ugh, that really stung. Christ. What happened to him?"

"Meet Banja Rouge's father, Kwaban Rouge. As you know, he is a Haitian national on his way here to be with his family."

"Jesus." She rubs her fingers together, both hands. "I remember reading the short file, but, at the time, nothing jumped out at me without an image."

"However, now you have not only seen but felt it jumping out at you. Didn't you? When I touched his image in a similar manner, I received a formidable shock for my efforts. It gave me the same creeps you are experiencing right now."

She shudders. "Well, Michael, we've both profiled and hunted unknown subjects with the capacity to torture and even dismember their victims. Was he tortured? Is this wicked scar some form of punishment?"

He responds, "I don't think so. Not in the traditional sense of the word, anyway."

"Even before I touched his image on the screen, I sensed . . . I sensed an unfamiliar surge of energy. It was not evil, exactly, but it was certainly close enough. His resolve—his will— is quite extreme."

"I got the same impressions, but the word I'd use would be power. Energy, yes. But this man's presence is powerful; it is potent. As far as him having endured some form of torture, it seems a distinct possibility. At least, that is what Assistant Director Majors thinks.

When I did a little digging, I was able to get in touch with a Haitian historian named Minoche. Dr. Liam Minoche."

"So, you really didn't get any rest after all."

"Not a wink, but I feel much better. Exhilarated, actually."

"Hm. What did the doctor have to say?" she asks, unable to take her eyes from the monitor. Oddly, Agent Seward is forced to resist the temptation to repeat her painful experience.

"According to Dr. Minoche, this man was never arrested nor tortured. More than likely, Mr. Kwaban Rouge performed a mythical, gruesomely bloody ritual on himself. This obscure, two-part, blood ritual known as the Blood Fire and Fire-bonding, Collage au feu, is referenced only once in all his years as a historian. Supposedly, the scarring on this man's body is highly indicative of said ritual. Doctor Minoche claims that his historical findings lead him to conclude that the Rouge surname stretches very far, and is highly revered among the older Haitian generations. Dr. Minoche spoke of a hidden, sacred cave where Kwaban Rouge is reputed to have performed this ritual. In addition, Dr. Minoche mentioned the staunch death threats he received if he should ever try to go there. The man we are looking at is almost legendary, partner. What do you know about a group of mercenaries called the Tonton Macoute? Does the name Papa Doc ring any bells?"

She finally looks away from the image of Kwaban Rouge with furrowed brows. "Only that members of the Tonton Macoute were referred to as Haitian bogymen. They kidnapped, murdered, and enslaved many people at the behest of the country's leader. Was it François . . . something?"

"Duvalier. President François Duvalier, who, essentially, declared war on this man and his family during the mid to late sixties.

Although he was extremely reluctant to chat, Dr. Minoche told me some incredible things. In a way, I shamed him into talking by appealing to the logical, scientific side of his professional life. Still,

I sensed his fear of discussing such things. Whenever someone walked into the room, he went silent. At times, even when no one was present, his voice was barely a whisper."

Agent Lee Anne Seward touches his hand, her eyes moving far away from her body before whispering, "Duvalier's men attacked them on Kwaban Rouge's fiftieth birthday, murdering members of his family because he refused to join a bloody campaign of intimidation and terror on the Haitian people."

Amazed by her growing insights, Agent Sievert says, "Yes, all but Banjalanah Rouge. It is said that the ground of Duvalier's sugarcane plantation ran red with blood, and nothing has grown there since this man found out that his youngest son was captured and enslaved there. According to the local lore, Kwaban Rouge and several men of his village launched a night raid on said property, where he beheaded every man in Duvalier's service with a legendary, scythe-like blade. The doctor has rough sketches of it. Though he admits no tangible proof of its actual existence, he shared the name of the weapon used. Not the type of weapon, but its actual name."

"Like the Norsemen would name their swords of battle?"

"Exactly," Sievert says. "It is known as *La lame de l'ouragan rouge* or, by interpretation, the Blade of the Red Hurricane.

"*La lame de l'ouragan rouge*. Can there be any truth to this?" she asks, knowing her partner too well to think that the story ends here.

"Reputed as one of the most powerful voodoo high priests of the time, Kwaban Rouge was an affront to President François Duvalier's sway over the people, who began to mimic Kwaban's example.

Unfortunately, Duvalier's henchman discovered the boy's identity before his father could rescue him. It was told, with great caution, that none other than President Duvalier's son, Jean-Claude, used a wooden club to beat Banja Rouge within an inch of his life. When the distraught father found his nine-year-old son in ruins, broken, battered, and near death, he was enraged. They freed all of the captives that night, but slaughtered every guard in Duvalier's service."

"Hmm," she moans while gripping his hand. As she strokes his right hand, she realizes that Agent Sievert has finally let down his guarded thoughts. Not completely, but enough. There are still hidden things. "But it doesn't end here. There was a second son of the dictator, younger than the one who used the club on the boy."

"A five-year-old child named Jean-Luc Duvalier," Agent Sievert utters. "Hours later. . . ."

"Hours later, after everyone was freed and scattered, there was a calamity. Twin tornados, just like those at the hospital, ripped the presidential residence to shreds when they converged at the same point with the singular, focused purpose of something sentient. Something alive."

He nods and says, "The five-year-old son simply disappeared. His family never saw him again."

Agent Sievert takes a photocopy from his briefcase. This was faxed to me from Dr. Minoche. It is an old black and white photo of Kwaban Rouge walking among the children of his village in 1964. Notice, there is no evidence of disfigurement. Now look at these, carefully." He passes three documents to her.

A moment later, Agent Seward says, "Kwaban Rouge was fifty at the time of the attack. His youngest surviving son was nine at the time, but the birth documents just don't add up, Michael. According to these, Banja Rouge is only forty three to forty-four-years-old. His age coincides with that of the five-year-old that disappeared. He should be about forty eight or forty-nine-years-old It can be a mistake, a typo. Nonetheless, taking a child to replace a child lost in battle has been a common theme in many warring cultures, even here with the Native American Indians."

"Then why perform the whole ritualistic self-mutilation? According to the good doctor, who got the information regarding the disappearance of Jean-Luc Duvalier from retired service members who were there, the place was impossible to breach. After finding all of his slave labor gone in the wind, and every man guarding them beheaded, the presidential domicile was completely surrounded. I believe that Kwaban Rouge did this to himself during the Blood Fire ritual. If this was a simple case of taking a child to replace another, how could you choose the exact timing of twin tornadoes—converging on a single point—to do it?" he questions with his arms now folded. "The sheer exactitude . . . the precision of timing in both cases no longer allows for mere coincidence in this profile. During her initial statement following the disappearances of Stacie and Robert Mecklenburg, the mother attests that Banja Rouge said, 'one life forsaken for one life safe. One life dims for one shimmering soul to take. Can you now cry for them all, mother? Can you cry for our children now?'"

"It is reported that Banja Rouge's son died as the result of the willful destruction caused by Mayor Mecklenburg's youngest brother. It is rumored that, when there was still a chance to save Kilarin Rouge, the mayor exerted his influence to have Robert rescued first. Meanwhile, inside of the bus, Kysing Rouge saves Stacie Mecklenburg from falling to her death. Though severely injured, herself, she saved the mayor's daughter. That selfless young lady now languishes in a coma that quite possibly could have been prevented. Instead, she is damaged, broken, lying at death's door just like her own father approximately forty nine years ago. Her desperate mother is crumbling inside while watching her only surviving child slowly slipping away. What is a loving husband and father to do in this situation? Could this all be a desperate father's attempt to save their daughter through . . ."

"Transference?" she finishes.

"The Rouge family has powerful allies in this world, Lee Ann. I have received a warning that may be fatal to ignore. We must tread carefully while still working toward bringing Banja Rouge in safely."

"Who are you talking about, Michael? Ever since the hospital, you've been trying to protect me from something that has you rattled. Even when we made love, you kept me out of all the very dark places. Isn't this the point in time when you give me the information I need to make up my own mind?"

He takes a deep breath and nods his head. "I cannot protect you and expect you to do your job to your full capability. I'm sorry, but. . . ."

The simultaneous ringing of their cellphones startles the completely engrossed agents. The caller, Detective Peter Blake, reports very disturbing developments.

*   *   *

At 2:00 AM, Agents Sievert and Seward arrive at the police precinct in Tega Cay where an anxious Detective Peter Blake meets them. He guides the FBI agents to Chief Cramer's office. Chief Cramer is sitting alone in dim lighting, watching the television with the remote in his hand. When they enter, he pauses the video feed and stands to shake the hands of both agents, hoping to allay the previous disagreements of the evening. Still, he cannot be certain without making mention of it.

"Before we begin, I would like to know if we are beyond our small issues."

Agent Sievert and Agent Seward look to each other and back at Chief Cramer. With the shake of their heads, Agent Seward asks. "What issue would that be, sir?"

"Good. Good," says Cramer, who clears his throat. "Please, everyone have a seat. Pete, grab the chair from that corner. There are several issues to discuss here, so bear with us Agents Seward and Sievert. Several hours ago, one of my detectives went missing. Detective Blake, please explain the particulars."

Showing obvious signs of anxiety, Detective Blake sits forward in his seat. "Well, earlier today, my partner and I had harsh words about a certain situation I'm sure you are both familiar with. Later, I thought about things and decided that I owed my partner and friend an apology for the things I said. I figured he was still pretty pissed at me because he just ignored my calls and refused to acknowledge my messages, so I went looking for him. Because Arnie wasn't at home, I went by McCall's, but he had already left. Before leaving the establishment, he had drinks with a tall, blonde-haired woman with piercing greyish blue eyes that perfectly fits your description, Agent Seward. I must admit that I asked Kerry to check the receipts for a name, thinking that maybe he had just gotten lucky with some hot chick. Never in a million years would you have been my first guess. No way."

Chief Cramer clears his throat to redirect Detective Blake's focus.

"I attained permission to do a spot check on my partner's phone, which was stationary in the vicinity of the Rouge home. Upon arrival, an officer on watch told me that Detective Reeves had come by and entered the home, but he didn't stay very long. He must have found a lead because he lit out like a shot. Still, he did not answer my call or anyone else's. After tripping his phone's GPS, we found it on a street in the same area. He must have placed it on the top of the car or something, maybe when he reached in for his service weapon or flashlight. It happens more than we like to admit, actually. As you can imagine, I became worried at that point so we checked the house out real quick like, but found nothing."

Agent Seward says, "I did go to McCall's to get some takeout, where I ran into Detective Reeves, but I left him there because we had lots of evidence to process. That's what we were doing when you called."

"I know you left him there. Anyway, we pinged his unit's GPS, which had moved out of the immediate area. By broadening the search pattern, we were able to locate him. Now Charlotte, North Caronia is just a little over 290 square miles. Mecklenburg County is about 546 square miles. Detective Reeves was clocked doing over one-hundred MPH on Interstate-85 in Granville County, one of the northernmost counties of North Carolina heading into Virginia."

"What?" she responds in amazement. "Where was he going?"

Agent Sievert asks, "Did you finally catch up with him? Did he discover a new lead in the case by revisiting the suspect's home?"

"All of a sudden, his unit just stops. Apparently, he ran out of gas, locking up the power steering when the engine suddenly died on a curve."

"Oh my God," she says, feeling a certain sense of guilt. "Did he survive the accident?"

Chief Cramer says, "Technically, Detective Reeves is under arrest for DUI and disorderly conduct, allegedly leaving the scene of at least three accidents with injuries. What finally stopped him was hitting the water barrels used as safety barriers on I-85. It seems that the traffic safety measures, the airbag, and the fact that he had the sense of mind to wear a seatbelt, saved him from any serious injuries. However, he's been hospitalized and heavily sedated. Detective Reeves has since stabilized, somewhat, but remains highly agitated and uncommunicative. Precursory evaluations by a shrink strongly suggest some kind of mental breakdown or trauma before the wild excursion off reservation and subsequent accidents. Although I had to reason with a Chief Canfield, the state troopers, and the doctors, Detectives Reeves is presently remanded into my custody. Any damages or injuries caused by my detective will be assessed during a full investigation. In the end, I fear that all necessary restitutions will be met solely on our dime. As we speak, I'm having the detective transported back to an area hospital, where we may find the underlying cause of this—this—total butt-fuckery!"

With a deliberately calmer demeanor, right after hammering his desk, Chief Cramer swivels his head and neck until he hears that disturbingly satisfying crackle. He uses both hands to smooth his white hair backward, before resuming with a bit more color in his cheeks.

Agent Sievert asks, "Is there anything more you can tell us, Chief Cramer? Did he say anything at all?"

Agent Seward asks, "Why disorderly conduct? Did he resist arrest?"

Chief Cramer inhales deeply, exhaling a troubled sigh as he strokes his white mustache and chin. He looks at the three people seated before him and says, "Oh yes. There are lots more to come, and not all about Detective Reeves. However, his well-being remains the utmost priority. According to Chief Canfield, Reeves was just sitting there as if nothing happened. He was staring through the shattered windshield as if deep in thought on a warm, sunny day. When first responders climbed down the embankment and looked in the windshield, according to Chief Canfield, his eyes were so red they thought he was dead after suffering some extreme form of hypoxia. Although the first responder had a loaded weapon and a fully charged Maglite pointed at his face, ordering Reeves to show his hands, he never even blinked. They claim that he did not resist arrest, exactly. Surrounded by nervous State Troopers, sirens, blue lights, and floodlights that you could see from the freaking moon, he just started screaming when someone reached in and tapped him on the shoulder. He backed himself into a corner and continued to scream for no apparent reason. No elicit street drugs were found in his urine or blood. Of course, a complete psyche evaluation is par for the course in the wake of his completely uncharacteristic behavior." Chief Cramer sighs hard and shakes his head from side to side. As he pinches the bridge of his nose, he mumbles, "Oh so long and hard is the way. . . ."

As the chief drifts away to process the very words he just spoke, the others look to one another.

Detective Blake attests, "I know my partner like the back of my hand, but I haven't got a clue. Arnie is a good cop, and he will probably need our help if his career is to survive this fiasco. Maybe we can chalk it up to stress from the existing investigation, while trying to keep the more unique details out of our official reports should we find otherwise."

"Detective Blake, the simple fact that he was last seen at the Rouge home, whether something occurred there or not, makes it part of our probe. Of course, we must investigate, but don't ask us to keep looking the other way because we've already done that bit." Agent Seward adds, "That simply cannot be your main concern at this point."

Chief Cramer says, "To finish answering your earlier questions, Detective Reeves did utter three words while under sedation. He said the words, and I quote, 'Lee Anne, seek.'"

"What the hell does he mean by that?" she asks. "Are they certain, that's what he said, Chief Cramer?"

"This is one of the reasons I demanded that Detective Reeves be remanded into our custody. That idiot of a so-called shrink thinks Detective Reeves is distraught over a failed relationship, and he has suddenly become obsessed with finding some woman from his recent past named Lee Anne. While under the influence of alcohol, he simply jumps behind the wheel and sets out to find her by flying through bad weather. Of course, we all know better. That part is probably all guesswork and hogwash. Therefore, I need you to talk to him. See what you can find out when he arrives. It's possible that something you discussed at the bar left some lasting impression."

"Of course, Chief Cramer. It's the least we can do," says Agent Seward. "When I saw him hours ago, he apologized for his attitude towards us both. Detective Reeves reluctantly expressed that he felt he has lost his objectivity while investigating this case and should remove himself by asking for reassignment. I tried to convince him that he did the right thing concerning the situation with Officer Plant after being told to his face that we weren't going to pursue the matter any further, which I feel makes him a good cop and person. We actually had a few laughs while I waited on my dinner order. I sensed no psychotic episodes coming on. In fact, sir, Detective Reeves thanked me for the talk. All in all, I'd say he was in a pretty cheerful mood when I left." "He had been drinking, of course," says the chief.

"We both had a few," she admits. "But when I asked if he was okay to drive, he seemed comfortable enough. The person you have been describing is not the same man I spoke with at McCall's Bar and Grille. Not in the least. Sure. He was down on himself, but he seemed to come out of the tailspin with just a few words of encouragement."

Agent Sievert is staring at the back of Chief Cramer's computer monitor, which doesn't go unnoticed. His field of vision keeps switching from the back of the monitor to the television, even though he cannot see either.

Chief Cramer looks at Detective Blake and Agent Sievert. He hits play as he turns the monitor 180-degrees so they can all see. "Do any of you recognize this man like the back of your hand?"

Agent Sievert is the only one that doesn't gasp at the sight of those terrified, red eyes. He says, "The cops and doctors believe that his eyes are blood red because of the impact with the airbag, but that's not really the case." Agent Sievert ponders aloud, "Is it possible that Detective Reeves found some previously undiscovered clue in that house? He seems to be exhibiting extreme panic even under heavy sedation. Something is scaring the hell out of him. He's mind-locked, trapped in his own brain."

"The guys surveilling the Rouge property saw nothing out of place, other than the fact that he left in a hurry. He even waved as he passed," Detective Blake reports. "Even so, as a precaution, I took three guys inside the home with me. We covered every corner of the home and saw nothing new. The K-9 team found zilch. In fact, the animal refused to enter. The handler said it seemed afraid, something he has never experienced with Wolf. We got the same results from the second K-9, which attacked its handler while being forced to enter the home. They had to put her down at the scene."

The agents find this bit of information interesting.

"Nothing was found in Reeves' car or pockets. His weapon was unused and locked in the glove box, where most off-duty officers leave them. We encourage taking them inside the home or leaving them in the trunk for safety issues, but you know how it is. Because they have already taken cast-off paint scrapings to prove or disprove contact with those alleging that their accidents are due to direct contact with Detective Reeves' vehicle, I'm having it towed so forensics can give it a go with expert eyes. Before they ship the vehicle down here on a flatbed, it will be shrink-wrapped to keep the weather out."

"How long?" asks Agent Sievert at the same instant that Agent Seward does.

The phone rings. When Cramer hangs up, he says, "It almost seems as if you two knew that someone was about to answer that very question. The police escort just called to tell me that the ambulance is approximately twenty minutes out. Our potential material witness is not too far away. I hope and pray that he recovers with a plausible explanation for this aberrant behavior."

Agent Sievert looks at the image on the screen. Those doped, faraway eyes still seem too fearfully alive with the amount of drugs they have pumped into his system. Strapped and cuffed to the gurney, Detective Reeves, should be fast asleep.

Agent Seward wants to reach out and touch the screen. When her partner clears his throat, she realizes that her right hand is paused in midair, reaching for it.

When she catches herself, Agent Sievert notices how Chief Cramer is becoming increasingly observant of them both.

Therefore, he asks, "Chief Cramer, sir, after you've shown us what you have paused on the television, would you allow Agent Seward and myself a few moments alone in your office? I realize how highly unusual this request may sound, but I think it best."

"Of course," Cramer agrees. He sits back in his chair with the remote in hand and says to the FBI agents, "You know, I believe I'm finally beginning to see why you two are so highly regarded by your section chief. Detective Reeves may not be the only man to apologize this night. I know you both want to see Reeves because you need something from him, something only his physical presence will provide. But this—this—may just split your infinitives right down the seams as you prepare to boldly go where no one has ever gone before. This little tidbit has already gone viral as a failed alien abduction caught on live television." He rewinds a bit, swivels the screen and hits play.

While a single bolt of lightning separates inches above Stacie Mecklenburg's forehead to oscillate all about her, she stands ankle deep in wet grass. With her arms spread wide, and her eyes gleaming white orbs, she screams amidst another strike with enough electrical current to fry her inside out. Within those azure oscillations, her feet begin to rise from the ground as a cobalt blue pulsation emanates from her body, knocking out the camera that captured these incredible images.

"Jesus!" Detective Blake says, "I heard the rescue call over the band, but I was too concerned with Reeves to pay much attention. Did you see that? She just stood there with lightning all around her, soaking wet no less!"

"I can see by the intense scrutiny that you two haven't seen this news clip. Still, Agent Sievert, you at least seemed quite curious. How do you do it, both of you? How?" Because they seem hesitant to hazard an explanation, he waves a hand to let them off the hook.

Without warning, Chief Cramer tosses the remote between them, smiling because Agent Sievert doesn't blink as his partner snatches it from the air like a hungry bird picking a bug from the sky.

Detective Blake looks at his watch, blowing an impatient sigh. Understandably, he is worried about the condition of Detective Reeves.

Chief Cramer shakes his head with a wily grin on his face. As he rises from the seat, he shakes a finger at Sievert and Seward to say, "You two are quite the team—yin-yang—the perfect investigative unit that moves nearly seamlessly through all contradictions to even nature itself. I admit my initial skepticisms, but no longer. I have a sneaking suspicion that you have a real shot at solving this thing right down to how a seventeen-year-old girl withstands two lightning bolts thrown directly at her by Almighty God himself. The room is yours. Take as long as you need. Come on Blake. While we are waiting, you can buy me a coffee. Afterward, I want you to stick to them like glue because you can learn a lot from these two."

The importance of quiet forgoes the fact that they are being watched through the blinds in the dimness of Chief Cramer's office. Agent Sievert whispers to Agent Seward, "Yes. I know they are watching, but we can't let that stop us." He sits on the corner of the desk, hitting the button to kill the intercom.

She replies, "Maybe I should have allowed the remote to hit the floor, spilling its guts and batteries all over the place. He was testing us."

"Doesn't matter now. Chief Cramer's very intuitive, and kind of sneaky, but no longer a hindrance. Before we begin, I need to warn you of something. Whatever happens, no matter what, we must share all things together."

She looks at the screen and then at him. "Okay, we both know that this situation would usually require us to split up to cover more ground. Most likely, they will be in the same local hospital. What has you so spooked, Michael? You've been holding things back ever since the incident at the hospital, whatever landed you in the ER. I want to know what happened, and why you feel we shouldn't split up to cover both Reeves and Stacie Mecklenburg simultaneously."

"I believe my overall apprehension started before the incident at the hospital. The closer we got to the town, the more it grew in intensity. Remember when I drew my weapon as you approached me from the rear at the Rouge family home?"

She draws her hair behind both ears, nodding an affirmation. "Yes. I was wondering about that because it has never happened before. Please stop trying to protect me, Agent Sievert. Just tell me everything." He glances at the slightly open blinds and says, "Take my hand." She does when their backs are turned. "I believe I know where the father is hiding. Because you never entered that laundry room, you did not experience the sense of vertigo that I did. It was suffocating, dizzying. I now believe that my unique perceptions were purposely blocked or distorted. There are extremely powerful forces at work here, Lee Anne, but before we go after Rouge, we need to know the why of it. We must, at the very least, know the why, even if the how never reveals itself. However, I wouldn't depend on that."

"You want to save him from harm because you do not believe his intent is malicious, but a desperate attempt to rescue the daughter and what's left of his family. The photographs will tell us some things. Even the one I doubted. However, we must first chance the touch of darkness with both Reeves and the Mecklenburg girl."

"Yes. We must stay together. Hopefully, these interviews will prove fruitful. I just want to survive the encounters. I've got a bad feeling about the future of things to come."

She cringes, shutting her eyes with a shudder. "Eyes. Eyes in the darkness. Teeth, like daggers. The floor made of obsidian glass, sulfur water, sand." Agent Seward shakes her head, wishing to shun the flash of images and smells. She suddenly withdraws from his touch. Her skin crawls as fibers of her Cashmere sweater bristle and rise from a sudden onslaught of static.

"It is intensely unsettling, but true. I was there, and I was terrified. Their warning was potent, yet we have a job to do. Before we go there, we must know more because I believe Rouge is holding vigil. He's not going anywhere. These two images will confirm the need to interview the detective and the girl. In turn, whether they communicate or not, Detective Reeves and Stacie Mecklenburg will produce something. I was trying to protect you, but it may be you, who protects me in the end. I was warned that interfering will only invite destruction, madness, and death. Whatever seeped through the fear was not evil, exactly, but it was close enough. What eked through was more like the potential for evil and destruction, and something else. . . ."

"What is it, Michael? What else did you discern?"

". . . fierce loyalty. Love even," he whispers. "The Rouge lineage holds great meaning for these beings, while they feel an utter disdain for mankind in general."

"I understand," she replies. "You could be right. We should stay together until the end, gathering the pieces together." Agent Seward rubs her thumbs across her fingers. "Jesus."

"Take your time."

"Okay. Okay." She takes a long blow. "I've got a feeling I'm gonna want that same long, cold shower like a baby screams to be fed." "Are you ready," he asks. "I'll understand if you don't want to do this because the personal experiences we are going to face may be exponentially worse."

"I'm with you, partner. All the way in, I'm with you."

Together, they reach for the image of Detective Reeves on the computer monitor. Moments later, when they finally emerge from the office, Agent Seward runs to the nearest trash bin to vomit. Chief Cramer does not question them. Rather, he directs the female agent to the restroom where she can compose herself in privacy. He notices that Agent Sievert is sweating and breathing hard. Whatever they experienced in his closed office seemed to be physically taxing.

When he places a hand on the FBI agent's shoulder, he retracts because of the intense heat.

On the way to the hospital, the meteorologist warns radio listeners to prepare for wave after wave of the foul, northbound weather being generated by two massive tropical storms that have suddenly formed in the southeastern Atlantic and the Gulf of Mexico. Until further notice, flood warnings are in effect for several counties.

Chief Cramer admits, "I hate rainy weather. It makes things grow and fortifies the earth, but it can wreak havoc when accompanied by wind, electrical discharges, and multiple automobile accidents.

Detective Blake agrees. "It's a good thing that everyone can't make detective. There wouldn't be any traffic cops to carry the load." He wants to chuckle, but he holds it when he glances at Chief Cramer's expression.

Ignoring Blake's comment, he grunts at the unwelcome news and scoffs, "Tropical storm cast-off, miserable weather for days to come, and failed alien abductions. On top of all that, a crazed, drunken, decorated law enforcement officer goes on a potentially deadly vehicular rampage. In addition, let us not forget the miracle child, who survives a tragic bus accident and two lightning strikes just days apart. Demon-possessed young Black girl in a coma floats in midair after summoning mother earth's total upheaval, complete with two freakish tornadoes. Mayor's son and daughter completely disappear without a trace and reappear without a clue. Christ, what will the headlines read tomorrow?"

When Detective Blake blasts through a swath of water, spraying the trees to the right, he adds to Chief Cramer's inquiry by saying, "Dangerous kidnaper takes own life when cornered." He looks at the agents in the back seat with a grin, hoping to lighten the mood with very poorly chosen words.

Agents Sievert and Seward simply look at one another, thinking the same thing as they turn their heads to look out the windows. Each wishes they had not allowed Chief Cramer to convince them to ride along instead of following in their own vehicle.

Though concerned about Detective Reeves, their thoughts reek with vengeance and deception. Chief Cramer is curious and wants to ask how they knew he was eavesdropping, but that would only serve to incriminate him. His fascination with their mental astuteness perplexes him to the point of childish envy. What the chief does not know is that they both recognize most of his flattery and charm as a facade. It oozes from him like drying mud on the deck of a rocking boat. For different reasons, neither can be fully trusted.

"Agent Seward, are you feeling better? If you don't mind my asking, what happened back there?"

Agent Seward politely says, "I'm feeling much better, sir. I appreciate your concern."

Agent Sievert tries to keep a smile from curling his lips.

"Well, Agent Seward, don't leave me hanging."

She clears her throat to say, "It's nothing, Chief Cramer. I just hate the sight of my own blood."

The confused look on their faces is priceless, but fleeting. It is quickly replaced by a sudden wave of revulsion when they finally get it. Now an uneasy burst of hilarious laughter comes.

She winks at her partner and smiles. "Got you there for a second, didn't I? The local boys have got to learn to keep up because my twisted sense of humor is just as twisted as I am."

They turn in, stopping under the canopy to let them out before Detective Blake pulls to the curb. Security comes out to tell them they cannot park there, but quickly changes his mind.

Moments later, Doctor Talal Baki begins to explain his preliminary findings in comparison to examinations done in Granville County. As he looks at the vital stats and lab results on the clipboard, he shakes his head.

"I'm afraid that Detective Reeves is completely uncommunicative at this time, and unresponsive to any treatment. He's got enough sedatives in him to put an elephant to sleep, but his heart rate remains extremely high. BP and histamine levels are also elevated. According to the EMTs, the patient has been this way since they began transport. The closer they got to this facility, the higher the BP and heart rate became. We have performed an EKG, but strangely enough, his synapses are firing like pistons in a runaway speedboat. We are applying eyewash to keep his eyes moisturized because he simply will not blink. Not even once since arriving. Blood tests show no detectable toxins, amphetamines, cocaine in his system. Other than a diminishing amount of alcohol, his blood chemistry is way off. If I didn't know better, I would swear that this man has just escaped a burning building."

"What do you mean by that," asks Chief Cramer.

"There is just too much carbon dioxide expelling from his body. I am talking about levels almost as high as you would find in a suicidal person, who locks himself in a garage with the car running. He is receiving oxygen, of course. His white blood count suggests infection. He is sweating profusely, but he has no fever, and shows no sign of pathogens, bacteria, diabetes, nor viruses."

Chief Cramer asks, "Don't you people have some clue as to what's going on?"

Dr. Baki rubs the combed over hairs of his balding scalp and shakes his head. He looks down at the medical stats and says, "By all indications, it is as if Detective Reeves is having a waking dream. More accurately, he seems to be having a nightmare with his eyes wide open. We are going to perform more tests, including a CT Scan and, if necessary, a Magnetic Resonance Imaging Scan to see what may be going on inside. There is no sign of stroke. Physically, for someone who has been involved in several accidents, he has only sustained a few minor cuts and abrasions. Otherwise, Chief Cramer, he's really as healthy as a well-kept horse. The problem may be of a psychological nature. That's certainly possible."

Blake comes out of the room just as Chief Cramer says, "Doctor, these are FBI Agents Seward and Sievert. I would like to give them a moment with your patient after I've gone in to let him know that we are behind him one-hundred percent."

"Yes, of course, but please keep it brief. Although the detective is not speaking, he is in a highly agitated state of shock. We've got to find a way to safely bring him down, or he is going to burn out like a matchstick. We are checking the databases for resembling signature symptoms. I have also contacted several of my colleagues, two of which are on the way to consult."

Detective Blake is shaking his head, while scratching an itchy wrist. "It's no use, Chief Cramer. My partner is not in the building. I don't know what caused this, but someone will pay. When I looked into Arnie's eyes, it felt like I was invisible. And then he...."

Doctor Baki asks, "Yes, what is it? Did he suddenly respond in some way?"

Blake averts his eyes on the cusp of tears. "Arnie . . . he just lays there and urinates on himself."

Dr. Baki scratches his scalp, absently, and replies, "That is the second time since arriving here, I'm sorry to say. I will have a nurse clean him up. We will take further precautions against repeated incontinency. I'm sorry you had to witness that, detective."

Chief Cramer strokes his mustache and says, "Dear God in heaven. I'm going in now, but I want you to make sure my officer gets the best care possible. I want you to keep my office apprised of his status the moment he shows any improvement. Is that clear?"

"Of course, Chief Cramer. You have my word that we will do everything in our power to help him. Please excuse me. I need to authorize more tests and have the patient cleaned up."

Chief Cramer goes inside and stands beside Detective Reeves' hospital bed. He sighs and says, "Arnold, if you can hear me, you have my every sympathy and support. I promise you that we will find the underlying cause of this. You just concentrate on getting better. We need you out there. I will pray for you, son."

He walks away and gives the FBI agents a shot. They approach and draw the partition curtains closed before Agent Seward asks, "Detective Reeves, do you know who I am? Do you remember what happened to you? It's me, Lee Anne. Remember?"

For the briefest moment, Detective Reeves almost smiles, but those red, terrified eyes quickly resume staring holes in the ceiling. Still, he tries to speak, only managing a series of sputters that produce nothing coherent. His eyes want to return to her face, but they are drawn back to the ceiling with every attempt to pronounce a single word. Seek.

She is about to touch his secured arm, but Agent Sievert stops her from making physical contact.

"Not yet. Not alone. Maybe, not at all. He is much too hot for either of us to touch," he warns. Agent Sievert's attention is drawn to the red spot in the middle of Reeves' forehead just above the bridge of the nose.

"What's the matter?" she asks.

"Haven't you noticed anything about each person that comes in contact with Detective Reeves?"

"You're right. They are all scratching some part of their body. Could this be an allergic reaction?" Agent Seward suggests.

"It's a distinct possibility, but he is trapped in a living nightmare. I get the sense that he's somehow . . ."

She says, "Caught in a loop?"

"My thoughts, exactly. Look at the red spot between his eyebrows. In the Hindu culture, that spot would be considered the chakra *Ajna*, the third eye. The Sankrit interpretation of the term chakra stands for wheel or turning. However, in what is known as the Yogic Culture, it translates into vortex and sometimes whirlpool."

She says, "Wow. You actually took yoga and metaphysic lessons. I mean, how else would you know that, besides dating Hindu women?" He smiles and says, "I was looking for answers when I didn't fully understand who and what I was. Please stay out of my head. Stop digging around and let's concentrate on his disconnected mind."

"You're right. I apologize. As much as I hate to do it for some inexplicable reason, do you think we should touch him now? There just seems to be some form of barrier, something keeping me out somehow. It is difficult to read him."

Agent Sievert stops her from touching him. "There is a barrier. We don't have to touch him. In fact, I strongly advise against it." He pushes the call button. "There's only one piece of information he can provide us at this point. But it's unnecessary to make contact because we already have that answer. You just haven't thought of it yet. It's Stacie Mecklenburg who we must penetrate. Doing both people in one night may short out our circuits, Lee Ann. I'm almost certain of it now."

A voice asks over the intercom, "This is Nurse Johansson. May I help you?"

Agent Sievert asks, "Nurse Johansson, this is FBI Agent Sievert Can you ask Dr. Baki to come in when he is available?"

"Yes sir. He's right here and on the way."

"Thank you."

"What are you thinking, Michael? Talk to me."

"When you—we—touched that screen, it overwhelmed you and that's why you felt so ill. It got to me, also. Imagine physical contact with him right now as being exponentially worse. It will be unimaginably worse for us both."

Dr. Baki walks in quickly. "Has something happened? Were you able to get any answers?"

"Not verbally," Agent Sievert says. "Doctor, you said his blood chemistry is out of balance. Correct?"

"Yes it is."

"Can you get someone from dermatology to see if they have a Wood's lamp or ultraviolet light?" asks Sievert.

"Yes. In fact, if I am not mistaken, I believe we have just such a device on this floor. Why, what good would that do?"

"Please be patient with me. It's just a theory."

He calls the desk and asks the nurse to bring it. When she shows up five minutes later, Chief Cramer and Detective Blake follow.

"Please kill the lights. Now, draw his gown down. Thank you. Can you turn it on and hand it to me? Thanks."

When he passes the light across Detective Reeves' head and chest, the others are shocked.

Chief Cramer says, "Good Christ in heaven. What the hell is that, doctor?"

The purplish light illuminates what must be millions of squiggly strands covering Reeves' body from head to toe. Barely above a whisper, Dr. Baki looks at the pinkish-white fibers on the man's body and humbly admits, "I have seen similar fungal colonies on the skin. It resides on the upper torso and arms, but his body is literally covered with it."

Sievert says, "On his forehead, they are concentrated at a much higher density. Dr. Bakki, are you at all familiar with Hindu philosophy?"

"Yes. Yes, of course. That would be *Ajna*, chakra of the third eye. But what does that have to do with anything?"

"Do you have anything with sulfur in it, like a lotion or shampoo?" Agent Sievert asks.

"Yes. We have several, like Selenium Sulfide two-point-five percent lotion slash body shampoo that's prescribed to patients with the fungal outbreak that I just mentioned."

"If it comes in a slightly stronger concentration, have it rubbed copiously on his body from head to toe with cool, wet sponges. I want it spread over every square-inch of his body, hair, and armpits. Pubic areas included."

"Before I do, I must know why. Can you tell me that, at the very least, agent?"

By placing her hand at the center of Agent Sievert's back, Agent Seward's trancelike words are, "*Ajna*—the Third Eye Chakra—the wheel is turning. There is great turmoil in the vortex, circling like a whirlpool. He is being driven mad, beset by visions so horrible that he cannot take his eyes away from them. Skin feels like biting mosquitoes, angry ants, swarming wasps."

The mystified doctor makes the pharmacological request. "Go on," he says.

Agent Sievert instructs, "These fibrous materials are alive and driving him mad. Notice how his fingers are the only moving parts of his body. Even though his wrists are secure to the side rails, he is still trying to scratch the itch he cannot reach. You mentioned that his blood chemistry is off kilter. Dr. Baki, are you still monitoring the histamine levels in his blood work?"

Dr. Baki says, "Yes," even before looking at the chart in his hand. "I noticed the elevated levels, but according to Detective Reeves' medical history, he has never had any allergies or allergic reactions to anything."

"It doesn't matter. Just administer anti-histamines and apply the Selenium Sulfide Solution. Leave it on for at least thirty-minutes to an hour. Be warned, he may react violently at first. If so, allow it to subside before gently scrubbing his skin down with a soft brush. I think a shower is out of the question at this point. Please, be warned that hot or warm water will only exacerbate things. Make sure your people don't neglect to get his back. It's one of the worse areas of aggravation. We must go, now. Please let me know how it turns out."

"Do you have a medical background, Agent Sievert?" Dr. Baki asks.

"Not in the least. Trust me, doctor. It will work. Besides, this is a noninvasive procedure so what have you got to lose? What's he going to do, hit you with a malpractice lawsuit for bathing him?"

The doctor implements his request with Chief Cramer's approval.

Before walking out, Agent Seward says, "Detective Blake, you told us that you guys are more than just partners, right?" When he confirms, she says, "If this works, Detective Reeves may be a bit disoriented, not knowing where he is. It will be better if you stay for a reasonable amount of time just in case. As his partner and friend, yours should be the first face he sees because of the trust and friendship factors of your relationship. Can you handle that for us, and send word if there are any changes?"

Sievert adds, "There is a very good chance that he may simply drift off to sleep from the sheer exhaustion. Even if he doesn't talk to you before drifting off, it will still be a positive sign that he's coming out of it."

"Yeah, sure, you got it. Chief Cramer, sir, I would like to be here for him just in case this works."

"Certainly, Detective Blake. What are partners for? Let me know what happens."

Blake hands over the keys to the car.

When the nurse returns from the pharmacy with several bottles of the Selenium Sulfide Topical Suspension, Agent Sievert asks, "May I borrow a few of those?"

She looks at the doctor, who nods his head.

"Thank you, doctor. Of course, this may just amount to a wild shot in the dark. When I was much younger, I had a similar fungal outbreak called pityriasis versicolor. It was a slightly worse form of tinea versicolor. Every spring or summer, it returned with a vengeance. The itching drove me crazy. It was worse when I sweated, especially on my back where I just couldn't reach to scratch. However, even in the places that I could reach, scratching never seemed to help the itching. The third dermatologist that I was forced to see, showed me what was causing it under a UV light. I was horrified when I saw those squiggly little white lines everywhere. They weren't moving about, but they looked like tiny little worms. I must admit that I felt dirty and unclean. He said, 'those pinkish-white strands are actually fungal colonies. The symptoms include round areas of hypopigmentation, caused by the colonies that we cannot see with the naked eye in regular lighting. These colonies produce acidic waste that causes the relentless itching, but only on the upper torso, arms, and face.' They returned several times, until I finally realized that I never washed my scalp with the smelly solution. It took about two to three weeks to regain normal pigmentation with more exposure to direct sunlight. I hope this will help Detective Reeves, although, I have never seen such a widespread outbreak. Still, it is a positive place to start. Sulfur seems to be a central theme I this case, playing both good guy and culprit."

Agent Seward approaches the other nurse at her station, inquiring about Stacie Mecklenburg. A moment later, she informs that the physician released the Mecklenburg girl after arriving at the trauma unit by ambulance earlier. Miraculously, she suffered no ill effects of the incident. Apparently, Robert Mecklenburg was also released into his parents' care.

Chapter 24

Father, Mother, Sister, Son

While Chief Cramer drives, he makes the call. When a woman answers, he asks, "Is Mayor Mecklenburg in? Please tell him that Chief of Police Cramer is on the line. Thank you. Yes, I'll hold." A moment of silence passes. "Larkin, this is Cramer. The reason I'm calling is to inform you that I'm heading to your home with Agents Sievert and Seward. Yes, I understand that this may be an inconvenience, but it is important that they be given access to your daughter in an effort to resolve issues surrounding the kidnaping. Be that as it may, you should know that I'm turning into your driveway as we speak. As they stated previously, 'Mr. Rouge is still out there. If his daughter dies, what's to stop him from taking your children, again?' Now, do you want this thing resolved or not?"

Mayor Mecklenburg protests the intrusion, stating several reasons for not forcing his daughter to face questioning after such traumatic events. Of course, his dead brother's wake is tomorrow evening.

"Mayor Mecklenburg, I understand that these are stressful times for your entire family. I do. Nevertheless, do you really think I would subject myself to this godforsaken weather in the middle of the night for absolutely nothing? Please, let these people do their jobs because there are simply too many odd occurrences surrounding this case for it all to be fucking coincidental. We just left the hospital where one of my detectives is . . . I see. I am yet to release that bit of information to anyone, so who told you? Uh huh, well it really doesn't matter because we are trying to help. We're here."

Agent Sievert, who sits in the backseat, says, "Sounds like the Mayor Mecklenburg still has issues, embarrassment being one of them. We will exercise as much discretion as possible."

Chief Cramer replies, "Just being a father trying to protect his daughter from any further distress. I'm sure you can understand that." "Certainly."

* * *

Rain tapping against the triple-paned window is deafening, but there is no thunder and lightning. The rhythm of the clicking and thumping sounds tell her that Robbie approaches with the assistance of crutches. Stacie is lying on her right side, sweating and scratching. Robbie knocks, lightly.

On the verge of tears, Stacie tells him, "I'm alright, Robbie. Please just leave me alone."

He adjusts his balance to try the doorknob, surprised to find it unlocked. In the cold room, she has kicked the black and white comforter to the floor. Seeing his sweaty sister lying under a sheet, rocking back and forth, breaks his heart. He turns slightly to the side to enter anyway.

Robbie lumbers clumsily to her bedside. He says, "You're going to catch a cold in here. Let me turn on your fireplace."

"No," she begs through clenched teeth. "Don't do that. Heat only makes it worse."

He finds a spot and sits, behind her. Putting the crutches aside, he turns to his agonized sister and strokes her damp hair. He caresses Stacie's cheek and says, "Hey, it's just me. Please tell me what I can do to help you, Stacie. I'll do anything. I can't stand seeing you this way."

She shifts onto her left side. "I know, Robbie, but I'm fine. Please just leave me alone. Please." Her eyes are practically begging. She is shaking her legs slightly, which he feels.

"No, sis. I will not go until you talk to me. What can I do?"

"There is nothing you can do, okay? No one can help me, so please just go away!"

As she weeps quietly, tears begin to spill from his eyes. He strokes her arm and moves closer to whisper, "I'm so sorry. I know you must hate me for trying to run away, leaving you behind. I panicked. I have never been so scared of anything in my life. Please don't hate me forever."

Stacie sits up and hugs him, stifling her tears as she says, "I don't hate you, Robbie. You're my brother, I love you. It is one of the reasons I volunteered for this, so you wouldn't have to. You probably would have died. Don't you see that? All the things I know about you as my brother would have been deleted like a file from your hard drive."

"What he did to you—what she's doing to you—is wrong, Stacie. We've got to tell someone."

"No!" she shrieks at him. "God, it hurts so bad at times, I just want to die. I just want it to be over, but we still can't tell." She cries openly now, no longer trying to hide her distress from him.

"I hate them for this. I want to kill both those bastards!" he declares. "If I ever get the chance, I swear to you I will."

She releases him, sitting back to look her brother in the eyes with pity. "Robbie, no. It's not her. She's hurting just as much as I am. We bear it equally." Stacie scratches her tingling scalp and itching arms in torment.

"What you're going through is killing you, but you don't owe them anything."

"Now you sound like your father, Robert. It was your own kin, who nearly killed all of us. Or don't you remember that part of this tale? My parents watched my brother fall to his death when he could have been saved. He was not able to hold on to that cable, as were you. Even though your selfish father treated me with utter contempt, I no longer hold your family accountable. My agonizing father is a good man, who only wishes to see me live. Even as a cowardly White boy, if necessary!"

Robbie holds his breath because this is the first time Kysing Rouge speaks to him through his sister's lips. In a way, even though he declared his anger for what the transference is doing to Stacie, a part of him still seeks to deny the fact.

"My God, it's really you," is all he can say.

"Yes, Robert, it is me. I am Kysing Rouge. My mother's name is Yara. My father's name is Banjalanah Rouge. My dead brother, whom I still love dearly, is Kilarin "Killer" Rouge. My sister is Stacie Mecklenburg-Rouge, whom I love for this unprecedented sacrifice. You do not have to worry about Stacie for very much longer because I cannot stand what my presence is doing to her.

The pain, at this moment, is not as bad as you think for either of us. The impending agony that surely builds within is like awaiting the return of the lamenting winds. The waiting, knowing not when it comes again— that is true torment. However, even as I speak, I feel my vacated body slipping toward the outer boundaries of the *Reach*. I am dying, little-by-little, moment-by-moment, right before my languishing mother's eyes. Like any other person, I also fear death, but I will soon choose it so that my sister may resume her life upon this earth. My death will be my gift of gratitude for her brave sacrifice. Rather than allowing my continuing presence to cause harm, I will go willingly, hoping that I will find Kilarin in the afterlife. There, we will be together forever because the love between a brother and sister can never truly die."

"No. Please don't give up on my account, Kysing," Stacie asks of her guest aloud. "Give yourself a fighting chance. I can take it. I will not just let you die. We have to hold on a little longer. I'm begging you to do that for me, but even more so for your parents' sake."

Witnessing this verbal exchange between two minds in one body stuns Robbie Mecklenburg. He is speechless, as two completely different sentient beings converse from the same set of lips. It is simply overwhelming, nearly impossible to process.

"I . . . I'm . . . I'm sorry. I was just angry. I never really meant what I said. I feel so helpless, and all I want is to help."

Stacie smiles. This time, when the vessel speaks, there are two distinct, overlapping voices. It is deeper, darker, most penetrating. "You already have, Robbie. Robert. You have distracted us from the discomfort."

"Jeez. As if this whole experience hasn't been weird enough, I never imagined that you could actually speak at the same time."

Stacie asks, "Kind of cool and creepy at the same time, huh? Think of it like the ultimate game of hide and seek, Robbie." The smile dissipates, and without warning, her eyes take on an eerie, opaque quality. She says in that deep, combined tone, "Seek. Seek the shadows of the mind. The seers are here, and we fear that they wish to harm our father."

"Are you talking about the cops?" Robbie asks. "What can I do? Would you like me to stall them or leave the room so you can act like you are sleeping?"

As Robbie reaches for his crutches, Stacie touches his arm. "No Stay. When they come upstairs, we should appear to be having a funny conversation as if nothing is wrong."

Her skin crawls. The anxiety revives that exasperating itch.

* * *

Downstairs, in the huge living room, the three visitors are invited to sit. Rock Hill's Chief of Police Archie Mecklenburg is present. They have been discussing the final arrangements for Mac's funeral. Before he stands to shake hands, Chief Mecklenburg closes an open folder on the coffee table and turns it over.

After guiding the guests in, Neara Jones is walking out. Pauline stops her from leaving the room, so she takes a seat nearby. Her husband's look of disapproval does not sway his wife. To prove it, which is a clear sign to Larkin that she is in no mood for his bullshit, she says, "Neara, dear, come sit closer. Come on, right next to me. You are as much a part of this family as I am. You have been my rock and shelter in these trying times, and I need you with me."

The surprised housekeeper does not feel it her place to take part in this meeting. She glances at Mayor Mecklenburg, who displays his acquiescence with but a hand gesture. Therefore, as requested, Neara sits close to Pauline Mecklenburg, who holds her hand. Mayor Mecklenburg stands and rubs his forehead in frustration.

"Before we begin, can I offer you some water, perhaps, or a drink?

I certainly need one. How about you, Archie, ready for a refresher?"

"Sure, why not?"

"Chief Cramer, Eddie, please indulge me by joining us."

Chief Edward Cramer considers it for a second, "I'd be happy to. Again, Larkin, I apologize for the ungodly hour. It is fortunate that you are all still up."

"That's fine. We are just finishing some personal family matters. Now, agents, would you like some coffee?"

Agent Sievert surprises him by saying, "Actually, mayor, I'd like some of that cognac you are having. I think my partner would like to sample the twelve-year-old Scotch that Chief Mecklenburg is drinking." To further their confusion, he adds, "I know that civilized people are sippers. We don't usually drink on the job, but this has been and extremely stressful, though enlightening, day. For what we are here to do, please don't skimp on either one. Go long."

Mayor Mecklenburg does not know how to react. He cannot tell if this is a poker-faced jokester or if Agent Sievert is serious. He finds himself stuck, standing in the middle of everyone like a human statue. His brother, also curious, casts a quick glance about the room for something specific.

Chief Cramer smiles despite himself. In all the years of knowing Mayor Mecklenburg, he has never seen the man so completely dumbfounded.

Pauline clears her throat to give her husband a kick-start. As Neara stands to accommodate them, Pauline rises with her. She gives Agent Sievert a wink and smile, wondering if they are together in ways other than just being partners.

"Neara, I will handle the drinks. Can you go upstairs and look in on the children? If they aren't asleep, please make sure they are decent. Hurry back."

Pauline depresses the button that opens the double doors of the hidden bar. The mayor notices the look on Chief Cramer's face and

asks, "What are you grinning about, Edward?"

Chief Cramer asks, "You mean you haven't noticed?"

"Noticed what, man?"

He looks at the mayor's brother to say, "Go on. Tell him, Archie."

Larkin looks at his brother to ask, "What is he talking about? I'm in no mood for mind games. The entire fucking world has turned on its ear, and he is acting as if everything is one big joke!"

With her back turned, Pauline says, "Calm down, Larkin. Please don't swear like that in front of our guests. Tell him, Archie."

Chief Archibald Mecklenburg looks at his red-faced brother and answers, "FBI Agent Sievert walked in here, and in a matter of seconds, he tells us exactly what we are drinking right down to the age of the Scotch in my glass."

"What?"

"I looked to see if the bar was open or if the bottle was sitting in plain sight. Obviously, there was no way of knowing because the liquor was not in sight. I think the fact that you never noticed is really what amuses Edward."

"Is that what this is all about, parlor tricks?"

"I believe the agent was simply proving a point. The point is not meant to simply demonstrate that the joke is on you, Larkin, but that they know their stuff. It might be best to hear them out."

Chief Cramer's cell phone rings. He answers and listens for a moment, thanking the caller before hanging up. After doing so, he looks at everyone in the room with his left brow arched in contemplation. He says to the agents, "You know, don't you? You already know what that call entailed."

"What's going on, Eddie? Seriously, what's this all about?" Chief Cramer says, "Oh, the things I've witnessed tonight alone. This team, these two, have amazingly acute insights into human nature. Among a myriad of other talents that I am yet to fathom. I doubt I ever will, but I believe they are getting close to answering questions we haven't even asked. So I implore you to accommodate them in any way they may need."

"I just don't know if I can do that, Eddie," says the mayor, while Pauline distributes the drinks.

Chief Cramer turns his attention to Agent Sievert and Seward to say, "I don't know how you did it, but, by God, it worked! That was Dr. Baki from the hospital. He informed me that Detective Reeves has responded favorably to the treatment you suggested. It seemed to make things worse for the thirty-minutes while the solution dried on his skin, during which, Detective Reeves behaved like a rabid animal. Then, his blood pressure and heart rate finally normalized. Reeves does not remember what happened, has no clue, but the doctor thinks it will return in time. As you suggested, he just wanted to go right to sleep. They put mittens on his hands to keep him from scratching himself raw. They will continue the same treatment as needed, until it no longer bothers him. I owe you both a great debt of gratitude. Detective Reeves is going to be okay. Thank you both."

"There's no need to thank us, sir. We are just doing our job," Agent Seward says.

"No need to be modest, agent. We don't always get to give credit where it is due. That being said, I think I'm going to enjoy this drink because I will probably see the sunrise in this uniform. You have the floor. Take it away."

Neara Jones comes down, closing the stain glassed interior French doors as instructed. She sits exactly where she was, and Pauline hands her one of two glasses of brandy.

After two huge gulps to finish off the drink just handed him, Agent Sievert stands before the fireplace. He has an idea, but he must get some cooperation, first.

"Mr. and Mrs. Mecklenburg, it is extremely important that we speak to your daughter. I am aware of the astonishing events that took place on your front lawn, as are we all. In any other case, this would have ended in tragedy. However, this case is anything but routine. This investigation has taken on a completely new meaning. It is vital that we speak to Stacie alone, without hindrance or interference of any degree."

Pauline asks, "Neara, are they asleep?"

"No. Robbie is paying his sister a visit. They are just sitting on her bed talking and laughing. Lord only knows, after everything those children have endured, this is a very good sign. Maybe things can finally return to normal for them."

Mayor Mecklenburg emphatically states, "Well there you go. That's it then. If they are in such good spirits, and finally communicating again, I'll not see them put through anymore. Not tonight. I'm afraid my parental duty to my kids' mental and physical well-being must take precedence over your investigative needs. The answer is no."

"Listen to them, Larkin. They mean the children no harm, I assure you," argues Chief Cramer.

"I'm sorry you feel that way," Agent Seward says, joining her partner near the fireplace. "As family members, we understand that you're being protective. Any parent worth his or her salt should be. However, you need to know something."

"What is it?" the mayor asks. His wife becomes very concerned at this point.

"No, sir. Why should I tell you anything, when you have been a bully and an obstacle to this investigation from the start? I know the secrets you're hiding, Mayor Mecklenburg, and I can prove it to you with but a few words. Because I am not here as the enemy, I will not speak of it. If you wish, go ahead and call the governor, or Assistant Director Majors. That is what you were just thinking, weren't you? When Agent Sievert surprised you by accepting a drink instead of coffee, you were caught off-guard—stuck—but not for the most apparent reasons. You were wondering how you could hold it over our heads if he was serious about having a drink."

Pauline Mecklenburg stands at this point. Her reaction seems hostile, but she knows that this woman is right. Because of it,

Larkin is about to kick them out, forbidding them to ever talk to Stacie. It is his parental right because she has done nothing wrong.

"Don't bother telling us to leave, sir. We will go and never come back. In fact, we can drop the entire matter and classify it as unsolved and closed. My partner and I have busted our asses, working our way through a maze of lies and total bullshit during the course of this federal investigation. However, we have experienced things, the likes of which would swallow you whole. And I promise you, Mayor Mecklenburg, that when we leave you to your own devices, it will consume your tidy little lives because this is probably far from over."

"How dare you speak to me like this? In my own home, no less," Mayor Mecklenburg shouts. "Get the hell out of my house. You're drunk. Just because you can't handle your liquor . . ."

"Shut up, Larkin," Pauline demands. "I want to hear her out."

"What did you just say?"

"You heard me loud and clear," his wife barks.

"You should put your pride aside, my good friend. I don't have a clue as to what they really need from your daughter, other than a more in-depth statement. Whatever it is, I suggest giving them the latitude. If I had ten more like them, we wouldn't need any detectives from Rock Hill to Charlotte. I've gleaned a few things since they arrived, and if you don't want this issue of the kidnappings resolved, one will be forced to wonder why. As I stated before, Mr. Rouge is still out there. And if his daughter should die, there is no telling what he may do. Be mindful, he's already proven once that nothing we do can stop him from taking them again and returning them dead next time."

The other white-haired chief of police clears his throat. He says, "Brother, those are mighty tall words from your own police chief and long-standing friend of the Mecklenburg family. Maybe you should listen to his endorsement."

The mayor turns on his brother to complain, "Not you, too!"

Chief Mecklenburg says, "I'll tell you what. I don't know about you, but this young lady has piqued my curiosity. What say we give her a chance to tell us something unexpected? If what they have to say or do doesn't pan out, then I'll escort them with their bag of parlor tricks to the door myself."

"Pauline says, "Go ahead, Agent Seward. Regardless of my husband's irrational objections, those are my babies up there, too. Please."

Agent Seward glances at her partner, who nods the go ahead. She approaches the bar and rudely pours herself another drink of excellent whiskey.

While she does so, Agent Sievert advises, "From this point forward, you should all consider anything you hear or see as highly classified information. In fact, Agent Seward and myself are both considered classified. We don't even exist to anyone outside this room."

Now Agent Seward looks at the worried mother to say, "Before I do anything, I will tell you this, ma'am. Neara, your dear friend and housekeeper, is mistaken about your kids. What she thought she saw and heard upstairs was staged for her benefit. They waited until they heard footsteps approaching to start talking loudly and laughing as if nothing is wrong because they are hiding something because they knew we were already here. Think back please."

Neara furrows her brow as she considers the agent's words and rewinds the mental tape. She says, "You know, she may be right. It was quiet as a mouse when I first went upstairs. I thought they were both in their own beds fast asleep, until I got closer. Just as I was about to open the door, they laughed so loud, it gave me a start. As loud as they appeared to be, I should have heard them long before I got there. The more I think about it, you may be right." "Why, that proves nothing," the mayor protests.

Pauline looks to the female agent, who informs, "Mrs. Mecklenburg, your daughter has answers we need, and she is the only one who can supply them. We promise to do her no harm. In fact. . . ."

Pauline says, "Yes, please go on."

A quick thought leads to the omission of Agent Seward's own fears. Instead, she says, "My partner has something Stacie may need, desperately. Has she shown any signs of scratching or a constant itch, as if she is having an allergic reaction to something? Is she displaying any subtle, but odd behavioral patterns?"

By the look in the mother's eyes, every word holds true. With deliberation, Agent Seward walks slowly around the room, coming to a stop to the right of Chief Archibald Mecklenburg.

She now states, "If what I do next holds absolutely no meaning, please put us out and never let us darken your doorstep ever again."

She reaches down to pick up the chief's unfinished drink, and rudely downs it as if she were merely drinking a glass of water. "You should all know that I can't seem to get drunk. Not even a little, no matter what or how much alcohol I consume. My partner is the same. It only drowns out some of the background noises in our heads because we are both crazy."

With everyone, other than Agent Sievert in suspense, she holds the attention in the room. She goes quiet for a few seconds, staring at the decorative pattern of the stained glass of the French doors. Without looking, she places her right hand at the center of Chief Mecklenburg's back, gently stroking it in a circular motion. She slowly points downward with her left forefinger until it rests on a file Chief Mecklenburg closed as Neara guided them into the room.

Agent Lee Anne Seward simply states, "This is where it all began for most of you."

Mayor Mecklenburg slumps onto the opposite end of the couch. His brother sits erect wordlessly.

She continues. "Classified information given to you through back channels by someone who owes you his life. DEA must pursue suspect to rescue a wounded, deep-cover operative. High-impact blood splatters on the window . . . drug contraband . . . weapons cache . . . *Hombre Muerto* . . . high explosives . . . deaths on the bridge . . . school bus . . . Kilarin Rouge . . . Banja Rouge swims a river of blood only to find his son dead . . . Mac . . .Mackenzie . . . Manuel Mendez Drug Cartel . . . connections to—M. . . ."

"Enough! Enough, no more," the mayor finally shouts. "I beg of you, no more. Please, that's quite enough."

With her eyes still affixed, Agent Seward removes her finger from the surface of the file. She looks straight ahead, raising the same hand before her. When she utters, "There is too much blood. Help me," Agent Sievert hurries to her side, gently taking her hand in his own. When the fugue passes, Agent Seward slips, seamlessly, back into the relevant. She remains quiet for a moment.

The mayor's brother glances at Chief Cramer, who arches his eyebrows and nods.

Chief Mecklenburg asks, "How could you know all those things? Even with Federal access to information, how could you know what's in this particular file? I deliberately closed it and turned it over before you could see any of the graphic photographs?"

"Jesus, Joseph, and Mary," whispers the mayor. "I could have done without all of that." Mayor Larkin Mecklenburg dusts off his drink, contemplating concerns that are his alone. He worries about the unnerving events that have already turned his family on its ear. The mayor is aware of a Federal probe into the financial connection with his recently deceased brother, McKenzie Mecklenburg. As if these recent events are not enough, from time to time, he detects a discrete, squint-eyed sort of loathing in the eyes of a daughter who used to worship him. It has been growing in intensity; he can almost feel her watching him, plotting behind those eyes.

Pauline Mecklenburg caresses Agent Seward's arm with a tearful smile as she makes eye contact. She nods her head and sits next to her husband. "Larkin, baby, what choice do we have? In light of their remarkable abilities, we owe it to everyone that died on that bridge to give these agents whatever they need to bring an end to this."

Chief Mecklenburg adds, "Larkin, you called in a favor with the governor, who used her influences to get the best people sent down here to find these kids. Even though the kidnaper returned your children, he remains at large. I reiterate the fact because you must face the fact that his ability to take them in the extraordinary manner in which he did, proves that there is little we can do to stop it from happening again if his only surviving child perishes. He may have done all of this to simply prove a point. He may have experienced a great measure of remorse, which forced him to return them both. That fact, within itself, technically, is still another mystery we may never solve because no one else saw him do it in broad daylight. There again, if his own daughter dies, who knows what he's capable of doing?"

Chief Cramer says, "Let's face the facts here, Larkin. There are unique aspects to this case that center, exclusively, around your family that no one is prepared to place into context. Typically, no young girl stands barefooted in the rain, at the center of multiple lightning strikes and survives the ordeal. Nor do their eyes glow as their feet float above the ground. We simple folks are not equipped to deal with the disturbing details of this case. As Tega Cay's Chief of Police, and I'm sure Police Chief Mecklenburg can agree, we defend our jurisdictional territory with a fervor and passion that alienates members of the Federal Justice Departments as though they are some kind of invading horde of marauders. Unfortunately, the same attitude trickles down through our ranks, which often hinder and sabotage investigations by simply leaking the details of federal probes to the media or worse. We can no longer afford such anti-productive attitudes, even where our own children are concerned."

Chief Archibald Mecklenburg feels a sense of shame. He nods his head and sighs. "As much as I hate to admit it, he is right, Larkin. It is time that we shed such ignorance and suspicion, and learn to accept the help that we often ask for."

Pauline Mecklenburg rubs the mayor's hands. She reaches up to brush his hair away from his forehead. "Okay," he agrees with those downcast eyes. "What do you require, Agent Sievert?"

"Ideally, Mayor and Mrs. Mecklenburg, we need to be alone with Stacie. It is important that there are no distractions. You have my word that this will not take very long. By the way, is this the only fireplace in your home?"

"What?" the distraught father asks.

Pauline Mecklenburg answers, "No. There are fireplaces in every bedroom. The others work with propane gas, not wood like this one. It's just not safe to leave the care of an open flame in the hands of children, no matter how responsible they have proven themselves to be. Why is that so important?"

Agent Seward replies, "Throughout history, staring at flames has always held a sort of calming, semi-hypnotic effect. Many arsonists, who have been apprehended, swear that staring into a flame is how they came to be what they are. We would prefer it if one or both parents escorts us up to her room, reassuring that it is okay to speak to us. If there is room enough, we will require three comfortable chairs—one facing the lit fireplace. Encourage Stacie, and leave us alone with her so she will feel more relaxed, unencumbered by your presence. If she asks that you stay, tell her that you are busy planning the funeral and leave anyway. If she insists and you stay, it probably means that she already intends to hold back information. Not that this is the case, but a girl who has been raped will always find it difficult to discuss the most vital details of it in front of her parents. You must reassure Stacie, and leave her with us."

"No, absolutely not," Mayor Mecklenburg says.

Agent Sievert looks directly into the eyes of Mayor Mecklenburg to say, "If she has had any issues with either of you, say a sudden change in attitude, you will be the one she will cling to most. Guilt will not allow you to leave her, but that won't change the way she feels about you."

He squints at the agent in awe of this remarkable statement.

"Larkin," says Chief Cramer. "Please comply. They are only trying to gather the evidence necessary to break this case. I have learned to trust their judgments, and the need for complete privacy. I have seen the results of their unique techniques, which always seem to yield dividends. If you don't trust them to be investigators with your daughter's best interest in mind, then please trust me as a good judge of character, old friend."

Pauline Mecklenburg asks, "Agent Seward, a little while ago, you mentioned that this isn't over. You also mentioned that your partner has something Stacie needs. Can you elaborate, please?"

Agent Seward looks at her partner. He approaches and asks Pauline Mecklenburg and Neara to join him. Agent Sievert reaches into his coat pockets to retrieve the bottles, "Ma'am, is your daughter behaving as if she's having allergic reactions? Scratching a lot, showing some dermal hyper-sensitivity that only worsens when she sweats?"

Pauline places her hand across her mouth. Neara, however, confirms that there is truth to his inquiry. "I have noticed reddish, irritated areas on her skin. She is showing signs of extreme discomfort." "This is Selenium Sulfide Lotion. It's more like a shampoo, really. I want you to make sure that Stacie uses it as a body wash at least twice a day, using cool or tepid water. It helped Detective Reeves, and it will alleviate the itching discomfort for a while. Get more from your healthcare provider and use as much as needed to cover her entire body. Most likely, she will need it after our interview. In fact, if she is reluctant to speak to us, apply this lotion to her arms, shoulders and back. I must admit that it has an acquired smell, but it will help. Agreed?"

"Yes. Anything you think will help, Agent Sievert. Was my daughter and the detective, who fell through the wall at the hospital,

exposed to something dangerous? Were they poisoned?"

Her trepidation is apparent.

He says, "This is just precautionary, ma'am. This will help her to think clearly. As my partner mentioned before, we don't think it is over. All the anomalous phenomena—Kysing Rouge's comatose body floating in midair behind an invisible barrier—for example, are somehow connected. You witnessed what you described as a thunderstorm in Stacie's hospital room, while there was a raging sandstorm in your son's room at the same time. The very way they disappeared and suddenly returned, your daughter's instantaneous healing, and her subsequent survival of two direct lightning strikes has to lead you to the conclusion that there is something extremely unusual going on here. The physicians cannot explain why Robert returned with his leg still broken, while Stacie's broken arm is completely healed. The titanium bolts and plates used by the Orthopedic Surgeon to stabilize your daughter's broken ulna and humerus bones have completely disappeared from her x-rays. Even the surgical scars have vanished. No one fully understands what is happening, but it directly involves Stacie Mecklenburg. These are all crucial issues that we need to address. We have theories, but your daughter will help the direction of this investigation, whether she answers our questions or not. Technically, this is no longer an active kidnaping situation. However, Agent Seward and I have a duty to continue the investigation because of all the disturbing, unresolved developments surrounding the original case. I'm asking you to trust us."

On the verge of tears, Pauline Mecklenburg depends on Neara to speak in her stead. The Black woman, who helped raise both children, says, "When Stacie first arrived from the hospital, her mother thought it best not to push. By the look in her eyes, we both got the feeling that she didn't recognize this home or me, for that matter. The doctor described it as PTDS or something like that."

"Yes. It is known as Post Traumatic Distress Syndrome, but you both believe it to be more than that."

"Mister, I have known those children all of their lives. If they ever felt they couldn't go to their parents with problems, they always sought my advice. Nowadays, they just smile and pretend as if absolutely nothing has happened. Stacie never speaks about her recent experiences, and we believe that Robert knows more than he is saying about what really happened to them when they disappeared from the hospital. You can tell that he wants to talk, but for some reason, he just will not open up about it. Now, what we saw earlier tonight defies all reason. May God bless her soul, and forgive me for saying so, but that young girl up there should be dead right now. We are all happy and very thankful that Stacie survived, but you must admit that this isn't normally the case."

With sad, downcast eyes, Pauline Mecklenburg nods and whispers, "I trust your judgment, Agent Sievert. While I cannot speak for my husband, I do have a say in what needs to be done in their best interest. Sometimes parents wish to protect their children from the truth of a disturbing matter, when it is facing facts that holds the very key to defeating it. Sometimes, a parent is actually protecting him or herself, instead of doing the hard thing to protect the child. I learned that particular lesson years ago from my dear friend here. I know that the pain of loss prompted that man to take our children in the first place, but he returned them for some reason. However, nothing has been the same since they returned, so I am going to take the doctors' advice by seeking professional counseling for my children. Seeing a shrink myself, doesn't seem like such a bad idea because nothing I've experienced jives with normal, everyday reality."

Agent Sievert looks at the woman, feeling her growing anxieties. "It may be a good idea to get all of this off your chest. I have no doubt that seeking professional help will benefit your children, greatly."

"Speak to my kids in any manner you wish. Do not concern yourselves with my husband. I think Agent Seward's little display, her so-called parlor trick, has placed the big bad bully in his proper place for once." She glances across the room where her husband now stands in front of the far window, quietly talking to his brother.

With their backs turned, staring out at the rainy weather, Chief Cramer approaches to join the conversation.

"Eddie," says Mayor Mecklenburg. "What's on your mind?"

"Larkin, we've been friends for many years now. I can tell you that it isn't what's on my mind that you should worry about, but what's on your own," Chief Cramer says with a discreet glance over his shoulder.

Just as Agent Seward answers her phone, and quickly retrieves her laptop from her bag, Mayor Mecklenburg whispers, "What the hell is that supposed to mean?"

Chief Cramer looks into the suspicious eyes of Chief Mecklenburg and says, "Well, let's just say you should stay out of their way. In fact, you should stay away from them period. I caution you to avoid thoughts concerning anything that you would never choose to divulge publically, at all costs. If there is anything you don't want coming to the attention of the Feds, put it as far away as you can because these two crack investigators are much more than they seem. Agent Seward's ability to tell you what is in that file and the way her partner knew exactly what you were drinking, serves warning that they are endowed with special gifts and exceptional qualities. Larkin, I'm not suggesting any wrongdoing on your part. Just consider it words of wisdom from a sympathetic ally."

"What are you telling us, that they are mind readers?" Larkin asks with skepticism.

Chief Cramer looks over his shoulder and says, "If you didn't notice, she just glanced this way the moment you had your little emotional outburst. Remember, they knew you were in my office as I tried to get rid of them. There was no reason to suspect that you were at the bottom of that call, but she sensed it. I believe he probably did, too. Earlier this evening, I allowed them use of my office to discuss some film footage. To my own discredit, I admit I was discretely planning to listen in on the discussion. However, as if he already knew, Agent Sievert immediately reached across my desk and turned the intercom off to keep me from eavesdropping. They have the aptitudes to see beyond the surface of things, and the shit I've seen tonight would absolutely blow your minds. I can tell you without a doubt that Agent Seward is a brash, straightforward, ass-kicker of a hot bitch, while Agent Sievert is the calm, methodical thinker. He displays less emotion, but those discerning eyes and honed instincts are sharper than the Punji sticks we faced in the war. As an investigational team, they complement one another's abilities, creating balance and very focused insight that is neither rushed nor typical. I've been with them for some time now, afraid to allow my mind to wonder toward some of my more youthful mistakes because I think it unwise. I suggest you try practicing the same. Let them do what it is they came to do and leave. It's as simple as that. Screw with these two in any way and they will probably shove a microscope so far up your ass, you'll be able to see your own bodily functions from a very unflattering perspective. I have friends at the bureau. One of which is actually an Assistant Director, but not even she could get past their names and badge numbers. Simply doesn't have the security clearance."

Before Chief Mecklenburg can ask his brother what he has to hide, Agent Seward asks, "Mayor Mecklenburg, sir. Is there a private area that my partner and I may use to engage in a conference call with our superior?"

"Yes, of course. You can use my office down the hall. Neara, can you see to it for me?"

"Yes sir, Mr. Mecklenburg," the housekeeper says.

When Agent Sievert asks, "What's going on?" she picks up her bag and moves toward the door to follow the housekeeper without answering. He assumes by the look in her eyes that it would be inappropriate to discuss this matter in public, and that he should know better than to ask.

Pauline Mecklenburg asks, "Agent Seward, is everything alright? Does this involve our situation? Has there been some new developments?"

Agent Seward turns toward them all to belie their concerns. "Ma'am, I'm sorry, but this is classified information involving another case. We can't discuss it openly, but I can tell you that it has absolutely nothing to do with this situation."

Mayor Larkin Mecklenburg clears his throat to say, "Ah, better yet. Neara, dear, let them set up in the drawing room. There is better lighting and more room in there."

Chief Mecklenburg refreshes his and Chief Cramer's drink. He is a bit disgusted, knowing that his brother has specific reasons for shifting the agents away from his office on the heels of Chief Cramer's advice. He decides not to bother raising the subject, knowing that honest answers will not come straightaway.

Pauline Mecklenburg looks up at her husband with a weary smile. He returns the gesture and places his arms around his wife for a hug that seems long overdue.

"How are you holding up, Paula? I know the world has spun out of orbit, but we are due for a good turn. Aren't we, dear?"

"God knows, I can only hope so." Pauline pats him on the chest and says, "I'm going upstairs to check on the kids. You want to come?"

"Huh? Oh, not right now. I think it would be best to stay down here with our guests. Archie and I still have a detail or two to go over. Besides, I don't think Agent Sievert appreciated my interruptions when he spoke to Robbie in the hospital. I was just being a little overprotective, as you said earlier. I defer to your judgment when it comes to the kids' wellbeing. Whatever you think best, honey."

"Okay." She lets go and heads for the stairs, giving Neara instructions along the way.

* * *

Robbie dips a towel in the cool water, wringing it out before daubing Stacie's sweating forehead, neckline, and itchy arms with it. He whispers, "You have got to stop scratching, Stacie. You are sweating like it's the fourth quarter, sis."

Her hands quiver, moaning as she tries to speak. "I can't help it. The more it itches, the more I sweat. The more I sweat, the worse it itches. Christ, it's driving me crazy."

"Quiet. I think someone's coming." He nearly loses his balance while hastily sliding the ice bucket and towel under the bed. She grabs his left arm to keep him from falling when the bare heel of his casted leg slips under his weight.

As Pauline Mecklenburg ascends the stairs, she notices the quiet. However, as soon as she approaches her daughter's door, the teenagers begin to speak loudly. A mother knows the sound of her own children's fake laughter. Especially since they have been so quiet of late. Although the concerned mother promised that Stacie would never have to speak to anyone she doesn't want to, Pauline Mecklenburg believes it important that she sees the FBI agents. She knocks before entering to find her son and daughter smiling.

"Hi, mom," Stacie says.

"Hey, mom," says Robbie. Following suit, he states, "We were just having a couple laughs."

"Don't, Robert. Just don't lie to me. Please," she scolds, sharply. "Your uncle Mac is dead and will be buried soon. Both of you nearly died a few days ago in a devastating accident that he caused because he was running from the law while committing several felonies. Someone kidnaped both of you, took you right before our eyes. Your sister returned completely healed of a broken arm. Hours ago, Stacie just walked, barefooted, out into a raging thunderstorm, screaming like a banshee. Two bolts of lightning came right at you to scorch the earth, but you are untouched. You claim to have no knowledge of the details surrounding the kidnaping, but I know better. So please don't bullshit me with anymore lies about having a laugh because I haven't seen anything funny in days."

"Mom," Stacie says with a sinking, depressive expression on her face. "What's the matter?"

"Yeah, mom, what gives?" her brother asks. "We are back. We're both okay, so I don't get why you're not happy."

Pauline Mecklenburg's eyes go dark and even more serious when she says, "See, that's exactly what I'm talking about. You both just asked what my problem is, as if you didn't hear a single word from my lips. Both of you are acting as if you are in complete denial. On the other hand, are you just playing dumb because I appear to be as stupid as you would like to believe?"

Stacie rubs her arms, trying to resist using her nails.

"Robert, go to your room. I don't want any backtalk, young man. Leave, now."

"Okay, mom. I'm sorry we upset you." When Robbie reaches for the set of crutches, their mother hands it to him and helps him to his feet. As he stands, Robbie looks into his sister's eyes, wishing he could do more.

As he sidesteps his mother, she cups his face in her hands and looks him in the eyes. "I love you, son. You remind me so much of your father in our younger years, Robert. However, his deceitfulness is not a quality that I want my children to emulate. Do you understand?"

"Yes, mom. I'm really sorry. I was just trying to help."

"Just trying to protect your sister, right?" He can only nod, as she hugs him. "I know. Of course, I'm happy that you two are home where you belong, so please don't ever question that. Now go take your meds and get some rest because it is very late. There's no need to worry. Go on."

"I love you too, mom," Robbie says as he turns to leave. "You, too, Stacie. See you in the morning."

Pauline turns toward Stacie, seeing a pleading desperation on her face that causes greater disquiet as far as a mother's instinct goes. As she steps closer, she notices the dark stain of spilled water beneath the bed. She reaches underneath and draws out the ice bucket and the cool, wet towel.

"What on earth are you doing with this, baby?" the mother asks. She is now close enough to notice Stacie's drenched nightgown and sweating forehead through the dim lighting. "Are you sick? Do you have a fever, Stacie?"

The teenage girl is sitting with her legs crossed. Her hands are between her legs, fingers scratching at the back of both hands. She says nothing, rocking back and forth until her forehead nearly touches her sheet.

"Stacie, what's the matter, baby?" Pauline asks again. She raises her daughter from the stupor and tests her sweating forehead for a sign of fever. When she finds no abnormal heat, she says, "Please talk to me. What's the matter, honey? Are you in pain?"

Stacie bravely stifles her tears as she continues to rock in her mother's arms. Finally, her quivering voice pleads, "Mom, help me. Please. Please...."

Extremely worried now, Pauline seeks an answer to what ails her child. "What is it, Stacie? You can tell me anything, anything at all."

Stacie can stand the invisible assault no longer. She scratches her back, trying desperately to get at a spot she can't quite reach. She scratches her neckline and arms with an audible sound of futility escaping her lips.

"Itching is driving me insane," she whispers. "I can't stand it, mom. Please tell me what to do before I rip my skin off."

Pauline feels helpless. She places the cool towel on Stacie's forehead. The girl takes it and dabs the wet clothes across her body. Now Pauline remembers the three bottles in her pockets. She removes them, looking at the name on the solution.

"What's that, mom?"

Pauline looks at her tormented child and says, "Something the FBI agent gave me to help you." She opens one of the smelly concoctions and lets her daughter sniff. "God, it reeks, but it might help," says her mother.

She pours the light-brownish lotion in her hands and applies it to Stacie's arms. For a moment, the young woman reacts as if it burns, writhing with the heightened stinging sensation that almost seems angry. She muffles a cry into her mother's shoulder as Pauline rocks back and forth with her.

"I'm so sorry, baby. I hoped it would help you. We'll have Doctor Avery come out an take a look at you."

A moment later, a small, quivering voice says, "More. Please, mom. More."

Tears burn Pauline's cheeks. She moves behind Stacie to lift her gown and undo her brazier. She rubs the lotion on her daughter's back, shoulders, and neckline. Stacie reacts the same way, as if paying the price for shaking a short stick at a nest of angry hornets or standing on the mound of defensive red ants. For all practical purposes, the sting is fighting back. It is fighting to survive, not fighting to continue its torment.

Slowly, very slowly, the itching subsides. Stacie discards the bra all together, pouring some of this smelly stuff in the palm of her hand to rub it all over her upper torso. Once the final, stinging battle ends, she leans back in her mother's arms.

Both mother and daughter shed tears of relief. Pauline embraces her daughter and whispers, "Thank you, God. It's working just like he said."

"Mom, those people downstairs, did they really give it to you?" Stacie Mecklenburg asks. "Did they?"

Pauline sniffles and answers, "Yes, baby. They are not the enemy, you know. Agent Sievert brought it from the hospital just for you, sweetheart."

"But how could he possibly know?"

Pauline turns her around and says, "I don't know, but he did, and that is why I want you to talk to them. It's important that you do, baby."

"I'm afraid," Stacie whimpers. "Please don't make me."

"Now listen to me, child. I love you so much, and I can't stand seeing you in agony. You've been smiling and acting as if everything is fine, but I know better. They only want to help you, Stacie. I truly believe that now. Will you do it for me, please?"

After a moment, Stacie agrees. She says, "Only because I hate seeing you cry, mother."

"Thank you, Stacie. This is necessary, or I would not ask you to talk to them. Before you do, why don't you go and take a cool shower using this stuff all over your body. Try it with the soft brush. Use it on your scalp, too. Don't worry about how it will affect your hair, go on now."

When the girl goes into her private bath, her mother strips her sweaty bed to find that Stacie has urinated on herself. A hint of pink suggests that she is still on her period. She fights back the tears, calling Neara to help her clean up the mess. They spray the wet spot with disinfectant before flipping the heavy mattress.

The bed will be remade with fresh linens by the time the lengthy, relieving shower is over. Pauline Mecklenburg lights the fireplace, but not too high because the heat may agitate her daughter's skin condition. While breathing just a little harder than usual, she and Neara arrange the chairs as instructed.

Pauline has already decided to call the dermatologist to order a case of the lotion, if that is what it takes.

* * *

In the drawing room, Agent Seward enters her password to boot up the laptop. The phone, set on speaker, sits on the white table between the two. She pulls up the file and tells Assistant Director Majors, "My unit is up and running, sir."

FBI Assistant Director Majors says, "Good. We are conferencing with Homeland Security Regional Director Dawn Fender-Holst. Go ahead, Director Holst."

The older woman clasps her fingers together before saying, "Agent Seward and Agent Sievert, this conversation is classified. It is not fodder for idol chat. Is that clear?"

"Yes, ma'am," Agent Sievert says.

"Of course, Regional Director Fender-Holst," says Agent Seward. "What can we do for you?"

"Director Holst will do just fine, agent."

Assistant Director Majors reminds, "As we are all viable and answerable components of Homeland Security, I convinced the Regional Director that this classified information may hold some significance to both investigations."

Regional Director Holst clears her throat to say, "Due to unexplained incidents on Flight 111 from Haiti to Miami International Airport, I'm hoping that, together, we can solve some very perplexing questions concerning a man named Kwaban Rouge. When we cross-referenced the name, Rouge came up as an open investigation in South Carolina. It didn't take long to connect the dots. In the greater name of cooperative interdepartmental lines of communication, we made your director aware of this man's recent arrival in the continental United States. His inquiries concerning the Haitian national were brought to my attention, so I approved sharing the abbreviated dossier you have seen earlier. Frankly, agents, we are at a loss as to this man's connection to certain ongoing phenomena. That's why. . . ."

"Excuse my interruption, Regional Director Holst. Are you still holding him in custody?"

Though slightly annoyed at the disruption of her diplomatic song and dance, the woman says, "At this moment, agents, all information concerning Kwaban Rouge is compartmentalized classified. However, with your security clearances and your boss's fervent belief in you, I must say yes. Yes we are presently holding the person in question at a highly classified super max facility in south Florida."

The agents join hands and Sievert says, "At the Dardis Biomedical Facility."

There is a moment of silence, but unmistakable whispers are in the background. "If I may ask, just how would you know that, Agent Sievert? How have you come by this information?"

"Is that really important Director Holst? Please continue."

"We will have to revisit that question at a later time. I'm calling because this facility is wired for sound, quite frankly. The technicians monitoring the detainee in question have stumbled on disturbing energy readings that seem to be directly connected to this man. In fact, spectral analysis shows, conclusively, that an unusual, multidirectional energy source is not only emanating from the detainee— it is growing in strength and frequency."

Agent Sievert sends Assistant Director Majors a text message.

Assistant Director Majors interjects, "Listen, Director Holst, it would help us all if you would get to the point and stop treating my people as if they are potential threats to national security. And while I'm at it, please tell those assholes from the military's weapons development and the Central Intelligence to either learn to whisper more quietly, join the conversation, or just shut up all together."

Agent Sievert is pleased by the response when she shouts, "Who the hell do you think you are talking to? I won't stand for insubordinate behavior or your vaunted cowboy tactics, Assistant

Director Majors. I'm aware that you and your units have access to highly sensitive knowledge of things that most will never know, but I don't have to bow down to anyone."

"Thank you Agents Seward and Sievert. I'm sorry for wasting your time with this bureaucratic browbeating. You may continue with your investigation."

Agent Seward says, "Yes, sir. We will. Are you ready to go upstairs, Agent Sievert?"

Agent Sievert adds, "Yes. Let's go because we don't have time for this speakeasy."

Frantically, the word, "Wait!" comes across the speaker. "Wait, just wait. It seems all of your reputations are highly deserved."

"We're listening, Regional Director Fender-Holst," says Assistant Director Majors.

"Agents, are you still with us? Agents?" she asks.

"We're here. Please continue," says Agent Sievert. "You mentioned a multi-directional energy signature of some kind. Have you determined the nature of it?"

"The detainee is putting out massive amounts of what closely resembles upper band electromagnetic energy, which seem to radiate in three distinct directions. My people have determined that one of those emanations transects areas very close to your vicinity. For some indeterminate reason, there appears to be a dampening field that curtails our ability to pinpoint an exact location. As I understand it from Assistant Director Majors, you are working a case circa the Tega Cay and Fort Mill areas of South Carolina."

"Yes that is correct, Director Holst," Agent Seward answers. "What makes you think there is a dampening field, which would suggest anything but a naturally occurring event? Could it be that the unusual energy signature has just reached its maximum range?"

"The energy pattern simply disappears approximately five miles from your location. However, by following the established trajectory from Florida, assuming that there is no undetected deviation, the straight line cuts right through Fort Mill and Tega Cay. Which, as I understand, are now actually one township. Anomalous events and unusual weather patterns lends credence to a connection."

Sievert asks, "How are you tracking this anomaly, exactly."

"We have several means of doing so. Satellites. Aircraft telemetry."

As Agent Sievert writes another text to his superior, he allows his partner to see it. It simply says, "They have boots on the ground, here somewhere close."

"Most disturbingly, the other two are aimed southwest and southeast of us. This energy signature matches that which our satellites detected when we tracked the flagged Flight 111 days ago. Please look at the file. I feel that this situation is a danger to many lives and we are contemplating whatever means are at our disposal because the energy that is not concentrating to the north is directed at the hearts of the two hurricanes now located in the Atlantic and the Gulf of Mexico. These instantaneous tropical storms formed almost simultaneously, and became Category 3 Hurricanes with 120 mile an hour winds within a matter of hours. The power of these violent weather patterns are growing at an unbelievable rate, culminating with the energy readings we are monitoring at this facility and the detainee. Meteorologists estimate that these massive storms may reach Category 4 or even Category 5 in a matter of twenty-four hours. The highly pronounced feeder bands are casting off huge amounts of precipitation. But the strangest thing is the fact that the energy isn't dissipating, but reaching out for the other storm, respectively. This is difficult to believe, agents, but the storms are feeding off one another in ways we have never experienced, exactly. They are growing to deadly proportions, as if this man is controlling them, himself. It seems as if he is the very nexus of their existence. The preliminary projected paths of both storms places them squarely on top of this facility. Our scientific experts all agree, no matter how crazy it sounds, that he is either directing these storms or has some kind of major connection to them. When we detected the anomalous energy signatures, we stripped him of all his clothing and scanned his entire body only to have our instruments short out, catch fire, or even explode. People were injured, and most are experiencing a growing dermal hypersensitivity when in close proximity to the detainee. Whatever this is, it's spreading in all directions, but the sensors are detecting no known chemical agents, and no advanced technological enhancements. And yet, there are moments when he sets off Geiger Counters. Christ, I can't believe I heard those words from my own lips. When Mr. Rouge isn't repeating words that have no clear meaning in the presence of our interrogative linguists, he demands that we release him. He has mentioned a grandchild in dire need of him, and family emergencies. But most of all, and quite emphatically, he promises the destruction of us all if he is not released."

Agent Seward clamps down on her partner's hand and says, "A flash of pinpointed light. Seeking destruction as they seek my doom. The Blade of the Red Hurricane will draw innocent blood for innocent blood. Release me . . . or perish as the wheel turns!"

"Jesus. What's she saying?"

"Authorizing. Authorizing lethal force to subdue. Continue to detain or attempt to murder me and the Harbingers will come ashore as a phalanx of annihilation!"

With her eyes wide, Director Holst asks. "Where the hell are your people getting this classified information?"

Assistant Director Majors intercedes by saying, "Director Holst, we are on the same side here."

She clears her throat. "I see. So it is true. You are employing bona fide clairvoyants, also known as Sensitives. Or the ever unpopular term, Ghost Talkers. Shit!"

Agent Seward looks at Agent Sievert, who says, "Are you contemplating killing this man? Have you tortured him in any way?" "That's classified information, agent. You know better than to ever ask such questions," Regional Director Holst scolds.

"Jesus," growls Agent Seward. "She actually means to do it, Assistant Director Majors. She's going to execute Rouge."

Agent Sievert clears his own dry throat and says, "Director Holst, if this is the case, I strongly advise against any collateral measures. If you believe such drastic action will render a swift conclusion to this situation, you may be wrong about that. I mean catastrophically wrong. Please. Can you tell us anything more about these deadly storms? Anything that shows extraordinary differences from what we consider to be natural weather formations?" The silence returns. "Ma'am?"

Director Holst decides to give them a part of what she has been holding back. She finally says, "Open the files being uploaded now."

A moment later, Agent Seward stands. "Oh my God. What is this?"

"That, dear girl, is exactly what you see. Our newly designed E2C2 Hawkeyes took these photographic images as they approached the eye of both cyclones. Their readings, while heading into the storms, were all over the place. Nothing could be trusted as the crews attempted to accurately gauge the data parameters. I can hardly believe it myself, but the evidence is undeniable at this point. Notice the condition in which the Hawkeyes returned from their initial recon mission. Because the pilots couldn't see, they were forced to trust the erratic instruments and autopilot to guide them back safely. The instruments eventually failed. The pilots had to land manually or they'd be dead due to mechanical malfunction. Still feel the same way?"

Assistant Director Majors whispers, "These hurricanes are actually blood red. I thought this was some form of heat signature."

Agent Sievert whispers, "*La lame de l'ouragan rouge.* Blade of the Red Hurricane."

In awe, Director Holst says, "That's exactly what the detainee often repeats, even with tears in his eyes. This is by no means ordinary, agents. This isn't exactly some charlatan promising to bring rain to a Midwestern township during a drought, so we must give serious consideration to prejudicial action because we cannot seem to even sedate the subject. He seems impervious to any of our non-lethal, airborne neuro-agents or direct injections with our most powerful neutralizing sedatives. Our efforts just seem to piss him off. Short of putting a bullet in his brainpan, we are at a complete loss."

Sievert warns, "Director Holst, please consider what may happen. If he is somehow controlling these storms, as your team of experts hypothesize, how will they react when there is no one controlling them? They may not simply go away, as I am certain you are betting on. It would be best to do nothing for the moment. What are your projections for landfall?"

"Both storms are definitely building in strength, but they have stalled over the Gulf and the Atlantic. I will almost swear that they are waiting for something, like permission to unleash total havoc. If the projected paths of both storms bear out, a great portion of the Florida peninsula will not survive them both. That is exactly what our scientists theorize. Also, if all of this isn't disturbingly frightening enough, they are polarized storms. Polarized, as in negatively and positively linked like two magnets. They are not forcing each other away from our coasts, but drawing one another toward it like twin buzz saws. We are demanding a statewide evacuation, but there is too much panic. Floridians are used to fleeing the full brunt of such storms, but not fast-moving twofers. We have seen storms in both the Atlantic Ocean and the Gulf of Mexico many times before, but no one has ever witnessed anything like this in our history. Unbelievably, that wasn't red paint on those E2C2 Hawkeyes. There are actual traces of red clay and human blood. As far as the DNA found on the fuselage of both airplanes goes, I will give you one guess at a biological match."

Assistant Director Majors asks, "Agent Sievert and Seward, your thoughts please."

Agent Sievert says, "We were about to interview the Mecklenburg girl. The parents were very reluctant to give us access. Without doubt, we believe this will shed light on the cause of these disturbing events. I believe I know where Kwaban Rouge's son is hiding, holding a ritualistic vigil that is geared to helping his comatose daughter. We need some time before any action is taken against the ninety-year old grandfather in custody. Once we have interviewed Stacie Mecklenburg, we may have a much clearer picture for an immediate course of action, which may include a visit to Dardis with access to the detainee."

"Absolutely not!" shouts Director Holst.

"I understand your apprehension, Director Holst, but taking summary action against this man may prove more disastrous. Please, ma'am, this is a bridge you shouldn't cross without accepting the fact that it may exacerbate the situation far beyond your control. If releasing him into our custody holds the key, how can you not consider it? Let the man join his family. I beg of you."

"If this man is what he seems, Agent Sievert, he is a threat to national security. I should think that is amply clear by now. Anything or anyone who seems to control violent weather patterns is much more than a potential risk. He is a weapon of mass destruction." With growing horror, Agent Seward says, "They want to dissect him like a bug to see what makes him tick. She's afraid that someone has engineered a human weapon bent on our destruction. You could all die if you continue to hold this man against his will. Kill that old man, and you may have the son's rage to deal with. If you find a way to destroy the head of the hammer, it just may reappear on the other end of the handle!"

"Agent Seward, I'm offering you the strongest caution right now. You had better rein her in, Majors, or I will!"

"Are you threatening us, Director Holst?" asks Agent Sievert.

In the absence of Assistant Director Majors' scolding voice on the line, Agent Seward continues. "Although you are aware of the existence of clairvoyant assets working in service of this nation, actually talking to—not one but two of us—the only thing on your mind right now is protecting the Dardis Biomedical Facility's filthy little secrets. As if we are potential enemies of the state, you fear we might just accidently glean the depths of your hidden treasures or most heinous crimes against humanity. With all that transpires before your freaking eyes, your most pressing concern is keeping us as far away from that place as possible. Get a fucking clue, Director Holst. You can't control every aspect of nature. Nor can you reverse engineer this! What if Kwaban Rouge's Haitian god, is real? What if he or she, happens to be more powerful and proactive than the God you hypocrites have been worshipping for thousands of years? Even worse, Director Holst, what if his God is actually your own? If that is the case, the crucifix wrapped around your bloody fingers just may strangle you with your own ignorance."

"Control your fervor, agent. I will do what I can to get you access, but I cannot guarantee his release," Assistant Director Majors advises. "She has already begun to reconstruct and redeploy her firewalls against us."

Angry at their disregard, Director Holst cautions them on trying to gain access to her prisoner, a word that more appropriately describes the disposition of Kwaban Rouge.

"Clearly, you have grown overconfident in your importance in the grand scheme of things, Assistant Director Majors. It would take a full military escort to breech these walls to see a detainee that's being held five stories down if I do not grant access."

Agent Seward says, "With all due respect, Director Holst, he's eight stories down. Maybe you need to take a look at the gigantic red stains that are now looming over both your coasts. If our interview proves fruitful, you may have no choice. If simply releasing him is the path of least resistance to abating the combined destructive force of the twin hurricanes converging on your regional jurisdiction, you may find yourself out of time and options. If you fail to hit some sort of kill switch by murdering that old man, how many more lives will be lost? We must go now."

In the background, they all hear Assistant Director Majors say to his assistant, "Get me a direct line to FBI Director Comey, the Director of National Intelligence, and the White House. ASAP!"

He now redirects his words to the conference call. "Get to work on the girl, agents. I will back your play no matter where it leads. Sometimes people with an ounce of power forget that in the grander scheme of things, human beings are truly nothing in the face of Mother Nature's fury. Furthermore, what are we, if she even begins to display hints of sentience in her angry fists? There are simply things that we will never explain or quantify by scientific endeavors alone. This woman knows absolutely nothing of the unknown truth of this existence." Click.

Interstate-95 North, I-10 West, and the I-295 bypass of Jacksonville are jammed pack with panicking Floridians, who only wish to flee what is being called the end of the world on the internet. As these families sit in stop-and-go traffic that is more stop than go, even at this great distance, the seventy to eighty mile an hour wind gusts are causing their automobiles to rattle and shiver as blood droplets begin to fall from the sky!

Stripped naked, the eyes of Kwaban Rouge are pearly whites in a room where they have him strapped to a cold, stainless steel table. He is surrounded by medical equipment. Surgical equipment to be exact.

The voice of Banja Rouge reaches for Kwaban's mind, begging, "Father, where are you? I cannot contain it all. My daughter's body lies upon the cusp, even though she is absent of spirit!"

The thick strap across Kwaban Rouge's forehead begins to smolder, leaving a void between his eyebrows, just above the bridge of his flaring nostrils. Through the intermittent static, those who hold him are trying to film every second of his captivity.

While standing safely behind six inches of pressure and impact proof glass, government scientists witness as he speaks aloud.

"Seek, Banjalanah. Time grows nigh for us all because the blade cuts both ways, my son. Even though a great fury builds unto the threshold of obliteration, continue to seek for we have not abandoned you!"

The titanium clamps securing his wrists begin to twist and break. With his arms suddenly free of their cold despair, Kwaban Rouge remains in a lying position. As his outstretched hands slowly rise from his sides, the energy level in the enclosure spikes. The closer his palms come to touching, the more his observers' skins crawl.

The compression-proof glass begins to crack, shatter lines run to-and-froe. Now, the fear in his observers begin to build to almost paralytic degrees. Doctor Bachmann finally hits the com linking him directly to Regional Director Holst. She answers the buzz, looking at the screen. When Bachmann begins to scratch his skin raw, he shouts, "He's broken free. We cannot contain this man. We must release him. We must!"

She bites her nails, and scratches her neck where the ragged nail of her left middle finger splits her skin to draw blood. She shouts,

"Use the Cyanide. Gas him. Gas him, now!"

"But the glass, it may not be safe."

"Do it now, damn you. Now!" she shouts.

On the television monitor in her office, a well-known televangelist looks into the camera with earnest conviction to say, "The recent earthquake that devastated Haiti is God's punishment of a wicked people, who have made a pact with Satan. This was God's own retribution."

Kwaban's palms clap together with a resounding boom!

Dr. Bachmann hits the button, flooding the enclosure with a thick cloud of cyanide gas. Three doctors and two armed guards stand before the glass, holding their breath with their gas masks in their trembling hands. There is no movement in the room, only silence amidst a deadly cloud. The sensors no longer detect the captive's heat signature. Most of the EKG leads have burned out long ago. The two that still work, show nothing. There is no detectable brainwave activity or heartbeats.

Finally, they breathe collective sighs of relief. They believe it is over, until a beeping alarm warns them and inanimate objects in the observation room begin to chatter. A small tremor causes an empty coffee cup to vibrate across the surface of a stainless steel tray. Dr. Bachmann looks at the readings, shaking his head in disbelief.

"My God," he shrieks. "The wind speeds have jumped beyond Category 5 for both anomalies. We are now looking at super typhoons with sustaining wind speeds over two-hundred MPH. We were wrong. He had no control over this. We killed that man for nothing!"

When he places his trembling fingers to his forehead in bewilderment, another doctor depresses a button to vent the gas cloud. Only one of the five air scrubbers seems to be functional. When Dr. Bachmann raises his remorseful eyes, Kwaban Rouge suddenly rises before the glass with those white eyes ablaze with rage. He bears his teeth as the good doctor and the others recoil in fear. The glass shatters. Enough lethal gas remains to claim them all while Kwaban Rouge inhales deeply with his mouth open wide and his nostrils flaring. He wears the look of madness about him, a look of unkempt, inconsolable rage.

Director Holst initiates a Level-10 Lockdown, dispersing armed men to dispatch the tortured prisoner, who seems to defy logic as if only to spite her. However, the detection of the gas by automated sensors lowers the bulkheads that ultimately protect Kwaban Rouge from the armed assault teams dispatched to eliminate him. They must bypass these safety protocols to reach the target.

"Seek!"

On the east and west coasts, Hurricane Mala and Hurricane Siena begin to climb onto the beaches of South Florida. As if they have been hurled from the angry fists of God, they churn like gargantuan blades to lay low all things that lie within their destructive reach. No longer are these massive storms looming colossi, but moving now as one to eradicate everything within their path. Hundreds of enormous, violent tornadoes precede their seething seventy-mile-an-hour pace up the defenseless peninsula.

The ground, which secures and harbors the hardened lower levels of the Dardis Biomedical Facility, now quakes. Homeland Security Regional Director Dawn Fender-Holst looks about as the walls of this facility begin to shriek, crackling like brittle twigs beneath the full weight of hell's fury in motion. When the buzzing lights spark and suddenly abandon her office to total darkness, she tries to feel her way to the door. When the emergency lighting engages, they crackle and explode. While her back oozes blood from the exploding glass, she crawls forth, wishing to take the secure elevator deeper into the underground facility where many atrocities have been committed in the name of science and national security. However, her own safety protocols have trapped her in a black world where plus 200 MPH winds are sheering the concrete building into disintegrating shrapnel.

When the roof of the upper floor strips away bit by bit, the wailing walls are sure to follow as she whimpers a prayer to a deaf

God. While holding onto a concrete pillar encased by beautiful woodwork that begins to crack and splinter, she screams as blood rain crashes down from the sky!

Her watch catches on the metal rail as her feet are pulled skyward. The agony of having her left arm slowly ripped away from her body causes her to scream and scream!

Chapter 25

Kysing Mecklenburg

Neara Jones, the sixty-year-old housekeeper, leads the FBI agents up the stairs. In a more pleasant mood, she says, "Lord knows, I have got to get used to the idea that this home actually has two elevators. It is high time I start using them, too. I personally want to thank you for bringing that smelly potion to help my baby girl. Thank you, sir. I thank both of you."

Agent Seward says, "You are very welcome, Mrs. Jones, but my partner deserves any credit you may have to offer. He's a very special man."

"Handsome too," she looks back to smile at Agent Sievert, who blushes slightly when Neara nods and winks at Agent Seward.

"Thank you, Nessa," he says, quite inadvertently. "I meant, Neara. Sorry, ma'am."

At the top of the rounded staircase, Neara Jones suddenly pauses. With furrowed brows, she turns to him in amazement. "Nessa? Oh, Mister Sievert, that is a name I have not heard in many a year. My grandfather took one look at me as a newborn and called me Nessa until his dying day. I loved that man, dearly. He used to bounce both my brothers and me on his lap, telling us interesting stories about the days of old. The love of a father's father is a precious jewel of the memory. We all should take them out of the dusty attic from time to time, shine them clean, hold them up before the enduring light and just smile a smile from deep inside the soul." She smiles and wipes a tear from her eyes. "I wonder, Mister Sievert. How did you know?"

He cannot help smiling back at the woman, touched by unspoken outpourings of her fond childhood memories.

"I told you he is a very special man. He's very kind, and gentle, too."

Neara beams, knowing Agent Seward's admiration of her partner to be based in truth and maybe something more. She says, "Well, what does it matter anyway? That's enough about me. I hope you two find the answers you need so this family can move on. I would love to see these children grow to adulthood, marry, and have grandbabies of their own someday. Stacie's room is just down this hall to the left."

"Thank you," Agent Sievert says. "Mrs. Jones, may we take a moment to talk to you before going in?"

Neara looks over her shoulder at the closed door and says, "Sure, if you think it will be of service to you. We can sit down here in this cozy little nook."

As they sit in a room fit for antiques only, Agent Sievert explains, "I want to do this now in case there is no time later. We don't wish to continually impose, and it is already quite late. You seem to have the pulse of this family, judging by the way Mrs. Mecklenburg allows to you to speak for her. She even bristled a little when her husband disapproved of your close proximity to this beyond being an employee."

"He's a very proud man, the mayor. Too proud if you ask me because he's no more than a sickly sweet angel. He may do all of the growling in here, but Paula has the teeth. Whatever you need. Just ask."

"Is there anything you wish to add to your earlier statement concerning our reason for being here? No detail is too small or unimportant."

Neara purses her lips in thought. With great empathy, she replies, "I'm just worried for the family, sir. I worry that this beautiful young woman is going to be forever scarred by this messy affair. She doesn't deserve that. To answer your question, I have observed her emotions as well as her motion. Since Stacie has been home, subtle changes seem to surface from time to time— by accident— I think. Recently, before the lightning storm, and a scream of pain that was fit to shatter

a parent's soul, I happened by her open door."

Agent Sievert asks, "Did something happen?"

Neara looks around the corner. "I heard voices coming from Stacie's room. It was almost . . . as if she was carrying on a full-fledged conversation with both herself and other people. I haven't told her mother about this, not sure that it will help her state of mind any better. Still, I feel in my own heart that Stacie has some kind of secret, something that her brother has been bound to keep. You see, I know those kids better than they know themselves. It shames me to admit this because I would never actually eavesdrop on anyone, but that voice was not her own. Her tone, her way of speaking . . ."

"Her inflection, perhaps? Is that possibly the word you are looking for?" Agent Seward suggests.

"Yes. That is the perfect word for it. Strangely enough, it ekes out at times when you least expect it and it scares me some. I believe I have heard her speaking with almost . . . well . . . it's like two voices at the same time. I know it sounds crazy. I do, but I must admit to you that it has happened when Stacie was looking me squarely in the eyes. It seems as though some small part of her wants me to hear or know her secrets. I'm sorry, but I just don't know any other ways of putting it into words, agents. Her mother and I have been friends for many years, so you must understand that I'm afraid to mention what I just expressed to you. I don't want Pauline thinking that Stacie has developed some kind of split personality, or whatever the term is, that will get her placed on some mind-altering drugs and such. That child is as dear to my heart as my own grown children. She is a kind soul, with a very strong spirit. She is one heck of a ball player, too. Nevertheless, there again, that other young Black girl, the one in the coma, was the same. She swore me to secrecy, but Stacie snuck out and went Columbia that night to watch her win the state championship out of pure respect. Stacie is a mature young woman. Mature enough to admit to me, that even though she believes her father tried to fix their game, that Stinger girl beat her fair and square because there was no quit in her. She greatly admired that. Stacie also told me that they share the same birthdate. I fear that she harbors a deep hurt inside because that same young woman saved her life on that bus. She is bereft with guilt that threatens to swallow her whole if that other girl dies or never recovers. Her mother feels that none of this would have happened if Mayor Mecklenburg had not treated those folks so poorly. She spoke of the scene in the hospital's chapel after he insulted the parents of the ill child who saved his daughter's life. She described a rage in Mr. Rouge's eyes with a bent meant to curdle blood and shatter bones. She said she has never seen her husband so terrified in their entire lives together."

Agent Seward asks, "Did anything else happen?"

Neara looks away for a moment, searching for Pauline Mecklenburg's words. "Paula said that Mr. Rouge attacked Larkin after his indignant remarks in the chapel. Any one in his position would probably do the very same. The mayor can be a bit abrasive at times. According to Paula, even when two police officers were restraining that man, he seemed to possess an unnatural power. Mr. Rouge dragged them right up to the mayor with a gaze that he even described as a physical touch. His anger was so prevalent that it radiated from his body like . . . like static. She swears it made her hair stand on end, and that's not all. She said Larkin was cold as ice, as if he had been locked in a walk-in freezer. I sense something bad in the air for these people. Please do what you can. Still, even though I am bound to this family, I pray for that poor child and her parents. Until I had all of the story, I found no pity in my heart for anyone who was a potential threat to this family."

Agent Seward leans toward her, looking into Neara's eyes to ask, "There is something more, isn't there. Something that truly scares you."

As tears begin to well in her eyes, Neara heathers to hold them back. However, the attempt will ultimately fail.

Agent Seward reaches for her right hand, stroking it gently, knowing that the woman's cascading emotions will comingle with her own. Neara Jones truly loves and fears for Stacie Mecklenburg.

"That day, when I overheard Stacie talking to herself in that room, I swear that I distinctly heard a man's voice. It wasn't Mayor Mecklenburg, but Stacie called him father. Then, as if she knew I was in the hallway, things went silent. I feel sick to my stomach. Everything seemed to . . . well, I became dizzy for a second. And then her door suddenly slammed shut so hard it made the floor shake. The air went cold enough to see my own breath."

Neara shivers as if her own tears were frigid.

Drawn to her pain, Agent Sievert kindly reaches out to touch the housekeeper's left cheek. As she allows her emotions to flow, what she feels is her grandfather's gentle caress upon her skin. For an instance, she even sees his smiling face before her eyes.

"Please help her," she openly weeps. "Please, dear God, help them to help her."

"We understand, Mrs. Neara," Agent Sievert says. "We understand, Nessa."

Neara rolls her cheek in his palm, holding his hand close to her skin. She looks into her grandfather's face through the eyes of memory and says, "Thank you. Thank you so much." When they withdraw from the emotional woman, she gathers herself, wiping her tears with a handkerchief. "Now, I've got to get it together. Can't let the children see me falling apart. Sometimes, when we cannot be the wood, we have to be the glue that holds it all together."

Sievert says, "Take your time."

"I wasn't going to go in with you, but I think I will step inside to show support to them both."

They rise and go to Stacie Mecklenburg's room, where her mother is standing at the window. Pauline Mecklenburg is staring out at the rain, noting how slanted it seems to be coming down. There is a click when Stacie opens the bathroom door, toweling her wet hair. She is wearing a white housecoat and fluffy slippers, feeling clean. Feeling free.

Pauline greets Stacie with open arms, knowing instantly that she feels better because her smile is now genuine. She kisses her daughter's cheeks and lips, looking into her euphoric blue eyes.

"I love you so much, mom. Thank you. Thank them."

Pauline holds her daughter tight and says, "I love you, too, Stacie, but I would like you to tell them yourself."

She slowly turns toward the handsome agent and his beautiful partner. She smiles at them and gives thanks for the relieving topical solution.

"Stacie Mecklenburg, I am FBI Agent Lee Anne Seward and this is my partner, Agent Michael Sievert. We only need to talk to you for a few moments, and we want you to know that you have nothing to fear from us. Okay?"

"It's very nice to meet you," she politely states. Stacie looks into her mother's eyes and nods. "I'm ready, mom. You can leave us alone." She looks at the table in the corner. Her mother and Neara have removed three of the chairs, and rearranged them near the middle of the large suite.

Surprised at the change of heart, Pauline asks, "You sure, honey?"

"Yes, mom. In fact, I think I would prefer it that way. I'm a big girl. Besides, they have already proven good intentions."

Pauline opens her arms and smiles. "Oh, well, there you have it. Neara and I will be just downstairs, okay?"

"Mrs. Neara, I think I can eat something when this is over. Is there anymore peach cobbler left?"

Taking the return of the absent appetite as a good sign, Neara and her mother both smile. Neara Jones replies, "Sure, child. Anything you like."

Her mother and the housekeeper can leave them alone now. As she approaches the chair facing the fireplace, Neara gives her a brief hug before leaving the room with Pauline.

The girl looks at the fireplace as the agents circle her, interrupting her view of the fire with a most deliberate pace. Around and around they go, never looking away from one another's eyes. They sit on either side of her, with their backs toward the fire.

In a calm, trancelike voice, Stacie says, "Musical Chairs was one of my favorite games when I was a child. What is it you wish to know?"

Agent Sievert says, "We want to know your secrets, Stacie. We need to understand what you are going through."

As she continues to stare at the fire, she contemplates the flames with her head slowly tilting to the left.

"You are the seers of the unapparent and hidden things, are you not?" she asks without fear.

"You can say that," Agent Sievert answers. "But we still don't know everything. You have nothing to fear from us."

"And yet I do fear that you want to hurt my father."

Agent Seward reassures, "You don't have to worry about that. We don't want to hurt the mayor."

Stacie's head slowly tilts toward Agent Seward, as if listening to her heartbeat or thoughts. She raises her right hand to point toward the door in the general direction of the people downstairs. She says, "Not him." She slowly points to her own heart and pats her chest. "Him."

The agents look at one another. "Who do you mean, sweetheart?" Agent Seward asks.

"My dad, Banja Rouge, is a good and loving father. You want to put him behind bars for his love and pain. You want to destroy my family, which is already decimated by the anguish of loss. I miss my mother and my brother so much."

Noticing tears that now fall from her eyes, both agents clearly sense Stacie's duality. Both minds and souls are fluctuating together and then apart, able to flow and speak as one or individually.

"You know, don't you?" she asks the agents, who are immersed in an enormous sorrow.

"What's that, Stacie," Sievert probes.

"I am one of two souls, separate, and yet whole." Now both souls speak as one. "We are Kysing Mecklenburg. We are Stacie Rouge, made of Banja Rouge, who was made of Kwaban Rouge." A slight tremor rattles Stacie Mecklenburg's basketball trophies in the glass case. Though no one downstairs feels it, the entire room seizes.

Agent Seward looks about the room, placing a palm to her lips. Her heart leaps when she looks in the corner of the room. There, a dark-skinned man with gleaming white eyes sits. His legs crossed on his perch atop the table. He is there, phasing in and out like the wings of a dove in motion. Agent Sievert senses her fear and follows her eyes to that area. He sees Banja Rouge sitting there with his finger meshed, forefingers pointed in their direction.

Stacie no longer tilts her head, still staring into the fire.

"My God, are you seeing this, too?" Agent Seward asks in a whisper.

"He does," a heavier male voice says to her from the girl's lips. "As do you, he sees and also feels."

"Don't leave your seat, Lee Anne," Agent Sievert warns, feeling her desire to draw her weapon. "Don't move."

He looks to the girl and says, "We do not wish to harm you or your father, Kysing. We only want to understand how and why these things are happening. However, we do know that there are others who feel very differently about his safety."

The heavy voice says, "Like your people, who have taken and ravaged my father? You were once warned that there would be consequences to further intrusion. Now, my father before me is in the wind. I no longer hear his voice or sense his strength. I only feel and hear the great maw of death creaking wide open as hope for you all flutters like paper-thin wings before its jagged teeth."

When the room seizes, again, a whistling breeze ruffles the pages of an unread newspaper.

Agent Seward looks to the girl to explain, "We would like to know how you can do what you have, apparently, done. We are trying to save Kwaban Rouge from those who now hold him captive. Please, you must know this to be true. I mean, haven't you been watching us all of this time? I have sensed your presence, but you remained hidden until now. Why have you chosen to reveal yourself, knowing that we mean her no harm?"

"Because a moment of choice is fast approaching. As are Mala and Siena the Harbingers of Life and Death . . . of light and dark," says Banja Rouge. "You should seek to distance yourselves from those who have willfully harmed my family. I need not threaten you, but I feel you should heed this as a warning."

"My body is dying, as has my brother and maybe my father's father before me," says Kysing Rouge.

Tears fall from her eyes as the voice says, "Then you know, daughter. I am sorry that my efforts are failing you. I wanted so much for you to live, but without my father's guidance and strength, I have not the power to do it alone. And yet, if I so choose, I can rend this evil world in two!"

This time, when the world inside Stacie's room seizes, it is a bit violent.

Agent Seward and Agent Sievert both place their fingers over their lips with the realization that these are truly the abject tears of the father falling from the eyes of the mayor's daughter. Kysing Rouge's tears and those of her host now join his. Being in such close proximity, both agents find their sorrow almost overwhelming.

"What can we do to help you? Tell us, please," Agent Seward begs as she fights back her own tears.

Agent Sievert asks, "Is there nothing we can do? We are trying to get your father out of that place. I swear it!"

The voice of Banja Rouge says, "There is nothing for you to do now. That inconspicuous prison and its torturers are no more. They have been razed to the ground by a will the average rational-minded person cannot understand."

"No," Agent Sievert says. "Are we too late?"

The television comes on. A bewildered meteorologist stands before a green screen where viewers can no longer see the southern regions of the Florida peninsula.

"As my grandfather chose to exist free in life, long ago, he chose to live free even if the death of his enemies claimed him!" Kysing Rouge says. "Father, may I show them the story of old—the legends we thought to be fairytales when we were merely children?"

Banja Rouge states, "Daughters, you favored them enough to freely reveal yourselves. In such cases, it is the right of every seed of Rouge to tell the story of our making."

"Thank you, father." She looks at the agents. First, she addresses Stacie Mecklenburg, saying, "Sister, because you are also touched by the Harbinger's of Life and Death, of light and dark, it is also your story to tell. No matter the future for either of us, you are forever Rouge. Shall we show them, together?"

"I would be honored, sister," Stacie Mecklenburg answers in her own voice.

Stacie looks from one agent to the other. That eerie double voice asks, "Would you like to know the Words of Beginning?"

Agent Seward clears her throat, "Yes, I would. I would like to know and understand more because I feel connected to all of this, somehow."

The girl says, "You are in many ways." She now looks at Agent Sievert to ask the same question. His answer is the same. Stacy looks at the fire and states, "I warn you. There will be pain."

For the first time since entering this room, there will be physical contact between them. Stacie raises both hands and grasps the arms of both people, who suddenly find themselves facing the fire. They are still seated next the girl, but on different sides in the opposite direction. She releases them.

"Are you certain?" she asks. With their positive answers, she again warns, "There will be pain."

"We understand," Agent Seward says. Her partner feels more apprehension because he has already experienced its depth. At least, he thinks so.

When Stacie offers both her hands, which they take, she tightens her grip with their fingers meshed together. Her manicured nails feel like iron talons digging into flesh. The pain is immense, causing both agents to quiver. They are certain that they have cried out, but no one rushes upstairs to their rescue.

"Seek, for this is nothing compared to what awaits when the greatest storm approaches. Give your pain to the light," the voices state. "Release it into the light."

When they see the pinpoint forming within the flames, the pain begins to subside. Kysing Mecklenburg smiles when a cool breeze brushes the hair away from her eyes. Standing atop a small hill, the sunlight warms their skin as the sweet smell of Hibiscus and Orchids mix in the air.

Long ago, even when the slave ships came to trade on the far side of the great island, there was happiness in life and honorable death, as it should be while this world revolves around the glorious sun. Life was good for a young fisherman named Emman Rouge, who fed his family, as well as the old and infirmed, people of his village with equal generosity during bountiful and lean times.

Emman was a crafty fisherman, creating his traps from wild sugarcane stalks and split bamboo that he wove with the leaves of palm trees and hanging vines. Taught by his aging father, he excelled at making his traps stronger than most. He was a man of the seasons, knowing when to dive deeply to gather clams and conch to add to his catch. He knew to avoid the waters when the tigers of the sea made their seasonal runs up and down the Haitian coast. The dolphin and porpoises allowed him to touch them and their young, something that no one else has ever done. They were wild, but curious beasts. Often, they allowed him to swim among them. Many times, when Emman sat along the beach watching for signs, groups of dolphin or porpoise would suddenly surface. They circled wildly, trapping shoals of fish against the shore as they fed. They even tossed fish onto the sand, allowing Emman and his kin to fill their baskets. Yes, these were happier, simpler times.

Lemay, Emman's young wife, had given him a daughter called Ella and a son, Meaco, which meant big fish. By the time he was seven, Meaco loved the ocean as much as his strong father did. Life was good for the family, and Lemay was newly pregnant with their third child. She was hoping to give Emman another strong son so that, one day, he would not have to work so hard.

Soon came the year of death and pestilence, when a coughing sickness spread across the island, moving from village to village. It took the young, the strong, and the elderly alike. Emman protected his family by keeping them away from everyone. His children were sad because they missed playing with their friends. Some of which, did not make it after falling ill. Lemay and Old Mother kept close watch, careful not to let them stray from sight.

As if the earth was sick, even the animals knew to stay farther offshore because the fishing was so poor this year. His traps were often bare, and even the turtles did not come to lay their eggs on the beaches. Emman Rouge was desperate to feed his family. Therefore, he tamed fire to hollow and fashion a boat from the large trunk of a fallen tree, which he used to venture further into the perilous ocean.

Meaco often cried because he could not join his father, who set out for a small strip of islands that his ailing father had taken him to when he was much younger. He paddled for nearly two days, finally coming to rest upon a beach where he started a fire and slept beneath the thriving palms.

The fishing was much better there. He dove deep and found many clams, lobsters, crabs, and conch. He cleaned and cured his catch so they would not spoil before he made it home. When he spotted some wild pigs, he set off to the hunt with a spear. As Emman Rouge returned to his camp with his quarry draped over his shoulders, he smiled and thanked
Great Creator for this bounty of blessings. Then, without warning, a shadow crossed the face of sun. A great ball of fire and smoke came from the heavens to crash into the ocean. Where it landed, a plume of smoke rose from the boiling water. Emman was afraid.

Though his fear was great, his curiosity was greater, so he anchored his boat and catch offshore to be sure that it would not drift away when he dove into the ocean's depths. Down he went, following a trail of bubbles until he came upon a curios orb. It was smooth and so perfectly round, he had to have it. It was too heavy to bring up, so he surfaced. After taking huge gulps of air, he dove repeatedly. Each time, he walked along the bottom with the warm orb in his hands until he got to shore. When he finally got close enough, he rolled it onto the sandy beach and lay beside it. Exhausted from his great toil, Emman Rouge fell asleep with his hand upon his warm prize. While dreaming of great battles between mighty gods among distant stars he often cried out. When a great, horned beast, with large eyes and sharp teeth came at his dreaming mind, Emman Rouge awoke drenched with sweat and sand clinging to his entire body. He ached all over, as if he had been fighting. To his great despair, when he woke he could not see his boat. Apparently, it had drifted away. He had slept so long that he thought he would have to wait until morning to search for it, hoping against all hope that the tide had beached it on another side of the island.

He soon realized that the light was not fading in the west. It was growing in the east because Emman had actually slept until the next morning. When he heard sounds coming from the round orb, which moved at his touch, he was startled and ran toward the water's edge. There, miraculously, the bow of his boat was beached with its anchor ashore as if someone had swam out and brought it to him. He looked at the orb and lost his fear, taking this good fortune as a sign from Great Creator. He carried the orb to the water's edge and placed it at the center of his boat. The catch that he had not yet dried or smoked, which he had lashed to the side of his wooden boat, was still fresh and floating in the salt water. No tigers of the sea had ravaged his fish.

Again, Emman fell upon his knees to thank Great Creator, promising to be good and caring all of his days upon the earth. He promised that he would teach his children and his children's children to live with the same love and charity in their hearts.

His good fortune continued. With calm tides and the favoring wind at his back, he reached his home in only one day. His family was happy to see him return safely. That night, they roasted the fat, juicy pig. While it roasted in the pit, Emman took a great portion of his catch and shared it among the hungry, less fortunate villagers.

Each night, as his family slept, Emman Rouge looked at the curious orb, touching it as it spoke to his mind. His son, Meaco, had taken a liking to it even though it first filled him with great anxiety. Soon, the young boy shed his fears. He played with the orb, rolling it around in the soft beach sand. Then, one night, it spoke to him too.

Listening to his father's friends inside, Meaco rolled the sphere inside the family home, placing it at the center of the sleeping chamber. The next morning, to their great astonishment, everyone had awakened with their hands touching the great sphere. During deep sleep, it told them the story of its existence, where it had come from, and why.

Ever since the orb was brought to the home of Emman Rouge, wondrous things occurred. The fishing was much better for the Rouge family, who fed nearly everyone in the village. The turtles returned, and the tigers of the sea had taken the lives of no one in many years.

One day, Old Father's mind sickness was simply no more. To the delight of Old Mother, he began to talk and walk, again. His steps were hard and unstable at first, but he made it to the sphere at the center of the room so that he may touch it. He thanked Great Creator and walked into the light of day under his own power for the very first time in many years. There was no more pain, and he even looked younger than his years. When Emman returned from setting his fish traps with Meaco, who had seen his thirteenth season upon the earth, they were happily surprised to see Old Father standing in the water with his arms stretched wide to greet them home.

For years now, Emman and Meaco had been using the orb, which seemed unbreakable, to crack open ripe coconuts. Whenever they slammed a coconut against the surface of the orb, it would split down the center, but none of its sweet milk was ever wasted. It was a curious thing to them all, especially when they held it upside down. One day, it spoke to Emman Rouge's mind, asking that he hit it with a coconut as hard as he could. Emman was thirsty so he did, but this time, the surface of the orb cracked and the shell of the coconut shattered. The rich milk spilled upon the orb's surface. However, the milk never touched the ground. It began to flow inside of the fractured orb. When it asked for more, Emman fed it with fresh fish and goat's milk until whatever moved inside was ready to break free.

Lemay was afraid, but Emman and Meaco were not. When the orb finally parted, its inside was a smooth black, glassy surface. Swimming in the thick silvery liquid of each half, there were small, winged, serpents. Even in their infancy, their power seemed immense. They caused the hair and skin of every family member to bristle and sting painfully. When they rose out of the ooze by standing on their tails, a small beam of light came from their horned heads, touching every member of the family Rouge.
Suddenly, the pain and the fear were gone from their hearts.

When Emman reached down to touch them, the winged serpents slithered forth to coil around his strong arms. They made a cooing, somewhat purring sound before suddenly leaping to the ground. They scurried from the hut and disappeared beneath the warm surf of the ocean. Emman and his family felt a great sadness as those of his village, who saw the creatures, questioned what manner of beast he had captured in his traps.

Soon, he and Meaco took both halves of the sphere to the water's edge to wash them clean. When they were done, they dried them and placed them upon an altar in the corner of the sleeping room. Lemay filled them with fresh flowers.

Emman never expected to see the serpents again. Yet, as the morning sun rose in the east, Emman yawned himself awake and sat up to greet the coming light. A quiet purring sound came from *one of the halves upon the altar where he was happy to find the creatures he had named Mala and Siena sleeping together. They seemed somewhat larger than before. He quietly roused each member of the family, including Old Mother and Old Father, showing them that the creatures had returned. Their hearts filled with joy.*

Soon, word of the shy creatures spread to the villages where the land was rejuvenated and peaceful. The fishing was good, year round, and then . . . they came. Traders with great sailing ships had come to the other side of the island with wondrous things like mirrors, sharpened metal, wheels, and nets made with strong mesh. Emman Rouge attained all these things from traders because the little ones, Mala and Siena, told him to in his mind. However, when the great ships left, something they had not traded for stayed with the islanders. A terrible, black coughing sickness swept through the island just as the season of the great storms gathered to hurl angry fists at the people.

Emman Rouge used the sharp metal to make wooden planks, from which he formed carts. He used the wheels, which were such simple but wonderful things, to make it move up the hill. Emman, endowed with the memories instilled during his youth by Old Father, gathered his family's stores of food, and supplies into the carts he had made. The nets held everything in place as he hurried his family up the small mountain to a secret cave with a red clay floor. Even though the sickness had taken hold of many, Emman would not leave his neighbors to the mercy of the furious ocean borne winds.

With Mala and Siena's instructions spoken into their minds, Emman and Lemay used items from their supplies and wild plants to make a powerful medicine. Up there, in that cramped cave, they withstood the worst winter storms of memory as the sick and dying slowly regained their strength.

When the winds finally calmed upon the turbulent waters, those who survived in the cave, came down from the mountain to find devastation and death. The storms captured many of those great sailing vessels and drove them ashore. Those that sought safe refuge from the deluge in sheltered coves on the far side of the great island were also smashed to bits; their crew members swept into the muddy brine.

Emman's people found the shorelines reshaped and forever changed. Although the earth had chosen a violent path, the sun seemed to shine all the brighter.

As villagers returned to rebuild their vanquished homes, tales of the miracles on the mountain spread across the island. Before the healing powers of the medicine could be made in greater quantity to help the suffering, the darker nature of humanity's fear, envy, and spitefulness, grew far faster.

A vengeful man, once known for his veneration, led vigilantes against the people of Emman Rouge. This man, who once had many sons before the storm winds came, had lost all but two children to the sickness and the tempests of the air. Because Emman Rouge's people had regained their strength and thrived in the aftermath of devastating circumstances, they repelled those who were simply driven mad by the sorrow of mourning. They coveted the wisdom and power of Mala and Siena, attacking those who once shared their fire and food. It was a bloody time of upheaval.

Soon, as Mala and Siena began to grow larger, they seemed to suffer their own ills. They became quieter in Emman and Meaco's minds. As if something called to them, they spent more and more time alone on the western beach, staring to the south from daybreak until dusk.

When the earth yawned and trembled, clouds of ash filled the far away sky. The creatures whispered to Emman. Siena spoke, "Earth Father, it is time we left these shores. Take us away so that you may remain safe with a chance to return to peace amongst your own people. We do this with great sorrow, but because we are not of this world, our power to destroy is ever upon our lips. My brother and lifelong mate grows angrier at the petulance of your people. I fear that I may not hold him to stillness much longer."

Emman looked over his shoulder where Meaco wept. As he joined his father, Mala and Siena climbed into their arms. Mala said to them both, "We are the children of gods fallen in a great battle far away the shores of Saint-Domingue, this land of mountains. Our time among you is at its end, but you and yours will always prosper in our love and appreciation. Because your Great Creator has spoken his commandments to our hearts, we must leave you now. Nonetheless, we are forever bound to the family Rouge alone. We are your Harbingers of Life and Death. Whenever there is need of us, call and we shall answer. We have pledged our service to the lord of this world, bound by his words except where the family Rouge is concerned."

Meaco asked, "But why must you go away? I love you, Mala, my best friend. I love you both."

In unison, their voices became one in the mind of the father and his eldest son, "We are of another realm that may be recreated upon this plane of existence, young ones. However, we have no desire for humankind to worship us as gods upon this world or any other, which was the very reason for the great wars across time and space. Our great powers are nearly limitless. We are ageless by comparison, far older than Old Father. Because of all the things we have spoken to you, our continued existence amongst your kind will bring naught but despair. Although we have been granted the privilege of being the Harbingers of Life and Death, the Harbingers of Light and Dark, we shall only wield the blade of vengeance for the family Rouge. Dance for us. Let your blood fire rain, and we shall answer to save one who slips toward the boundaries of the Reach when damaged by an enemy's hand. Your kind was never meant for an immortal life, but you are to be long lived. We love you, Meaco. Big Fish. However, only your father may travel on this journey. As it was in the beginning, so must it be in the end."

Emman looks at his feet with sadness. A glint of metal shone into his eyes. As he picks it up, Siena climbs upon his shoulder and says, "Wield this power with temperance and respect for life. Name it as you will, but only after it must draw blood to save your own. Etched upon its haft is the story of our existence, how our falling parents blew us across the cosmos with their final breath. Below it is the symbol of Rouge, the diver of the deep, the keeper of his people even at the peril of his own life. We are forever in your debt."

Mala speaks only to Emman to say, "Take us to the burning mountain. Climb to its peak, fearing not your life, for we shall protect your coming and going. Upon the summit, bid us goodbye and cast us in without care of our safety for it is closest to our own fiery realm. Smile for us when the calm returns to the belly of the earth, for it shall never rumble its discontent as long as the line of Rouge continues upon this land."

The father and son wept together. Emman set sail at dawn with the favorable tide and wind at his back. Two days later, Emman Rouge climbed to the summit of Saba, where they said their final goodbyes. In his boat, he looked over his shoulder and smiled as the grumbling volcano went to sleep. This was in the year, 1640.

When he returned to the familiar beaches of home, Emman was struck dumb, falling to his knees in a pool of Lemay's blood. His home was scorched to the earth and his family was dead. Only Meaco still clung to life, clutching the bloody blade that Emman Rouge would soon name *La lame de l'ouragan rouge. Meaco whispered the names of those who assaulted them in the night, and Emman wept as he gave his son a drink of water.*

Emman carried his dying son in his arms to the secret mountain cave, where he called upon Great Creator. Kneeling at his son's side, he called upon Mala and Siena, who answered with raging sorrow.

With a pinpoint of light forming before his eyes, Emman Rouge first danced the Harbinger's dance. There was much blood spilled when the howling wind rose to take that which had been taken by those who participated in the butchery. Then, before slipping beyond the boundaries of the Reach, Meaco's choice was made. Still, for many, those who murdered his family, sorrow ruled when their children were lain low. Years later, Meaco begets a son so named Sienmala, who begets Shaumua. And so on, the line continued until Gaul begets Kwaban Rouge, reputed to be the greatest to wield La lame de l'ouragan rouge. Long-lived is the family Rouge, which now threatens to break into shards and dust. If the line is broken and lost, there will be a most dire consequence."

"Seek!" Kysing Mecklenburg says. She releases the agents' hands, staring into the flames as they slide from their seats to the floor to writhe in something twisted between agony and euphoria. As if they just leaped from the windows of a burning home, their clothing smolders. Both agents are steaming as though they have just been hauled from a boiling cauldron.

The white eyes of Kysing Mecklenburg seek the ivory gaze of their father, who still sits with his legs crossed upon the tabletop.

"You have done well, my children."

The girls say, "Thank you, father. We hoped to do our family proud."

Banja's gaze falls upon the FBI agents, who are slowly recovering from a most taxing experience. Although, Banja Rouge, begotten of Kwaban Rouge, stares down at them, his words are directed to Kysing.

"And so you did. I will go now, ever watchful over thee. You need only whisper, and I shall hear for I await your decision, my love. Mala and Siena are approaching, and their anger is greater than ever before. It seems that Great Creator has given them reign to exact vengeance as they see fit. Even I may fall to their fury. There will be blood. There will be lightning. There will be agony, but you must remember to give it to the light. You should rest now, climb into your warm bed and sleep, children. Dream your sorrows into your mother's slumbering mind. Tell her of your undying love so that, in memory, she may find a measure of comfort."

"Wait," Agent Sievert whispers. "Please, can you tell us what we can do? I beg of you. This goes beyond our investigation into the kidnapping. We had an accurate assessment of your motives long before we came here, even before we saw Detective Reeves in the hospital. We know you are a good man, who never wanted to hurt anyone, which is evident by the fact that you didn't harm these kids or kill a drunken cop. You just sent him away."

Banja's gaze washes over them, releasing both from the nauseating feeling that has taken form within their bellies. As Agent Seward holds her hair back to retch into the wastebasket, he smiles at them.

"You are wrong about one thing, Agent Sievert. I was willing to rip the very soul from either of Mecklenburg's children because my pain was too great to process reason. It was so great that I would have done anything to save the last of my children. Thusly, salvaging what I could of my beloved wife's spirit and will to live.

Now that you have been truly touched by our way, your lives will never be the same. You should know, as seers yourselves, your kind—your very existence—is directly due to Mala and Siena's presence upon this world. To answer your question, soon you may have no choice but to do your duty. Your insistent meddling, truly, has no bearing here where the wheel yet turns as foretold my Mala, the angry one. However, the abduction of Kwaban Rouge by others now invites deadly destruction. Even my own fate is out of my hands. Only my daughters can choose their own paths, but we are all at the mercy of the wheel."

"I do not believe that the future is written in stone. I do not believe in fate," Agent Sievert says with great conviction.

Banja Rouge smiles at him. "Were you and your lover not fated to be together, or was it just a decision made by your superiors. Alone, during separate investigations, you both hunted a seasoned bi-coastal killer. He was profiled as a class-2 personality, a psychopathic sadist known as "the knife" because he completely skinned his victims and hung the eyeless carcass facing its own skin with eyes intact. Alone, your partner tracked a remorseless pedophilic collector from the east coast. When he was done with those precious, defenseless children, he ground them into paste. Bones and all. He smeared their remains into near perfect renditions of sketches he made of them in public places without ever being seen or having his image captured on camera. The only color used in his macabre artistry was always blood red. DNA was the only means of identification. You both met in the middle to capture a bi-coastal human monstrosity with two perfectly separate, yet equally deadly personalities. With absolutely no collaboration, no similarities in modus operandi, you met for the very first time at the same ugly green door at the same moment with weapons drawn to kill him. Not capture, but to kill him. Four years ago, Agent Seward and Agent Sievert met the only person upon the face of the planet that either one could ever truly love. You have only recently allowed the barriers built over a lifetime to come down to enjoy that which normal people experience every day."

Ever so gently, Kysing Mecklenburg kisses both agents on their sweating foreheads. She climbs onto her bed and draws the clean, dry, sheet to her neckline.

Agent Seward asks from her knees, "How can you know such things?" For some reason, maybe because this has been her first actual touch, Agent Seward is having a harder time recovering. She is dizzy and a bit disoriented by waves of vertigo.

"I know many things, Agent Lee Anne Seward," Banja Rouge says. "Lee Anne, the only begotten child of the high-school sweethearts Leland and Anna Beth Seward, parents who were told that neither of them could conceive children together. Nor apart. As adventurous archeologists, they once climbed mountainous terrain in the Caribbean to make camp near the rim of a volcano called Saba. That is where and when you were conceived. Their miracle baby.

Even as a child, who excelled very early in school, you had only one friend. A blue parrot named Sammy. As you grew up to become a stunning young woman, you felt like the loneliest girl on the planet. Among all of those voices, you were afraid you were insane. Please pardon the depth of my intrusion, but puberty was an extremely awkward and confusing time for you. Was it not? When you were seventeen. . . ."

She holds her upset stomach and cuts her eyes at him. In a flash, Banja Rouge appears right before her eyes.

He touches her head, running both hands down both sides of her body to her hips. He says,

"Peace, be still, child. I mean you no harm."

The nauseating, disorientation lifts, fully restoring her senses. "Thank you."

"Should I continue?" he asks. When she looks at Agent Sievert, she decides to give the nod after much consideration. Banja looks at him and returns his gaze to the woman. He says, "You lost your virginity at age seventeen to an older boy whose name is no longer important to you. The experience, however, was the very first time that you realized that you were not insane and that the voices were real. You felt alive and excited, as your hormones were a raging inferno. Your sexual inexperience with a school athlete became an issue when he thought of other girls he had bedded. You recognized those names, had even seen him talking to them. Your infatuation grew despite the fact, and he took advantage of your innocence. When certain names entered his mind along with the story he just couldn't wait to tell his teammates about you being a slut, you gave him a black eye. Later, when you found out that you caught an STD from the only boy you had ever been with in in your senior year, you gave him another and a swift kick with a specially chosen pair of shoes. You were suspended from school that day, but you've been wearing that type shoe ever since."

Now that the shoe rests squarely on the other foot, there is a bit of amazement in Agent Seward's eyes. Banja, sitting between them, now looks at her partner.

"And me," Agent Sievert says.

Banja's demeanor is serious, again. His white eyes are brighter. His face is upturned as if listening. When he finally looks at Agent Sievert, he says, "The time for parlor games is over. They are coming." "Who is coming, Mr. Rouge?" asks Agent Seward.

"Your people are coming. They have been using your own electronic devices to spy on you since my father called from the shores of Florida. Before Mala and Siena ripped that evil bitch to shreds, she gave two orders. One was to have you monitored or even captured and turned. The other order was to have my father murdered."

"What?" Agent Sievert says in disbelief. "They want to turn us into human weapons. Spies and assassins if necessary. But we are federal agents."

Agent Seward says, "So are they."

"With Siena—the patient one—at Mala's side, and in total congress with him, I fear many lives will be castrated from existence. Because of the many evils of those involved, know that the God of this universe will do naught to dissuade the wrath of Mala and Siena. Even now, he turns his eyes away."

"What can we do to stop this?" Agent Seward asks as she looks at the blinking light on her phone. He is doing the same.

"Do your job, and then, maybe, you can die well," Banja Rouge replies with a sad gaze upon the sleeping girl. "I hear my name upon the lips of the famished winds of the reaping, Agents Sievert and Seward. I cannot discern the message that follows from so far away, but I know within my heart that the line of Rouge will somehow survive the calamities to come. My family is truly made of good people, and now, so are you. Believe in fate, Michael. Whether or not you know it, you may already have spoken your own. Do not look for it, for it shall appear without challenge. Cling to your woman for

whatever there is of time yet to come and pass. Seek."

Banja Rouge fades away to vapor.

There is a knock at the door. It opens slowly as Neara enters with a tray of warmed leftovers from dinner. She looks at the sleeping teenager, disappointed that she arrived too late to see Stacie enjoy her favorite meal. She leaves the tray on the table, setting it right where Banja Rouge sat only moments before. Now she hands two disposable containers to the agents.

"I hope neither of you is allergic to peaches, apples, or pineapples, seeing as how I used all three in this cobbler. The children love it."

They thank her, although their recent experience renders a healthy appetite as something to be desired.

Agents Seward and Sievert gather themselves to leave the girls room after learning many unexpected things.

Chapter 26

Devil in the Details

O n this ordinary Friday, at an ungodly late-night hour, when Dr. Silver would much rather be at home with his family, he peruses the weekly reports with concern about the progress of a few patients. He expects little to no change in most. However, a peculiar human curiosity plagues him with more questions than answers. He knows that he has seen something in this particular patient's weekly progress reports that does not jive. Some small factor still escapes him. It nags him because he knows it is there. It may be basic, but extremely significant. What eludes Dr. Silver is something that others should have noticed right away, as a part of simple medical protocol.

"What could it be?" Doctor Silver whispers, as if asking the question aloud will produce the answer.

This chilly, rainy weather is transforming spring into an uncharacteristically dismal time of year. In the very last days of April, the trees, the flowers, and even the unhatched eggs of aggravating Cankerworms seem unsure of themselves. It seems as if nature is traumatized, afraid to peek out even when the sun shines through.

In the gloomy office, beneath the warm, soft light of a reading lamp, Dr. Silver runs both index fingers down two separate reports for the same patient. He searches for some atypical little thing that causes his scalp to tingle. No longer reading notes written by attending physicians, he combs through raw data for any inconsistency. His eyes are intense as he starts over from the very beginning, finally placing his fingers on that which he seeks as the phone startles him.

At 1:53 AM, Allison Silver's sleepy voice asks, "Joseph, is everything okay? I fell asleep while reading this awful novel chosen by the book club. When I woke, you weren't lying next to me. Are you still at the office, honey?"

He looks at his watch with a wince. "Yes, sweetheart. I'm sorry. Just lost track of time." He sighs.

"That bad, huh?" she asks.

"To be perfectly honest with you, I don't quite know how to answer that question just yet. I cannot seem to nail it down. It keeps gnawing at me because it's so simple, yet it's very important. Basic science, but crucial, nonetheless."

She says, with concern, "You sound pretty stressed, baby."

"Yeah, I suppose that's accurate. Allison, have you ever known that there is something terribly wrong, but you do not even know what it concerns?"

"Like the day I called my mother out of what seemed like an irrational fear? Moments later, while we were talking and laughing on the phone, she has a massive stroke. I have asked myself every day since if it would have happened the same way had I not called. Yeah, I think I know what you mean."

Tears well in Allison Silver's eyes as she turns her head away from the phone.

"Oh, Ally. I never meant to take you there. It was insensitive of me. Are you okay?"

His wife sniffles and stifles her tears in an effort to abate her husband's unnecessary feeling of guilt.

"I will be fine. I just wish you were here right now, but it's totally unreasonable for you to think that you can anticipate everything that may send my memories toward my mom's death," she says. After shaking it off, Allison asks, "So you've stumbled into a real mystery."

"Well, sort of. Yes. I have to figure out what I'm looking for, first. It is in the basic biological science of it all. Important, yes. It may even be dangerous, but it is elusive; like a ghost, you can only see from your peripheral vision. I feel so strongly that there is something just staring me in the face and I cannot see it for all of my efforts. On the other hand, it could be a compilation of years of data sifting simply stacking up in the old attic."

"Baby, maybe you should take a step back and come at it with fresh eyes. Listen to me. God that must sound so self-serving."

"Not at all," Dr. Silver says with another long sigh. "Maybe you're right. It is getting very late." He taps the left index finger on the file in the very same spot it was in when the phone startled him.

"Joseph, do what you feel is best for the patient's sake. I was just concerned you were out having a tawdry affair with some young, sexy intern."

He chuckles with her. While leaning forward to close the files, he takes one last glance at both and there it is!

"Oh my God. That's it. That is it. Shit me out and spread me onto burnt toast."

With a yawn, Allison perks up. "What? What is it, Joseph? Joseph?"

"Hm. Oh, I really got stuck on stupid. Someone else's stupidity, that is."

"What do you mean?"

He double-checks the data and answers, "Someone in the blood lab must be dipping into the sauce because the baseline data for this patient of week one states that her blood typing is A-negative. However, this week's blood work shows B-positive. How can they have made such a colossal mistake?"

His wife responds by adding, "It's been a long time since basic high school biology classes, but I'm certain that's the kind of screw-up that could cost a patient's life."

"Very true. With all of the extraordinary distractions surrounding this case, this could become much worse in an instant. Well, at least there is one positive aspect to this."

"You mean besides finding the discrepancy?" she asks.

"Yes," he says with a distant and studious voice. The blood samples were drawn at the same time of day, and the same staff members were on duty. The same person typed them. Honey, I'm going to be a little longer. To be certain, I'm going to check this patient's transferred records. I'll, also, order my own lab work just to be on the safe side."

"I'm happy you solved your mystery, honey. Just drive safely on your way home in this crazy weather. Do you know there was red hail reported in three different counties today? It's April in South Carolina for God sake."

"And yet the Republicans still swear that there is no such thing as climate change."

She chuckles. "Those professional screw-ups don't know a weathervane from thumbs up their asses. If it refuses to give them a kickback, they will deny weather even exists. Okay, be safe. I love you."

"Love you, too. See you soon."

Dr. Silver goes about checking the patient's medical history as soon as he hangs up. The confusion grows as he digs into Stacie Mecklenburg's medical history. The girl's latest blood work suggests that she is B-positive. However, the lion's share of her life indicates that she has always typed A-negative.

Morning comes after a night of restless sleep. At 8:15, the phone awakens Joseph Silver, who has fallen asleep with a chart on his chest. Rising from the couch in his office, he groans his way into consciousness and shakes his head from side to side to clear his mind of dreadful sleep and dreadful dreams.

"Good morning, Martha?" he yawns before snatching the phone away from his ear. His calm secretary is now a bit hysterical.

"Dr. Patel says it is urgent she speak to you. It seems that "screaming girl" is at it again. This time she got loose, somehow!"

"Okay. Just lower the volume and put Luna through."

"Joseph?"

"Yes, Dr. Patel? What's going on?"

"Martha told me you slept here last night."

"Yes, I fell asleep while going over your status reports. I found some disturbing inaccuracies, so I ordered a few tests. What's going on?"

"What kind of inaccuracies?" Dr. Patel asks of her meticulous reports. Before Dr. Silver answers, she says, "Oh, never mind that for now. I really need you on the ward. Please come to my office. We can discuss other matters then."

"I need coffee."

"Please, Joseph. Come to my office as soon as you gather yourself."

"Okay. Okay, I'll be there posthaste."

"By the way, I noticed that you ordered a rush on extra blood work for the Mecklenburg girl. My own test results came back. However, they're as useless as they are inconclusive."

"How can that be? Are they having problems with the lab techs or the equipment?"

"Dr. Maynard assures me that there are no problems on their end. Frankly, I do not know what to make of all these anomalous readings and symptoms."

"Are we still talking about the same thing, Luna?"

"Whatever do you mean?"

"The inconsistencies of her blood typing. Earlier labs suggest she is Type A-negative. More recently, lab work suggests B-positive." "What?" she asks.

"It nearly slipped by me, but the old subconscious wouldn't let it go until I tracked down the discrepancy."

"Thank goodness she never required a transfusion. How did that escape my attention?"

"I'll sort it out shortly."

There is an urgent whisper in the background.

"I've got to sedate this disruptive patient. Please join me as soon as you can."

"I'll be there in a few moments."

"Thank you," Dr. Patel says, while ordering the powerful meds for the young woman that some have begun to call "the banshee" or "screaming girl."

"As Dr. Silver stretches his back, he looks at the file that had fallen to the floor when he woke to the ringing phone. The pair of eyes in the photo causes him to shudder as he bends over to pick it up. His skin prickles as static cling causes a slight spark to pop his index finger when he touches the metal clip that holds it all together. He recoils, annoyed as though the shock was some malicious contrivance.

As he holds his index finger, surprised at how painful the little zap is, he flinches when his secretary taps lightly.

Martha Graves enters with a freshly pressed suit in plastic. With a smile, she says, "Good Lord, you look like something the cat would drag out of the house." With a chuckle, she hangs the suit in the corner of his office. "Your wife dropped this off on her way to a meeting. She was concerned about you not coming home last night, but she understands. I really like her, Dr. Silver. She is so dutiful and patient. You really ought to marry that woman, someday."

"You mean . . . again?"

"Again."

The two share a chuckle.

"Thank you, Martha. I'll shower and change after seeing Dr. Patel. I need coffee, and I want this godawful couch condemned to death-by-crushing." When the assistant laughs aloud, he reconsiders. "On second thought, just have someone pick it up as a donation. I'm certain someone can use it."

She smiles at him and walks out only to return with a steaming cup already made just the way he likes it.

"Martha Graves is all-knowing, Doctor Silver. That ghastly couch will be replaced by the midweek. Shall I put the replacement on your credit card or requisition it through the expense department?"

He looks at her and says, "Put it on my card. It will be much faster. In fact, you should take two hours for lunch so you can find a suitable replacement today. I trust your judgment and I don't want to wait until midweek."

She smiles as she takes his credit card. "I know just the place to get you something that's much more comfortable, Doctor Silver. Who knows? Maybe I'll buy a new car." She gives him a devilish little smile and a wicked chuckle.

* * *

The ward is quiet. Much too quiet. It is most disconcerting, all this peaceful tranquility where things tend to turn disruptive quickly. In this environment, one agitated patient can seem to affect the mental status of a multitude.

No sound comes from those double doors. Not a single peep. He turns left, knocking on the third door to the left.

When he enters, Dr. Patel is standing behind her desk. She faces the window, studying a file in her hands with intensity. When she turns toward her boss, he sees concern on her face and a bit of confusion in her eyes.

"Good morning, Luna. Now then, what seems to be the problem?"

She places her hands on her hips with the file open at her side. Her eyes reflect deep thought. Before she can answer, the phone rings. Moments later, she says to the caller, "Yes. When the mother arrives, please bring her straight to my office. I may not be here, but I will be on the floor with Dr. Silver. Thank you."

"Okay. What has you so flustered this morning?"

"This patient is becoming highly troublesome. I'm afraid I will have to recommend relegating her to extreme isolation."

"What's going on? Has she displayed violent tendencies toward the staff or while interacting with other patients?"

"Not exactly. However, at 5:30 this morning she began to scream as if in unbearable pain. It is the same every time. Her disruptive behavior coincides, invariably, with the onset of violent weather patterns moving through the area. The Mecklenburg girl is displaying all the precursors of a severe psychotic break, Dissociative Disorder, or even MPD. Something happened to her, which may be of a psychosexual nature. However, nothing I can think of accounts for other anomalous physical symptoms that tend to crop up overnight. I'm running every test I can to determine a reason for the abrupt physiological changes she is undergoing."

"What changes, exactly?" Doctor Silver asks with growing interest, now that he knows the subject's name.

Doctor Patel approaches her desk and lays out four photographs of the patient. Two of them are left face down.

"This first photograph represents her features over six months ago. She is a smiling, normal, happy teenager. This photo is representative of the first day her parents admitted her for a psyche evaluation— right after she bit her father. She waylaid Mayor Mecklenburg like a rabid animal in their kitchen, where she was being consoled by her mother and the housekeeper. She was highly upset about something, but when he came in, she attacked without warning. Took twenty stitches to close him up. Another inch or so higher, and she would have torn out his carotid. She has been here for two weeks now." Dr. Patel turns the third photo over and further explains, "Week one, patient undergoes rapid Heterochromia. As you can see in these photos, she has blue to blue-grey eyes. Now she has one blue-grey and one that is dark brown. This transformation, quite literally, happened overnight. Eye exams show no trauma."

Dr. Silver first saw those eyes as he reached for the file copy on the floor of his office, but they were the same color.

"Overnight?" he asks. "Highly unusual and unlikely."

"Yes. I was shocked, but this photo shows what she looks like right now. Last night, she has transmuted, displaying highly advanced and extreme Vitiligo."

"What?"

She overturns the last photo of a young woman with blue-grey and brown eyes. Her skin is splotched white and tan, almost as if she had her body painted to look like camouflage. She resembles a calico animal."

Obviously, Dr. Silver is not prepared for such a rapid transformation. He winces and says in a near whisper, "Twenty-four hours? This happened overnight?"

"Yes. I suggest running a panel of tests to rule out perinicion anemia, and hypothyroidism, Lupus, and Type 1 diabetes. Any of which could be a plausible explanations, but. . . ."

"I concur with your plan of action. However, don't rule out skin cancer. Dr. Armen Dice is a great oncologist. I've worked with him before and he fosters an entire unit of brilliant specialists with wide-ranging experience. I'll give him a call to consult."

"Of course, but the sudden onslaught of Heterochromia and rapid skin depigmentation do not explain what I'm about to show you right now. Please follow me."

They walk out of the office to traverse the labyrinth of shatterproof glass used to safely observe patient behavior without disturbing them while at rest. As they approach the units housing the mental patients at a pace suggesting urgency, he asks, "What are we missing here?"

She answers, "I was forced to sedate the patient with haloperidol– promethazine. The reaction was positive, but it did not put her down. Not completely. What you are missing here is noise, regular old human sounds. If you think you are creeped out by the silence, then I don't suggest you look into these units as we pass."

It is impossible for Dr. Silver to ignore the presence of patients standing to the left and right behind transparent enclosures.

Each patient, whether heavily sedated or not, is erect and motionless behind a glass wall. Each is the very picture of silent serenity. They're almost trancelike, while staring in the general direction of Stacie Mecklenburg's room. It seems as though they are all listening to a sound indiscernible by the doctors, or waiting for something to happen. Dr. Silver has never seen this sort of behavior. Nor has Dr. Luna Patel, until yesterday morning when she thought she could handle this strange trend. Frankly, they are both highly disturbed. As they approach, their skin begins to crawl and sting.

Each patient turns his or her head to look at the doctors with the same blank, emotionless stare before returning their gazing eyes in the same direction. No one pounds on the glass partition to get his or her attention. No one pleads for help. No one asks for food or meds. No one asks to go home. Absolutely no one.

As if they will hear her, Dr. Patel whispers, "This is really weirding me out."

Merely inches from her eyes, he taps on a female patient's glass, only to have her ignore him.

"You and me both," Dr. Silver says. "These patients seem to display an almost hive-like mindset. They are listless. Distant. And yet...highly focused."

"Disconnected." She agrees, adding, "The patients are quite dismissive, but at the same time, they are acutely aware of our presence. They seem content and normal, in an eerie sort of way. No one is exhibiting the usual neediness we are accustomed to seeing. Especially in the morning. They are all calm and quiet. Much too quiet for my part, Joseph. I rather prefer the ranker of a riotous asylum where the inmates are merely inches from running the establishment."

"They seem to be waiting for something," Dr. Silver says. "Like drones awaiting their next dose of a pheromone or a new, highly addictive street drug."

"Yes. My own conclusions, exactly."

"Why do I get the distinct feeling that there is a big *BUT* coming, Luna?"

"Very perceptive of you, Joseph. As you just stated, they seem drugged while awaiting the next dose. However, in this case, that thing they crave seems to be quite painful."

When the lights flicker, Dr. Patel stops in her tracks, looking upward. Her respiration increases.

"Luna? Doctor Patel, what's the matter," asks Dr. Silver.

Resuming the walk to the end of the corridor appears to be a difficult decision. Her eyes dart about as the lights buzz and flicker. "The meteorologist predicted wave after wave of thunderstorms throughout the week."

When the lights begin to glow brightly overhead, with an ominous sizzling, static crackle, a terrified nurse turns the corner and hurries in the opposite direction. She keeps her eyes to the floor, excusing herself. Fists tightly clenched, her neck recedes between her hiked shoulders as the static builds.

Dr. Silver cannot help noticing the nurse's urgent need to be elsewhere. "Rain . . . yes," he says absently.

After a quick glance at the ceiling, Dr. Patel pauses, again. With her eyes shut, she whispers, "Shit. Shit. Shit." Now wrenching her hands, she says, "We're too late."

"Too late for what?" Dr. Silver asks

The thunder rolls, preceding a chilling cry!

Dr. Silver recoils, looking overhead as if he expects the ceiling to come crashing down. The surrounding atmosphere hisses, charged with foreboding static as hairs begin to walk the air along invisible wires. Doctor Luna Patel, a brilliant student of the mind, freezes in her tracks. Her fists clench at her sides. Her eyes shut, and her jaw clamps down on those pearly whites.

Now comes another wretched scream.

With his scalp tingling, Dr. Silver's curiosity forces his feet to hurry toward the cry of a patient in obvious distress. When he rounds the corner, his heart seizes. His breath halts. There, behind the glass partition, she floats in defiance of gravity, slowly turning clockwise in midair. Her matted, wet, blonde hair is almost black from the roots to the ends. Her ragged nails have scratched the thin hospital gown to ribbons. It is also soaked with sweat.

A rumble precedes a wicked clatter from an angry sky. She spreads her arms and screams as the lightning blurs the small window above the bed and finally releases her pain. A brilliant flash engulfs her room, forcing Dr. Silver to cover his eyes with a forearm. Tendrils of electric blue are unleashed, seeking every conduit, and living soul of the psyche ward.

In unison, other patients of the ward begin to scream a haunting chorus as the crackling tendrils round the corner to touch them through the thick glass partitions.

This is utter madness; chaos, running amok within a cloak of suffocating fear.

Silver can do nothing. He turns his head to see the other doctor of the mind still standing there, rigid. His own feet want to retreat toward her, but he fears that something will follow. Doctor Silver is rooted in stone. He cannot seem to move with any form of decisiveness.

With disbelief, he looks back at the patient slowly turning in midair like the hands of a clock on the wall. After a brief flash, he blinks his unbelieving eyes because there are two girls floating in midair. They are identical, but one floats horizontally while the first patient turns vertically. The lamps overhead, once functional and soft, shatter or explode in a parade of sparks.

In a flash, one charged electric tendril stabs at his chest!

Silence.

Darkness envelops all, until a flash of lightning reveals the darkling's splotched skin and red eyes staring back at him through the glass. Doctor Silver's knees buckle as he drives a fist into his mouth to muffle the audible expression of a grown man's sudden fright.

When he opens his eyes, the teenage girl curls into the fetal position on her bed and quietly drifts into the waiting arms of peaceful slumber.

Moments later, without having entered Stacie Mecklenburg's room, Doctor Silver staggers back down the corridor. Luna Patel holds on to him. Without the sense of mind to remove it, she limps along with one broken heel. Meanwhile, Doctor Silver, missing his left loafer, stumbles along on paralytic legs. He has no clue that the left shoe is missing from his foot. Nor does he care to look down at his disobedient legs.

Try, as they might, neither could resist glances at the now vacated glass walls. Most curiously, the other patients are also placated. Some have gone back to sleep. Others sit quietly on their bedsides, smiling while staring at nothing of particular substance.

As they pass through the double doors, Dr. Silver collapses. His heart is dysrhythmic as the walls around him seem to collapse and recede.

Silver clenches his eyes shut, but when he opens them, he is faced with the unsympathetic glare of Stacie Mecklenburg. Her scream stabs at his scientific mind. He clutches at his chest and seizes. Heart attack!

* * *

Eight miles away, during a break in the stormy weather, a small jet lands at Frontage Airfield in Rock Hill. Five very large, very serious looking men in civilian clothing exit the plane with duffel bags. The leader, Carl Magnusson, removes his dark shades and surveys the surrounding area.

A special helicopter transport soon lands nearby. As the rotors begin to slow, a nerdy looking technician exits and meets Magnusson. He walks toward the helicopter with the technician, opening the other door as a leggy woman in white waits for the rotors to come to a complete stop. Now she exits, looking at readings on a pad.

She looks at Magnusson and says, "We are in the zone alright. These readings are erratic, but deceptively so."

Magnusson asks, "What do you mean?"

She simply says, "I see a pattern here, Magnusson. One which seems purposely misleading." As three black SUVs pull up, she asks, "Have your men been briefed?"

"They have."

"Then I suggest you get to it. Remember, we are here to watch, listen, and learn. Locate the subjects and report back to me. I'll let you know when to move on them." A scarf holds her raven black hair in place. She removes her glasses to look across the pavement, musing at the red streaks on the jet Magnusson and his men just vacated. As the technician removes her equipment and bags from the helicopter, she says to herself, "This is the place, indeed. Director Holst may have been a heartless bitch, but she always followed her nose."

Finding his spine amidst her luggage, the technician asks, "Mrs. Vincent, if it's true that Regional Director Holst is dead, is it wise to pursue her most recent agenda without further oversight? I mean, rumor has it, that it's what got her killed and the Dardis Biomedical facility leveled to the ground."

Sierra Vincent gives a sharp reproachful glare at the aide she often treats no better than a walking doormat. Her voice is sheer venom when she says, "We've been paid well to do a job, and do it well. If you don't have the belly for it, maybe I'll have you dropped into a deep, dark hole with the people we came here to observe and snatch because they are threats to national security. Are we clear on that, Leach? This case, the people involved in it, have caught the attention of very powerful people who need to know how these phenomena developed. Emphasis on the term develop."

Paul Leach cowers from her vicious glare, simply nodding affirmation as he squints into the rising sun. He walks away to toss her bags into the back of one of the SUVs. While doing so, he curses under his breath.

He sighs hard before whispering to himself, "That's your wakeup call, kid. Everybody is expendable to those who are the real threats to national security. I'm gonna have to watch my ass with this spawn of another heartless bitch."

To Be Continued

Blood of Banja Rouge: Book 2 The Red Hurricane

Made in the USA
Columbia, SC
18 June 2025

59547042R00276